ARÖN

TALES OF KHAYAAL

BOOK 1

by

REHAN KHAN

Story concept by Peter Gould

UHIB
BOOK

Uhibbook Publishing
Sharjah Publishing City
U.A.E

www.uhibbook.com

First published in United Arab Emirates by Uhibbook Publishing FZC 2025
Approved by U.A.E National Media Council
Media File Number: MF-02-6662024

Paperback ISBN: 978-9948-684-73-2

E-book: 978-9948-686-71-2

To Neil King, who connected the dots.

CONTENTS

CONTENTS

Frozen North
ICE RIDGE
Kuor Araz
Northern Waste
JUTES
Varini
Njars
Gepids
Angari
Teuton
Turones
Helisii
NORTHERN OCEAN
Nar
As-samum
RIFT
Shimshian
Lootini
Qwaqitul
Koemox
Sylish
Afaraskan
Gamzak
Kermon
ZANJ
Gor
Arön
SUSA
Dvin
URUA
Hatra
Onogur
Shabaran
Tawj
CHENGDI
EAMIN
XI'ZU
DUTONG
ANYAN
Cin
YEH
TANG'AN
Aybateh
Jamarca
Vitkuz
Atzlan
KUZRO
Peesak
SOUTHERN OCEAN
Southern
Waste
Frozen South

What has been foretold in legend of the Final Standing will come to pass, for it is written on tablets of light, placed within a chronicle, upon a dais on a celestial plane.

Every generation lives with this knowledge; all expect to see its signs, yet few can claim to have seen anything at all.

-1-
DVIN

*For a seed to sprout and become a tree of significance,
it must be buried deep in the soil.*

THE WISDOM OF THE WAY

WINTER ARRIVES EARLY IN ARÖN; a cool breeze ripples through the flanks of the northern army. Long-range acoustic cannons roll across muddy fields. Each infantryman carries a sonic rifle, and some have handguns and steel sabres. A light rain-shower ends and the clammy air stinks of sweat and fear.

Alifa observes the wet sheen on the fields of Dvin. She adjusts her white headscarf; some of her silky black hair falls across her forehead. She stands silently by the flap to the entrance of the medical tent, where the cold air snatches at her apron. The sun remains a spectre, low in a cloudless sky.

Under the heavens, the armies of the northern sultan assemble for battle with the southern sultana. In all her sixteen years of life on Ikleel, Alifa cannot remember a time when she was not in a medical unit. *Men will die today,* she thinks. *Far from their homes. Others will be injured, and for what? A fight between two cousins.*

'Alifa.' It is the voice of Kira, the head nurse.

'Coming,' she replies. Alifa takes a deep breath, the air cold in her lungs, stares at the soldiers, shakes her head, then ducks back into the suffocating tent. Inside, soldiers sprawl on stretchers, and in the dim light, she is being asked to attend to an injured man.

'Says he has a wrist sprain – see what you can do,' says Kira, before leaving her.

'How did it happen?' Alifa asks the dejected soldier.

'Does it matter?' he mutters.

'It might,' Alifa replies.

'It's a sprained wrist – my sword hand as well, can't lift my bloody weapon.'

'I see,' Alifa says. *He wants any excuse to avoid fighting. One less soldier won't make a difference.* Alifa starts to wrap the man's wrist.

'How long do I need to rest it?' he asks.

'Until you don't feel any pain,' Alifa says.

The soldier nods.

'Alifa,' Kira calls out. 'Need your help.'

She leaves the soldier, attends a new one slumped on a stretcher. Kira crouches over the patient, who has a nasty gash in the side of his stomach. Blood oozes out.

'Lad got caught between two rivals having a sword fight. Farmer's boy, by the looks of him. Hold the gauze,' Kira instructs, then walks away.

'Kira?' Alifa calls after her.

The head nurse takes out her scroll-light, unwraps the canvas cloth with the meshed liquid algae display, slides the *kamish* made of ironwood from its side and taps the greenish-blue screen. Writing right to left, Kira scribbles something on the scroll-light, looks back at Alifa, shakes her head, moves on.

Probably the death entry for this fellow, thinks Alifa.

Alifa studies the bleeding soldier. *He's not going to make it. Who does he he leave behind? Distraught parents, troubled siblings, a sweetheart perhaps? What a waste.*

Unless.

She looks around: no one is close. Alifa uses her healing.

Immediately a tingling fills her hand, then surges into the dying man. She trains her attention on his injury, willing it to heal, then feels her own energy draining. Hesitantly, she withdraws the gauze from the wound. Blood no longer leaks. It congeals and the wound starts to seal. The soldier has a fighting chance. He remains unconscious, oblivious to what is happening. *By the Will of the Creator, I pray it is enough*, Alifa hopes.

'You! Come here.'

It's an angry voice and when Alifa turns, she recognises one of the fearsome Black Axes, loyal stalwarts of the Sultan of the north. Dressed in a mixture of leather and metal armour with black greaves, his broad belt housing several knives, the man is of middling height, rippling with muscle. Two taller, broader Black Axes come in after him. The Black Axes are elite martial warriors, favourites of the Sultan, and they know it.

'Coming,' Alifa replies, sounding obedient. *No need to rattle the Black Axes*, she thinks. *But this poor fellow hasn't fully recovered. I need to give him another dose of healing when I regain my strength.*

'*Now*, girl!' the Black Axe roars, as he slams the flat of his palm on a table and sends a bundle of bandages and a wooden jar of water tumbling to the floor.

The medical tent is suddenly empty, apart from injured or dying soldiers. Even the fellow with the sprained wrist has disappeared. Alifa realises she is the only member of the medical staff present. *The others, they must have seen the Black Axes approaching.*

'Come on Vartez, the fighting starts soon, we need to get going,' the tallest Black Axe grumbles.

'I want this shrapnel out of my arm. Otherwise how am I going to kill southerners?' Vartez says. 'Girl, why aren't you here!'

The wounded soldier: if he doesn't get a second dose of healing, he won't make it.

'Please, this man is dying, I'm just trying to help him,' Alifa implores.

Vartez glares at the soldier spreadeagled on the stretcher. Marches over, takes out his knife and in one swift movement, slams the weapon through the soldier's heart. The man's body convulses, eyes open in shock, before he lies still. Vartez withdraws the blade, cleans the steel on the bedroll.

'Well, he's dead now, no need to help him,' Vartez bellows, to cheers from the other two Black Axes.

'You ... killed him,' Alifa exclaims.

'He looks like some useless farmhand who didn't want to be here. I've sent him on his way.'

'But ...' Alifa says.

'Bah! Stupid girl, I'm the fighter. Help me, not him.'

Alifa doesn't let her anger show but it rages. She stares at the ground, calming her thoughts. *There are other ways to get even with men like Vartez*, she thinks.

Vartez grabs Alifa by her apron, hauls her up. 'Get on with it, girl! I have a battle to fight. Take this shrapnel out.' The Black Axe motions to the metal protruding from his right arm.

Alifa glances at the dead man. No amount of healing will bring him back now. *I was so close. If only I was stronger, I could have healed him.* But she wasn't and she doesn't even know what healing is, or why she has it, but it's useful, like the other little gifts she has.

'All right,' she says. 'Sit there,' she motions to Vartez, pointing at a wooden stool.

The Black Axe lumbers across and lowers himself. Alifa focusses on the stool, then nudges it. It moves out from under Vartez, causing the Black Axe to hit the ground. His comrades erupt in fits of laughter and Alifa cannot help but smile.

'What?' Vartez says, grimacing as he gets up. 'You!' he howls at Alifa. 'You did that deliberately, gave me a broken stool. Why, I'm going to gut you.'

The Black Axe unsheathes his knife again and lunges at Alifa, who leaps back, then nudges another stool to come between them, Vartez trips over it, falls flat on his face.

'Hah!' the Black Axes roar. 'If you can't keep your feet, Vartez, you won't last long in the battle,' the tall one says, slapping the other fellow on the back as they explode in laughter.

'Damn nurse, I'll skin and gut you,' Vartez growls, kicking the stool.

Just then, a deep bellowing horn sounds.

'We need to go: we're being summoned,' says the third Black Axe.

'This will only take a minute,' Vartez spits as he comes for Alifa.

The tallest Black Axe is now beside Vartez. 'Later, after the battle. She's not going anywhere, we know where to find her. Do what you need to after the real fighting.' The Black Axe glares at her with distaste.

'She's not worth our time,' says the third man.

Vartez seems to calm down. 'All right,' he says. He points at Alifa. 'You're dead.' With that the Black Axe marches out, kicking over a table of medical supplies, sending bottles and scalpels flying. With cold stares, the other two Black Axes also leave.

Alifa lets out a long breath.

Moments later the doctor and the other nurses return as though nothing happened. They simply set about their work, barely giving Alifa a look. Even the injured soldier with the sprained wrist saunters back, finds an empty stretcher and lies down.

Alifa returns to the dead soldier. 'Sorry, friend.'

'Wrap him up,' says the doctor, appearing by her side, barely looking up from his scroll-light as he uses his *kamish* to fill out a report. 'Take him out back. There is a grove nearby, bury him there. There will be plenty more going to the same place after the fighting. Better get the gravediggers busy.'

'Yes, Doctor,' Alifa replies, wondering whether she will ever own a scroll-light and *kamish*. She doubts it: she can't afford it. The scroll-masters charge an extortionate amount for the privilege of calibrating a person with such tools.

Alifa wraps the soldier in the bloody bedroll, then wraps him again in a white cloth, before dragging his body on a bamboo stretcher out the rear to the nearby grove. The gravediggers have already prepared some burial holes and Alifa leaves the dead man in their company. She prays that the Creator will take the soul of the dead man and reunite him with his loved ones in the Gardens of Liyuün. As Alifa returns through a thicket of trees she hears voices coming up the path. Black Axes. She ducks low, hides behind the trunk of an oak.

Alifa notices a man approach from the military camp, the tallest man she has ever seen. The Sultan of the north, Artay! He is rumoured to be seven foot tall and seeing how he looms a full head above all around him, Alifa can believe it. He is immensely broad, his shaggy black beard bounces against his breastplate, and his coal-black hair sticks out from under his helmet. The emblem of a Black Axe is embossed on it. Artay strides up the gravel path, flanked by Black Axes, before stopping yards from Alifa's hiding place.

'Your Majesty,' says a Black Axe, with a bow.

'What news, Commander?' Artay asks, his voice deep and powerful. If a bear could talk, it would sound something like this, Alifa thinks.

'Gamzak has been raided by the Zandal,' the Commander says.

'What is the status of the port?' Artay asks.

'They looted, then burned the city.'

Artay clenches his gauntleted fist. The veins on his massive forearm tighten.

'Do we have it under control?' Artay asks.

'Yes, Your Majesty.'

'Is there a chance of another raid on Kermon or Gor?' Artay enquires.

'Possibly. It is difficult to say. We have sent ships out to patrol the coastline and raise the alarm should the Zandal be spotted once more.'

Artay is silent. He shuts his eyes and all around him wait. Alifa holds her breath.

'General,' Artay instructs another Black Axe. 'We cannot lose face with the Sultana, my dear cousin Negin. Send out our most disposable regiment.'

'The Nanga Pagaals?'

'Yes,' Artay continues. 'Let the drugged fools cause mayhem. No need to equip them with any sonic weapons. The Vanimal assassination team is already deployed; let it fulfil its mission to kill my cousin. If, as I suspect, she has Conduits protecting her, it will be another matter to take up with the Emperor. After the raid, withdraw all forces, and march back north, double time. We need to protect our own territory.'

'Yes, Sire,' the general replies.

'And General, don't do anything rash. Follow me north as soon as you have word from the assassination team,' Artay says.

The general winces.

'Is there something else?' Artay asks.

'The Vanimals are ...'

Artay cuts him off. 'Unpredictable beasts, I know, but expendable mercenaries, wouldn't you agree?'

'Yes, Sire.'

'Good, I would rather lose some Vanimals than men in this situation.'

'Yes, Sire.'

The giant sultan marches towards an enormous black vehicle with tractor-like wheels. Artay gets inside and it starts to slowly roll away, as other Black Axes mount similar vehicles and still more follow on horseback.

When the coast is clear, Alifa emerges, and trudges back to the medical tent. *Who – or what – are Conduits?*

-2-
BREAKING THE SEALS

Until you are tested, integrity is but a label.

THE BOOK OF HERALDS

THE ARMY OF ARTAY, the Sultan of the north, assembles on a flat expanse of land. The mountains of Dvin lie to the east, beyond which the jagged straits lead to the Middle Sea. Comprising one hundred thousand soldiers, the northern force is spearheaded by the fearsome Black Axes.

Wrapped in a dark grey cloak, his face hidden under a hood, Zorar sits on his brown mare, watching the northern army. His keen dark brown eyes take in the formation as he assesses the troop numbers. A gust of wind buffets his riding cloak, dancing around his steed. Zorar thinks: *This battle can be avoided, should be avoided, but it requires dialogue.*

A middle-aged man about Zorar's age approaches, on an open-topped algae-fuelled vehicle with wide tractor tyres that churn the grass. The driver brings the vehicle to a halt in front of the woman to Zorar's left.

'Your Majesty,' the newcomer says.

'General Ramin, your assessment?' she asks. She is Negin, Sultana of the south, the woman Zorar deeply loves, and who loves him.

Both know they can never be with one another.

Her bright brown eyes twinkle and although she is in the fourth decade of her life, her olive-coloured skin retains the suppleness of youth. A fine floral design runs up her breastplate and greaves. Her helmet shines gold and a red cape hangs from her shoulders.

The General glances over his shoulder. His soldiers are arranged in a phalanx facing the enemy who are in a similar arrangement. 'It is an odd formation,' Ramin says.

'Odd?' Negin asks.

'Too defensive,' Ramin says. 'Sultan Artay is known for his aggressive risk-taking. I expected him to set up his notorious wolf-snap manoeuvre.'

'Should we not be grateful if he means to fight a conventional battle?' Negin asks.

'We should, but something doesn't add up.'

The General is right to be cautious, thinks Zorar. In fact, Ramin is an able military commander, loved by his soldiers and no stranger to hard work.

Turning to Zorar, the General's tone is cold and formal. 'Zorar, I trust you will remain as an observer. We do not need the intervention of *your* kind.'

'He is here at my say,' Negin retorts.

Zorar exchanges an affectionate look with Negin.

'I mean no offence, Your Majesty,' Ramin says. 'But we know that Conduits are outlawed across the Empire. If Emperor Behrooz were to hear about any intervention ...'

'You know as well as I do, Ramin, that the Emperor is fixated on dancing girls and intoxicants, paying little heed to what is happening here.'

'Your Majesty knows best.' The General tilts his head.

'I will remain an observer,' Zorar says.

The General nods.

Then Zorar adds, with an impish smile: 'Unless the unexpected happens.'

'Humph!' Ramin mutters, before motioning for his driver to

turn the slow-moving vehicle back towards the main body of his troops.

'Don't pay attention to him, Zorar. Conduits will always be welcome in my dominion,' Negin says.

Then more softly she adds, 'You will always be welcome.'

'Thank you,' he whispers.

Fondly they contemplate one another, before Negin raises her chin, looks to the horizon and says, 'But we do need to lift this nonsensical imperial ban on Conduits.'

'Yes, Your Majesty,' Zorar says.

'If only my cousin Behrooz ruled effectively, it would rid us of disunity, but even rulers are slaves to history.'

Negin regards her armed forces. Zorar wants to press the matter of the ban but considers now is not the right time. *When will be the right time*, he wonders.

Horns blare across the battlefield and a riotous cry goes up from the northern forces. Zorar surveys a rabble dressed in loincloths breaking away from the main force. Nanga Pagaals. Dishevelled men, high on drugs, with white paint on their brown skins, wild hair, beards untrimmed and untamed. Each is carrying a spear; they holler as they sprint towards the southern forces.

Within minutes they cross the verdant meadow separating the two armies. General Ramin's southern infantry steps up, rifles are aimed and then the *pop-pop* of the sonic weapons is followed by line upon line of Nanga Paagals hitting the ground. Those who survive charge toward the southern force, waving spears, uttering defiant war cries. Those not mowed down by the sonic weapons are impaled on lances held in defensive positions. And Zorar considers: *What is Artay playing at? Unless.*

The *whoosh* of an axe flying through the air alerts Zorar to the

danger. Immediately his hand reaches out, whipping his cloak away. Semi-transparent lines only visible to Conduits leap from his hand to deflect the axe from striking Negin. Two more axes come at the Sultana. Zorar leaps onto the back of his horse, balances on the saddle and threads the other axes away from the monarch. Two beastlike men approach at remarkable speed, scattering the royal guard. Vanimals!

The Vanimals, humanlike but a head taller than most humans and possessed of animalistic features, slash with swords and daggers, leaving a bloody path. The Sultana's royal guard crumple before the hideous onslaught. Vibrations in the air cause Zorar to spin to the right. Half a dozen arrows fly at Negin. He deflects another dagger thrown at her. He cannot reach the arrows.

He sees more semi-transparent lines appear, propelling every arrow away from its target. Azadeh runs through a mass of southern soldiers. She has that familiar determined look on her face, her hair tied back in plaits, the hood of her cloak thrown back. Two Vanimals head towards her, drawing sonic rifles from their backs, as another Conduit, the muscular Nimar, rushes in to help her.

Zorar leaps from his horse, lands nimbly on the soil, unsheathes his sword, falls into a defensive crouch before Negin. A Vanimal breaks through a line of terrified soldiers, leaps like a predatory tiger, baring sharp white teeth, eyes wild with the thrill of the fight. The Vanimal lands before him, skids on the ground, hoping to catch him by surprise, boots aimed at Zorar's shins. Zorar leaps into the air, backflips, lands, and his sword flicks out at the Vanimal, whose axe comes up in a defensive block. The steel of the blade meets the iron of the axe, setting off sparks.

The Vanimal is almost two heads taller than him and broad as an ox, but is on his feet fast, leaping at Negin. Zorar launches himself, wraps his arms around the huge frame of the Vanimal. They both land, roll over one another. Zorar untangles himself, draws a dagger, aims at the Vanimal's jugular. His opponent pushes him off: the Vanimal is faster than expected. The Vanimal rolls forward and two daggers appear in his hands. He thrusts at Zorar.

Zorar leaps back.

The guttural steel voice of the Vanimal is distinctive as it rasps. 'Human filth.'

'Look who's talking,' Zorar says, sniffing the stench coming off the beast.

The Vanimal springs. Zorar deflects one dagger with his weapon, the other he smacks away with his hand, before he drives the Vanimal down with a knee in the neck. Zorar rolls forward. Drawing on his Conduit strength, he drags the colossal beastlike man behind and over him, before slamming him into the ground, headfirst, snapping his neck, breaking his spine. The Vanimal spasms, then goes still.

A fourth Vanimal, hidden till now, sprints towards the Sultana. The Vanimal takes several heavy sonic blasts in the chest from the royal guards, but his sturdy armour deflects the impact. A group of soldiers defends Negin against the approaching Vanimal. Invisible threads fly from Zorar's hand, yanking his sword from the ground, before he sprints at the Vanimal. The assassin, spotting the oncoming Zorar, swings his mighty spiked mace. Zorar ducks, opens a gash in the belly of the Vanimal, spins in mid-air, then in one swift movement takes off the Vanimal's head.

Zorar shifts his gaze toward Nimar and Azadeh and is relieved to see they have overcome the two Vanimals, who now lie still on the ground.

'Your Majesty,' Zorar says, approaching Negin.

Boom!

A crack of thunder, as though the sky has split, is followed by an ongoing chorus of blasts. The ground shakes, judders, vibrates. Men and animals topple, vehicles tip. Overhead the blue sky begins to change and an unnatural darkness creeps up from the horizon till the sky turns pitch black.

The thunderclaps and the earthquake cease. Silence. A comet soars overhead; as high as an eagle climbs. Emerging from the north, it heads south in a fiery inferno, lighting up the battlefield. The comet dips over the southern horizon. Disappears.

Zorar's heart races as terror fills every part of his being.

The Final Standing!

Then as suddenly as it came, the darkness steals away, following the path of the comet. The sky is restored to its natural blue hue, the sun is visible once more, the wind can be felt and slowly men and women across the battlefield turn and stare at one another. Shock is visible on every face.

Zorar kneels down. Palms flat on the earth, head lowered, he trembles, every fibre within his body fearful, on edge.

Mörtan, the Corroder, rises!

He feels for the source through the soil. He lost connection when darkness filled the sky. Was he blocked from it? Trembling hands clench into fists. He stands, composes himself, walks unsteadily towards Sultana Negin, offers his hand to help her up. She gratefully slips her hand into his and for a moment they look into each other's eyes. Zorar lets go.

Negin smooths down her dress. She is shaking. 'Is it really …
are we truly in the end time?' She studies the look of consternation on his face.

All around them, soldiers rise to their feet. Slowly the sounds of men, animals and machines return. The army of the north has remained where it was.

'It would seem like it,' Zorar replies.

'Do you not know?' she asks.

General Ramin scrambles up to the Sultana, wiping mud off his uniform. 'The northern army retreats, Your Majesty,' he says, pointing across the battlefield. 'But ...' He turns to Zorar. 'Is it truly the Hour?'

This time Zorar remains silent. He merely nods.

'Damn unlucky, is all I'd say,' Ramin declares.

He thinks once more of the Final Standing. *Oh, by the Creator, not in my lifetime!*

'Shall we rout them as they retreat?' Ramin asks. 'We may not get a better opportunity.'

Negin considers his request before replying. 'No, leave them. Whatever caused Artay to retreat may end up being the cause of our two peoples coming together. Besides, if the world is coming to an end, let us at least be in our own homes when it happens.'

'But ...' the General says.

'No,' Negin says. Her steely gaze silences Ramin. 'Remain vigilant and camp in Dvin. Send scouts to track the progress of the retreating northern army. When we are sure they have left, demobilise and return to Urua.'

Negin exchanges a concerned look with Zorar, before departing with her military officers. As she does so, the Hefter, Nimar, comes up beside Zorar. His penetrating black eyes stare at Zorar, as the Threader Azadeh joins them.

'The Final Standing approaches,' Nimar says.

'I wish it were not so,' Zorar says.

Azadeh whispers, 'The end of time.'

'How long have we got?' Nimar asks.

'That was the first sign. "A comet will turn the sky black as it flies north to south." After that, we do not know. It could be years or even decades before the Final Standing itself. It could be less. We simply do not know. But the signs will come quickly, like grains of sand slipping from your hand.'

'I wish it were not so,' Azadeh laments.

'There was something else,' Zorar says.

'More?' Nimar arches an eyebrow.

'When the horizon turned pitch black, I sensed a pulse from a Grand Conduit in the northern army.'

Nimar says, 'Sultan Artay does not have Conduits.'

'Who could it be?' asks Azadeh.

'Maybe someone who doesn't know they are a Grand Conduit. If Mörtan is about to return to Ikleel we will need all the Conduits we can find,' Zorar replies.

-3-
UNCOVERING
A CONDUIT

*Deprivation can be a gift,
for it is a doorway to awareness.*

THE WISDOM OF THE WAY

To ALIFA'S SURPRISE the medical tent does not see an influx of the newly-injured. *Perhaps*, she thinks, *the southern army capitulated*. She takes a stroll outside, observes the retreating northern army. *So soon.*

She recalls the shock when the thunderclap sounded, the earth shook, and the entire sky went black. Like others, she thought it was the end of the world. But unlike others, she felt a stabbing pain in her heart. As she watched the fiery comet pass overhead, she thought her heart was going to burst and she fell to the ground.

I need to leave. But where can I go? Alifa considers her role as a nurse: it provides her with regular food and shelter, a modicum of dignity. *What more do I want?*

She thinks about the death of the young soldier earlier, stabbed by the Black Axe. She had almost healed him. Almost, not quite. *What is this healing gift?* she ponders, not for the first time. It comes in trickles; she has little idea how or why. *Someone must know what it is. Who?*

'Alifa,' the Doctor calls.

'Coming,' she replies.

'Tell the gravediggers not to expect any more bodies except for those of the Nanga Paagals. No more graves need digging.'

'I will, Doctor.'

For the second time that day she visits the gravediggers and conveys the message, whereupon they put down their tools and take a break under a sycamore tree. Before returning to the medical tent, Alifa sits on the stump of a felled tree and looks around the silent woods. Time passes and she thinks, as she often does: *I wonder what the south is like.* Ghastly tales of Urua, the dark malevolent southern capital, have dissuaded her from finding out.

I need to get back, she counsels herself, as she stands up, then halts once more. Something is drawing her south, a magnetic resonance. She turns, looks south again. Shakes her head.

Hours have passed, for when she heads back, few soldiers remain. There's a field between her and the medical unit when three men with black axes appear.

Vartez.

Instantly they surround her, the two larger men lifting her by either arm, running with her back into the forest, toward the closest tree.

'Thought you'd make me look stupid,' Vartez snaps in her ear. 'Thought I would forget!' The Black Axe punches her in the stomach. The other two wind a rope around her, pulling her against the tree trunk. Her back is pressed against the tree, her arms pinned on either side, the rope tight around her neck. She cannot move her head. The rope is looped several times, pinning her legs as well.

The other two Black Axes snigger as they consider her situation.

'Had to catch you unawares girl, didn't want you using trickery,' Vartez says.

Although her face is jammed to one side, Alifa feels an overwhelming sense of calm wash over her. She should be terrified. She isn't.

'What trickery?' Alifa asks.

'Don't play me for a fool, girl,' Vartez snaps. 'Your kind are known for it. A little nudge here and there, make things move a few inches, trip people up. It's no wonder you people aren't welcome in the north.'

There are others like me? Alifa thinks.

'Who are we?' Alifa asks. She should be panicking, but she is filled with a soothing sensation.

Vartez yanks a long hunting knife from the scabbard on his belt. 'But once a cold shaft of steel goes through the heart you all end up the same. Dead.'

Vartez pulls the weapon back and drives it at Alifa. Unexpectedly the weapon and Vartez's arm catch in mid-air. Wide-eyed, Vartez tries to pull his arm down but it's immobile.

'What are you doing, girl?' Vartez growls.

Nothing. But she cannot tell him that.

'Slit her throat,' Vartez barks at the others. They draw knives, but before they can take any action, the blades fly from their hands, disappearing into the undergrowth. Both men are flung against tree trunks, arms pinned back. Legs parted.

'What!' the Black Axes exclaim, heads turning wildly from side to side.

Vartez, held paralysed, strains to break free. Sweat streaks his brow. The knife he holds starts to turn back towards the Black Axe himself. Eyes wide with horror, Vartez releases the blade.

'Why you ...' Vartez says, launching himself at Alifa. His body is yanked back, as though he were a puppet on a string. Thrown against a tree trunk opposite, Vartez is now restrained by invisible threads. He flails his arms, screams, curses Alifa. She is as surprised as he is. Then, as she gazes in wonder at the Black Axe, he is rotated upside down, so that his head is now inches off the ground. The sight is comical, but Alifa is not sure whether to laugh or cry. *Did I do this*, she asks herself.

Three robed figures approach across the field. One is a man in his late forties. Immaculately dressed for such a setting, he wears a mischievous smile and there's an astonishing air of confidence in his stride. To his left is a woman, her hair in ponytails and a determined look on her face. Her long fingers make movements and if Alifa didn't know better she would say invisible threads connect her and the three Black Axes. To the other side of the man is a dark-coloured fellow, powerfully built, with a generous smile. His beard has a distinct point to it.

Who are they? When Alifa makes eye contact with the man in the centre, a tremendous feeling of calm swells within her once more.

The newcomers approach Alifa. In one swift movement, the dark man flicks out a knife, cuts the ropes binding her.

'Better?' the other man asks.

'Yes,' Alifa stutters.

'Good,' he says, turns to the Black Axes. 'You know who we are?'

The Black Axes stop struggling. Nod.

'You know what we can do.'

Again, nods.

'In keeping with the spirit of a day where there was no significant fighting,' the man announces, 'you may go. Return to your army with your weapons.'

The Black Axes are stunned. Whatever pins the men to the trees is removed. They fall to the ground. Vartez lands on his head. Grumbling, but relieved. In a softer tone Vartez says: 'We will do as you command.'

'You may leave,' the man tells them.

With that the three men collect their weapons before running north. Minutes pass.

The woman tilts her head to one side, as though listening for something. 'Ah, here it comes,' she says, as Alifa hears a whoosh in the air.

The woman waves her hand as though swatting a fly, after which Alifa hears the thud of an arrow in a tree trunk behind her. The Black Axes just tried to kill her.

'May I?' the dark man asks the other.

'If you must,' the other replies.

In one swift movement, the dark muscular man removes a bow, nocks an arrow, draws back the bowstring and fires. He rapidly repeats the manoeuvre two more times. Alifa hears cries of pain from the forest.

The bowman smiles, his brilliant white teeth showing. 'Just in the thigh; they'll remember it.'

'One got it in the backside,' the woman adds with a wry smile.

'My aim must be off,' the dark man says.

The other man turns to Alifa. 'They won't be bothering you again.'

'Thank you,' Alifa stutters.

'Zorar. You may call me Zorar,' he says. 'And this fine lady with the nimble fingers is Azadeh and our less than precise bowman is Nimar.' Zorar grins at his companions before turning back to her.

'I am Alifa,' she says.

Zorar smiles. She senses that coolness and serenity enter her heart once more. He asks, 'Do you know who we are?'

She shakes her head.

'We are Conduits, part of the *Nurani Kha* Order,' Zorar says.

She now recalls hearing stories about Conduits from childhood, that they are some kind of witches and warlocks. Something inside her triggers and before she knows it she says, 'Aren't *Kha* Orders mixed up with Mörtan the Corroder?'

'Some are,' Zorar says. 'They are *Dhulmi*, serving Mörtan. Our *Kha* Order is a *Nurani* one. We oppose Mörtan.'

'How do I know you're telling the truth?' Alifa asks.

'The girl has a point, Zorar,' Nimar says.

'You can't know, Alifa. Not here. But if you come with us to Urua, to the south, then I think you'll realise we are with the noble Heralds. We uphold the criterion, established by the Creator.'

'Come with you!' Alifa exclaims. 'Why would I do that?'

'Because you are one of us,' Nimar interjects. 'You are a wielder of *Kha*: a Conduit.'

Alifa, takes a step back. 'I ...' She struggles for words.

'Have you ever been able to move objects, Alifa, just by thinking they should be moved?' Zorar asks.

'I ... yes,' Alifa replies.

'Or been able to make a wound better, simply by placing your hand on it and willing it?'

'Yes,' Alifa says. *But I couldn't save the dying soldier,* she reminds herself.

'There are many things you can do, which you do not even know of. But come south with us and we will teach you,' Zorar says. Alifa feels that wave of serenity wash over her once more.

Alifa remains silent. *There are others like me. I want to learn, but can I trust them? Yet they saved me, saved me from certain death.* Letting out a deep breath she says: 'I haven't got anywhere else to go.'

'Your family?' Zorar asks.

'There are none that I know of.'

'You are welcome to join us, Alifa,' Zorar says. 'We can be family for you, if you want us to be.'

Family, she would like to be part of a family. *How can I be sure they have my best interests at heart?*

They wait silently.

I cannot be sure, but then I cannot be sure of anything else either.

'I ...' she pauses, stares north. *There is nothing for me there.* 'I will come with you.'

Zorar's face lights up. 'There is much to learn. The work is hard and unrewarding at times: you will be pushed to your limit. No matter how many you help or save, no one will know you, no one will thank you for what you do.'

'I think I understand,' Alifa says.

'You will come to understand.'

'Is Urua as awful as they say it is?' Alifa asks.

'What do they say?' Nimar asks.

'In the north they say Urua is a nasty city, filled with flaming terraces, smoky walkways, foul odours and most of all, rude people.'

The three Conduits exchange looks with one another.

'Why,' Zorar says. 'That's exactly what we heard the capital of the north, Zanj, is like.'

-4-
URUA

*Become balanced like a mountain and
you will be unmoved by storms.*

THE BOOK OF HERALDS

EVERY BUILDING IN THE STONE CITY OF URUA, capital of the south, seems fragrant, the air infused with sweet-smelling incense and slow burning perfumed *oud*. Tawny-coloured buildings, ancient libraries, craft souks, entire quarters brimming with artisanal knowledge, all rest easy in the shade of cedars, oaks, minarets and spires. Mystics, metaphysicians and scientists, polymaths of world renown, all meander along cobbled pathways heading to dervish lodges, universities and centres of knowledge and learning. Merchants' horse-drawn carts and slow-moving vehicles with wide tractor tyres carry fresh produce picked daily on farms surrounding the city. Urua is a self-reliant marvel; the city seems to inhale and exhale, at peace with itself and all who occupy it.

In one intricate alley, where the footpath is a mosaic of azure tiles, and fountains supply citizens with crystal-clear drinking water, Alifa waits. Her mouth is wide open: she is amazed at the sights around her. In the night she had not taken in the marvel of Urua, but now by day, it overwhelms her. This is not the city described by northerners; this is a land of dreams. Then she remembers once more the stabbing pain in her heart when the comet flew overhead. Zorar mentioned it has something to do with the Final Standing. She does not know what this is but suspects she will soon learn of its consequence. *It has an ominous air to it – the Final Standing. What are people standing for and what is final about it?*

From the far end of the street, beside a green flag with an outline of a hoopoe bird, a tall, well-built man casually strolls in her direction. As he draws closer Alifa is mesmerised by his good looks and winning smile, his chiselled jaw, his perfectly coiffed hair held back by a red headband. Two-day-old stubble covers his lower face and as he comes closer, she notes his eyes are like a deep well.

Two young women on the other side of the street halt, stare at the passing man, whisper to each other, smile as he walks past them. They give him a shy wave, to which he graciously bows, flashing that charming smile. One woman almost topples and is supported by the other. A slightly older woman, walking with her husband, promptly stops to take in this most gorgeous man, and lets out a long sigh. The husband walks on. This dashing figure, in his buccaneering boots and belt, a sword in a sheath by his side, places his hand on his heart and bows to the woman.

For the second time that morning Alifa reminds herself to shut her gawping mouth.

The fellow now turns his penetrating gaze on Alifa and the young northerner gulps. Her mouth goes dry and she can feel the heat rising in her cheeks.

'You must be Alifa?' he says in a deep resonant voice.

Alifa is silent.

The man arches a perfect eyebrow. 'Or maybe you are not?'

'I am she. I am Alifa.'

The man places a hand on his heart. 'Goodwill to you, Alifa.'

'Goodwill,' Alifa replies.

'I am Jamshi. Zorar asked me to collect you from this spot. He had an important matter to attend to this morning. Come, let us go,' he says, as Alifa joins him and they continue down the street.

Heads turn as Jamshi strolls by. He acknowledges most well-wishers with either a sparkling smile, a hand on his heart, or when they are close enough, he utters the traditional greeting of the Arön empire: 'Goodwill.'

'How was your first night in Urua?' Jamshi asks.

'Restful,' Alifa says.

In truth she has never slept in such a comfortable bed and the novelty of a room to herself, with clear running water and a toilet, was not lost on her. She woke several times in the night, wondering why it was so quiet.

'You seem uncertain,' Jamshi comments.

'I'm not used to the silence,' Alifa replies.

'Zorar said he found you with the northern army.'

'Yes.'

Jamshi rubs his chin. 'Uncertainty, noise, danger, death – I suppose these are the only certainties when you are in an army.'

'Something like that,' Alifa says, preferring not to think about it, as she regards a green-domed building they walk past, sparkling sapphires set into its walls. *Will this new life in the south be better than my time in the north? It must be. Oh, by the Creator I pray for it.*

Jamshi tells Alifa to wait as he enters the premises of a scroll-keeper and takes out his scroll-light and *kamish*. He deposits the device with the scroll-keeper for maintenance, before returning to the footpath. Moments later, they stop once more, at the Dallah Wala, where Jamshi collects two cups of *kahwa*, offering one to Alifa. They sip the sweet-tasting beverage, before continuing.

The pair turn into a small square where a group of old men sits together and a large crowd of children dances and jumps to the sound of the music they play. One elder plays an *oud*, a fretless stringed instrument; beside him is a *duff* player, tapping the ends of the drum, and then there is a flute player who conjures a harmonious melody.

When the *oud* player notices them, he immediately stops and waves them over. 'Jamshi!' the musician exclaims.

Jamshi smiles, glances at his watch. 'We will be late, if ...'

'*Sayyidi* ... the children want to hear the world's greatest troubadour play,' the *oud* player says, hand on heart, beckoning them again.

'Next time Sidi – I have to go, but I will return,' Jamshi says with a dramatic twirl of his hands.

'But you promised ...' a voice calls out.

Jamshi stops. Winks at Alifa, turns to the crowd and sings in the most harmonious voice she has ever heard:

> *'The promise I made; I commit to.*
> *The songs I sing, I sing for you.*
> *The promise I made I commit to.*
> *The songs I sing, I sing for you.*
> *But today this is all I can do.*
> *I will return with songs anew.'*

Alifa notices the looks of disappointment on the faces of the musicians and children. Several children wave and Alifa returns their gesture.

'Keep moving, Alifa,' Jamshi says. 'If we stop, I will forget the time and Zorar does not like to be kept waiting.'

'You are a musician?' Alifa asks.

'I have some skill,' Jamshi replies, but she thinks he is hiding the extent of his ability.

'The man called you the world's greatest troubadour.'

'I've been promising to play something, but recently the demands of the royal court and our other ... commitments, and now this situation with the Final Standing, have meant I've done fewer impromptu performances for the public.'

'You perform at the court of the Sultana of the south?'

'They have some uses for me.'

Alifa is about to ask another question, when Jamshi turns sharp right down a narrow pathway. It slants downwards, then they turn left, descending a set of stairs and entering a courtyard with a syca-more tree at its centre, around which there flows a stream of water. Several sand-coloured and reddish-brown buildings form a colour-ful ring around the courtyard, which is bedecked with a dazzling display of marigolds, hibiscus, jasmine, roses and bougainvillea.

Jamshi leads her towards a light tan two-storey building with intricate wooden panel carvings on its façade. It has several stained-glass windows and azure tilework. They enter a large hall with a high ceiling. Mosaics in shades of ink blue, rose red and sunflow-er yellow run around it, and hallways branch off in four directions. They go straight past a set of stairs and up to the next level. Walk-ing down a corridor, they see that paintings featuring calligraphic brushstrokes adorn the walls. They arrive at a large circular *majlis* with twelve high-backed chairs.

'Ah, we're early. Take a seat Alifa. Let me pour some hibiscus tea.'

Floor to ceiling windows run the length of the room and Alifa notes the lush verdant landscaped garden where trees grow: man-goes, papaya, guava and figs. Around a pond are beds of hyacinth, marigolds and lilies, and elsewhere banks of hibiscus and lotus pro-vide colourful cover.

Alifa stands silently by the window. *The south is unlike anything I was told*, she thinks. *Why did I ever doubt myself about moving here? Yet can it truly be so good? Nothing in life tends to be what it seems.*

'Here you go.' Jamshi passes the tea to her.

'Thank you.'

'I hear you're a Nourisher?' Jamshi asks.

Alifa's expression is blank.

'Ah, the look on your face tells me you're not familiar with Conduit abilities.'

'I am not,' Alifa replies. 'Do you have a … an ability?'

Jamshi nods, rubs his chin. 'I am known as a Clarifier.'

'What is that?'

'Through words, music and art, Clarifiers remind the soul of its true purpose, which is to return to the Creator.'

'I see,' Alifa says, though in truth she is not sure what Jamshi is saying. 'But you are a troubadour.'

'We all need to pay the bills. My employment with the royal court allows me certain privileges, but when the work of the Order comes up, it takes priority.'

Another man appears in the doorway. He looks to be in his late forties, possibly older, slightly portly, with a moustache and goatee beard, wavy hair down to his neck and the cheekiest of smiles. He wears loose khaki-coloured trousers, a baggy shirt, and a reddish-brown waistcoat. A patterned scarf is tossed casually around his neck.

'Durayd,' Jamshi says. The two men clutch elbows before hugging.

'Found the right woman yet?' asks Durayd.

Jamshi turns a touch red. 'There are so many to choose from, it's quite an ordeal.'

'Bah! You fool. You'll never find the ideal wife that way. Just marry the best one available, and work with her to make yourselves perfect for each other.'

'You make it sound so simple,' Jamshi says.

'It is, my friend. Don't complicate matters.' Durayd roars in laughter, slaps Jamshi on the back and turns to Alifa. 'New Conduit?'

'Apparently a Nourisher,' Jamshi says. 'Her name is Alifa.'

'Alifa,' Durayd says. 'Goodwill to you.'

Alifa replies. She can smell the aroma of *kahwa* coming from Durayd. A sense of calm falls over her. Alifa thinks that Durayd is such a kind, generous dignified man, the very thought of upsetting him is suddenly anathema to her.

'Durayd! Go easy on her,' Jamshi says.

'What!' Alifa exclaims.

'I'm just making friends,' Durayd retorts.

'By manipulating emotions,' Jamshi says.

'Merely drawing out the innate kindness that resides in the girl's heart,' Durayd replies.

Alifa looks from one man to the other. 'You made me feel calm? You can do that?'

'Durayd here is what they call a Calmer,' Jamshi says.

'Oh!' Alifa says. 'Are you still calming me?'

'No, you just needed a touch and your good character surfaced quickly. Rarity these days: most people are harder work.'

Jamshi pours Durayd a glass of tea, after which Azadeh appears by the doorway. She still wears the steely look of determination Alifa noticed the first time they met in the forest of Dvin. Her hair is tied in plaits, and her long fingers remind Alifa of the twigs of a tree.

'Gentlemen and lady,' Azadeh says.

'Goodwill, Azadeh!' cries Durayd. 'Been too long. How are your husband and children?'

'Goodwill, Durayd, they are well. Thank you.' Turning towards the troubadour Azadeh asks: 'Married yet?'

Jamshi bends towards Alifa, a guilty smile on his face. 'They have my best interests at heart.'

'Find a wife, before I find one for you,' Azadeh declares.

'Worth taking Azadeh up on the offer, Jamshi – she is an agronomist after all. Cultivation is her forte,' Durayd adds, winking at Alifa.

Surprisingly, Alifa cannot help but like these people; they have a certain companionship with one another. They even treat her like a long-time friend.

'You should know, Alifa, the garden back there is Azadeh's handiwork, but to see what she can really do, you should visit her in her food-forest south of Urua,' Durayd says.

'How are you, Alifa?' Azadeh addresses her.

'Well, thank you,' Alifa says.

'Nourisher apparently,' Durayd adds.

'I know. Always need a good Nourisher in the forest: lot of animals and plants to take care of. A little bit of extra healing at times is never a bad thing,' says Azadeh.

'I can use my … abilities on animals and plants?' Alifa asks.

The three of them look at one another in bemusement.

'She's new,' Jamshi adds.

'She is!' a voice announces from the doorway.

Zorar enters, elegant and imposing, in a long dark blue robe with golden seams and a mosaic pattern running along the edges. His face shines with a serene smile, which he shares with Alifa.

'Goodwill to you all,' Zorar says. He turns to Alifa. 'Rest well?'

'Yes, thank you.'

Nimar appears at the door, his muscular frame filling it, and further greetings are exchanged. Two more join them: first, Kaşifa, Chief Librarian of the royal court, who dresses like an austere scholar in sombre shades, despite only being in her late twenties. Tall and thin, Kaşifa has a solemn serious-minded look to her. The man who enters next is Belal, an in-demand apothecary and acupuncturist who has a surgery in Urua. His concoctions of herbs and cures are known far and wide, according to Durayd. He is a Nourisher. Belal is of medium build, with silky hair fashioned into a long ponytail. His beard is wispy, and he wears several rings set with an assortment of stones, as well as a variety of necklaces.

The eight now seat themselves in the *majlis*, around the circular table.

'Everyone is here, except for Cinan. He was called to court for the commission of a new observatory,' explains Zorar.

'Another one?' Durayd asks.

'The Sultana is a patron of the arts and sciences,' Zorar replies.

Alifa thinks: *Sultana Negin invests in art, culture and the sciences, whilst her cousin Sultan Artay wishes to wage war upon her.*

'One other person needs to attend this meeting,' Zorar says. 'I asked him to wait a few minutes. Nimar, please ask him to come in.'

The Hefter departs, returns with another man. The newcomer is dressed in a tight grey and black suit, with a military cut. He is short and wears a worried expression. His hair is cropped and his face clean-shaven.

'Wait a minute! Is that …' Durayd says.

'General Ramin, you are most welcome,' Zorar says. He stands, shakes his hand and directs the General to a chair, before pouring him a glass of tea.

Ramin accepts the tea, turning the hot glass around in his fingers. Observes those seated with the eye of a clinician assessing the sick.

'What is he doing here?' Azadeh asks Zorar. 'He abhors Conduits.'

Ramin's face twitches. He sips the tea.

Zorar says: 'After the assassination attempt on the Sultana, she asked that General Ramin and I should put aside our differences. A matter has come to her attention that requires our collaboration.'

'The Final Standing maybe?' Durayd asks.

'Another matter,' Zorar says.

Durayd arches an eyebrow.

The General turns to Durayd. '*Dallah Wala Kahwa*. I've visited your outlets several times. Never knew you were a Conduit, Durayd.'

'And knowing it, will you continue to visit?' Durayd asks.

'I will embrace this new spirit of comradeship.'

Durayd nods.

The General eyes Jamshi. 'I should have suspected, for your words are so powerful and clear, your music enough to make a man weep or cry. You recently played at the autumn festival. I and my family were in the audience. There was not a dry eye in the hall, including my own, after you finished the performance.'

'I will take it as a compliment,' Jamshi says.

Ramin scans the others, recognising Kaşifa. 'Chief Librarian,' the General nods.

Kaşifa's austere expression does not change.

'The General has assured me that your identities and these discussions will remain within these walls. Is that not so,' says Zorar.

'Most certainly.'

'Go ahead then, General,' Zorar encourages.

Ramin takes another sip of the tea. 'Good tea,' he says. 'Hibiscus, I think.'

Jamshi nods.

'In recent months,' Ramin declares, 'a group called the Syndicate, made up of Teutons from the north, has established a commercial and political foothold in Arön. It would seem our Emperor likes them and has bestowed several lucrative commercial arrangements on them.'

Ramin examines the hibiscus tea. Twirls the glass slowly in his fingers. 'By all accounts the Emperor is addicted to the narcotic Opius. The Syndicate is now the largest global supplier of Opius, farming it at industrial scale in the Northern Wastes. They have made some arrangement with the Zandal and have flooded Cin, leading to an Opius epidemic. Now they enter Arön.'

'Opius is highly addictive,' Belal the apothecary says. 'After only a single shot, the body craves it.'

Ramin nods before pressing on with his case. 'The Syndicate has tabled several reforms with the Emperor – some relate to agriculture and farming, some to industrial mechanisation, and some, in my opinion, are criminal, such as flooding our cities with Opius.'

'What is the Emperor's response?' Kaşifa asks.

'Favourable,' says Ramin. 'The Emperor has appointed advisors from the Syndicate into every ministry. He has issued an imperial decree instructing Sultana Negin to facilitate the Syndicate's entry into the south. As you know the Teutons are opening an Embassy in Urua this month. To all intents and purposes this will be the commercial centre for the Syndicate in our capital.'

'This is all statecraft,' Durayd says. 'Hardly our area of expertise.'

The General glances at Zorar, who nods. 'Indeed, but there is another connected matter that has come to our attention.' Ramin pauses; the twitch is back under his left eye. 'The Syndicate use Conduits, like you,' he declares.

A hush fills the *majlis*.

'Whoa!' Durayd cries.

Ramin presses on. 'The Syndicate used Conduits to great effect in Cin. At this time we do not know how many they have in Urua, but they have them, we know this.'

'Any Grand Conduits?' Nimar asks.

Ramin shrugs. 'Maybe, I wouldn't know.'

'That's why you need us, General,' Durayd says, cocking his head to one side. 'But what do we get from this arrangement?'

All heads turn back to the General.

'As you know,' Ramin starts, 'the Sultana has kept Conduits close. When the time is right, she will make the necessary representations with the Emperor to lift the empire-wide ban on Conduits.'

'Is that a promise?' Durayd probes.

'It is a commitment from your ruler,' Ramin says.

'Umm,' Durayd looks across at Zorar, his expression uncertain.

The *majlis* is quiet once more.

'What do you need us to do?' Nimar asks.

'Use your abilities,' Ramin says. 'Get close to the Syndicate. Find out about their plans for Arön. What are they going to do, when, how, who? Share this information with me, and together we can repel these people from the empire and send them back to the north.'

Alifa remains silent, studies the faces. Zorar sits forward, rests his arms on the table. 'If the Syndicate uses Conduits, we need to level up the field. If the Syndicate's Conduits follow the *Dhulmi* Order, they are servants of Mörtan. Recent events have shown that the Final Standing is coming and with it Mörtan will return.' He stops and looks at Ramin. 'Let us just say we cannot allow *Dhulmi* Conduits to flourish in Arön.'

Zorar gently twirls the agate stone ring that adorns his right index finger.

'I can't say I trust the military,' Azadeh says. 'But if you think this is the right thing to do, I'll follow you.'

Zorar nods.

'Nimar?' Zorar asks.

'You have my support.'

He looks at Jamshi.

'I suppose it's an opportunity to write some new songs, more upbeat perhaps. I'm in.'

'Durayd?'

'I don't have a good feeling about this, Zorar. Many of us have kept our abilities hidden from men such as Ramin. If the military turns on us *again*, where do we go?'

'Durayd, do we have a choice?' Zorar says. 'Should the Syndicate get their way, they will topple the economy of the empire. Some profit, most lose. Besides, the Teutons hate *kahwa*, they drink tea! What would happen to Dallah Wala?'

The stout man rubs his chin, laughs out loud. 'Well, now that you put it that way, count me in.'

'Belal?' Zorar asks.

'I know the effects of Opius,' the apothecary says. 'And though I do not trust the General, in the interests of keeping Arön clear of Opius, you have my support.'

Zorar nods and turns to Kaşifa who says: 'I will start researching the Syndicate and what else the Teutons have been up to recently that may impact us.'

'Thank you,' says Zorar. He looks at Alifa.

Taking her cue, she nods enthusiastically.

Zorar swings his gaze back to the General. 'You have our support,' he says.

-5-
ELEMENTAL

There is a light deep in your heart which He has sent from an invisible realm. Polish your heart and you will become that light.

THE WISDOM OF THE WAY

A FTER LUNCH, THE OTHERS LEAVE. Zorar remains at the lodge with Alifa. Zorar has hinted she is more than a Nourisher. Alifa thinks: *I don't understand these people. I want to understand them.*

'Alifa, I want to begin your training now.'

'Here?' Alifa asks.

'Not quite here,' Zorar replies. 'But nearby.'

He leads Alifa out the dining room, down the corridor, back to the central entrance hall, then along another corridor. They pass a library – its doors are open, Alifa marvels at the thousands of books, filling shelves from floor to ceiling. Tomes encapsulating centuries of knowledge, in green leather jackets, or with dark brown spines and sand-coloured covers.

The corridor ends at a plain-looking door. Zorar opens it to reveal a metal grille which he pulls to one side.

'Go on,' he invites her.

The space is tight, with stonework on either side. Alifa steps in and Zorar follows, shuts the door and pulls the grille back into place. He unlocks a mechanism, pulls a lever. The lift judders, then descends.

When they reach the basement, Zorar reattaches the lock on the lever, then opens the grille, and the door. They step out into a well-lit corridor sloping downwards. At the end of the corridor is an entrance to another room.

'Come on,' Zorar encourages Alifa.

They emerge into a large circular room; mosaic tiles intricately decorate the domed ceiling. Geometric patterns are carved into walls around the room. Elsewhere maroon calligraphic brushstrokes appear against a sandstone finish. Azure and topaz inlaid tiles run around the edges of the room. In the centre is an enormous circle. The floor is a complex geometric design; the degree of craftmanship mesmerises Alifa.

To one side, seven waist-height glass cylinders contain elements in varying colours.

'This is the training circle,' Zorar says. 'We learn how to access the Source through the seven elements.' Noticing the absent look on her face, Zorar pauses. 'What do you know of *Kha* and what we do?'

'Nothing,' she says.

'Do you know of the Heralds?' Zorar enquires.

'I have heard of them.'

'And what of the Primordial Promise?'

She shakes her head.

'Let us begin with the Primordial Promise, for this is our divine history,' Zorar says. 'It is an ancient commitment every human made to the Creator. When we were created, He, the Creator, asked us to recognise Him. We all affirmed Him as our Lord.'

'I don't remember,' Alifa replies.

'None of us do. This elemental bond was made by our spirits before we were given physical bodies,' Zorar says. 'From what we know of our ancient history, a descent took place from the heavenly abode. Three types of beings were sent to Ikleel – Humans, Vanimals and the Djüne.'

'I've seen Vanimals: the Sultan of the north keeps some,' Alifa says. 'But the Djüne, aren't they just folk tale and myth?'

'If only it were the case.'

'Oh.'

Zorar picks up a book. 'I want you to read this later. It's a history of Ikleel. As you know we are in what the historians call the third epoch. This book contains the histories of the first and second epochs. It's important for you to understand, especially now that ... the Final Standing approaches.'

'This ... Final Standing, what does it mean?'

Zorar lets out a long sigh. 'We do not really know; our records are buried deep within vaults which no one has accessed for millennia. Kaşifa is now investigating the imperial archives. Yet the major sign, the one that starts everything is what you witnessed at the Battle of Dvin. As to what that everything is, possibly it's the end of human life upon Ikleel. As to when, we do not know. Anyway, read that book. Perhaps you might uncover something useful which I have forgotten.'

'I will,' she says.

Zorar strides over to a wall upon which hangs a large map of the world.

'Ikleel,' Zorar says.

Alifa notes that the continents, land masses and oceans are etched onto the brass plate hanging there.

Zorar looks at the map. 'As far as we know a Herald was sent to every people and nation on Ikleel. Some Heralds brought oratory, others stories, some songs, artwork, others books of revelation.'

'How many Heralds were there?' Alifa asks.

'Tens of thousands, possibly more. What we do know is that every Herald was a Grand Conduit and of their descendants, some manifested the abilities of Conduits and fewer developed into

Grand Conduits.'

'Am I … descended from a Herald?' she asks.

Zorar nods enthusiastically. 'You are a very special person, Alifa. In fact, you are probably descended from two Heralds, since we think the chance of a Grand Conduit appearing becomes greater when two Heraldic bloodlines merge.'

Her throat is dry and she feels a tear well up. In wonderment and awe, she stares with renewed interest at the map. *I didn't even know my parents; how can I possibly learn my ancestry?*

'We draw our power, this thing we call *Kha*, from the Source, a spring which we think emanates from the ocean surrounding the throne of the Creator. We cannot touch the Source; it is too much for any human to bear. We must use the elements to channel *Kha*, this ability we have. Hence, we are sometimes called Conduits.'

Zorar pauses.

'I think I understand,' she says, when she realises he is waiting for her to say something.

They walk back to the central circle with the mosaic floor. Zorar stops beside the line of waist-high cylinders. From the first cylinder he draws a handful of dark rich soil and rubs it between his fingers. It crumbles. 'Soil is made of several elements,' Zorar says.

Moving across to a cylinder brimming to the top he clutches a handful of the contents. 'Sand,' he says, as he takes some granules, places them in the palm of his hand and with the fingers of his other hand rubs them into his palm. Moments later there is a glow, like a firefly dancing over his outstretched palm. It lasts mere seconds. Alifa is unsure whether her eyes have deceived her.

Zorar turns to look at Alifa, and she is overwhelmed by a sense of relief. She felt the same when first meeting Durayd. 'You're calming me with this *Kha*,' Alifa says.

'That's right,' replies Zorar. 'I wasn't very subtle about it, I just hit you full on. The more subtle you are, the less someone knows you're calming them. The best effects by practitioners of *Kha* like Durayd are imperceptible. Now you try.'

He directs her to the cylinder and she takes some sand, placing it into her left palm.

Zorar continues. 'As a Grand Conduit, you can tap into the Source to strengthen your *Kha* through the sand particles. But you can only reach it through your heart.'

'My heart?' she asks, staring at the grains of sand in her hand.

'Yes, the illumination of the heart is more powerful than the eyes, for when you access the spiritual heart, the light, the *Nur*, which the Creator has placed within you, you gain access to the realm of the metaphysical, beyond the material world. This is where the powers of *Nurani Kha* reside, in the metaphysical, that which can only be accessed by the spiritual aspect of your person, and the organ in the body that is most connected to the spiritual realm, to the Source, is the human heart. Learn to see with your heart and you will connect with the Source. Try it.'

Alifa is unsure. She rubs the sand particles in her palm, waits for something to happen, to see the glow. Nothing.

'Take it slow, no need to rush. Breathe, calm yourself, try again, with the heart,' Zorar reassures her. Zorar slips a green agate ring off his finger, places it in an inside pocket.

Listen with my heart, feel with it, see with it, she tells herself.

She presses down on the sand particles. A sudden surge produces an incredible sense of elation. Despite herself, she smiles. From the particles of sand, a glow forms, like a firefly rising from the palm of her hand.

'Oh!' she exclaims, then watches the glow go out.

—

'Yes, you have it,' Zorar says. 'Now direct that emotion at me.'

Alifa, beaming from ear to ear, thrusts the feeling in his direction, like a river boat leaving one shore to cross to the other. She imagines ripples moving across a placid lake.

'Yes!' Zorar says. 'I feel great!'

'How long can I keep on making you feel calm?' Alifa asks.

'Length of time is less important. When you nudge a person's emotions, their own internal mechanism will take over and the sense of calm will unfold. If you need to calm a group of people, then you will need to draw more of the Source. There are many factors at play: the capacity of the Conduit, and the litanies invoked. You will learn more as you progress. In time you may be as proficient as Durayd.'

'Once I draw on the Source, how long can I keep it, before it extinguishes?'

'Good question,' Zorar says. 'It remains as a reserve within until you use it.'

'I don't feel it anymore,' Alifa says.

'That's because you hit me with a full dose of *Kha*. With experience, you'll learn to release your energy incrementally. That way you keep your reserves for longer.'

Zorar moves to the next cylinder. The substance is white and clear.

'Silica,' says Zorar. 'A component of sand. When you reach for the Source through silica, you access another of the emotional abilities, that of a Clarifier.'

'What does a Clarifier do?' Alifa asks.

'A Clarifier reminds a person of their true purpose.'

'Which is?'

'From the Creator we came and to the Creator we will return.

A Clarifier removes distractions from the human heart, reminds a person of their journey back to the Creator. It is a very delicate and elusive skill, which Jamshi is best placed to teach you.'

Alifa collects up particles of silica from the cylinder, places them into the cup of her palm, then rubs them with her fingers.

'With your heart,' Zorar whispers.

The glow appears, rising from her palm, before it winks out seconds later.

Alifa closes her eyes, reaches for the Source. An overpowering sense of detachment hits her. She is like a reed shorn from the riverbank, lost from its home, cast down river, when all she wants is to return home to the safety of the riverbank. Her eyes open and tears pour down her cheeks.

'What happened?' she fumbles the words.

Zorar casts a sympathetic look at her. He places a hand on her shoulder. 'You just became aware of your spirit.'

'My spirit,' she whispers.

'It has been veiled from you,' he says. 'Possibly your entire life. Now you know what the spirit yearns for. It aches to return to the Creator, to be in the divine presence. This is what Clarifiers do: they remind a person of their spirit, by lifting the veils around it. We are spirits having a physical experience in this world but when we die we return to our true form.'

'What does a spirit look like?' Alifa asks, wiping tears from her face.

'The Heralds speak of the spirit as pure light; it is the size of a large ant. Tiny, compared to our physical bodies, but it is who we are. It is our essence.'

The size of an ant!

'The spirit within you is tethered to another realm, tap into it and you will access all the beauty and majesty of that which is hidden,' Zorar studies her carefully, gives her time to regain her composure before he says, 'are you ready to move to the next element?'

Taking a deep breath, Alifa nods.

They approach a cylinder containing a very pale brown substance.

'Corallite,' Zorar says. 'Another element, though it is found in the soil of the sea.'

Whoosh! Alifa turns to witness a sword fly through the air before Zorar seizes it. He raises his other hand and a shield flies off a wall into his grip. 'Threading. When you tap into the Source through the corallite you learn to thread objects around you. You can tug in your direction, as I just did, or you can ...' The sword soars from his grip and embeds itself in a wooden beam at a cross-section of the dome. 'Thrust.'

Alifa places some of the corallite in her palm, rubs with her index finger. The glow forms.

Zorar takes several steps away from her.

Alifa reaches for the Source through corallite. Faint white lines appear around her, like the web of a spider. A thread!

'Now, tug this shield from my grip,' Zorar instructs.

Alifa reaches out with her hand, aiming for the shield, and notices a single thicker thread appear in her vision. It attaches to the shield and she tugs. The shield slams into her, knocks her off her feet.

Zorar is beside her, offering a hand up. 'Are you all right?'

The shield is in Alifa's hand, but she also feels a bruise coming up around her knuckles.

'It takes practice. You tugged too hard, when a softer tug would have done. The heavier the object the more force you need to apply, but then the heavier the object coming at you, the more precise you need to be.'

Zorar takes ten paces away from her and says, 'Now, thread the shield to me. Remember, moderate your effort.'

Alifa holds the shield in her hand. In her mind she draws a straight line to Zorar. Immediately faint white lines, like iced spiderwebs appear, heading towards him. One line is particularly thick. She thrusts the shield along that line. It flies from her hand, but at a speed that makes it easy for Zorar to catch.

'Yes, you have it. It normally takes a novice much longer to get to grips with thrusts, but you have a natural affinity for it,' Zorar says.

Alifa smiles. Thinks back to the time she knocked over the Black Axe in the medical tent.

Zorar strolls across to a sword stand, beside which is a set of ten black *meels*, hefty clubs with short handles, used by warriors for training. He motions for Alifa to pick up the second one from the right.

She lifts it. It's heavy, but manageable.

'Can you swing it over your head?'

She tries and just manages it, before putting it down again.

'Now try the fifth one,' he says.

Alifa hesitates. She tries, all the while knowing she won't be able to lift it over her head. She grips the handle of the *meel*. She cannot even move it from its stand.

'I can't,' she gasps.

Zorar walks back to another cylinder.

'Ochre,' he says. 'This gives you physical strength, allows you to lift heavy objects.'

Alifa places the ochre in her palm, rubs it and the glow appears. *With my heart, see with my heart*, she reminds herself. A surge of *Kha* flows through her muscles.

'Oh!' she exclaims.

'Try the fifth again,' Zorar instructs.

She strides over to the *meel* stand. Grips the fifth *meel* by the handle. Draws it with ease and without much effort lifts it high over her head.

Zorar smiles. 'You are a quick learner.'

Alifa swings the *meel* around, like she has seen northern wrestlers do, switches it from one hand to the other. It feels light.

'Try the eighth one,' Zorar encourages.

Putting the other *meel* back, she hesitates: the eighth *meel* is large, very chubby.

'Go on,' he says.

She tries and lifts it clear over her head in a single movement. With an effort she swings it between her arms before placing it back in the stand.

Alifa puffs out her cheeks, suddenly feeling tired.

'That was a very good first attempt. As with the other elements, over time you will learn to draw more *Kha* and maintain higher levels of reserve. I suspect you will be able to lift two of the heaviest *meels* at the same time and swing them around. But remember, you must learn when your power is draining, because if you're carrying a heavy load when it goes, you'll be crushed. An experienced Hefter like Nimar knows their limits.'

Zorar walks back to the set of cylinders and stands beside the cream element.

'Limestone,' Zorar says. 'This is where we access our healing abilities, to be what we call a Nourisher. You already have some experience of this, but you still have much to learn. Belal is the best Nourisher I know, and I'll let him train you.'

Zorar gestures to the next cylinder, containing a jet-black element. 'Obsidian. We access this to imbue. An Imbuer like Kaşifa can infuse an inanimate object with memories, so when another Imbuer touches it, they can also access the memory. Let me demonstrate.'

Zorar strides over to a table where pens and scrolls are kept. He lifts one of the pens. Holds it between the tips of his fingers, shuts his eyes for a short while, then opens them and hands the pen to Alifa.

'I have imbued or planted a memory in this pen. See if you can access it.'

She accesses the Source through obsidian, then feels with her heart. Alifa examines the pen. A picture appears in her head. She sees the three Black Axes surround her, tie her to the tree before Vartez lifts his weapon.

'I saw myself and the Black Axes, but … through your eyes,' she says.

'That's right. Imbuing can be very useful when you need to send someone a message, or you want to send a message across time.'

'Across time?'

'We have objects that were imbued hundreds, maybe thousands of years ago.'

Alifa shakes his head. 'But how do I know if a memory has been left inside an object?'

'You don't,' says Zorar. 'Which is what makes the role of an Imbuer tedious work: you have to search through hundreds of objects which have no such memory to perhaps find one that does. Fortunately, Imbuers have developed a system over the years, whereby they are more likely to imbue certain types of objects, such as an astrolabe, or a compass. This makes it easier for another Imbuer to access the memory. If of course you are trying to hide your memory for a specific person alone, then there may be other forms of cryptography that can be used. I will ask Kaşifa to show you more.'

She nods, thinks about the possible ways she can use the skill of an Imbuer. 'So, someone from the past could compose a specific message for me?'

'Yes,' Zorar says.

Only no one would want to send me a message, she thinks.

Zorar looks at the final cylinder. 'This cylinder contains volcanic ash and is used by a Revealer. Cinan is the most experienced Revealer I have worked with, as Chief Architect of Urua. It is better he shows you what a Revealer can do.'

He guides Alifa to a set of *tasbeah,* ceremonial beads linked together. *Tasbeah* sets are arranged on a table, are of different colours and sizes but each has ninety-nine beads strung along a single strand.

Zorar picks up a set. 'The elements are not always around us, so we carry these *tasbeah.* Each bead contains the element that a particular Conduit can use. So, in this one,' he picks up a brown set. 'All of the beads are filled with sand particles for a Calmer to access.'

Zorar selects the last bead closest to what would be the conjoining section at the top of the *tasbeah,* moves it along, till it passes through a ring at the point before where the first bead is located, where it then comes away from the remainder of the set. Once in the palm of his hand, Zorar rubs the bead with his fingers and Alifa notices sand particles in his hand, the bead has emptied its contents though the bead itself remains intact. The now familiar glow forms.

'Each bead is painstakingly made. When one bead comes away from the others it begins to empty, allowing you to access the element within and so tap into your *Kha* abilities.'

'Wouldn't it be easier to keep the elements in a phial?' Alifa asks.

'You could do that,' Zorar says. 'Indeed, the *Dhulmi Kha* Conduits keep their elements in ironwood cartridges which they wear like belts around their waists. We use the *tasbeah*, because the beads also serve as part of the daily litany you will perform as a Conduit. The more invocations you pronounce over your beads, the longer the element contained within will last. Once a bead has been emptied, you will later need to refill it and reattach it to the set.'

Zorar withdraws a magnificent *tasbeah* from within the folds of his robes. It is rosewood in colour. The ring around which a bead is removed is brass. He holds the *tasbeah* in his hand. 'Some of these beads in this set, I have been reading litanies over for months, others for years.'

He guides her across to another table, containing many *tasbeahs*. 'These are the *tasbeahs* of a Grand Conduit. Each bead contains particles from all of the elements. I will show you how to make your own beads and fill them. This is an important craft to learn and it will serve you well in your function as a Grand Conduit. For now, I want you to pick one.'

She is taken aback. *He offers me a priceless tasbeah.*

'Whichever one you recommend,' Alifa says, as her eyes stray to a camel-coloured set, with white and gold trimmings.

Zorar examines the dozens of *tasbeah* sets on the table. After glancing at her, he looks at the *tasbeahs* once more. He takes a step towards one, hesitates, then picks up the camel-coloured one which Alifa had had her eyes on. 'This is the one for you,' he says.

Alifa takes it in both hands. The beads are smooth and cool to touch. She moves them between her fingers.

Zorar steps back. 'Yes, I think that suits you very much.'

'Thank you,' Alifa says.

'No need to show off when you're walking down the street: people might get the wrong impression. But always have them on your person. They will serve as a doorway to the Source. You can access your full *Kha* powers when you remove a bead. Just remember to keep the bead in safe place, so that you can reuse it later once filled and reattached to the set. As for the invocations to read over them, I will share these with you. The more you moisten your tongue with the litanies, the deeper your connection to the Source, the more you can harness your *Kha* as a Grand Conduit.'

Alifa nods.

Zorar takes out the agate ring he had slipped into his robe and puts it back on his finger. From his other inside pocket, he takes out a similar ring encased in silver and hands it to Alifa.

'Wear this at all times,' he says. 'It will disguise you from other Grand Conduits.'

Alifa turns the green agate ring around in her hand. 'Disguise me?'

'Grand Conduits of the *Dhulmi* Order wear chromite rings. If you come across one of them, they will only have one thought in mind.'

'Which is?' she asks.

'To convert you or kill you.'

EXPECTATIONS

Whoever said money doesn't buy happiness,
doesn't have enough money.

A FOOL'S PARADISE

THE FIRST-FLOOR CASEMENT WINDOWS at the rear of the Teuton embassy in Urua, capital of the south of Arön, offer an eye-catching view of the verdant gardens, bristling with magenta foxtail orchids, snow-white lilies and fluffy pink lotus flowers. There are several banyan trees with glossy green leaves in prominent positions and tall spindly acacias along the perimeter walls, as well as a clutch of neem trees known for their medicinal properties on the left-hand side of the gardens, close to the property. It has been two weeks since Hale arrived in this land of colour and life, a stark contrast to the lifeless grey skies of Jutes, province of Teuton and home to his people. Despite the gradual onset of winter, he has witnessed endless blue skies and a molten gold sun on most days.

Streaks of sunlight catch his wavy blond hair and he relishes the warmth of the low winter glow on his face and arms. His pale skin is a contrast to that of the people of Arön and he has promised himself he'll add colour to his wardrobe. A magenta scarf, a terracotta cravat, a red cummerbund – these might suit better, he thinks. In Jutes he would not dare wear such outrageous colours; his people are known for dour grey and black attire and the women wear either white dresses or black ones in the evening.

Outside, workmen navigate the grounds of the embassy, conveying items newly arrived from the port of Shabaran and transported up the Rulers' Road to Urua. All large items from the imperial capital of Susa are sent by sea from the port of Hatra. He stayed in Susa, the centre of the Arön empire, a city with fabulous jewel-bedecked palaces, ornate buildings, and ornamental arched bridges. It is, as Aunt Orinda has pointed out on several occasions, awash with the wealth of centuries.

On the windowsill are four small cylinders, each the size of an index finger. Hale picks up the one which has a label on it that says 'Green algae'. He holds it up to the light, observing the green contents. He places it back and picks up the cylinder with the blue algae, once more holding it to the light, then returning it. He repeats the process with the golden algae. Finally, he picks up an empty cylinder, which has a label that says 'Red algae'.

'Where in the world is it?' Hale says.

He hears footsteps coming up the corridor and turns to see his aunt's handmaiden.

'Sir,' she says. 'The Lady Orinda is ready to receive you. They are in the annexe, where the library is to be built.'

Hale thanks the woman and makes his way out of the room and down the spiral staircase. The female servants who notice him pass, stop their work and curtsy; the male servants bow. He is not royalty, so he considers this a strange custom, but he acknowledges them with smiles and continues to the annexe. Hale hears voices coming from inside, knocks on the door and enters.

Paxon rises, welcomes him, as do the other two in the room.

'Ah Hale, good lad, do come in,' Uncle Paxon declares. He is in his early forties, tall, angular, thin, with dark black hair and a pencil-line moustache, which can be missed from a distance. Hale's uncle always dresses with the utmost care and presents himself with immaculate precision, as he does today in his royal blue three-piece suit with red stitching.

His Aunt Orinda, who is his late mother's younger sister, embraces him warmly. She possesses the signature smooth blonde hair of the family, which she wears in a high bun. Like Hale she is tall, with elegant features, and shares her husband's habit of dressing with dramatic flair, as her boat-necked dress testifies.

'Auntie,' Hale says, kissing the older woman on the cheek.

The third person in the room is unknown to him. He looks to be in his early thirties, with a thick mop of reddish-brown hair, which cascades down one side of his brow. His face is gaunt, with high cheekbones and a milky-pale complexion. His reddish-brownish eyes are surprisingly narrow for a Teuton, for he is a Teuton without doubt, in Hale's estimation, though possibly from the east of the continent. Hale speculates he is from Helisii.

'This is Brant, your uncle's new deputy,' Orinda says before she turns to Brant. 'My adorable nephew, Hale.'

'It is a pleasure,' Brant says, extending his hand.

They shake hands.

'Good day to you,' Hale replies.

Seated once more, with Hale taking a position beside his aunt, the group waits for a servant to finish pouring cinnamon tea.

'Like you, Brant, my nephew is newly arrived on the shores of Arön,' Orinda says.

'How are you finding it?' Brant asks him.

'Quite overwhelming,' Hale replies. 'It is so different from Teuton. But I like it.'

'Once you get past all of the strange customs, habits and rituals of these people, then it is, I grant you, a tolerable place,' his uncle states. 'What do you say, Brant?'

'Like young Master Hale, I am also astounded by Arön, but more

by the opportunity it presents to the Syndicate,' Brant says with a chuckle.

'Brant is a lawyer,' Orinda says. 'By all accounts a very successful one: he has his own practice in Teuton.'

'It is nothing, madam, just an insignificant firm of grim-faced notaries and solicitors,' Brant says.

'Do you specialise in any particular type of law?' Hale asks.

'Shipping law, actually.'

'Is that wet or dry shipping law?'

Brant is surprised by the question and looks at Hale with fresh eyes.

'Actually, it is dry. Nothing too exciting: contracts, sale and purchase agreements, that sort of thing.' He turns to Orinda. 'You have a very informed nephew,' he says.

'Hale is always in his books or out looking at rocks. I really don't know what he's reading, but it seems to be the law, though I thought geology and phycology was his interest.'

'It's just curiosity, Auntie, I really don't know very much,' Hale says.

'It would seem we have a potential lawyer and amateur geologist, come phycologist in our midst,' Brant says. 'If at any time you want to know more about the law, please ask. I know my firm would love to recruit someone with your level of … curiosity.'

Paxon clears his throat, glances at Orinda, who nods. 'All right, I suppose we can discuss this in front of our nephew, particularly if he'll be a lawyer one day.' He turns to his deputy. 'Brant, this is an untapped market for Opius. That's one of the reasons we're here. The Syndicate has made strong inroads into the Cin empire and profits are very healthy in that territory. Headquarters want a similar growth curve in Arön. What do you say?'

Discussing the narcotic Opius makes Hale uncomfortable. He knows it has fuelled the rapid rise of the Syndicate these past two decades. Before Teuton explorers discovered the drug in the Northern Waste, it was not harvested at scale. Only the Zandal used it, recreationally. Now, an entire industry mass-produces the intoxicant for export around the world.

Brant sips his tea. 'In Cin, where the market is centralised, we entered via the merchants' guilds and were able to penetrate all regions through their subsidiaries. Here, the market is split between territories the Emperor controls, and those of his two cousins, Artay, Sultan of the north, and Negin, Sultana of the south. To gain a foothold, we will need to use a different approach.'

Paxon leans back in his chair. Eyes Brant judiciously. 'Go on.'

'The Emperor's own territory we can penetrate by buying off junior ministers in the Department for Trade. My affiliate Konrad has identified three potential targets to approach – they are all personally over-leveraged and in need of cash. We also need to reach out to those bankers to whom the Emperor is indebted and convince them that their commercial interests are better aligned with the Syndicate. With your permission I will broker a meeting with Almas, the chief banker.'

'You have it,' Paxon says.

Brant continues. 'The north will be harder, due to the heavy influence of the military and Artay's own Black Axe division. To break into this market, we will need to use the officers within the legacy Imperial Unit. They are not aligned to the Black Axes. In fact, they are a regiment whose soldiers were gifted by the Emperor to Artay's father. When Artay usurped his father, he saw very little need to work with the Imperial Unit but he has kept them, so the Emperor does not lose face. As such, the old Imperial Unit has many disgruntled soldiers. We have identified a few senior officers within the Imperial Unit we'd like to talk with, who will potentially turn a blind eye to Opius being distributed. As we know, once we have reach, usage goes up, sales tend to be steady when it comes to existing users and the numbers of new users snowball. It is the nature of the narcotic.'

Brant has only been here a few weeks, thinks Hale. *Yet he has a grasp on the politics of this empire. He is shrewd and cunning. I can see why my auntie wanted me to meet him and called me down for this meeting. She has high expectations of me.*

Paxon puffs out his cheeks, glances at Orinda. 'Impressive, Brant. You have some workable ideas. What of the south? Negin was reluctant to grant us the opening of the embassy. Only when the Emperor applied considerable pressure did she acquiesce.'

'The south possesses some unique historical artifacts. It is a bastion of culture, with learned men and women, guilds for craftsmen, and farmers' co-operatives. It also has some inimitable – dare I say *peerless* – light-guards, who are close to the Sultana. They will be a major inconvenience. I have some ideas about how to neutralise them as well as secure the south but would like to do a bit more field research first.'

'Light-guards, you say. I did not see them in any of the regiments I inspected when General Ramin gave me the tour,' Paxon says.

'They do not come under the General's purview,' Brant says.

'Not under the army, light-guards,' Paxon says.

'Umm, I think I may have described them in the wrong way. They are more an Order of elite warriors, who report directly to the Sultana. They interest me as they have certain abilities which they have honed over time.'

Paxon and Orinda exchange a look.

'And you can take care of this *Order*?' Orinda asks.

'It will require a particular skill set, but I think I know some people who can manage it,' Brant says.

'All right, keep me informed,' Paxon declares. 'We've organised a state dinner at the embassy for the Sultana, her ministers and other important guests in four weeks' time. Do you think you'll be ready by then?'

'Possibly,' Brant says, sipping his tea.

He is astute, this Brant, thinks Hale. *He does not overcommit at this stage for fear of disappointing.* Hale catches sight of the chromite ring encased in silver on Brant's finger. *What a unique design,* he thinks. *I wonder where he got that from?*

-7-
AGITATING
AN AUDIENCE

Choose your thoughts with your soul in mind.
Choose your words with honesty in mind.
Choose your leaders with order in mind.

THE BOOK OF HERALDS

WEEKS GO BY. To Alifa it feels like days. She has trained every available moment, honing her physical and mental abilities, grappling with learning the basics of the law, the way and path of excellence – the trivium of the order. At times she feels like a woman who just noticed the ocean, when in fact it was present all along. She receives encouragement from Zorar and Nimar as well as others. She thinks back to her life in the north and the person she was: that person no longer exists. She is becoming someone else. She *is* someone else.

The algae-powered vehicle, emitting a blue glow from under the bonnet, trundles along on its rollerblade wheels, steadily making progress towards the Teuton embassy. Inside, Zorar and Cinan sit opposite Alifa, and beside her is Azadeh. Streetlights fuelled by green algae emit a warm glow, illuminating the magnificent mosaic-tiled walkways of Urua. Everyone she meets is content and not a bad word is directed towards the Sultana. In fact, Alifa would go so far as to say her subjects adore her.

It's a far cry from the north, and how Artay rules his subjects, Alifa thinks. *Brute strength and fear keep the populace compliant. The streets are filthy compared to the south; there is little concern for the poor and destitute.* She thanks the Creator for bringing her south.

—

Alifa turns her gaze to the interior and Cinan offers her a fatherly smile. The famous imperial architect is now in his sixties. With
his white hair, silky beard and broad forehead, he has the look of an
erudite scholar. Even in the north, they know Cinan. His designs
are copied by lesser architects. Alifa looks forward to spending
time with him and learning the skills of a Revealer.

The vehicle draws to a halt: there is traffic on the road as they
approach the Teuton embassy.

'All right,' Zorar says. 'Once inside we split up. Alifa will stay
with me. Azadeh, be discreet, but see what you can find out about
the Syndicate's plans.'

Azadeh nods. Zorar continues: 'Cinan, be yourself. Your fame
will give you access to most people.'

'I will try,' Cinan says.

'Who knows, the Teutons might even ask you to design a building for them in their lands,' Zorar says.

'Buildings in Teuton,' Cinan ponders. 'Worth considering, I
suppose.'

The vehicle crawls along before it stops.

'As far as it goes,' announces the driver in the front cabin.

They get out and head towards the embassy which is a short
walk away.

At the entrance gates, Zorar presents the guard with their invi-
tations. Names are checked against a register before they are ushered through. Beyond the gates is a lush garden. A path paved with
sandstone leads to a sizeable three-storey building. The embassy is
decorated with algae-fuelled bulbs, giving off a green hue against
the marble walls. The entrance hall is circular with staircases curv-
ing around the edges to upper levels. Shimmering chandeliers hang
from high ceilings, fitted with multicoloured stained glass along

the edges.

Beyond the foyer, they split up at the entrance of the grand hall to the rear of the embassy. It accommodates two hundred and is quite full. Cinan is immediately recognised and drawn into several conversations, whilst Azadeh melds into the background; Alifa soon loses sight of her.

'Come.' Zorar ushers Alifa towards a drinks counter.

The server offers them several options. They both choose the lemon with lime and Zorar directs them up a few steps, towards a marble pillar on a raised dais wrapping around the hall. Behind them is a corridor leading to what Alifa assumes is another entrance to the building. The position offers a panoramic view. A server approaches with some starters: prawns and orange capers. Zorar declines, as does she, taking his lead. *Is this a dream? Will I wake up in the medical tent any moment, to see the Black Axes standing over me,* she wonders, not for the first time.

'The Teutons have invited the elite of Urua society,' says Zorar, studying the room, with its well-dressed occupants. 'All the major families are represented; they cannot afford to miss this after Negin confirmed she was coming. I know many families, like their ruler, have reservations about the Teutons and the role of the Syndicate.'

Last week, Kaş ifa as chief librarian to the imperial archive, briefed them on the history of the Teutons, whose recent accumulation of fabulous amounts of wealth has been thanks to their trade in the drug Opius and in weapons. The Teutons have gone from divided tribes – the Gepids, Helissii, Njars, Turons, Varini, Angarii and Jutes – at each other's throats for centuries in blood feuds and death pacts, to becoming a commercial entity in which the Syndicate is the uniting force. Yet as Alifa observes these Teutons now in their fine livery, she would never suspect they used such exploitative underhand methods to accumulate their wealth.

'Many of Negin's junior ministers are present, and a few senior ones.' Zorar points them out. 'General Ramin, I expect, will be arriving with the Sultana.' He glances back down the corridor behind them, then continues: 'He does not trust the Teutons and has placed a personal guard around her.'

'Would the Syndicate try to harm her here?' Alifa asks.

'No,' Zorar says. 'The Emperor will not tolerate such behaviour and the south would be up in arms. However, slow poison in her food or drink would be hard to pinpoint.'

Alifa looks at her drink.

'Oh, don't worry, these drinks are fine, they're serving everyone. Besides if there was a small dose of poison you could access your healing and recover. If it was very severe and you became incapacitated, another Nourisher would assist you.'

'We're immune to low-level poison?' Alifa asks.

'Yes, as long as you know it's entered your body, you can do something about it. If you are not aware, that's different,' he says.

A bugle sounds behind them and Alifa turns to see the corridor filling with the Sultana's royal guard, who line up along it, all the way to where Alifa stands with Zorar.

She asks: 'Should we move?'

'We're fine,' Zorar says, and she suspects he knew precisely where to position himself when they arrived in the building. Soon Alifa sees General Ramin enter through the far doorway, and beside him is the Sultana, strong and firm in her features, wearing a crown. And Alifa wonders: *I have seen both the ruler of the north and the ruler of the south within a matter of months. I might be the only person to have done so!*

The entourage with other royals trails behind. As the Sultana

draws close, she glances at Zorar, who smiles. The monarch returns the gesture. It is a smile of comprehension between the two of them, thinks Alifa. Very warm, it lingers. The party does not stop and soon enters the grand hall, where they are met by the Teutons, to polite applause.

A man, tall, angular, thin, with dark black hair and a pencil moustache, and a woman with long blonde hair and elegant features appear through the crowd to greet the Sultana. Pleasantries are exchanged, before they guide the ruler and her party towards a private dining area at the rear.

'Governor Paxon and his wife Orinda,' Zorar says, pointing to the man and woman who are welcoming the ruler. 'An ambitious couple, keen to replicate the success the Syndicate had in Cin.'

'By flooding Arön with Opius?' she asks.

'Undeniably,' he says. 'It's only the beginning. They have drawn up plans with the Emperor's blessing to revolutionise our agricultural methods by replacing traditional farming methods with chemicals and machines. They have plans for educational reform, beginning with shutting down all existing centres of traditional learning. There are many proposals – economic, military, social – none good for Arön, all profit-driven to make money for the Syndicate.'

A glass shatters. Alifa whirls to see a drink has been spilt on a man wearing a white *sherwani*. His trousers are soaked. The culprit, a tall thin fellow in blue, does not apologise, but sniggers. The soaked man takes offence, says something. The sniggering man responds.

On the other side of the room, a similar altercation takes place, this time between women. Soon other voices around the two women are heard, as people take sides. Alifa glances back at the first altercation. The man in the white *sherwani* shoves the other.

'Light and Kha. He's agitating them,' Zorar whispers. Alifa follows Zorar's stare and spots a smartly-dressed Teuton wearing a black jacket. He is in his early thirties, with a thick mop of reddish-brown hair, a gaunt face, high cheekbones, and skin almost like snow.

Zorar reaches into his robes for his *tasbeah*, undoes a bead. The glow it emits remains hidden to all, but Alifa can see it. *He reaches for the Source. Calming.*

Guests in the hall are on edge, a murmur washes through the room. *Dhulmi* energy dissipates like sludge across a pristine ocean. More become agitated.

The Teuton closely monitors the disturbance, then his gaze swings in Zorar's direction and he locks his eyes on him.

The Teuton smiles.

Animated voices grow louder. Alifa feels a huge sense of calm wash over her. All her troubles disappear. It is Zorar's *Kha*, not subtle, rather a blast of cool air in the face. It does the job. She observes the room. It's grown quiet; those being agitated are calming down.

The Teuton thrusts a wave of agitation – impulsiveness, aggression, confrontation – like surf breaking on the beach. Zorar follows with calming emotions – love, compassion, kindness – an appeal to the higher soul.

Unseen, the duel continues, wave after wave: agitate, calm, agitate, calm. Fierce forces are at work. Alifa is buffeted between the two, coming up for air, then being thrust into the murk. Like the crest of a wave she rises and falls.

Zorar and the Teuton do not break eye contact. Then abruptly it ends. The Teuton releases his grip on the guests. He flashes a smile at Zorar, as if he recognised an old acquaintance. Casually, he steps down from his position and saunters towards them.

The guests are quiet. The man who spilled the drink profusely apologises to the other man. The two women say sorry. People reach out to one another, connect, shake hands, hug. The madness has passed.

Zorar heads toward the Teuton. Alifa follows.

They meet the red-haired man in the centre of the hall, as guests mingle around them. The Teuton has collected a drink from a server and sips it as he comes to a halt before Zorar.

'Remarkable,' he says. Then follows up with: 'Brant. The name's Brant.'

'Zorar,' her tutor replies.

Brant's eyes turn to her. 'Alifa,' she says in a whisper as though her voice is caught in her throat.

'Apprentice.' Brant assesses Alifa, notices the ring on her finger. Momentarily his eyes sparkle. 'Grand Conduit.' Brant smiles. 'Plenty of time to decide whether you want to pursue the path of *Nur* like your master, or *Dhulm*, which is of course the superior path.'

Alifa remains silent.

'Why are you here, Brant?' Zorar asks.

'I work for the Syndicate,' Brant responds.

Zorar corrects him. 'You work for Mörtan.'

'A man must earn his keep and the Syndicate pays well.'

'By selling Opius,' Zorar says.

'Opius, weapons, slavery. Livelihoods of ordinary people. But we know these are mere distractions, and organisations like the Syndicate are passages in the play. Nothing stands before the power of Mörtan. Mere mortals must prepare for the coming of Mörtan. We are simply paving the way, preparing. You know this as well as I do.' Brant takes a sip of his cocktail.

'Mörtan is using the Syndicate to achieve his aims?' Zorar asks.

'The Syndicate today, someone else tomorrow. You see, Zorar,' Brant pauses to grin, 'the world has forgotten about Mörtan, which means my Lord has succeeded. He is the corroder, the manipulator, the shaper from the shadows, yet none notices how he steers them. That is real power, when the one being manipulated does not even know it.'

Zorar is about to respond when they are interrupted.

'Mr Brant.' It is a young man, a few years Alifa's senior. His striking blond hair rests comfortably on his nape. He is tall and broad and his suit fits his body well. 'I've been wanting to speak with some uh ... locals. Perhaps you can introduce me to your friends?'

'Ah yes, my friends,' Brant smiles, turning to Zorar and Alifa. 'This is Hale, nephew to Governor Paxon and his wife Orinda. Hale is newly arrived in Arön: bit of an amateur geologist and phycologist who also has a working understanding of shipping law. I sense he has a keen mind and is very willing to embrace local customs.'

'Welcome to Urua,' Zorar says pleasantly.

Brant adds, 'My friends are Zorar and Alifa. They appear unassuming but don't ever doubt them: they have great *influence* here.'

'Zorar, Alifa,' Hale says. 'Lovely to meet you. Urua is such a beautiful city. But I have barely left the embassy. I am keen to explore.'

'There are ...' Zorar begins, when a servant approaches.

'Sir, Zorar, the Sultana requests your presence.' The servant turns to Brant. 'Mr Brant, the Governor also asks for you.'

Zorar and Brant exchange a look and Zorar says, 'Perhaps, Alifa, you and the young man can keep each other company till I return.'

'Yes, of course,' Alifa says.

'If you will excuse me, Hale,' Brant says, tipping his head forward. He and Zorar walk side by side through the crowd to the private dining area, disappearing behind the screens.

Hale looks at her. 'Alifa, how long have you lived here?' he asks.

She has never spoken to a Teuton before, let alone one so handsome. She tries to hide her nerves but is sure she is blushing. 'I am new to the city, having arrived two months ago.'

'Oh, I just came a month ago. Where were you before?' Hale asks.

'I was in the north,' Alifa says. She notices a few Teutons looking at them, exchanging words with one another. She blushes.

'What did you do?' asks Hale, who seems enraptured by her, ignoring the Teutons around him.

'I was with the army,' she says apologetically.

'A soldier?' Hale takes a step back, eyeing her carefully. 'You don't look like one,' he adds with a disarming smile.

'No, more a nurse. Nothing much, nothing important.'

'You cared for people,' Hale says, with an earnest look. 'Helped them when they needed it. That, in my humble estimation, is a lot.'

She thinks, *he is unlike what I expected the Teutons to be. Hale is considerate and affectionate.* 'I played a part,' she says. 'What about you, why did you come?'

'After my parents passed away, my mother's sister, Auntie Orinda, took me in. When Uncle Paxon was posted to Arön as Governor, I soon followed.'

'I am sorry about your parents. Your uncle and aunt are important people in Teuton; they will take care of you.'

'Important people tend to be busy people,' Hale says, 'who have little time for family. Oh, I know that sounds harsh – my uncle and aunt are downright lovely, but so consumed by work they barely have time to check on me.'

'I see.'

'Is Zorar your ...'

'He is my teacher,' she says.

'Teacher? What does he teach?'

Alifa thinks it over. How can she describe the order to someone who does not know what it is? 'Zorar teaches the science of the heart.'

Hale listens attentively, ponders, asks, 'What is such a science called?'

'*Kha*,' she says. She is not sure why she says it, but there is something about this Teuton that makes her want to trust him.

'*Kha*,' he moves the word around in his mouth. 'Has a nice sound to it.' Hale takes a step closer. 'Can you tell me something of it, this *Kha*?'

She feels drawn to him and before thinking it through, says. 'I am a beginner, but I will share a lesson from *The Book of the Way*, a line I memorised this week. The book says: *It is for the aspirant to ask, yet it is for the Creator to answer in a manner and time He chooses, for He knows the aspirant better than the aspirant knows himself.*'

'What do they mean, these words?' Hale enquires.

'My teacher explained it to me: it is our responsibility to make the effort, yet only the Creator can deliver the outcome.'

'I see,' says Hale. 'Well, at least I think I do.'

'What is your occupation?' Alifa asks.

'Having completed my studies, I'm trying to find a suitable profession. One that agrees with societal expectations. It's terribly difficult and most of the work is rather boring or disagreeable. Yet, what I enjoy the most is ...' He pauses.

Alifa waits, a smile on her lips. *I do like this young man.*

'Geology, the scientific study of rocks and phycology, the study of algae.'

'Oh,' Alifa replies.

'I know it sounds archaic, scouring rocks and elements from the past, as well as algae but there is a lot more to it than you'd think. It was geologists who discovered how we could use algae, green, blue, and gold and put it to use in our cities. Without algae fuel imagine what society would be like!'

'I suppose you have a point,' Alifa says. 'No lights, vehicles, energy to power objects.'

'Exactly,' Hale says excitedly. 'But what's really of interest to me is the discovery of red algae.'

'Red? I never knew that existed.'

'Well, technically it doesn't exist, the red algae. However, there have always been legends about its existence and its potency. It's meant to be far more powerful than any other form of algae we have ever discovered. It could transform society, the economy, the world itself.'

'You want to discover red algae?'

'I know it sounds fantastical, but wouldn't it be great to be the one who finds it, who puts it to use, helps uplift the lives of the poor? I'm not interested in the fame of it, more the application of it for the common good of humanity.'

Alifa is about to reply when a Teuton approaches. He is tall, dressed all in black. 'Master Hale, your aunt requests your presence.'

Hale nods. Turning to her, he says, 'I do hope we have another opportunity to meet. I enjoyed our conversation.'

'As did I,' she says.

Then Hale leaves with the tall Teuton who looks down at her with a condescending stare.

Alone, Alifa strolls over to the pillar where she originally took up position. Another waiter presents her with a platter: this time of avocado quiches. Feeling hungry, she takes one. She finds it odd for the Teutons to serve their guests whilst they stand. It appears inhospitable. Perhaps it is the custom in Teuton to eat whilst standing, she thinks.

'Alifa,' a voice whispers.

It is Azadeh. *How did the Threader approach so quietly?*

'What did you find?' she asks.

Shifting her eyes around the hall and checking behind her, Azadeh says. 'Very little. But I did notice the Teutons have at least two, maybe three Hefters, and a couple of Threaders. Access to all private areas was blocked. I even tried from the outside of the building, but there were two Threaders patrolling and my movements would be noticed.'

'The Syndicate has come prepared,' Alifa says.

A plump gregarious fellow emerges from behind the private dining area. With him is an entourage. The group catches Azadeh's eye.

'Almas the chief banker,' Azadeh says. 'He bankrolls the Emperor. Without him, the imperial treasury would be devoid of cash, so poor is the Emperor at managing his administration. His ministers regularly steal from him, others trick him into false schemes and now with the arrival of the Syndicate, I fear the impact of his poor decisions. Almas' presence here today means he is hedging his bets.'

The joyful banker shares some humour with one of his acolytes, who is careful to laugh at the right moment, before sharing the joke with others, who also giggle.

Azadeh asks: 'Alifa, where is Zorar?'

'With the Sultana and the Teuton Governor. The Syndicate also have a Grand Conduit with them, named Brant.'

'A Grand Conduit. How powerful?' Azadeh asks.

'You'll need to ask Zorar. He just tangled with Brant and calmed the crowd after Brant agitated it.'

'A powerful Grand Conduit!' Azadeh puffs out her cheeks. 'If they have another, we're done for,' she says, placing a hand on Alifa's shoulder, 'unless, my young friend, you learn everything there is to being a Grand Conduit, in no time.'

Alifa did not expect to leave the north, but then she did not envisage many things, certainly not becoming a member of an Order, but here she is and this is who she is. She doesn't feel ready, but sometimes you just have to be ready enough.

Ⓚ

-8-

ISTHMUS

When one lights a candle in a dark fathomless cavern
it brings hope, when two candles are lit, it affirms,
when three, then the darkness begins to recede.

THE WISDOM OF THE WAY

'TODAY, ALIFA,' SAYS ZORAR. 'We enter the Isthmus.' With those words he leads Alifa into the basement, via the lift, into the circular chamber with geometric patterns. Zorar meets Alifa's expectant gaze as they pass the training circle and thinks, *I wore the same look of awe the first time I entered the Isthmus.*

Striding towards the enormous brass map of Ikleel, Zorar reaches the wall and places his fingertips at a specific joint. The wall before him slides open and a dimly-lit corridor appears, at the end of which is a circular door the shape of a full moon. Zorar guides Alifa down the corridor, stops before the door. He removes a bead from his *tasbeah* and watches it empty in the cup of his hand. A glow forms, then winks out.

'You will need to do the same,' he instructs her. 'It will help you cross into the Isthmus.'

Alifa removes a bead. He has seen her reciting her litanies using these beads. She has taken well to being an apprentice. He prays they have enough time to get her ready for what may be coming. The glow emerges in the cup of Alifa's hand, and he can see her absorb the Source, before she safely tucks away the empty bead in her tunic pocket.

'Do we need one for the return?' Alifa asks.

—

'No,' he says. 'Exiting is easier than entering.'

Zorar takes a crystal from a set encased into the wall and places it into a niche in the door-frame. The moon door lights up around its edges and within its intricate carvings. *Click*. It unlocks and they pass through.

A bubble cocoons them as they pass between the two domains. The semi-transparent bubble blurs everything around them, but there are streaks of light around its edges and a reverberation in the air. Within moments another door appears, and Zorar pushes this. They enter a wooden cabin; a fireplace is opposite. But for a set of leather seats, an oak dining table and chairs, and a rug with a sun and moon on it, there is very little else in the cabin.

'Where are we?' Alifa whispers.

'The Isthmus is in motion. Like the cosmos, it is moving, so you cannot be certain where you will emerge. But the state of your heart will take you to a starting position. Today, it would seem fate has been kind.' Zorar looks out the window, seeing rolling hills lush with green grass. 'Come, let's go.'

'And the doorway?' Alifa asks.

'There are several gateways by which you can exit the Isthmus. However, to return to the place you entered, in our case the lodge, you must exit from the same gateway.'

They leave the cabin and stride out onto the crest of a mound. Around them are hills, stretching as far as the eye can see. Dandelions, bluebells and buttercups grace every incline. Overhead, the sky is deep blue without a single cloud in sight.

Zorar smiles. 'We have been fortunate,' he says, surveying their surroundings.

He observes Alifa's innocent bewildered look as she soaks in the ambience. He remembers that the first time he entered the Isthmus, he emerged on a rugged rocky tract, lifeless and barren. Nonetheless it had been beautiful in its own way.

'The Isthmus,' Zorar says, 'flows. It is a realm next to ours, but not of it. Today, only those who are Conduits can enter it, though that is not what it was like originally.'

'What was its original purpose, why did the Heralds design it?'

'Alas, it was meant to be a place of spiritual retreat, where humans could once in a lifetime spend forty days and nights in it – to pray, reflect, contemplate on the journey of the soul back to the Creator. Yet before it opened, Mörtan created, unbeknown to the Heralds a parallel *Dhulmi* Isthmus, and tied the two together in an inseparable bond. After that the Heralds declared the Isthmus unsafe for all but Conduits to enter and even then, with great care and thought.'

He looks up at the sky. 'There are no celestial bodies, like the sun or moon or even stars that I have ever seen in the Isthmus, and there is no night nor day, but there is darkness and light.'

'How do you mean?' Alifa asks.

'After the corruption sown by Mörtan the Isthmus is like a cone on its side. We enter it through the tip. If you seek the *Nurani* path you ascend the levels, of which there are seven. If you seek the *Dhulmi* path, you descend the levels, of which there are also seven. At each level there is a gateway which takes you to the next level. We refer to these levels as Mökam. As a Conduit ascends or descends Mökam, their powers amplify. In the outside world you may be able to thread a fifty-yard leap: here it can be five hundred, or even more. The Mökam become more cavernous as you ascend or descend. Which is why the analogy of a cone on its side is useful. A cone grows wider the further you move away from the tip.'

'What was it like before the corruption of Mörtan?' asks Alifa.

'More like a pyramid. There was only *Nur* and you could only ascend.'

'Can I go to a higher level, I mean Mökam?'

'Yes, but not today, as each Mökam has a unique station or rank, and you must in your heart be ready to ascend to it before you attempt to physically pass into it.'

'Oh,' says Alifa.

He notes the confusion on her face. *She will learn in time,* he thinks.

'There is also something else that changed when Mörtan corrupted the Isthmus.'

'Which was?' asks Alifa.

Zorar scans the plain. 'He lengthened the course of life.'

'How?'

'As you venture higher or lower your body ages more slowly, thus lengthening your life.'

'By the Creator,' says Alifa.

'You can see why so few *Nurani* Conduits venture beyond certain Mökam: the temptation to live longer may be too great for them to want to return to Ikleel.'

'Why did Mörtan do this?' Alifa asks.

'It allowed him to extend his already very long lifespan.'

He watches Alifa taking in the scene with some trepidation. He felt the same when he first came: he didn't want to lose any time in the outside world by becoming trapped in the Isthmus.

Zorar continues, 'On the plus side there are certain relics – ancient objects like thumb and signet rings, anklets and armlets, pendants and astrolabes, sky discs and tablets – located at the third level and above, or below if you take the *Dhulmi* path. These relics, when harnessed by a Conduit in the outside world, amplify his or her ability, making it comparable to the abilities they possess in the Isthmus.'

'I see,' Alifa says excitedly. 'Then if a Grand Conduit has a relic at their disposal in the outside world, and I have to confront them, what should I do?'

'Either have a relic of your own, or … run.'

'How can I tell whose relic is stronger?'

'All relics from a certain Mökam of the Isthmus are equal, so it depends on how well a Grand Conduit can channel the power. But if a Grand Conduit using a relic from, say, the fourth Mökam, were to encounter a Grand Conduit with a relic from the third, then the former would be at an advantage.'

Alifa nods.

'Cheer up,' Zorar says, noting her melancholy look. 'Do you feel all the elements within you?'

'Yes,' Alifa replies.

'Good. See that peak over there.' He points to a hill several hundred yards away. 'I'll meet you on that. Just remember, before you land, draw on ochre: you'll need its strength to make sure you don't break your legs from the impact of the landing.'

Zorar spins, crouches, leaps, threading through the air, the air whipping at his cloak as he cuts through it. Below him he notes the valley between the two hills is full of violas, deep purple. As he descends, the hillside approaches fast. He draws on ochre, strengthens his legs, lands, skids to a halt. He turns to look at Alifa. The girl remains motionless on the hill.

The first time Zorar leapt in the Isthmus, he barely reached one hundred yards. *Let's see what she does, I suspect she will land amongst violas. Not a bad place to touch down. I crashed into a barren Wadi on my first visit.*

—

He watches Alifa crouch, bend low as he has taught her, then leap. Alifa rises into a high arc, begins to come down, then to Zorar's delight, threads again in mid-flight, whooshing right over his head. Alifa shoots past him, landing on the sloping side of the hill.

'Oh dear,' Zorar says, threading after her.

Alifa rolls head over heels down the side of the hill, before slowing and coming to a stop on both feet. Zorar is beside her, placing a steadying hand on her shoulder. 'Give yourself a moment,' he says.

'I didn't realise I could leap so far,' Alifa says, panting with excitement.

Nor did I, thinks Zorar. *That was impressive for a first timer.*

'All right,' Zorar steps back, Alifa stretches her arms and shoulders. Other than a scratch on the side of her cheek she looks well. 'You can nourish any injuries away because an injury you sustain here you take back into the outside world. It's best to heal yourself here and avoid any awkward questions.'

A cool breeze whips through the valley between the hills and Zorar looks about expectantly.

'You said the Isthmus is like a cone on its side. Does that mean we can pass between the *Nur* and *Dhulm* domains?' Alifa asks.

'Good question. Let's leap to that hill over there. I can show you.' He points to a nearby peak. Adjusting his robe, Zorar crouches, threads into a leap. He senses Alifa is close and when he lands, she is moments behind him.

'How was that?' he asks.

'Better,' she says.

Alifa's abilities are impressive. It took me at least two visits before I was threading leaps this distance and landing safely. Observing her now, he regrets how distracted he has been. Searching for his missing wife and daughter has occupied much of his time these past few years. *Had I been less negligent in my duties as a Grand Conduit I would have noticed the plans of the Syndicate, the arrival of Brant and his Dhulmi Conduits.*

'Good,' Zorar replies. He stares out at the horizon, spotting something in the distance. 'To the west – can you see that ground fog?'

'Yes.'

'It represents an intermediate space. If you enter it, you will be drawn down into *Dhulm*. There are things in the fog that should not exist, abominations and corruptions of Mörtan. If they sense you, they will venture out and pull you in. Stay as far away as possible from the ground fog. Do not on any account go near it.'

Alifa nods. 'Can someone from the *Dhulmi* side come up into the *Nurani* domain?'

'Yes, when the Heralds realised Mörtan had contaminated the Isthmus by creating *Dhulmi* levels, they managed to re-engineer the design so that there will always be a beam of light emanating from between the clouds in *Dhulm*. A Conduit of *Dhulm*, if they have truly repented, needs only to step into these filaments of light and they will ascend.'

'And if they have not? I mean, *truly* repented?'

'The light will incinerate them,' Zorar says.

Behind them a shaft of cold catches their cloaks.

'It turns,' Zorar says, looking at the western horizon where the ground fog swells.

'It knows we're here?' Alifa asks.

'Perhaps. Mörtan is powerful. The fog is his way of existing within these levels of the Isthmus. His eyes watch, his ears hear. Come, let us not stay: we head south.'

'How can you tell which way is east or west? There are no celestial bodies.'

'Access your Revealer ability. It will show you north.'

Zorar watches Alifa's eyes widen. 'Quite something, but it lasts but a moment.'

'Threads of light, stretching in every direction like a map. North is a throbbing star,' Alifa says.

Threading between hilltops, they head south. Alifa remains beside Zorar, who keeps them moving for half an hour, till the landscape changes to a forest choked with towering pines. Snaking around the outer edge of the forest is a languid river. They stop on a rise to look down at the woodland.

'How do you feel?' Zorar asks.

'Tired, but I'm fine,' Alifa replies, tilts her head to one side.

'What is it?' Zorar asks.

'There is a sound I hear, like a harmony, even when I leap through the air. It's soothing my heart. At times it sounds like birds chirping, or the song of a whale, or the swishing of waves.'

Zorar smiles. 'Indeed, every Mökam has its own harmonics, some might call it music. As you ascend the harmonics change, becoming more aligned with the composition of the cosmos, bringing you closer to the Divine presence, to the primordial melody which is tuned in the heart of every human.'

'The primordial melody?'

'The ancient elemental song which every soul heard when it was created. These are not words, but resonances, vibrations, and tones emanating from the celestial realm, so that a spiritual discourse can take place between the Creator and created. I cannot profess to understand it, but this is what we were taught by the Heralds, who all received their individual divine disclosure in this manner.'

'I do not understand it, but I hope to one day,' Alifa says.

'As do we all,' replies Zorar.

He observes Alifa: she has sensed it. 'What is it?' Zorar asks.

'There is something unusual about that forest. As though there was a vortex of darkness in there. Everything around it seems to be collapsing into it.'

'You see it?' says Zorar.

Alifa nods.

'Good. You have sharp Revealer abilities, more than I imagined. Proficient Revealers like Cinan can detect metaphysical sensations.'

'What is in the forest?'

'Come, let us see with our eyes.'

Zorar crouches, leaps, Alifa beside him. Within four bounds they are at the perimeter of the forest. Ancient trees with gnarled roots stand like sentries. An eerie hush permeates the undergrowth. Few animals and birds occupy the Isthmus; those that do are not found in the outside world.

'It's quiet,' whispers Alifa.

'Places between two gateways usually are,' he says, leading her into the woods. Branches snag at their robes. They push forward to a clearing.

'You still see the vortex?' Zorar asks.

'Yes.'

'Lead the way,' Zorar says.

The clearing branches into several trails and the pines give way to aspen, birch and maple. Alifa takes a path: they enter a shaded part of the forest, where the moss is dense beneath their leather boots. Pristine white lilies, purple bellflowers and ruby willowherb grow in patches in openings between the trees. The terrain slopes downwards, leading to another opening in the forest, clear of any overhanging trees. At the centre of the clearing is an enormous smooth boulder, devoid of any moss or dew. It looks out of place. On one side of it is a circular iron door.

'The Gateway?' Alifa asks.

'The Revealer within you can see it with the heart, the metaphysical reality – it is a vortex, a point between two Mökam. Yet to the physical eye, it is an iron doorway.'

'I prefer the iron doorway,' she says.

Zorar smiles. *It does look ominous*, he thinks. He strides over to the gateway.

Alifa asks. 'Can Mörtan ascend through the *Dhulmi* gateways of the Isthmus and enter the outside world?'

'He can,' Zorar replies.

'What stops him from doing so today?' Alifa asks.

'The seals.'

'So, these seals, they're in place, right?' Alifa asks.

Silence.

She looks at him closely.

'They were,' Zorar says.

With a sharp intake of breath, she scans their surroundings.

'They were?' she repeats.

Zorar nods.

'What happened?'

'They broke, or at least we think they did,' Zorar says. 'The comet at the Battle of Dvin and the breaking of the seals are said to take place at the same time.'

'You're not sure?'

Zorar shakes his head.

'How long have we got?' Alifa asks.

'We do not know exactly.'

'I have much to learn,' Alifa says, her tone morose.

'Well, that we can fix,' Zorar says rubbing his chin. 'I think it's time you visited the scroll-master to be harmonised.'

-9-
SCROLL-MASTER

The spirit within you is like groundwater.
You must dig deep to get it out.

THE BOOK OF HERALDS

T HE ORNATE ENTRANCE to the Blue Souk of Urua greets the visitor, beyond which there is an azure tiled floor extending to every corner of the marketplace. Buildings are painted in varieties of blue, radiating confidence, coolness, harmony, water. Overhead periwinkle canopies shaped like the sails of a ship provide shade. Polished blocks of lapis lazuli are inscribed with helpful visitor information. Cool gusts of air channelled by narrow walkways ripple through the coats and shawls of shoppers.

Alifa takes the eastern path. She passes jewellers' shops. Wedding rings, talismans, necklaces, earrings and bracelets fill shop windows: sapphire, jade and turquoise being the most popular materials. Scroll-keepers who are servicing scroll-light and *kamish* sets come next, a pale blue algae illumination coming from their workshops.

At the courtyard of fountains, where even the water creates the illusion of coming out with a hint of blue, she waits for Jamshi. Moments later the troubadour arrives, all swishing robes and quiffed hair blowing in the breeze. Heads turn – some are made to turn back by watchful mothers and envious husbands. Jamshi pretends not to notice, but Alifa has been with the royal troubadour long enough to know he soaks up the adulation. It doesn't make him a rotten fellow in her estimation, just a needy one.

'Ah, young Alifa,' Jamshi says, drawing up beside her. 'Let us venture on, deeper into the souk. The scroll-master's abode is at the very heart of the market.'

He guides Alifa deeper into the labyrinth. The lanes narrow, and Alifa notices they are now surrounded by artisanal bookshops, astrolabe makers, calligraphers, *kamish* smiths, and watchmakers. The aquamarine-coloured walls of the outer souk give way to darker royal blue. Above the door of each unit within this part of the market is a turquoise plate bearing the name of the proprietor and when the venture was established, which in some cases Alifa notes was hundreds of years ago.

Oud and scent burners placed outside each shop infuse the narrow lanes with frankincense and other resins from the Boswellia tree. She inhales the aromas.

Her *tasbeah*, with its ninety-nine beads, clinks inside her robes, the metal ring catching her belt. She has an urge to reach for the beads and read her litany, strengthening their potency. But Zorar has asked her to be discreet and not to display her *tasbeah* in public. So, she recites on the beads early in the morning before the dawn prayer, late at night after the evening prayer and throughout the day when she is in the company of other Conduits or alone. Zorar has instructed her that when your heart is busy in the remembrance of the Creator it will not be distracted by the frivolities of the world. *Oh, Creator, verily make me one of your confidants, not a confidant of the dark ones*, she prays.

They enter a small courtyard. In the middle is a fountain, where crystal clear water pumps into a pool where azure-coloured mosaics form an intricate pattern, before branching out to smaller clusters and channels of water scattering to every corner.

'Here we are,' Jamshi announces. 'This is the absolute middle of the Blue Souk.' They advance, approach the dwelling of the

scroll-master. When they enter, a little brass bell rings above the door and the woody aromatic fragrance of myrrh greets them.

Inside, low sofas run along the walls, with wooden and brass tables at either end, on which ceramic coffee cups are placed. Other patrons wait, seated patiently, sipping their beverages. Jamshi wanders to the small counter, behind which sits an old man, more fossil than living, but with a twinkle in his eyes. They approach him.

'We have an appointment with the scroll-master,' Jamshi says.

The old man looks up. 'Ah yes, Zorar mentioned you'd be coming. Go through to the rear apartment – you know where it is. She'll be there.'

They rise, walk around the counter, along a corridor where Jamshi stoops to avoid hitting his head on the low ceiling. The room is entered through a circular oak door with iron plates running around its edges and a circular iron shield in the middle. Jamshi raps his knuckles on the wood. 'May we come in?' he asks.

'You may,' a woman's voice replies.

Through the door is a high-ceilinged storehouse, with dozens of oak shelves running along each wall. On each shelf sit hundreds of scroll-lights and *kamish* pens, each propped up and visible inside a glass container. There are scroll-lights of every colour, from dark purples and blacks through to light lilacs and greys. Alifa sees the calligraphic *kamish* pens, made of ironwood, in corresponding holder colours. Some even have designs on them.

'Jamshi,' the woman says, 'are you married yet?'

The old woman is as much a fossil as the man in the front of the shop, but she has a certain zest and energy to her, which Alifa finds infectious. She sits on coloured cushions on the floor.

'Elder Daria, I'm working on it,' the troubadour says. 'Making a decision is difficult,' he adds sheepishly.

'I have several beautiful granddaughters. Choose one. We'll have you married by the end of the week,' she says.

'I was thinking sometime towards the end of next year.'

'They'll all be gone by then,' she snaps, turning her gaze to Alifa. 'Who is your friend?'

'New apprentice of Zorar,' Jamshi says. 'Her name is Alifa. She needs to be harmonised with a scroll-light and *kamish*.'

'Well, you've come to the right place for that,' Daria says. 'Come here, girl, let me get a look at you.' The old woman rises as they approach. Her cotton dress has an intricate mosaic pattern and her blue headscarf is in keeping with the colours of the souk.

Daria takes Alifa's hands, studies them, observing the lines on them, tracing them with her index finger. 'May I listen to your pulses?' the woman asks.

'Yes,' Alifa replies.

She places two fingers on Alifa's wrist. 'Heart is strong,' she said. 'Kidney and liver are clean, but they would be in one so young. Ah …' she turns to Jamshi.

'As I said, she is a student of Zorar. She … has the same abilities as the master,' Jamshi says.

The scroll-master lets go, steps back, places her fingers to her lips, nods to herself. 'Have you ever been harmonised to a scroll-light and *kamish* before?' she asks.

'No, never.'

'I haven't harmonised a Grand Conduit since Zorar, and that was some thirty years ago. I had almost forgotten how strong your energy lines are.'

Daria moves away, the hem of her dress dragging on the ground. She takes stock of the shelves running the length of the room. Scrutinises them with a piercing look. Mumbles to herself.

'Is everything all right?' Alifa whispers to Jamshi.

He nods.

Daria paces down one aisle, pulls a movable ladder to a certain spot, climbs it, reaches for a scroll-light and *kamish* set on the top shelf. She returns to her desk and invites them to come closer. They wait cross-legged on the aquamarine carpet.

'Let's start with this,' she says, unwrapping the canvas, to display the liquid algae screen within it. She lifts the *kamish* and hands it to Alifa. 'Try and write something on the screen.'

Alifa takes hold of the ironwood *kamish*, its calligraphic tip cut at a gradient. The weight feels a little off in her hand, but she's never held a *kamish* before. She applies the nib to the screen, attempting to scribe a series of letters from right to left. Nothing happens. She looks at Daria.

'No,' Daria declares, taking the scroll-light and *kamish* back. 'Radiant field is too far off.'

Alifa looks at Jamshi, who smiles. Then, when Daria has risen to retrieve another set, Jamshi shrugs his shoulders.

Daria returns with another set. 'Try this,' she hands her the set.

Alifa applies the *kamish* to the liquid algae display on the rolled-out scroll-light. This time the *kamish* flies from her hand, like a projectile and bounces on the carpet.

'Oh,' Daria says. 'A clear rejection.'

'Sometimes it takes a couple of tries,' Jamshi assures Alifa.

Daria paces up and down several aisles, staring up at the shelves. This time she returns with several sets. She places them before Alifa. There is a scroll-light wrapped in a purple-coloured canvas, one in a sea-blue one and finally one whose tone is red-brown. Alifa likes the look of the last one. In fact, she feels it.

Daria studies her, notices Alifa's gaze linger on the red-brown scroll-light.

'Try it,' she encourages her.

Alifa picks up the *kamish*. Immediately she feels a connection to the ironwood calligraphic pen. It emits a vibration when she first touches it.

'Yes,' Daria whispers. 'Apply it.'

She places the tip of the pen against the liquid-algae screen and immediately the scroll-light springs to life. The screen switches on and she can see a data-stream loading. The screen winks out, resets itself, then changes to a dark ivory colour.

'It's harmonised,' Daria says. 'The ironwood radiates at a particular frequency when it harmonises with the wielder of the *kamish*, who must also be at the same frequency. Only you will be able to use this scroll-light from now on.'

'What can I do with it?' Alifa asks.

'The scroll-light is a portal to access information held in electronic catalogues. It is like entering a walled garden. You have access to certain stores of knowledge within the wall, but not others, which are outside of it. This ensures that each person uses their scroll-light purposefully.'

'How do I know what I can access?' Alifa asks.

'Zorar will register your profile with the Information Ministry. This will permit you access to what you need to know. If you need access to additional information beyond your profile, then a request can be made to the Ministry. If the cataloguers think it is valid, they will allow you access, otherwise they will decline.'

'I see,' Alifa says.

'And of course,' adds Daria. 'With the scroll-light you can send a dispatch, whether it be a short message or a longer one. Everyone registered with the Information Ministry can be found and you can contact them. Here, let me set this up for you. Jamshi, you have her details?'

'Yes,' Jamshi says, handing over a card.

Alifa has seen dispatches sent on the battlefield between officers and headquarters. It seems a fast way of communicating. She is not sure whether she will have much use for it. *Surely I would want to speak to someone in person, rather than sending a dispatch?*

Daria takes out her own scroll-light and sets about registering Alifa's device for dispatches on the Ministry network.

Jamshi removes his scroll-light and *kamish*, in a mauve-coloured canvas. 'Look, Alifa,' he says. The liquid-algae screen comes to life and Alifa sees iconic symbols on the ivory-coloured screen. 'The royal musical archive,' Jamshi says, pointing to an emblem. 'The storytelling archive, a catalogue of musical instrument makers in Urua. These are all the things a troubadour at the royal court needs.'

'Your profile has been accepted by the Ministry,' Daria declares. 'You'll see an emblem appear on your screen. When you open it, you can send another registered person a dispatch.'

'Can I send one dispatch to many people at the same time?' Alifa asks.

'Many? No, no, no, they don't permit that. One dispatch to one person only. Otherwise, we would be inundated with useless dispatches which we have no reason to read. This way, the sender must be very specific and the receiver knows the message is for them and them alone.'

'I see,' Alifa says.

There is a knock on the door.

'Yes,' Daria calls.

It is the assistant they met at the front of the shop. 'Scroll-master Daria, there are some Teutons here to see you.'

'Teutons?' Daria says, raising an eyebrow. 'What do they want of an old scroll-master?'

The three head to the front of the store. Alifa feels a sense of pride as she carries her new scroll-light and *kamish*.

As they emerge into the main shop, Alifa is surprised to see Hale and his Aunt Orinda.

'Alifa,' Hale declares, a smile breaking out on his face. 'Auntie, this is Alifa. Remember I told you about her.'

'Oh yes,' Orinda sighs, studying Alifa with a hawkish eye, before her gaze takes in Jamshi. 'Oh, and who is this?' she purrs.

Jamshi places a hand on his heart. 'Jamshi, troubadour to the royal court. At your service, Madam.'

'Oh, I would like you to be at my service. Next time we throw a party we must invite this dashing troubadour. I'm sure, Jamshi, you know a song or two to make the heart swoon,' Orinda says with a wink.

'Hale, it's good to see you again,' Alifa says.

'Do you work here?' Hale asks.

'Oh no,' she says. 'I came for my harmonisation.'

'You've never had a scroll-light?' Orinda asks.

'No, Madam,' Alifa replies.

'Poor girl,' Orinda quips.

'Auntie,' Hale says, turning to her with a firm look on his face.

Daria clears her throat.

'Ahem,' Jamshi announces. 'This is the proprietor, scroll-master Daria.'

'How may I be of assistance to our Teuton guests?' Daria asks.

Alifa detects an edge of irritation in her voice. Few in Urua welcome the presence of the Teutons. She glances at Hale and they exchange smiles. *Hale seems like a nice Teuton*, she thinks.

'Since arriving in Urua,' Orinda announces. 'My scroll-light has been playing up. I've taken it to the scroll-keepers but they failed to fix it. I wonder if a scroll-master of this land can help me reharmonise it.'

Daria sniffs. 'Reharmonisation is possible, but you are not registered with the Information Ministry in Arön, which means your scroll-light, even reharmonised, will not be able to access anything within the walled garden of information in Arön, nor can you break out and access any catalogues in Teuton. It will be all but useless.'

'It is all but useless now. Can the Information Ministry contact its counterpart in Teuton and obtain my profile?' Orinda asks.

'Yes, of course, at the level of the Ministry this is possible: it is how diplomatic dispatches and information are exchanged. But it will mean logging your scroll-light into the central catalogue-frame of the Ministry. It will take a bit of time. And of course, it will require approval of a senior government official to make it possible.'

'I'm happy to give it a try,' Orinda says. 'See what you can do.'

Daria receives the scroll-light and *kamish* from Orinda. 'I cannot make promises.'

'Thank you, that's all I can ask for,' Orinda says.

Hale takes out his scroll-light and *kamish*. 'Alifa,' he asks. 'Are you on the dispatch system?'

'I think so,' she says.

Daria nods.

'I would very much like to send you a dispatch,' he says and clicks the emblem for a dispatch. Hale locates Alifa on the Urua catalogue then sends her a dispatch. 'Done.'

Alifa unrolls her scroll-light, clicks the dispatch emblem. 'It came through!' she announces. 'My first ever dispatch.'

'Now you can write back to me,' Hale says.

She looks confused. 'I can say what I want to right here: you're next to me.'

'Not now!' he smiles. 'Some other time.'

THE RIDER

Oh, what wonder and delight
there is to start a fight.

A FOOL'S PARADISE

TWO LEAN FIGURES dance with nimble feet on top of a plateau within the Isthmus. A breeze caresses them, wraps them in its embrace as the hum of melody vibrates around, as they thrust and duck with a set of weapons.

Zorar, robe flapping, leaps into the air, twirls a red oak Bo Staff, forcefully strikes down, cracks it against another of similar shape and size gripped by Nimar. The Hefter uses his formidable strength to block him, before slipping his staff off the edge of Zorar's. He falls into a roll, comes up fast, and backswings his weapon, which Zorar blocks, both his hands gripping one end of his staff. Bone-crunching strikes are exchanged, thrusts and feigns, blocks and counter-blocks. Each assault is enough to immobilise the opponent. But they have performed this drill hundreds of times; even blindfolded they can complete it without injury.

Nimar is powerful, thinks Zorar. *Yet he is not a Grand Conduit. The Syndicate have at least one in their ranks. Do they have more? Alifa has potential and learns fast, but she is young, inexperienced. We cannot risk her too early in a live environment. But with Brant so openly flaunting his abilities the choice might be made for us. And with the Final Standing approaching, can we wait?*

They weave and skip across the plateau, keeping in tune with one another. High and low the blows fall from these old practice partners. *Brant is powerful. I barely suppressed his agitating; any longer and he would have broken me. How would Brant have fared against Durayd?*

Duelling, they approach the edge of the cliff. The drop is several hundred feet. They stop to reset their positions; Zorar spots an unusual dark hue to the ground fog.

'I have never seen such a thing in the Isthmus,' Zorar says, lowering his Bo Staff, gripping it in one hand, placing the other end on the ground. To Zorar it looks like the ground fog is pulsating, throbbing like a heart. He has seen many strange things: this is just another. Or is it?

Nimar turns to peer at the ground fog in the north. 'Nor I,' he says.

'When Alifa and I were in here last, the ground fog turned in our direction. We were far enough from it, but it noticed us and there was a foul smell in the air, as there is now.'

'The Isthmus is changing,' Nimar declares.

'It would seem so,' he says. 'Even the music of the Mökam at times is off tune.'

He stares at the dark grey swell of the fog. The darkness within its very centre is black on black. He imagines the screaming wind raging within, the voice of Mörtan riding on it, planting fear in men's hearts. Zorar pictures the wraiths that roam the fog. He shivers, thinking about the Conduits of *Dhulm* who never left it, becoming enslaved to Mörtan, the trickster who now uses them as pawns. He thinks about the Final Standing happening in his lifetime and a cold sweat breaks out on his forehead.

'Mörtan's power grows,' he says aloud.

They stare at the fog in grim silence.

Nimar clears his throat. 'A dispatch from Conduits in Cin confirmed they also witnessed the comet, the day the sky blackened.'

'When did you learn about this?' Zorar enquires.

'Recently,' Nimar replies.

'But that battle took place months ago.'

'The Dispatch was held up by the Information Ministry in Cin, as well as in Urua. You know how little information is exchanged between borders, until it is verified. It would seem this news had a high classification and the authorities in question did not want it shared at the time.'

Zorar grips his Bo Staff, his knuckles making a cracking sound. 'Send a dispatch to Aztland if you have any acquaintances there. Find out what they witnessed and whether there is anything else they can tell us. I will try to reach an old friend in Koemox, but we know very little gets in and out of its Information Ministry. It is a shame we no longer have access to the Obsidamids in the Isthmus, it would make travel so much easier."

Zorar detects movement behind and whirls, as does Nimar, who falls into a crouch.

A hooded man, whose charcoal-grey robes touch the ground and swish about his ankles as the wind catches them stands, erect and tall, his face hidden within the folds of his hood. Impenetrable. He is a shadow.

'I am Zorar, of Urua, Grand Conduit,' Zorar declares in the time-honoured fashion of greeting another Conduit in the Isthmus.

'Nimar of Urua, Hefter,' his companion declares.

The hooded figure remains silent. They wait. Nothing.

'State your name,' Zorar says.

Silence.

They exchange a look and Zorar grips the Bo Staff, levelling it in a ready position. Nimar takes up a defensive position.

The newcomer cocks his head to one side. Zorar imagines him

smiling, but on what type of face does such a smile appear, for he is a shade within a shadow.

'Declare yourself,' Zorar says.

The robed shadow moves. Two palms slam into Zorar's chest. He has never seen anyone move so fast. He had no time even to raise his arms. Zorar is flung back, his Bo Staff flying out of his hand. He crashes to the ground, then rolls towards the cliff edge. The world turns upside down several times before Zorar finds himself clinging to the edge. His fingers grip the rock for purchase. Pain shoots through his chest, tears fill his eyes. Zorar tastes blood in his mouth.

Who is he?

Zorar draws on the ochre reserves he has stored inside his body, strengthens himself. The pain subsides and he threads himself back to the top of the cliff to find Nimar wildly swinging at the newcomer with his Bo Staff. The shadow in the robe moves with grace as though he knows every Bo Staff manoeuvre, every form, every rhythm.

The Hefter leaps, swinging down hard with this weapon. The hooded figure, for Zorar is sure now that he is a man, sticks out a hand, catches the staff in mid-air, and plants a beefy boot into Nimar's stomach. The Hefter is sent toppling head over heels. The Bo Staff remains in the assailant's grip, and he snaps it in two as if it were a toothpick, casually dropping it by his side.

Zorar is back on his knees, rising gingerly to his full height, as Nimar gets ready for another attack. Whoever the hooded figure is they are no match for him, but what does he want? A foul odour wafts from behind them; Zorar takes a glance, seeing how the ground fog has drawn closer, the pulsating darkness within it apparent.

The two Conduits draw closer to the hooded figure. Zorar tries a different tack, as he should have done before. He taps his sand reserves, draws on it, sends out a calming wave. The hooded figure nods as though acknowledging Zorar's attempt to calm him. Then Zorar is writhing on his knees. He has been hit by a tidal wave of agitation – Zorar grips the sides of his head, turning one way then another. Twisting his neck like a man possessed. The intensity of the agitation is a thousand times more than Brant produced at the reception. Zorar raises a barrier of calm to protect himself, but it is swatted aside and he is thrown to the ground, writhing in pain, head throbbing as though his skull is going to split.

Then he feels the rage rising in his heart, the venom in the pit of his stomach, the fury on his face. He wants to kill someone. *Anyone.*

Nimar too is thrashing on the ground and when the Hefter looks up their eyes lock. Nimar wants to kill him, kill Zorar! He fights the urge through clenched teeth. Zorar will not harm his friend, he tells himself. *I cannot.*

Nimar rises, drawing his scimitar from its sheath.

In slow pained movements Zorar shakes his head, imploring Nimar to regain control. Nimar draws closer, but his taut muscles tell Zorar the Hefter is trying to resist. Every muscle of his sculpted body is in danger of rupturing. Nimar approaches, closer with every step. Zorar forces himself to remain stationary. *Cannot, should not, will not.*

The hooded figure watches, like a statue in a museum.

Nimar is broken. He sprints at Zorar, scimitar raised, ready to bring it down on Zorar's neck and sever his head in a single clean strike.

No! Zorar strains. He will not fight.

Nimar's blade cuts down, slicing through the air like a guillotine.

Zorar threads himself into a roll, rising and turning.

'Fight him, Nimar! Light and Kha,' Zorar implores.

Nimar swivels, the blood lust visible in his eyes. He leaps at Zorar with his weapon. Zorar ducks, rolls away again. It is an absolute effort not to strike back. He knows his hand almost went to his own blade.

The hooded man is on the move. He casually walks around their fight, viewing it from a new angle.

'Get outside his head!' Zorar screams.

The robed figure says nothing. Watches from a new position, hands by his sides.

Nimar rages, hollers at the top of his voice, throws away his sword and barrels toward Zorar, who has seen Nimar ram his way through a wall before. As he draws close, Nimar pushes his fists out, jumps straight at him. Zorar threads upwards, pulls Nimar into a thread before sending the Hefter at full speed straight at the hooded figure.

Who does not move.

Nimar smashes into him. Zorar has seen Nimar bring down entire buildings with this move. Their assailant remains stationary. Nimar merely bounces off him, rolls away, lands in a heap, face flat on the ground. The robes of the hooded man part. On the leather sheath of his sword, Zorar spots an emblem against a silver circle. It is of a rider upon a horse, all in black.

The hooded man stops agitating Zorar and the Grand Conduit stands tall once more, tiredly removes his sword from its scabbard. Raises it before him.

The hooded man walks away, towards the edge of the cliff.

'Who are you?' Zorar shouts.

Silence.

As he reaches the edge of the cliff, he stares back at Zorar.

'Another time,' he says, his voice like harsh gravel.

The hooded man turns, crouches, then leaps an impossible distance. Zorar has never seen anyone thread themselves so far. The distance is so immense that it is as though he leaps to the very horizon, into the approaching ground fog miles away, into the screaming wind within it, into the shadow of Mörtan, into the very heart of darkness.

-11-
HEALING
HEARTS

Being in the service of others is the way of return.
THE WISDOM OF THE WAY

THE NEIGHBOURHOOD IS A POOR ONE, full of dilapidated rustic buildings, past their prime. Despite the state of disrepair Alifa sees no grim faces. The residents she encounters appear content. Alifa has lived with people of meagre means, but in the north there was an acrid edge to them, making their company bitter and perilous. In the south it is quite the opposite. She muses, not for the first time, about how Urua, capital of the south, is so different from Zanj, home of the Sultan of the north.

Beside her Belal the apothecary, acupuncturist and Nourisher, walks with an easy gait, his steps soft and almost reverent, mindful of vegetation and insects, avoiding harming anything. Zorar asked Alifa to spend a few days with Belal. Zorar says there is no better Nourisher in the empire. Alifa has learnt through the course of the day that Belal has a wife and two teenage boys, one of whom plans to follow in his father's footsteps. Belal wears his silky hair in a long ponytail. His khaki-coloured clothes are loose-fitting, with ample sets of pockets on trousers and sleeves. Necklaces and amulets dangle over his chest. He constantly twirls one of the rings on his fingers as they walk, and after a while Alifa realises he performs the litany when there is silence in their conversation. Each ring must, she suspects, possess some access to the Source. His multicoloured *tasbeah* shows every now and then as they walk. Like all *Nurani* Conduits, he keeps the *tasbeah* hidden in public.

With a tremendous sense of honour, Alifa carries the famous apothecary's medical bag, with its herbs, infusions and medications. Since the morning, every encounter with people on the street, in the park, or outside shops has been filled with smiles and warmth and a quick question about a medical problem, either the person's own or that of a relative or friend. Belal always stops, obliges, shares some suggestions and prays for them. He reminds Alifa that without the Creator there is no healing, no nourishing: we are simply the means.

Alifa has begun to grasp that smiling is also part of healing. It seems to lift his patients up when Belal projects a cheerful and bright demeanour, along with an empathetic ear. Alifa thinks *I spent years with medics in the army, with the doctor and the nurses – never once did I see any of them smile for a patient.*

Since the morning they have visited infirm patients who cannot travel to the surgery. On their first visit, to an old man who complained of itchiness, Belal identified his problem as one to do with his liver, and prescribed *namak-zaytoon*, salt of olive. To the old woman with the big grin on her face, whose joints pained her in the winter months, he prescribed the *kala-gound*, gum from an ebony tree. To the paraplegic former stone-cutter, who complained of indigestion, he suggested chewing *ajwain*, thymol seeds.

Alifa turns to the apothecary as they walk. 'Belal,' she says. 'I haven't seen you use your Nourisher ability with any of the patients this morning. Why is that?'

As they continue down the street, Belal smiles, says: 'The Source of any cure is the Creator. Everything is from Him. We are merely Conduits for His Will. Most patients will rarely be in need of our nourishing ability; more often they require someone to listen to their sorrows, or speak a kind word to soothe their worries, or offer a smile to infuse them with joy. This is enough to set them on the path of recovery. Others might need a specific herb or salt, to boost their internal organ function. The human body is remarkable: there is an entire universe inside us. The Sages tell us that we are part of the universe, and the universe is part of us. As such, the body can do much to heal itself when given a little nudge in the right direction.'

Alifa ponders his words. An entire universe inside of us? She struggles to comprehend what this looks like. She asks: 'Wouldn't it be easier to just use your nourishing ability and cure the person?'

Belal stops, places a hand on Alifa's shoulder. 'I warrant sometimes it would,' he says. 'But we cannot make patients dependent on us. Better they have the means themselves. That way, they feel less hopeless, they are more assured in themselves. And what they learn, they tell others. This is true healing.'

'I see,' she says. 'But there will be some patients where you must use your nourishing ability?'

'Yes, there will be, Alifa, but these will be few and far between. Much of what we do as Nourishers remains hidden from others. Conduits might be welcomed by Sultana Negin in the south, but they are banned throughout Arön by the Emperor and there are many in the south, even in Urua, who have no liking for what we do. They associate us with Mörtan, sure that we derive our abilities from the Corroder of Hearts.'

'That's nonsense,' Alifa replies, then remembers that she herself held the same opinion six months ago.

'To you and me it is,' Belal says, with a sympathetic smile. 'But we must deal with people as they are. No matter how much good you do, some people will still treat you as the enemy. It is for this reason we do not openly display our nourishing abilities. It would create civil strife and we do not want to be the cause of that. Remember, the Creator in His wisdom provides us with many ways to worship Him so we do not grow weary — the prayer, the litanies, smiling at others, giving charity, taking care of the sick — these are all opportunities to serve Him.'

They continue walking along a pebbled path, the street narrowing. Overhead, lines of drying clothes ripple in the wind. The path tilts upwards. They reach a dilapidated building, which has the look of an old mill. When they go inside, Alifa notices a large millstone, the type used in flour mills, left abandoned in the courtyard.

There is a queue of people there: when they see Belal, there are pleasant whispers, smiles, nudges and warm looks in his direction. Belal acknowledges these and walks along the queue, at the front of which several of his assistants wait eagerly for him.

'Goodwill, Apothecary Belal,' says a man with silky hair. He looks to be in his early thirties.

'Goodwill, Emad. How are you this morning?' Belal asks.

'By the Creator I am well,' Emad replies.

'This is Alifa,' Belal says. 'Zorar has sent her to me, to observe.'

'I see,' Emad says, smiling. He has a knowing look. 'You are very welcome, Alifa. May I take the apothecary's bag?'

Alifa hands it to him. It's heavy, and Emad stoops a little when taking it. Alifa had forgotten she was using ochre to boost her strength. She has grown used to tapping into the Source.

'You have hidden strength for one so slim, Alifa,' Emad says.

'Ah yes, thank you,' Alifa replies.

'Are we ready?' Belal asks Emad, who glances at his scroll-light and nods. 'All right, then, start sending in the patients. Alifa, come, join me.'

They walk to an adjoining room, where the wall has been

partially knocked down. A set of chairs and a small table are in the centre of it. Though the room is visible to everyone else in the queue, it is out of earshot. There is an adjoining room sealed off with a curtain which Alifa imagines is used if an examination is required.

Alifa takes a seat in one corner, whilst Belal occupies the seat beside the table, as the first patient walks in, a wizened old man, half-bent, shuffling along with his walking stick, who complains of a chesty cough he cannot shift. Belal recommends he gently suck *peepli*, long pepper, to contain his cough, then places his hand on the man's chest and together they pray. For the first time that day Alifa feels the Nourisher's pulse from Belal as he draws on limestone. The old man gradually sits up straighter.

'Apothecary,' he splutters. 'I feel better already. Thank the Creator.'

Belal dictates to his assistants a list of roots the old man should boil and drink morning and evening. Emad takes note on his scroll-light and another assistant writes out the prescription on a piece of paper, handing it to the old man, who leaves with a confident upright step.

Belal nods at Alifa, who acknowledges the subtle touch of the Nourisher, indistinguishable to all in the building except for her.

A middle-aged woman enters who complains of always getting sick when the seasons change. He suggests a concoction of *majoun*, a dried fruit paste containing infusions of blue lotus. Belal removes a small container from his medical bag, shows the woman what *majoun* looks like, a black paste, and instructs her to take a small spoonful twice a day for six months.

As the woman leaves, one of Belal's other assistants rushes in and whispers in Emad's ear. He turns to Belal: 'Apothecary, there is a distraught mother here who says her daughter is dying and she needs to see you now.'

In one swift movement Belal is out of his chair. 'Alifa, bring the bag,' he orders.

Alifa grabs it, using her ochre to heft it with ease, surprising the other assistants, before striding after Belal.

Meanwhile Emad announces to the patients that the apothecary will return after dealing with this emergency.

The mother who is waiting at the entrance to the surgery is distraught, but when she sees Belal, there is a glimmer of hope in her eyes.

'Apothecary,' she calls out. 'My daughter is dying.'

'Take us to her,' Belal says.

They follow the mother into the narrow winding alleys, eventually coming to a pitiful dwelling, which is hemmed in on all sides by other modest buildings. An olive tree grows outside, around which several men with bloodshot eyes sit, some swaying as though intoxicated. Others are barely awake.

Belal passes by them.

Inside, the mother takes them to a bedroom at the rear of the house. A man is there – the father, Alifa assumes. He weeps as he holds the girl's hand, but Alifa notices he also sways as if intoxicated. The girl lies on a bedroll on the ground.

'What happened?' Belal asks the father, as he sits down by the bedroll.

The man opens his mouth to speak, but words do not come. Tears run down his face as he looks at his wife.

'She ate the Opius packets thinking they were sweets.'

'Opius!' Belal says, looking at the father.

'He and his friends,' the mother says, 'took Opius, passed out, left packets around ... she ... is only a child ... she could not have known ...' The mother breaks down. The father looks at his wife and reaches out with his hand, but she flinches at his touch.

'Move back, both of you,' Belal orders. Turning to Alifa, he gestures with his hand in a downward movement and Alifa understands what she must do.

Her calming skills have vastly improved after time spent with Durayd. Alifa begins to calm the couple, soothe their anxiety. Belal approaches the girl. Her eyes are closed. White foam dribbles from her mouth and nose, running like paint marks on her cheeks. She barely breathes.

Belal places his palms over the child's body, making sure he does not actually touch it. He draws on the Source through limestone and Alifa senses the powerful pulse of a master Nourisher. Belal continues to draw on the Source, then as though he were pushing down he directs it at the girl. Slowly at first, then more. The girl does not react: it's worse than he thought.

'Multiple organ failures,' whispers Belal, so that only Alifa can hear. 'There is only one way to do this. Keep them calm, otherwise they'll panic,' he says, drawing more from the Source.

He amplifies the nourishing. A blast of pure light, white as snow, flows around his palms, enveloping the girl's body, bathing and radiating it. The mother squeaks, but Alifa hits her with a huge calming dose. The father's mouth hangs open as his eyes temporarily roll into his head. Alifa steadies him, hits him with a dose of nourishing to dissipate the Opius in his bloodstream. The *Kha* of Belal envelopes the entire bedroom. Belal is like a fountain of light, radiating in all directions.

The girl takes a deep breath, her chest rises. The light begins to fade. Belal lets go of the Source. The girl takes another deep breath, then another, before her eyes hesitantly open.

'Mama,' the girl says.

'My baby!' the mother cries, rushing forward to embrace her daughter. The father is now beside them, arms and legs still unsteady. Belal withdraws, sits back, cross-legged, studying the family.

'Opius,' Belal says with disgust. 'The Syndicate.' And for the first time since she has met him, Alifa sees anger on the apothecary's face. Belal cracks his knuckles.

-12-
ROOFTOP DANCE

The moral resolve of a few can affect the many.

THE BOOK OF HERALDS

IT IS DUSK. The streets of Urua's market district are busy with transactions, as shoppers and sellers exchange goods and services. Families chat, browse, rest, enjoy the eateries lining the central thoroughfare. Avenues are devoted to each of the trades: the jewellers, the hatmakers, the cobblers, the tailors, and other craftspeople. Each has their place, each benefits from trade as well as the mutual kindness of other merchants. When sellers reach a certain quota for the day, they close their shops so that others benefit. If a seller steps away from their premises, their neighbour, often a competitor, steps into their shop and completes the sale with the customer, leaving the takings for the absent merchant. These are unwritten conventions, and everyone prospers.

Zorar, his hood up, hugs the edge of the thoroughfare. He avoids the places where others know him: in his line of work it is better to go unnoticed. *May I be hidden from the people and known by the Creator,* he reminds himself. Shiny objects showcased in shop windows catch his eye before he counsels himself: *I want not to want.* Any worldly appetites he possessed, he lost after the disappearance of his wife and daughter several years ago.

At the next corner the sign for Dallah Wala is in brass lettering, against a green backdrop. All five of the Dallah Wala stores in Urua have the same design. Durayd attends to his true love, the numinous beverage *kahwa*, plying his patrons with its soothing fruity taste.

Durayd stands outside his store on the central boulevard, greeting customers who recognise the portly proprietor with the cheeky smile. Durayd notices Zorar, waves, then signals to one of his staff. By the time Zorar arrives a cup of the Dallah Wala *kahwa* is waiting to be served to him.

Thanking the barista and taking a sip, he asks Durayd 'How is trade?' as they stand on the pavement outside the establishment.

Durayd brushes back the whiskers of his moustache and smooths down his goatee before replying. 'Compared to last year, I'd say business is slow. But thank the Creator it is good enough for me to earn a decent livelihood.'

'What is the difference between this year and last?' Zorar asks, taking another sip.

Durayd looks right and left, leans forward, whispers. 'Opius.'

The comment surprises him. 'How so?'

'Normally I would have more men coming to the coffee shop, but Opius pervades the city. The single men who used to spend their money at Dallah Wala, are experimenting with it. In some places caches of the drug cost the same as several cups of *kahwa*. Someone is subsidising the market,' Durayd laments.

Zorar nods. 'The Syndicate will increase the price, so those addicted will spend more of their income on the drug. The Syndicate will increase their income from Urua, establish their supply lines and before we know it there will be an Opius crisis.'

'Why isn't the Sultana doing something about it?' Durayd asks.

'The Emperor has given the Syndicate trade licences for all of its imports into Arön, including Opius.'

'Yes, but ...' Durayd starts.

'You know how she is: familial duty will prevent her from disagreeing with the Emperor, no matter how appalling his decisions are. Behrooz is still her cousin.'

'They disagree about Conduits,' Durayd says. 'And what role we perform.'

'This is true, but the bond with the order runs deeper than Negin. It goes back centuries.'

Zorar finishes the *kahwa*, puts the cup on a table. 'Come, we need to talk in a more private place.'

They head down one of the lanes containing jewellers' shops. Gold, silver and a host of gems and ornaments catch the eyes of passers-by. The merchants recognise Durayd and wave to him; he returns the gesture. Zorar keeps his hood up, face partly-hidden within its folds. Passing down the lane, they enter another part of the city which is more open. Fabric stalls occupy a square which leads towards a public park. Cypresses and oaks are partly illuminated in the soft green glow of the algae-powered streetlights. Couples walk about; some sit and converse on benches, others hold hands.

When Zorar is sure they are out of earshot he says, 'Nimar is badly injured: all the bones in his hands are broken.'

'What!' Durayd exclaims.

Zorar tells him about his training session with Nimar in the Isthmus. Explains how the ground fog approached and with it a sense of threat. Then the appearance of the hooded assailant, and their subsequent skirmish, which ended with him propelling Nimar into the hooded figure; finally how the stranger leapt an impossible distance.

'How is Nimar?' Durayd asks.

'Belal says he will need a week to fully recover and that's with the apothecary providing intensive healing. It was a bad break.'

'Nimar is one of the most powerful Hefters I've ever known! Who could have done this?'

Zorar glances around. The branches on the nearby oak sway and leaves fall to the ground. Overhead there is a full moon, its light bathing the park in a sort of serene abstraction.

'I do not know, but he was able to agitate both of us, a thousand times more powerfully than anything I have ever felt before.'

Durayd arches an eyebrow.

'I know, that would make him more powerful than any Calmer we know – even you,' says Zorar.

'I'd like to see what he's got,' Durayd says.

'You may yet, but I hope we never encounter his like again.'

'Any idea who he might have been?'

'There was an emblem on the sheath of his weapon: a rider upon a horse, all in black.'

Durayd shakes his head.

'I have asked Kaşifa to look into it. If there is anything in the imperial archives she will find it,' Zorar adds.

They stroll along the lit pathway running through the centre of the park. Some men huddle close to one another under an oak.

Zorar notices them, realises they are from Cin. He glances at Durayd.

'Started arriving when the Syndicate appeared,' Durayd says. 'Keep themselves to themselves. The Cin embassy has been inundated with these new arrivals. Looks like they weren't expecting them.'

'What are they doing here?' Zorar enquires.

'Word has it that the new Cin arrivals are somehow linked to the Opius trade,' Durayd says. 'Don't ask me in what way; the Syndicate has already decimated the economy of the Cin mainland with the narcotic. Why these fellows would be here now, I don't know.'

The Cin talk amongst themselves, glancing over at Zorar and

Durayd.

'Make some enquiries, get to the bottom of who's bringing them in and why,' Zorar says.

Resuming their walk, they eventually emerge at the far end of the park into a residential district. As planned, Azadeh is waiting. Her hair is plaited, her long fingers like twigs hold a *kamish* as she writes something on her scroll-light. She looks up as they approach. Behind her on the road, rollerblade transports move along, their algae-fuelled power sources emitting a blue glow from their underbellies. The street behind her is crowded with people, and on its other side are three and four-storey tenements.

They exchange pleasantries. Azadeh jests that the quality of the *kahwa* varies in the different Dallah Wala outlets, which Durayd dismisses with a wave of the hand.

'I think you secretly calm your patrons,' Azadeh says. 'Make them feel the *kahwa* is better than it is.'

'Nonsense!" Durayd says. 'Though I admit I have calmed the odd fellow who has walked in with a grumpy look.'

'Other proprietors don't have a Calmer. It's a little unfair, don't you think?' Azadeh probes.

'I don't go looking for their customers, but if their customers keep coming back, what can I do, but serve them?'

'Is the reason the *kahwa* or the calming?' Azadeh smirks.

'All right,' Zorar interjects, smiling. 'Let's agree it's a bit of both, with Durayd only nudging his customers when he needs to. Fair?'

They both nod.

'Right, Azadeh, what's the strength of the Syndicate's Conduits in Arön?' Zorar asks.

The Threader glances at her scroll-light once more. 'It's not good news. I'd say they have more Conduits in Urua than we do. I've seen a couple of Threaders, several Agitators, and there are three Hefters – big guys, you couldn't miss them. At least two Nourishers, one Imbuer and most likely one Revealer, but you know how hard it is to track a Revealer when they don't want to be found.'

'Quite a collection,' Durayd comments.

'And Brant, the Grand Conduit who Zorar tangled with at the embassy,' says Azadeh. 'If they have more Conduits waiting to join them, we're in serious trouble, if we aren't already. The crackdown on Conduits over the past decade has reduced our numbers to a bare minimum, and though there might be others, we don't know where they are.'

'What are the Teutons and the Syndicate planning to do with so many Conduits?' Zorar asks.

'Well, this is the thing,' Azadeh says. 'When I followed them around for nearly two weeks, I realised they all report to Brant. In fact the other Teutons seem unaware they have Conduits at all. I couldn't say that about Ambassador Paxon: he must be in on it. Even Brant's number two is a Threader, a dangerous wiry-looking fellow called Konrad.'

'Brant works for the Syndicate but he pursues his own agenda. He made that perfectly clear to me,' Zorar says.

'The question then is, what does Brant want?' Durayd asks.

'Whatever Mörtan wants,' Zorar says.

'Was there another Grand Conduit?' Durayd asks.

Azadeh shakes her head and Zorar thinks, *Brant is my equal – maybe he's more powerful. Another Grand Conduit would tip the scale in their favour.*

Across the street voices are raised. They turn their heads. Zorar notes two men pushing each other. A third intervenes, then a fourth. Suddenly fists fly, a brawl breaks out, others join in. The entire street is filled with shouts, men diving in for a fight. Most people avoid the melee, but the assailants now number twenty or so. A man is headbutted by another and falls to the ground. Someone stamps on his leg. *Crack.*

'Someone is agitating them,' Durayd says. The Calmer looks down the street. 'And they aren't hiding themselves.'

'I see it,' Zorar says. 'Calm them,' he instructs Durayd, before he and Azadeh take off towards a pale yellow residential block. He has detected an Agitator's pulse coming from the fourth floor. Zorar and Azadeh enter an alley along the side of the building, then go left to the rear of the structure. There is another building, the back of it behind them. Zorar glances up and down the dark alley which has a ghostly algae-fuelled lamp at one end.

'Fourth floor,' he says, then releases a bead from his *tasbeah*, watches the glow form in the cup of his hand. Feels the surge of the Source. Azadeh, a Threader, uses corallite from her *tasbeah* to reach the Source. They propel themselves up four floors to land nimbly on the balcony of an apartment. It's dark and it's unlikely anyone has seen them.

The balcony door is open. They enter a bare living area, full of dust and debris. They move through the first room and make their way to the front of the building from which there is a clear view of the street below. The apartment is empty.

'Whoever was here, left,' Azadeh says.

Footsteps on the roof draw his attention. Zorar glances up.

'I'll take the stairs,' he says. 'Meet you up top.'

Azadeh heads to the balcony.

Zorar exits the apartment, hears voices in other apartments. Finds the stairwell, ascends, exits onto the roof. A water tank serving the building is on his right. Otherwise, the area is empty.

Azadeh lands neatly beside him.

On the roof of an adjacent building, a silhouette emerges from behind a column. A man, wearing a long coat. He is masked in shadow. Another figure steps out of the shadows on an opposite rooftop. He stands in the light, and Zorar can see the man's outline. It's Brant.

The first man, a Threader, leaps away.

'I'll take him,' Azadeh says, giving chase, threading herself off the roof, landing on the next, as her target springs from one roof to the next. Zorar turns towards Brant. The Teuton smiles, then threads himself away from Zorar, onto the next rooftop.

'A double chase then,' says Zorar, threading after Brant. *This has been planned*, he thinks. *They want our attention. Why?*

Brant soars effortlessly between buildings, some three storey, others four. He maintains a steady pace and it dawns on Zorar they are headed for the docks. Zorar keeps the width of a building between them. He does not want to be caught by a surprise attack. Their chase goes unnoticed by passers-by below. If he draws more *Kha*, he can thread himself over Brant. He resists. *What does Brant want? To talk or fight?*

With a slow inevitability the river comes into view, snaking north and south. The docks are quiet. Brant propels himself into a high leap, arching over the last building to land on top of a crane. The crane's extended arm juts out ten yards over the river. Fifty yards below are several berthed vessels. Brant perches crow-like on the end of one, as Zorar lands on the other side.

The wind whips at Zorar's cloak. The brightness of the moon obscures the starlight. Brant rises, dressed in dark black and blue pinstripe with red trimmings. He stands with his hands behind his back, grinning.

'Zorar, my friend,' he says and pauses to see his response. There is none. 'I do hope we can be friends.'

Zorar tunes in for any other Conduits emitting a pulse nearby. There are none. His attention is back on Brant. The crane hangs over the river, so there is no one to observe their stand-off. *As it should be,* he thinks. *Our business is better done without witnesses.*

'I'll take that as a yes then,' Brant chortles. 'Look, the situation of Conduits in Arön is diabolical. You, well, *we,* I suppose, are outlawed by imperial decree and the south only accepts us grudgingly. If General Ramin had his way you'd be banished entirely, perhaps worse. You barely survive and that you do is because of Sultana Negin. But ...'

A pause, a long pause.

'If something were to happen to her ...' Brant says.

Zorar takes a step towards him. 'What are you planning, Brant?'

Brant places a hand on his chest as though protesting his innocence. 'Me!' He shakes his head. 'Nothing. The Syndicate is here for purely commercial reasons. But monarchs become old. Some get sick, die early. Others just die unexpectedly.'

'Brant,' Zorar's voice is steely.

'No, no, no,' Brant gestures with his hand. 'You misunderstand my intentions. All I'm saying is that if something were to happen to your only patron in Arön, what would your precious little band of Conduits do? Where would they go? Who would help you, take you in, understand what incredible abilities you possess?'

It's a question Zorar has asked himself many times. *What will we do?*

'I'm not here to antagonise you, Zorar,' Brant says, taking a step towards him, his arms by his sides. Brant reaches out with his left hand. 'I'm here to offer you a solution.'

Zorar's eyes narrow, as he carefully observes Brant's out-stretched left hand. *He does not draw on Dhulmi Kha.*

'What?' Zorar asks.

'Things are about to change for Urua and its Sultana. The Emperor grows tired of her intransigent attitude – she dithers and delays, preventing the free flow of trade from Teuton and other Syndicate supply centres. Negin is too protective of the south and its culture. She doesn't want to integrate with what's happening elsewhere. The Emperor and his ministers see the folly in this. Sooner or later a change is coming in Urua and the Sultana will find herself relieved of her kingdom.'

'The Emperor would not do such a thing,' Zorar replies.

'A man high on Opius will agree to just about anything, so long as he knows where his next fix is coming from.'

Zorar clenches his fist. Brant studies the reaction. Zorar scolds himself. *Remain calm.*

Brant raises his hands in a conciliatory signal. 'Now look, Zorar, all I'm conveying is the reality of the situation. We both know the Seals holding Mörtan have broken. You saw the sign at the Battle of Dvin with the comet and the darkening sky – everyone did, but few accept its meaning. What will come to pass is inevitable and you will need to choose which side of history you want to be on.'

Zorar's silence tells Brant what he thinks about this. *There must be a way to stop Mörtan,* thinks Zorar. *The Vessels of Nur were used before, but they are all lost. If only we knew where they were.*

'In fact,' Brant continues in his commanding tone. 'As I'm such a generous fellow, I will offer you two alternatives.'

Zorar waits.

'When the south implodes – and it will, sooner than you can imagine, then you and your people will need to flee. This is where I come in. Let's combine our forces. Join me and the Conduits of Teuton. Imagine what we could achieve together, what territories we could conquer.'

He leaves the question unanswered, for he knows what Zorar will say.

'And the second option?' Zorar asks.

'Well, if that doesn't appeal to you, though I can't imagine why it wouldn't, when things go kaput here, I can offer you a haven in the Northern Waste. No one will bother you and your people there. In return for this favour, you will enforce Teutonic law and discipline amongst the tribes of the Waste. It's where our Opius comes from, as I'm sure you already knew, but the tribes of the Waste are an unruly lot, always fighting with us and each other. We could use more Conduits to maintain a steady hand, and a Grand Conduit, now, that would go far. We could even set you up as a sort of faux governor of the Waste. As long as the supply of Opius keeps arriving, no one from the Syndicate will question what you do or how you do it. Imagine – you and your people will be truly free.'

The so-called options are non-starters and Zorar knows that Brant realises this as well. *So, what is he really up to?*

'What do you say, Zorar?'

'To be a man of another man is to be no man at all,' Zorar says.

'Let us not argue about what kind of man you want to be, just be one,' Brant says, taking a step closer, a grin breaking out on his face, 'since only one thing remains.'

Zorar readies himself, draws on all the elements.

Brant leaps off the crane, hangs mid-air, threads himself right at Zorar. The Teuton lands a crunching blow which Zorar deflects with his ochre-strengthened arm. Brant cuts with his left fist; he ducks and counters with a strike to Brant's stomach, but the Teuton threads himself back, leaving Zorar's fists to strike air. Brant smiles, threads himself at him faster this time, draws a sword. Zorar's blade is out in an instant. Steel clashes on steel: sparks fly like fireworks off the top of the crane.

Brant is on the offensive, stepping up the attack. His sword rains down blows and all Zorar can do is defend himself with ochre-enhanced hefting. Zorar shuffles away, then threads back, but Brant leaps after him. Either side of the crane arm is a void, a plunge into a cold dark river. Brant swings left, then right, high then low. Zorar leaps up and over him, swings back with his arm, hoping to catch Brant, but the Teuton has copied the manoeuvre and by the time Zorar notices, Brant has kicked him in the back with the flat of his boot. Zorar skids across the top of the crane arm, barely keeping his balance.

Zorar places a hand on the cold metal of the crane arm to steady himself. Brant is already plunging downwards, his sword aimed at Zorar's hand. Immediately Zorar lets go of the crane, loses his balance, tips, falls. He threads out, seeing the thin white lines attach themselves to the crane, and Zorar threads under the crane arm, before swinging back and landing on the opposite end from where Brant stands.

Their combat draws an audience, as dock workers gather below: about a dozen, who probably live close by. Zorar can hear their banter and notices their excitable gestures towards the crane arm. *This is unwanted attention.*

'Oh look, we have an audience,' chuckles Brant. 'Why don't we put on a bit of a show, Zorar?'

Brant propels himself at Zorar, threads at high velocity, blade aiming for his neck. Zorar ducks, counters with his own strike, but Brant has threaded himself off the crane. He swings himself back at

Zorar, sword aimed at his chest. Zorar leaps up and high into the air in a backflip, before landing on the crane arm again. Brant's force has taken him away from Zorar, plunging towards the dark river, but he threads himself onto the crane arm, swinging up underneath it and landing on the opposite end to Zorar.

'Well, Zorar,' he says, sheathing his weapon. 'That was useful to know.'

He takes a few steps towards Zorar, stops. 'But I have other things to do this evening and really need to be on my way now.' He glances at the workers below, smiles, content with whatever he is thinking. 'Yes, they will do,' he nods to himself.

Brant backflips off the crane arm, arching away from it, then threads himself around it, taking a wide arc back over the river behind Zorar, before he propels himself at high speed, slams into the base of the crane with his ochre-enhanced legs, unhinging it. Screws pop out; the frame holding the arm creaks. The entire crane shudders. Brant leans into it, his feet digging into the ground. Hefting with every inch of power he has. Slowly at first, then with a terrifying screeching sound, the entire crane starts to collapse.

Zorar looks on in horror. The crane arm he is on plummets towards the river and the central column, along with the tons of cement slabs that held it in position, topples towards the workers. Zorar leaps off the crane, arms out, robe flapping, as he dives for the dockside. He throws out his left arm, threading invisible lines of *Kha* at the central column of the crane. Zorar threads under it, his momentum taking him out towards the river. He hangs in the air, twenty yards above the water, then pulls the threads towards him with all his ochre-powered hefting abilities. The central column shifts. He yanks it again, but his ochre reserves are almost gone. The column collapses. 'No!' he shouts.

Ochre almost gone. One last heave and he manages to shift the column several yards. His hefting and threading abilities are gone. Zorar plunges into the dark cold river below. The column crashes onto the dock but misses the workers. Debris splashes into the river.

Before he hits the water, Zorar catches sight of Brant threading himself away from the dock, back towards the city.

-13-
TAKING STOCK

Better to adjust the truth, than adjust yourself.

A FOOL'S PARADISE

ALIFA ARRIVES EARLY AT THE LODGE. Zorar has sent all the Conduits an urgent dispatch asking them to assemble first thing. *What could it be?* she wonders. She enters with her assigned key and makes for the central courtyard around which all the rooms are built. Collecting a glass of lemon water, she sips it, then finds a place on one of the many benches. In the centre of the courtyard is a fountain from which narrow channels run off in four directions. The frangipani is devoid of flowers in winter, but the desert roses and lilies are full of colour and life.

A pair of hoopoe birds hop around between the fig and olive trees. Watching them brings a smile to her face. She decides to unravel her scroll-light, placing it on her lap. Responding to her, the harmonised device momentarily vibrates when she activates the *kamish*.

One new dispatch, cleared for delivery to her scroll-light, awaits. She accepts it with the touch of her *kamish* and watches as the handwritten calligraphic strokes form on screen, all intricate waves, curls, brushes, the letters slowly forming, replicating the hand movements of the sender as they wrote it. The full message takes time to come through and she glances back at the hoopoes, but they have gone.

Hale has maintained a regular correspondence with her since their chance meeting at Daria the scroll-master's. Mostly he has described his exploits touring around Urua with his uncle and aunt, who are treated like royalty. Hale has visited places and people she can only imagine. He has also collected many indigenous rocks which he intends to analyse in the makeshift laboratory he is building. In his new dispatch he writes he is planning a dinner at the Teuton embassy for some of the new friends he has made in Urua and he would like her to attend. He very much hopes she will come and has mentioned her to others who also anticipate her company. He signs the letter off with his very best wishes.

Alifa closes the dispatch, unsure what to make of her acquaintance with a Teuton. He seems to like her, but she is an Arönite and Hale is a Teuton of some standing, so she is not comfortable with associating with him, let alone calling him a friend. *Yet are all Teutons as bad as they are made out*, she asks herself. To take her mind off the subject she looks back at her scroll-light and opens a paper written by Cinan on city planning. He puts forward an argument that cities must be designed with metaphysical aspects considered, so that they align with the physical and spiritual needs of the residents. This brings balance and harmony to a populace. Much of what Cinan has written she does not comprehend, but he has assured her he will personally tutor her on the paper and there are elements within it which will help Alifa develop her Revealer abilities. She has yet to use these to any great effect.

Engrossed in the paper, Alifa fails to notice its author, Cinan, appear and stroll across the courtyard with a cup of *kahwa* in his right hand, his left arm behind his back. When he is only a few steps away Alifa sees him. He is dressed immaculately in a pristine white shirt with a high collar, and a long jacket which swishes as he walks. They exchange morning salutations before Cinan sits down on the bench beside her.

Noticing what she's reading he says, 'Ah, yes – how are you getting on with that?'

Alifa puffs out her cheeks.

'Difficult?' Cinan enquires.

She nods. 'I don't have the formal education to understand your ideas, let alone use them.'

The architect smiles, sips his coffee. 'It would take a lifetime of study to comprehend half of what a Revealer can do.' Seeing the perplexed look on Alifa's face, Cinan continues, 'You see, with a skill like threading, you can pull objects and you can propel them. There are certain things you can do, based on your level of proficiency. Knowledge, as opposed to skill, is limitless. First, accept you don't know anything. Then accept that whatever you do know will always be less than what you don't know.'

'But you are a master: you must know a lot?' Alifa asks timidly.

'Ah, there is the nub of it. You and others may think me a master. I see myself as a student, a beginner on the path who has no preconceived notions of grandeur. This way, when I wake I am possessed of an insatiable curiosity to learn more, to acquire knowledge I did not know existed. If ever I consider myself a master, complacency will set in. We can ascend as far as our *himma*, our efforts, take us. I am already an old man; if the Creator wills, then to my last breath I will seek knowledge and share it with those willing to listen. This is my *telos*, my purpose.'

'Learning till the grave,' Alifa says.

'Yes, anyone who believes they have arrived at the epoch of their profession, is truly deluded. The one who sees himself on a journey filled with openings, will ascend to heights an egoist can never reach. In fact, the one with humility will experience an ascension in their soul and transformation in their skill, and give it no consideration, for it will be ordinary to them. Only a person who has not encountered them for some time will notice the change. It is better this way. Take no note of the good works you do, the compliments you receive. Be grateful for them, but don't dwell on them, or your ego will become inflated and your intention corrupted.'

Noticing the perplexed look on her face, Cinan adds.

'Look, the easiest way for you to develop your Revealer abilities is to first focus on your acoustic skills related to sound, then to optical skills related to vision, and finally to chimbiotic skills related to the interconnected nature of the universe.'

I have so much to learn, Alifa thinks.

Footsteps in the courtyard herald the arrival of other Conduits, including Zorar. Soon they regroup in the *majlis*. Alifa sits beside Zorar at the round table. The chairs are occupied by Nimar, whose hands are now mended, Kaşifa, Belal, Durayd, Jamshi, Azadeh and Cinan.

Zorar thanks the Conduits for assembling at short notice and tells them about his encounter with Brant as well as how Azadeh chased Konrad across the rooftops of Urua, until the Teuton Threader eventually disappeared. He relays his conversation with Brant, the two offers the Teuton made, then briefly mentions their fight on the crane.

The Conduits are silent. Even Durayd has nothing to say.

Eventually Nimar asks: 'What was Brant's motive?'

'I believe,' Zorar says, 'it was a test of strength.'

'And?' Nimar asks.

'We're about equal,' Zorar replies.

'Does he have a relic?' Belal asks.

Zorar shakes his head. 'I don't know. If he is in possession of a relic which comes from the fourth level of the Isthmus or lower, we are in trouble.'

Durayd asks, 'Is he the only Grand Conduit the Teutons have?'

Zorar looks at Azadeh. The Threader says, 'From what I can tell, yes, but who's to say others are not on their way? What's certain is that they have more Conduits in Urua than we do.'

'What are they planning for Mörtan?' Cinan asks.

'I do not know,' Zorar says. 'But deposing Negin is a stated objective of both the Syndicate and the *Dhulmi* Order. If she is out of the way, what Mörtan's acolytes plan is unclear.' Zorar turns to the troubadour. 'Jamshi, what have you seen at court?'

Jamshi leans forward, resting his elbows on the table. 'The imperial decree has emboldened the Teutons. New arrivals appear every day – politicians, traders, craftspeople. Why, this week there was even a musician who was commissioned by the royal court to build something called an Organ. I am told the music emitted by this instrument is morose and sorrowful. I'm sure this has something to do with the weather in Teuton, where I believe it rains most of the time and it's always dark and miserable.'

'An organ,' quips Cinan. 'Yes, I have read about these instruments. They are placed in large music halls with high ceilings and very little light.'

'Ambassador Paxon and his wife Orinda are at court most days,' Jamshi continues. 'The Teutons have been given an office within the Commercial Ministry: instructions from the Emperor, as I heard it.'

'And what of the bankers, Almas and his minions?' Durayd asks.

'I see them spending more time with the Teutons, often in the very offices the Sultana has assigned to the Teutons. There are also meetings taking place between bankers from Teuton and Almas, at the Central Bank.'

'Whose side is Almas on?' scoffs Durayd.

'On the side of money,' Jamshi replies.

'And the Emperor has very little left,' Cinan remarks.

'If the bankers were to switch sides and finance the Syndicate ...' says Zorar, letting the thought go unanswered, before adding, 'I will speak with Negin at my next audience with her, which will be next week.'

Alifa observes the concern on each Conduit's face. She does not know what the bankers do, beyond holding funds in vaults. But clearly if the bankers switch allegiance from the cash-strapped emperor to the Teutons, it will be a significant blow to Arön.

Zorar turns to the apothecary. 'Belal, what is the situation in the poorer neighbourhoods of Urua?'

When Belal rubs his palms together, the ten rings on his fingers clink. 'Opius addiction grows. The *khidmat-gars* receive addicts daily; some become violent, as the craving for the drug overwhelms them. Overall, the populace is anxious and less clear-headed than before.'

'We need to choke the supply line,' Azadeh says. 'Stop Opius getting onto the streets.'

Zorar nods. 'Nimar, make some enquiries. Use your connections in the trade to find out where the drug is coming from. We will need to pay them a visit.'

'Will do,' Nimar says, cracking his knuckles.

'Anything else, Belal?' Zorar asks.

'Yes,' the apothecary says. He rubs his chin with his fingers. 'A group of farmers from a village to the west of the capital told me that men from the Syndicate have been visiting all of the province's farmers individually, asking them to share any seed they have from previous years of their harvest.'

'Seed!' Azadeh asks.

'Yes, seed. Apparently, these men say the Syndicate want it for cultivation in Teuton.'

All heads turn towards the agronomist, but Azadeh is lost in thought, and silence takes hold. Alifa cannot see how seeds from a hot climate such as Arön's can grow successfully in a cold place like Teuton.

'What are they planning to do with *our* seed?' Azadeh asks, letting the question hang.

'All right, so the Syndicate is busy, opening an office in the Ministry, building an alliance with the bankers, importing Opius – now this seed business. Anything else?' Zorar asks.

'Yes,' Durayd says, chuckling. 'It was brought to my attention that the Syndicate is importing tea into Arön! Tea from Cin. Now, I know the Cin love their tea, but we are *kahwa* drinkers. Why switch to tea? Anyway, let the Syndicate bring tea. We'll show them where to put it.'

'Switch from *kahwa* to tea?' Jamshi exclaims. 'Never!'

The others nod and Durayd is content with the response of his fellow Conduits.

'Fine, we agree, but let's add this to the list of things to watch,' Zorar says. 'It all makes me uneasy, and we still don't know the plans of the *Dhulmi* Order.'

Cinan chortles: 'A plan within a plan.' He clears his throat. 'Zorar,' he says. 'I have officially been invited by the Teuton embassy to give some lectures at the Academy of Architects in Teuton. Apparently, Ambassador Paxon, trained as an architect and since arriving in Urua has marvelled at our designs. His office contacted me last week – what do you think?'

Zorar ponders the question, his brow furrowed. 'We could learn something about these people and the Syndicate if you were in Teuton. You may encounter Conduits in Teuton. They cannot all belong to the *Dhulmi* Order. I think it's a good idea. If you are willing, take up the offer.'

'My thinking precisely,' Cinan says. 'I will take some of my apprentices, so we can document our trip.'

'Good. Go sooner rather than later. We need to know more about the Teutons. Presently there is information asymmetry,' says Zorar.

Kaşifa quietly unravels her scroll-light. They all turn to look at the Chief Librarian of the Royal Archive. Her expression is sombre.

'The comet at the Battle of Dvin some months ago confirmed our worst fears: the Final Standing is upon us and the Seals holding Mörtan in the deepest levels of the Isthmus have broken. The question Zorar asked me to research is this: what can be done about it?'

Silence.

No one says anything. Alifa looks from face to face: all have a faraway look.

'Within the royal archive,' Kaş ifa continues, 'are books not touched for hundreds of years, possibly millennia. These manuscripts contain fragmentary descriptions of what may come to pass. Within them, reference is made to the Vessels of Nur.'

The Conduits nod.

'We know the story of how the Vessels of Nur came down to Ikleel at the time of the descent of humans, Vanimals and Djüne, and how they were used by the Heralds at the end of the first epoch, tens of thousands of years ago, against Volgorok, master of Mörtan. In the second epoch, thousands of years after the first, the Vessels went missing, stolen and hidden by Volgorok and Mörtan. Since then, there has been little or no trace of them.'

Kaşifa continues, 'At the time of the Final Standing, we will need the Vessels. It is why, according to our ancestors, they were sent. In total there are seven Vessels.'

The room remains silent.

How will we stand up to one such as Mörtan?

'The Vessels of Nur,' Zorar exclaims. 'The power to vanquish Mörtan. Only, we have no idea where they are. Some could be in Arön, or Cin, or elsewhere. Has anyone claimed to have found a Vessel?'

Kaşifa shakes her head. 'I cannot be sure. The dispatch network would have filtered out any such references.'

'This,' Zorar declares, 'is the priority. Find the Vessels.'

'Where do we begin?' Azadeh asks.

'First, we need to see with our own eyes the Seals in the Isthmus and how badly they are broken. This will tell us how much time we have left before Mörtan and his Djüne emerge.'

'I will go,' Azadeh says.

'I will go with her,' Nimar offers.

Zorar opens his mouth to remonstrate, but Durayd interjects. 'They are right, Zorar. Urua – no, Arön – needs you here, facing Brant and his Conduits, outwitting the Syndicate and their plans. We can't lose you in the Isthmus. If you were to get trapped for longer than you expected ...'

'He's right,' Nimar says.

'Fine,' Zorar says reluctantly. 'Make a visual sighting then get out as fast as you can. If Mörtan is on the move, the darkness will be like a plague.'

-14-
PLANTING A RELIC

Your heart is dead when you feel no remorse for your mistakes.
THE WISDOM OF THE WAY

NIGHTFALL IS A TIME FOR TRAINING, as Alifa has learned. Grand Conduits move across rooftops undetected. The early winter sunsets offer long nights in which to train. Zorar has pushed her hard these past few weeks. She needs to be ready, or as ready as she can be. The wind catches the inside of her scarf and the folds of her tunic as she threads herself fifty feet down, landing on a commercial building in the western district of Urua. In the evenings she wears charcoal, grey and dark blue. At times her clothes feel like a uniform.

Before her the low-rise buildings three or four storeys high stretch out in the direction of the central district where she can see the ornate pearl-white domes of the royal palace, lit up like a beacon. Around it are several government buildings. Her hand moves to her *tasbeah*. She is about to remove a bead, but her reserves feel fine, and she desists. Zorar has warned her against drawing too much from the Source too early, as the body needs time to adjust.

The flapping of robes draws her attention as Zorar lands close to her. Like her, he wears mostly darker shades, though there is a hint of sea-blue in his clothes. He pulls on the cuffs of his leather gloves as he approaches. His robes swish around his ankles.

'Zorar,' she says, reverentially.

He smiles but his face is knotted with worry. *I will be ready*, Alifa tells herself. *I have to be ready.*

'All right, Alifa, tonight …' he begins.

Alifa interjects, 'May I ask a question?'

Zorar nods.

'In the Isthmus, the hooded man you and Nimar encountered, was it Mörtan the Corroder?'

Zorar purses his lips. 'I have asked myself this very question several times.'

Alifa waits in silence. Below them on street level, two cats brawl in the evening air.

'No. He would not waste time on the likes of us. Besides, when he comes, Mörtan will not be alone. I suspect all the Djüne will be there. Till then his power will grow in the ground fog in the Isthmus and there will be other cracks and fissures within the Isthmus that will see his power seeping through to *Nurani* levels.'

The cats continue to scrap at street level, with persistent hissing and whining.

Zorar places his heel against the lip of the rooftop, stares down. The cats have scarpered as a couple of people walk by.

'People are oblivious to what is happening. I hope they never find out – it will paralyse them with fear. Nothing will stand in the way of Mörtan. Not the emperor of Arön nor of Cin, nor the Teutons. Someone like Brant is just the beginning. I expect more powerful pieces to appear on the board soon – like the one Nimar and I fought.'

'They're coming into our world?' Alifa asks.

Zorar nods slowly.

'Who was he?' Alifa enquires.

'A powerful advocate of Mörtan,' Zorar says. 'I have asked Kaşifa to investigate further.'

'When will she have a better idea?'

'It will take time; she is checking the archives as well as objects that may have been imbued with this knowledge. There are many artifacts in the royal archives, and Kaşifa is undertaking the slow and laborious task of discovering what she can by tapping into imbued items, as well as cross-checking the earliest written manuscripts within the vaults of the imperial library.'

'I have the skills of an Imbuer. May I help her?' Alifa says.

Zorar likes the sound of her suggestion. He grins. 'Thank you, Alifa. I think it will make a difference.'

She has been mulling over a question and decides now is the right time to ask. 'Zorar, the other Conduits in places like Cin, is there a way of meeting them in the Isthmus?'

He smiles. 'There is and we do on occasion. Perhaps we should do more. There was a time when Conduits could use the Isthmus to travel to Cin. They would enter a gateway in Arön and exit one in Cin.'

'Why can't we do that now?'

'Alas, there were porticoes hidden within the Isthmus. They looked like large mirrors, and when you stepped through them, you emerged in another part of the Isthmus and from there the nearest gateway took you to a different part of Ikleel. These were only to be used in an emergency and with right approvals in place, hence the knowledge of the porticoes was a heavily guarded secret known to but a select group.'

'What happened?'

'The language of deciphering the location of the porticoes and where they took you was written in the ancient *Ilkidee* script. There are none left, that I know of, who can understand *Ilkidee*. Besides we do not even have the maps showing which portico is anchored to what place in Ikleel.'

'The knowledge is lost,' Alifa whispers.

Zorar observes the couple disappear down another street.

Alifa feels a potent pulse coming from a rooftop nearby. She swivels to the west, as does Zorar. A figure emerges from the shadows three buildings away.

'Brant,' Zorar says. 'Must have followed me.'

Brant slips his ring back on and the pulse dies down. He leaps away to a further rooftop.

'Stay here,' Zorar says. 'Don't follow.'

Zorar takes off after Brant, threading to the next building, as Brant leads Zorar on a chase into the west of the city.

Alifa waits for Zorar to make the third leap. 'Stay here? I don't think so.' As she prepares to thread after him, movement elsewhere catches her attention. A group of Threaders is making its way across the rooftops towards the central district.

'Teutons!' she whispers. 'Three of them!'

Alifa observes the men leap in smooth arcs over buildings, briefly touching down on a roof, before propelling themselves forward once more. They head in the direction of the royal palace. She turns to see Zorar disappearing into the distance.

'Make myself useful,' she says. 'All right.'

She clenches her fists, sets off after the Teuton Conduits.

She synchronises her leaps with those of the Teutons. When they thread, so does she. Alifa remains three rooftops behind. Soon it is apparent they are heading for the royal district, with its clutch of domed governmental buildings. The Teutons are skilled Threaders, their movements graceful, easy to look at. She drops back a little, for fear of being spotted.

The Teutons land on the roof of the Treasury, an enormous structure. They hold onto the spire at the centre, converse, then each pulls out a balaclava which he slips over his head, so only his eyes show through narrow slits. Alifa hides two rooftops back, clinging to the side of the dome with her ochre-enhanced strength, and steals a glance at the resting Teutons. Below her is a squadron of soldiers. The night shift, she supposes. Otherwise, it's quiet.

The Teuton Threaders are on the move. This time there is no doubt about their destination – the royal palace. She follows. As the Teutons descend from a high arcing leap, glints of metal fly from their hands. Several soldiers patrolling on the rooftop collapse like sacks of wheat. Landing about twenty feet apart, the Teutons move quickly to finish the guards off. They reconvene. Alifa waits, hanging onto a nearby dome. *Are those soldiers dead?*

The Teutons disappear off the side of the roof. She lands, checks one of the soldiers. Dead. The others as well. She offers a prayer for them, then follows the Teutons. At the edge of the roof, she can see they have made an enormous leap and entered the inner palace. Between her and them is a courtyard, filled with magnolias, lilies and fern trees. She watches the Threaders. She needs to wait for them to move on.

They lift a rooflight, then drop down into the building. Immediately she threads herself further than she has before, crossing the courtyard below. Soldiers glance up, but Alifa has already cleared their line of sight. She lands, rolls, crouches low, runs after the men and drops down through the rooflight. She is inside the royal palace. *What am I doing?* she asks herself.

Ahead is a marble tiled corridor. At one end, a guard lies crumpled. She runs down the corridor, as quietly as she can, using her threading ability, barely connecting with the ground. As she turns a corner, she spots another felled soldier. Urgently, she chases the Teutons, and as she rounds the next corner, glances left into a generous oval chamber. Inside, the floor glitters with the colours of gold and brass in intricate tilework forming the shape of a phoenix. Remaining hidden, Alifa observes the Teutons examining several objects. One, the shortest in the group, picks up an item, shows it to the others two, who shrug their shoulders, before he bags it.

Thieves! Alifa thinks. *Is that all they have come to do, steal from the royal household? They're common crooks.*

They make their way back towards the doorway and she threads into an alcove. Crouches in the shadows, watches. They continue further down the corridor away from her, so she follows.

The Teutons are inside another cavernous hall, a banqueting one, Alifa suspects. Once more the shortest one picks up an item, checks with the other two, then bags it. The Teutons repeat this process in two other chambers. Having secured their loot, they head back to the rooflight. The Threaders are marching down the wide marble corridor when Alifa makes her move.

She steps out from her hiding place, blocking their passage. *Light and Kha*, she thinks.

Surprised, they freeze.

'Return everything you've taken,' Alifa orders, making her voice firmer than she feels.

'Get lost, kid,' the shortest one says, advancing towards her.

'Wait,' the masked Teuton in the middle says. 'This is the *one*, the other Grand Conduit.'

The advancing Teuton pulls up, takes a step back, examines Alifa. Up and down his gaze searches. 'Her?' he says, pointing a questioning finger at Alifa.

The one in the middle nods his head. 'Uh-huh. It is her.'

Alifa hears footsteps behind her. Three well-built men round the corner, coming in her direction from the other end of the corridor.

'Three Threaders, three Hefters,' says the Teuton in the middle. 'More than enough to take care of an inexperienced Grand Conduit.'

The three bulky Hefters approach. She swings her gaze between them and the Threaders. *Which way?* The corridor is wide, but not enough for her to slip around them. The walls are smooth on all sides, bearing only paintings and wall hangings, nothing that can be used as a weapon.

Alifa draws on the Source.

The tallest Threader propels himself at her, threading off the ceiling, using the height and the angle to come down rapidly on her. Alifa leaps straight at him, uses ochre, enhancing her shoulder, rams the Threader into the wall. When she lets go of him, he crumples. She spins. The short Threader yanks a painting off the wall, threads it at her. Alifa ducks and the painting smashes against the thigh of a brawny Hefter who has come up behind her. He barely notices as his mallet-sized fist piledrives a meaty punch at Alifa's head. *Whoosh!* It barely misses her as she twists backward, only to have the short Threader grab her from behind, as the third Threader also pins her in place. The Hefter who missed now swings at a stationary target. The blow is aimed at her stomach.

Alifa draws from her ochre reserves, propels herself and the two Threaders holding her backwards so the punch misses.

'Bah!' the Hefter says in disgust. Rolls his neck, advances.

Meanwhile, the two Threaders hold on. Alifa has thrust them high into the ceiling. They cushion the impact for her. She hears a bone crack. The two Threaders release her. All three fall to the ground. She lands smoothly, crouches, fingers out before her as the enormous Hefter makes a grab for her. She rolls through his legs but is then confronted with a second Hefter, broader than the first. He swings, she ducks, she hits him with an uppercut. He staggers, shakes off the blow, swings a backhanded strike. She hits the ground, kicks him in the shins and he doubles over. Alifa leaps onto his back, then propels herself away from him. Lands. The third and the largest of the Hefters waits. He smiles as he sees her stand back up. Only this Hefter remains between her and escape from this corridor.

The Hefter crunches his knuckles and takes large strides towards her. His arms pump out wide. His grin has turned to a snarl. Rather than wait, she draws on her corallite and threads herself straight at him. With all the strength she can muster, she lands a punch in his stomach. He stops. Again she pumps a round of blows, against stomach, body, chest. Panting, she looks up at the brute. He has a smile on his face. Exhausted, she stops. He leans back, then his giant boot smashes her full in the chest. Alifa is thrown back; only her ochre-strengthened torso prevents anything from breaking, but the bruises will be bad. Alifa lands on her back, slides along the smooth marble floor of the corridor.

The original Hefter who attacked her lifts her off the ground. Has her in a reverse bear hug. He squeezes. She channels more ochre, but she feels her reserves diminishing. Stars start to appear before her eyes as the largest Hefter now marches towards her, a look of satisfaction on his face. He presses his right fist into his left palm. Alifa swings her head back, smashes the Hefter in the nose. He staggers, but his vicelike grip remains. Again. Again. His grip loosens. Alifa is able to release her elbow and drives it into the man's stomach. The second Hefter whom she had forgotten about, makes a grab for her. She threads herself up towards the ceiling and with her other hand she threads a line onto the second Hefter. She yanks him with all her remaining strength, swinging him down the corridor straight into the path of the oncoming and largest Threader. Head first, the second Hefter barrels into the third Hefter. They both land on the ground.

Alifa lets go of the thread holding her to the ceiling. Threads herself over the two fallen Threaders, so that all the Teuton Conduits are now behind her. Only the corridor, now empty, is before her.

The way is clear. Using corallite she threads herself down the corridor, hearing the shouts of the six men behind her giving chase. Half a dozen soldiers come round the corner ahead of her. Armed with sonic-powered rifles, they fire straight at Alifa and the other Conduits behind her. A sonic wave slams into her. Alifa is launched backwards, skidding along the marble floor.

As she lands, an entire wall comes down. The largest Hefter has punched a hole through it and exited into the adjoining hall. The two other Hefters also punch their way through and are followed by the Threaders, who take the largest pieces of debris, stone and metal and fling them as projectiles at the approaching soldiers.

Inside the hall, glass smashes. Alifa leaps back up. Her chest and stomach aching, she glances at the hall. An entire glass window and accompanying wall has disappeared, along with the Teuton Conduits. Alifa gives chase, but then the sound of moans behind her makes her look back. All the soldiers are injured, two very badly, pools of blood forming around them.

Alifa remembers the young farmer in the medical tent at the Battle of Dvin. Her mind is made up. She sprints, slides to a halt beside the two badly-injured soldiers. One has a metal spike sticking out from his stomach. It looks like a piece of shrapnel has gone through the other's neck. The other soldiers hold his neck, trying to stop the blood loss.

When the other soldiers become aware of her presence, they reach for their weapons. Alifa threads the sonic rifles away to the other end of the corridor. She calms them, drawing on sand, a full blast. They quieten, their agitation receding as they watch her.

She draws on limestone reserves and the Nourisher within her sets to work. Swiftly she extracts the spike from the man's stomach. He screams, but her nourishing palm is immediately pressed onto his stomach. Blood seeps through her fingers at first. She applies the healing until she feels light-headed, but she persists. She has to save him. *I've practised with Belal, I can do it. I must do it.* She does not let up, till the blood stops gushing from the wound. She rips away the soldier's blood-soaked shirt to see the wound congealing. The soldier will live. Thank the Creator.

With bloodied hands Alifa turns to the soldier whose throat wound bleeds. He is blanking out, eyes flickering.

'Hold on,' Alifa says, calming him. 'It's okay,' she whispers.

'What's going on?' one of the soldiers behind her snaps. She hits them all with another round of calming. They quieten.

The soldier's throat wound is deep. But the jugular was not cut. Alifa places her hands over the wound, shuts her eyes, draws on limestone to reach the Source, removes the shrapnel, then directs a healing blast at the neck wound.

The soldier's tear-filled eyes look up at her.

'It'll be all right,' she says.

The wound starts to close. The other soldiers see what's happening. They gasp in surprise.

'What!' one of them exclaims, moving towards her.

Alifa calms the man, making him docile once more.

Her head spins from all the effort. She is going to pass out.

'Halt!'

Voices come from the other end of the corridor, booted feet tramp across the marble floor.

'No, wait!' she hears one of the soldiers who witnessed what she did cry out.

Then Alifa feels the thud of a weapon on the back of her head, followed by darkness.

-15-
SEEKING SOLACE

The true warrior is unassuming.
The true fighter is never provoked.
The true victor is magnanimous.
The true leader is humble.

THE BOOK OF HERALDS

SLIPPING INTO THE PALACE GROUNDS unnoticed is hard. What else does he expect after the recent theft? Zorar threads over the stone wall into the Sultana's private garden, where he crouches behind some cypress trees. He scans the surroundings, alert to any sound or movement. There is none, other than the song of the crickets and the dance of the fireflies. A solitary algae lamp in the centre casts a dewy glow. He rises, leans against a tree and waits.

He thinks about Alifa. It's been a day since the incident. She was taken away to a military prison, he does not know where., But what prison can hold a Grand Conduit? He prays the girl does not forcibly break out but waits instead until she is released. It will be soon. He hopes she has the patience: let procedure play out. They cannot risk another incident with the military, as dealings with them are edgy at the best of times. Despite his many failings, General Ramin did come to him and ask for help. Zorar wants to maintain this fragile alliance.

The night wears on and as it approaches midnight, he hears muffled footsteps on the stone path. The Sultana approaches, wrapped in a cloak with the fur-lined hood up, as well as a shawl around her shoulders, for it is a cold night. He marvels at her grace. Once she spots him, she heads towards him. He stands straight. She draws close, very close. He almost reaches out but restrains himself. Their eyes embrace with a deep longing, but both know their love cannot be. The Sultana shivers, only inches from him, and when she speaks, a mist of cold air caresses his lips.

'Your Majesty,' Zorar says, lowering his head so it is a little closer to the fur of her hood.

'Have you waited long?'

'Yes and no,' he replies, a suggestive smile on his lips.

She arches an eyebrow. 'So have we both.'

He would like to tell her how he feels, he would like that very much, but why start something that will not end well?

Zorar takes a deep breath, calms himself. *It seems to work more easily on others*, he thinks. 'Did they take anything?'

A momentary look of disappointment crosses Negin's face at the change of subject, then it is gone, and there is a presence, a formality. She leans back a little, still close, but the moment has gone. *It will never come*, he thinks. *Not for us.*

'A paltry catch, hardly worth the effort. I wonder why they bothered,' Negin says.

A thought occurs to him. 'Did they leave anything?'

'Leave?' Negin asks. 'Yes, an awful mess. Smashed antiques, shredded wall hangings, a broken wall and window. Glass all over the place. And …'

She pauses.

'One of yours.'

'Alifa,' says Zorar. 'Her name is Alifa, my apprentice.'

'I am told she was caught at the scene with the other Conduits who escaped.'

'She would not have been *with* the other Conduits. If anything, she would have been trying to stop them,' Zorar replies.

'She was in the palace uninvited. Did you know?' Negin asks.

'No,' Zorar replies.

'Then?'

'She must have followed them into the palace,' Zorar says. 'If I could speak to her ...'

'Little chance of that right now,' Negin says. 'For this Alifa, her saving grace is that she saved the lives of our soldiers, by ... what do you call it, 'nourishing' them. A miracle, in the eyes of those present. The other soldiers vouched for her. But it does not prevent the wrath of the military.'

'I understand,' Zorar says.

'You know I forced Ramin to visit you and ask for help, against his better judgement. Now this incident has put any alliance between the army and your people at risk. Some of his officers have been waiting for an excuse to move against Conduits. To eradicate them completely from the south as they have been eliminated from the north.'

'It would be a mistake. The Teutons ...'

'I know, it's likely they were Teuton Conduits who broke into the palace,' Negin interjects. 'I'm not blind to what is happening. I also know they have more Conduits than you. I've heard about your recent encounter with one of them – a peer it would seem – at the docks, and how you came off second best.'

'You heard about it?' Zorar says.

She leans forward a little, speaks more slowly. 'I'm worried about you, Zorar.' Negin places a hand on his arm. He wants to hold it but does not.

Zorar looks down at her. *So close, yet so far.*

'You have saved my life, Zorar, times I'm aware of and other times I don't even know about, I'm sure. I believe in you, I …' she stops. The words are caught in her throat. She grips his arm. 'I …'

'Yes,' he whispers.

They look into each other's eyes. How long for, he does not know, but he can feel her fingers around his arm. He raises his hand to take hers, but then lets it drop back to his side. He cannot.

The moment passes.

'Urua needs you and your Conduits.'

'We will always serve,' Zorar says softly. She loosens the grip on his arm, but still keeps her fingers over it.

'Years have passed since the deaths of my husband and son,' Negin says. 'It has grown harder to govern; I can only do so much by myself. Factions within the army want to exterminate Conduits, others want a war with Artay in the north. Some even hatch plans to topple the Emperor. It is at times ungovernable.' A tear forms in her right eye. She blinks and it rolls down her cheek.

Zorar takes a handkerchief from his breast pocket and dabs at her cheek. She holds his hand. He feels the warmth of her clasp. They remain silent, looking at one another. *If only it were possible,* he counsels himself. *But it is not.*

Zorar remembers what Brant told him, Negin will soon no longer rule the south. *No, I will not let such a thing happen.*

'I am here, Negin,' he says. 'I will always be here for you. No matter what.'

Bold words, he thinks to himself, but it is how he feels.

'I know,' Negin says and she leans into him, her head on his chest. 'I desired to change the world, remove injustice, uplift the destitute and poor, assist the sick. Yet I always stumbled, as I wasn't prepared to first change myself.'

'You have done much for your people Negin, Urua itself is a marvel and your subjects love you, as do we all,' Zorar says.

He has to use all his resolve not to wrap his arms around her. They remain like this, hands clasped, she leaning into him and he with his chin on the fur trim of her hood.

The Sultana whispers. 'We both bear the same loss.' He hears her sob.

Zorar remembers his wife and daughter. Years have passed since they were taken from him. He, with all the powers at his disposal, all his abilities, cannot find them. *Are they still alive?*

Negin turns her tear-streaked face up to look at him. 'I have lost much, I do not want to lose you.'

'You will not,' he replies.

'Yet I have not quite found you either,' she whispers.

'It is hard to let go,' he replies. 'Maybe they are still alive.'

'I know,' she whispers.

Eventually, Negin steps back, holds both of his hands. 'You have to be sure,' she says.

'I promise, if it comes to a time when it is apparent that I will not find my wife …'

'Hush,' she says, placing a finger on his lips. 'We will come to it, when we come to it.'

He nods.

'Then you will only need to ask,' Negin says.

They hold hands for a few moments longer, then she lets go. His heart stops racing and he wonders whether he should tell Negin about the breaking of the Seals. He wants to, but it is not the right moment. There will be another, he tells himself. The Sultana is already burdened with so much. Besides, he wants Azadeh and Nimar to confirm it, so they know how long they have to prepare.

Negin sighs.

Zorar knows they must return to matters of statecraft.

'Have you heard of the Custodians?' she asks.

He has not and tells her so.

'My vizier has been speaking about classified correspondence sent by a group who call themselves the Custodians. They appeared only after we returned from the battle at Dvin. No one has heard of them.'

Zorar mulls over the name. *The Custodians. Custodians of what?*

'You have not come across them, then?' Negin asks again.

He shakes his head but with an uncomfortable feeling.

'I'll get around to looking at what they want,' Negin says.

'Ramin came to see us,' Zorar says. 'He wants our help against the Teuton Conduits. We've realised that Ambassador Paxon and the other officials are not aware of the extent of the Conduits' plans. Nor are we at this time, but his Deputy, Brant, is a Grand Conduit and is the one I fought in the docks.'

'The Deputy Ambassador!' Negin begins.

Zorar nods. 'He made it clear to me that he was merely using the Syndicate to serve the agenda of another.'

'Who?' she asks.

'Mörtan.'

Negin shakes her head, says. 'We have to deal with reality, Zorar. The Syndicate is the threat we face, despite the comet and the talk about the Final Standing approaching, I don't see Mörtan appearing anytime soon. Do you?'

He wants to tell her more. 'Whether you believe in his imminent return or not, Brant is in his service and has more Conduits in Urua than I have. We are outgunned.'

'So, what are you getting at?'

'I need Alifa, I need my apprentice.'

'Why is she so important?' Negin asks.

'Because, like me, she is a Grand Conduit.'

The Sultana's mouth falls open. 'Oh, I see. And the Teutons, do they have another Grand Conduit other than Brant?'

'They may have,' Zorar replies.

Negin nods. 'She will have to remain in prison for a few days in order to placate the military, after which I will have her quietly released back into your custody.'

'Days?' Zorar asks. 'The Teuton Conduits may have caused other problems before then. Can she not be released sooner?'

'You have other Conduits, more experienced. Nimar, Azadeh – there must be more.'

Should he tell her where Azadeh and Nimar are about to go? Given her scepticism about Mörtan, Zorar thinks it better not to tell her. He tries another tack.

'Your Majesty. You realise that a Grand Conduit like Alifa can break out of any cell.'

Negin arches an eyebrow. 'Not this one.'

A chill strikes Zorar. 'Why?' he asks.

'We have a special military prison where Conduits are held. It is made entirely of metal. You cannot access the Source through metal – is that not correct?'

-16-
HIRING AN ASSASSIN

Possibly you could be in the service of others,
but not when you are in the service of yourself.
A FOOL'S PARADISE

THE SNOW-CAPPED PEAKS to the north of Urua are visible from the city. In winter the snow settles for weeks at the summits, as it has now. Brant can see why so few from the city attempt the ascent. The valley at the foot of the mountain range is treeless, with vast swathes of wetland, filled with blade-like grasses and spore-bearing ferns. Brant notes a murky river lies to the east of their position.

He dismounts from his steed, as does Konrad. The horses cannot cross the marsh, so they will have to go on foot.

Brant turns to their local guide. 'Take the horses and wait for us at the last village we passed. We will return by nightfall.'

'The marsh! It is certain death to try to cross it,' the guide says.

'We'll take our chances,' Brant says.

The guide makes a gesture with his hands.

Brant throws him a bag of coin. 'The other half when we get back,' he says.

'Humph! I pray for your return,' the guide grumbles, taking the reins of their beasts and setting off for the village.

Brant removes a cartridge from his belt. Uncaps it and pours the contents onto his palm. With his *dhulmi* heart he accesses the elements: a glow forms over the cup of his hand. He feels alive once more, as the Source surges inside him. He taps volcanic ash to ignite his Revealer abilities. Brant swings his gaze back at the marshland. This time he clearly sees footsteps, cleverly concealed but following a well-trodden path across the marsh.

'Let's go,' he instructs Konrad.

Moving swiftly, the two Conduits thread themselves across the marsh, crossing by the hidden solid places. Ten minutes later they arrive on firmer ground at the base of the mountains.

'Wasn't too bad,' Brant says.

'Can you do that at night?' Konrad asks.

'Haven't you been with me long enough to know the answer?' Brant replies, moving off towards the mountain.

Konrad shrugs and takes off after him.

Brant discovers another path, and they ascend at a steady pace. Whoever hid the path did a sterling job, thinks Brant, but not when an experienced Revealer is involved. The apex of the first peak is reached, with several bouts of threading to propel them up the more difficult parts. Hours pass and though the threading has made it easier, Brant still draws on ochre to strengthen his muscles. He glances across at Konrad. The man does not say it, but Brant can see the exhaustion on his face. Konrad does not have the luxury of drawing on ochre.

'Let's stop for a moment,' Brant says, planting himself on a boulder.

Konrad gratefully slumps onto another rock. Removes a canister from his pack, drinks it. Overhead the clouds are metallic grey and heavy, despite it being near midday.

Brant detects movement in the undergrowth. The sound of someone approaching, wearing soft and supple boots, quiet enough to avoid detection by most. He alerts Konrad with a movement of his hand, then motions with his eyes behind him. Konrad's hand moves closer to his weapon.

With his Revealer abilities tuned he knows four bodies approach, most likely armed. One is a woman. He lets them draw near.

Brant feels the tip of a sword on the back of his neck.

'Turn around. Slowly,' a voice rattles.

The voice of someone young and inexperienced, he thinks.

Brant gradually rises from the boulder, turns to face a hooded man. There are two others, on either side of him, and the fourth has taken up a position close to the seated Konrad.

'Go back to wherever you came from,' the young hooded man says.

'Actually,' Brant says nonchalantly, 'we came to see the Patriarch of the Peak.'

'Why?'

'We seek to hire assassins, but better ones than you,' Brant says.

The assassin's eyes widen. In one swift movement, Brant has snatched the assassin's sword and spun it around so that its tip is now against the assassin's throat.

'Huh!' the assassin gasps.

Before the others have a chance to react Brant spins the weapon once more, seizes the assassin's hand and firmly pushes the hilt back into its owner's grip.

'Now,' he says rubbing his palms together. 'Are we going to see the grown-ups?'

The shocked assassin looks across to his comrades.

They're all probably quite young, Brant thinks. *The Patriarch likes to surround himself with young people.*

'We pay well,' Brant adds cheekily. 'And if you're a good boy, I'll teach you that sword-swapping trick.' He grins.

The assassins exchange nods.

'Come on,' one of the other assassins says: it's the girl. 'We aren't going to slow down for you. If you can keep up, you get to see the Patriarch.'

The climb is treacherous. The assassins move swiftly over familiar ground, making the ascent, leaping from one boulder to the next, walking along edges below which there are drops of hundreds of feet. Despite the assassins' best attempts to outpace them, both Brant and Konrad comfortably keep pace.

This clearly annoys the assassins, who push themselves faster, till one slips on an edge and it requires Brant's intervention to prevent him from falling to his death.

'No need for that,' Brant purrs. 'Just face it, you kids aren't going to lose us, so let's all try to get to the Patriarch in one piece.'

The remainder of the hour is spent at a calmer pace. They approach a sheer vertical rock wall rising several hundred feet high. The assassins begin their climb, using hand and footholds.

Brant looks across at the frustrated Konrad, who could comfortably thread himself upwards, as could Brant. 'I know it's tempting, but let's just use the old-fashioned method for now,' he tells Konrad.

The two Conduits climb, following the assassins, to emerge on a plateau, speckled with snowflakes. A narrow stream, with unspoiled water from a higher mountain range, runs to the east. Brant smells the distinct fragrance of the Papaver flower, whose seeds are used by the followers of the Patriarch to intoxicate themselves after a kill.

'So this is where he grows it,' Brant says.

'Stronger than Opius,' Konrad whispers.

'Umm,' Brant says. 'I wonder how much of it there is?'

The assassins make their way across the plateau. Midday has turned to early afternoon and by the time they cross the upland, a cold wind has begun to bite. Before them is the next range of mountains: these are the snow-capped ones visible from Urua.

No wonder no one comes here, thinks Brant. *Most would die making the climb.*

On the other side of the plateau is a precarious crossing: a narrow stone bridge. Below the natural bridge is a drop of several thousand feet. Snowflakes swirl around in the vortex between the two mountain ranges.

The girl turns to him. 'You wait here. If the Patriarch wants to see you, he will present himself on the other side of the mountain. It might be tonight, or it might be at dawn. If he does come, then he will cross halfway on this stone bridge. One – only one – of you will be permitted to meet him halfway. Don't go further than that point. Then make your proposal. Is that understood?'

'Quite,' Brant says.

The young assassins sprint across the narrow stone crossing, disappearing behind boulders that mask what to Brant looks like an entrance to a wider cave system.

'I'm sure it's warmer on the other side of the mountain,' Brant scoffs. 'Alas, you and I will just have to make ourselves comfortable here.'

Brant clears some snow from the ground, puts his pack down and sits on it, taking up a cross-legged position.

'It's cold up here,' Konrad says, blowing into his hands.

'You're a Teuton: this is a spring day for you,' Brant scolds him.

Konrad shrugs. 'Got used to the warm weather in Arön.'

'Well, I suppose that was the downside of sending you a year ago. But the reconnaissance you managed to do, the contacts you made, are all coming to fruition. You should be proud of yourself, Konrad.'

'I suppose,' Konrad says in a droll tone.

'Let's rest, wait for the old man,' Brant says, as he leans back against a wall of rock.

Hours pass in the chill, but as the sun starts to set, Brant notices lights approaching: several burning cressets. Assassins march along the path and spread out on the other side of the mountain. Cowls hide their faces. Then the Patriarch of the Peak appears. *He is indeed old*, Brant thinks to himself.

A pulse! More powerful than anything Brant has felt. He leaps up. Konrad notices the urgency, prepares himself for combat. Brant scans along the line of assassins. *Do they have a Grand Conduit? Is there more to these assassins than I thought?* He exchanges a concerned look with Konrad. The Threader knows what it means; they are both alert.

Brant isolates the pulse. It emanates from a masked assassin, who crouches by a boulder, a Sarabi mastiff dog curled up by his feet. *A Grand Conduit, without doubt!* There is another pulse coming, not as strong, on the other side, from an assassin who flicks and unflicks a knife. *A Threader, at least*, Brant thinks to himself. *By Mörtan, does the Patriarch even know what he has?*

Using a wooden staff for support, the old Patriarch makes his way onto the stone bridge. Brant cautiously approaches, his eyes flicking to the two Conduits on the other side, watching for an attack. *The Grand Conduit must know who he is. But if he did, he would be wearing a ring.*

He clearly doesn't know who he is, then. Brant hides a grin.

The wind buffets him as he edges onto the narrow stone bridge. It whips around his clothes, stings any exposed skin. The old man's stride is determined, unruffled by the gale ripping at them. They stop a yard apart and then the old man sits down on the ground, cross-legged. Brant follows suit, glancing at the Grand Conduit with the dog beside him.

The Patriarch is dressed in a long robe, with his hood down, showing his scraggy hair and beard. His piercing grey eyes, like the moon itself, draw Brant's attention.

Brant shivers.

'Few make it this far,' the Patriarch says in a surprisingly firm voice.

'Few have the skills,' Brant replies.

'State your business,' the Patriarch instructs.

'Oh, I think anyone who comes to see you only has one thing on their mind,' Brant says jokingly.

The old man is not impressed. He remains silent.

'All right,' Brant says. 'Not one for humour, then.'

Brant removes an envelope from his coat pocket, hands it to the Patriarch. 'Inside are the names of officials we want assassinated. It is a long list, but necessary for my employer.'

'I will review it,' the Patriarch replies.

'Do you not want to know who we are?'

The old man shakes his head. 'Better I don't know. Tomorrow your enemy may come to me with the same request. What do I care? If I knew, maybe I could not take his coin. If I don't know, it is better.'

'Very well,' Brant says, taking out a pouch of gold coins. 'Half now. The remainder, when the list is done.'

The Patriarch shrugs, collects the pouch and puts it into his cloak. 'Everyone pays,' the old man says. 'No one wants to get visited in the middle of the night by one of my assassins.'

Brant glances across at the crew assembled on the mountain. He counts twenty. 'No, I suspect not. Tell me, the one with the Sarabi mastiff by his feet, who is he?'

'What does it matter to you?' the Patriarch asks.

'Curious. He has a particular quality that stands out.'

'He is my best. That is all you need to know, Teuton,' the Patriarch says and rises to his feet in one swift movement.

Brant also stands, saying, 'If you need to get hold of me—'

'We won't,' the Patriarch cuts him off. 'The names on this list are as good as dead. When the list is complete, we will find you and collect our final payment.'

With that, the old man turns and strides away, leaning on his staff. Soon the other assassins fall in behind him as they make their way through the pass between the two mountains.

The assassin with the Sarabi mastiff is the last to leave; he observes Brant with a penetrating gaze.

-17-
BOXED IN

You should be willing to give up any worldly position. If you cannot do so, then do not take up the position in the first place.

THE WISDOM OF THE WAY

IT'S COLD. The metal has a wintry feel on her skin, but it is her only companion. How long has it been? Five days, Alifa thinks, but she is not totally sure, as the cell is windowless with bare metal walls, ceiling and floor. Everything is metal: the chair, the bed, the latrine, everything. A low voltage algae light emits a greenish hue, as though she were stuck in a swamp at dusk. She thinks she has slept at night and stayed awake during the day, but after so many days her mind is jumbled. Without the sun and stars to guide her, she cannot be sure. She has recalled the events several times – her fight with the *Dhulmi* Conduits in the royal palace, then the blow to her head, next the cell. She has a fleeting memory of being in transit, and of how every time she tried to wake, she felt a pinprick in her arm and fell back into a deep slumber. They drugged her.

The cell is ten by ten paces with a high ceiling where a vent regulates the airflow. A sink and latrine are in one corner and once a day food is passed through a flap at the base of the door. The door itself has remained shut since she arrived. A pallet which she uses to sleep and sit on is furnished with a sheet and blanket. It's clean, and far better than anything in a northern prison.

Having tasted the power that comes from being a Grand Conduit, to have it taken away feels worse than not having had it in the first place. She is still dressed in her scarf, tunic, trousers, but her *tasbeah* and ring have been removed. She thinks about the injured soldiers in the palace, *I tried to help them all, but in the end, I couldn't even help myself.*

In her head she goes through the invocations Zorar taught her. She remembers the Creator. She performs the litany she has learned:

The Creator is all we need. What an excellent Guardian is He.

I ask for forgiveness from the Creator in His glory.

There is no Creator but the Creator, the King, the real, the manifestly apparent.

Oh Creator, extol the noble Heralds, their families, their companions and their followers and envelop them in perfect peace.

She repeats the litanies, one by one, throughout the day, so that by the end of it she has uttered each line thousands of times. It offers an inner peace and strengthens her resolve. Whatever happens, she is prepared.

The door creaks. She looks up as it swings open. Five armed men enter, faces hidden behind visors. An algae glow seeps around their goggles. They aim sonic-powered rifles at her. She knows a full blast from those weapons will destroy her internal organs, pulverise them to mulch. With ochre reinforcing her, she would feel the blow but quickly recover from it. Without the strength of a Hefter she has witnessed the deadly effect of such weapons on the battlefield. There is no outer wound, no ripped flesh, or gouged skin. Sometimes a trickle of blood leaves through the nose, eyes or ears of the victim. She doubts even a Nourisher like Belal could repair the damage caused by a direct sonic blast.

Another man enters behind the five armed ones. He does not carry any weapons.

'On your feet,' he says from behind his visor.

She rises.

—

'Take your things, you're leaving.'

She has only the clothes on her back and her boots, which she slips on.

A cool breeze comes down the corridor; it freshens her. She clenches her fists.

'Don't try anything,' the man says.

The four riflemen take a step forward, weapons pointed at her.

That was stupid, she thinks to herself. *Better to play meek and coy, till I know what they're planning. I still can't feel the Source and I don't have my tasbeah.*

'Outside,' the man orders.

Two of the riflemen approach, weapons trained on her head and heart. The other two slip out into the corridor, where she notices a metal box, just large enough for a grown man to squeeze into. It sits on a trolley.

'Get inside,' the man instructs.

Before entering the box through a front opening, she glances left and right up and down the corridor. There are dozens of cells on each side. Then she feels it. Pulses from other Conduits, emanating from each of the cells. *This is a prison for people like me, for Conduits, and this entire corridor is full of other Conduits. Who are they?*

Noticing her hesitation, the man barks, 'Hurry up.'

She crawls inside the metal box, before the other items she had on her are thrown in: the robe she was wearing, along with the belt, her *tasbeah* and ring. The door slams shut. It's pitch black.

'Move it,' she hears the man's voice through the metal. It is muffled; the box has a thick band of metal around it. She can no longer feel the pulses of the other Conduits in the cells. *How many are there,* she wonders. *And how many levels are there to this prison? It could mean there were hundreds of Conduits in confinement. Does Zorar know?*

She is transported down the corridor. It takes time to reach the other end. A lift takes her up for what seems like an eternity. Either it is a very slow lift, or they are very deep underground. Eventually they exit, and she is pushed along again. Voices reach her as whispers. She hears a door open, then she thinks she is outside. She cannot be sure, but it feels as though a weight has been lifted.

Thank the Creator.

The box tilts as it is pushed upwards. She hears the wheels of the trolley being locked, then a door shutting, followed by the start of an engine. They have placed her in an algae-fuelled vehicle, a truck, by the sounds of it.

The journey is a long one and she is unsure of their direction, altitude or location. She does not even know whether it is night or day.

Alifa resorts to the litanies, as they calm her. She knows that when the door opens next, she might have only seconds to react. She removes a bead from her *tasbeah*, it empties, there is the familiar glow over her palm, then with her heart she reaches for the Source. Nothing. She tries again. Nothing. Either it's the metal, or the drugs they gave her have stifled her ability. She prays it's the former. Hours pass. She has a sense of being driven up a winding mountain, then down again.

Eventually the vehicle comes to a stop. Its back door is opened. Her trolley is rolled out onto uneven ground. There are several muffled voices around her. The trolley is being pushed along pebbled ground and then it feels like they are on a wooden surface, something smoother, but not concrete. She thinks she hears the lapping of water. Can it be?

The trolley is rolled onto another surface and she immediately feels the sensation of being on a boat or ship. *Where are they taking me?* The fear returns. Her fingers hover over a second bead, ready to release it as soon as she is free from this metal cage.

The metal box is loaded onto the boat. The trolley is wheeled away. Then slowly she feels like they have pushed off and the boat is drifting out onto the water. There is no engine noise, so they must have some men rowing or pushing it with long poles if the water is shallow enough. The motion continues for some time, till they come to a stop.

Once more some muffled voices, then the sound of what might be another boat coming alongside hers. After which there is silence. She strains to hear anything. She wraps her robe about her, as she feels cold. Alifa's fingers hover over the bead.

When nothing happens fear takes hold, and once more she recalls the litanies and reads them aloud. Calm flows over her. She remembers her times in the Isthmus, where she leapt over verdant hills, over streams and rivers. She remembers yanking and thrusting objects over the city streets, falling at speed towards the ground then threading herself onto another rooftop, the wind whistling in her ears. She thinks, *Will I ever experience that again?* Then she recalls the words of Zorar: "*Still yourself, for you will hear the hymning of your heart and the natural world around you as it praises the Creator, for without it all hope is lost.*"

Alifa realises she must have gone to sleep, for she is woken by the sounds of voices. Several of them. Urgent in tone.

'Open it.' The voice is familiar to her.

Whack. She hears a padlock smash. The door is wrenched off its hinges. Cold wind rushes in. Three familiar faces, concerned, etched with fear, stare in, against the backdrop of the night sky. The moon appears as a silvery coin behind Zorar's head.

'Alifa,' Zorar says, his voice cracking with emotion.

'Come here,' Azadeh reaches for her, fingertips stretched out.

Gingerly, for she is not sure whether she is dreaming or awake, she raises her arms. Alifa's fingers touch those of Azadeh's and the older woman tenderly draws her out. Alifa clambers out of the metal box and falls into the embrace of the Threader, who holds her tight.

It is only then that Alifa bursts into tears. She has kept the grief, the dread, the sadness pent within her: she did not want her captors to see her break. But now, now she is with friends, her family, so it all pours out in deep sobs and cries.

'There, there,' Aazadeh consoles her. 'It's okay, we're with you, Alifa. It'll be all right.'

As she clings to Azadeh tears stream down her cheeks. She does not open her eyes but grips the Threader tighter.

'It's okay,' Azadeh whispers softly into her ear.

Eventually, the tears stop. Alifa lifts her head to see Zorar staring at her, attempting a smile, but doing a very poor job of it. Beside him Nimar has a determined look on his face. It is only then she realises she is on a barge, in the middle of a lake, surrounded by dense forest. On the edge of her vision she can see a range of mountains.

'Alifa,' Zorar says. 'I'm so sorry.'

She nods. It's not his fault, she knows it: he told her to stay where she was, but it was her decision to chase the *Dhulmi* Conduits.

'It's my mistake, I should have stayed put,' Alifa says, her voice hoarse from lack of use.

Azadeh provides her with a canister of water and she sips from it.

'Did they ...' Zorar starts, but cannot complete the sentence.

'No one touched me,' Alifa says.

'Thank the Creator,' Zorar says, releasing a deep breath.

'What happened after you were taken?' Azadeh asks.

'When I awoke, I was in a cell. I couldn't tell you where it was.

But I think it was deep underground, because when we left the prison, we came up in a lift, for a long time.'

The three Conduits consider her comment.

'How did you know where to find me?' Alifa asks.

Zorar's face twitches. 'After you were taken, I went to see Negin. She assured me you'd be released unharmed, but it would be after a week. I then received a dispatch from General Ramin this afternoon telling me where you had been left by the military.'

'Where are we?' Alifa asks, looking around.

'This is to the south of Urua, a desolate place of forests and lakes. Do you think you might have been kept inside a mountain prison stronghold?' Zorar enquires.

'Possibly.'

'I did not know,' Zorar says, 'they had metal prison cells for Conduits, until Negin mentioned it. I … understand it from their perspective, but for a Conduit not to be able to access the Source, is like chopping off both their arms.'

Then she remembers the pulses emanating from the other cells in the corridor.

'Zorar,' Alifa says quietly. 'There is something you should know.'

He arches an eyebrow.

'I wasn't the only Conduit in that prison.'

-18-
DOUBTS

A human lacking humanity is nothing better than a beast.
THE BOOK OF HERALDS

CRAWLING UP OVER THE EDGE OF THE MOUNTAINS, the morning sun is a haunted spectre behind a veil of snowflake-shaped clouds. Kaivan looks down from the ridge. Hundreds of feet below is the narrow stone bridge connecting two mountain ranges. The crisp morning air nibbles at his exposed skin and he pulls his grey tunic tight. Beside Kaivan, his dog Mushtar, a dependable Sarabi mastiff, sits on its haunches, staring down at the stone crossing.

Yesterday a Teuton visited, with a list of names of people marked for assassination. There was something about the Teuton, a certain resonance emanating from him. Kaivan cannot explain it, but he has always possessed an intuition, an awareness of a room, a sense of the crowd, an inkling of danger. It's what makes him an effective assassin. He listens to this voice, sees with this inner eye. Sometimes he feels his heart speak to him from behind a veil, but what can his heart tell him that his head can't? Whatever it is, it keeps him out of trouble, one step ahead. When people ask him how he knows something he can't explain it. When they ask him why he can jump further than others, why his strength at times is as much as that of two men, he can't explain that, either.

Kaivan opens the piece of paper the Patriarch gave him. It bears a list of names. His targets for assassination. In total there are nine names on his list. Most are military commanders, even a general. Two are religious scholars. The latter names make him uncomfortable. He does not personally know these men, but assassinating a religious person feels wrong. There it is again, that inner sense steering him. *But then, is it right to kill anyone at all*, he asks himself. *I must be the worst assassin in the world if I keep asking myself that question every time.*

This is the only life he knows. Trained from childhood by the Patriarch who found him disorientated, tired and hungry in the mountains as a child, he has never known any other way but killing for payment. Now, as he approaches his twentieth year, doubts creep in. He asks questions of himself. *Who am I? Where is my family from? What is my lineage?* These persistent questions are like an insatiable thirst: he wants to know, needs to know. Recently these questions have haunted him in his dreams. He tosses and tumbles in bed, wakes in a sweat. The last person he assassinated might have been a member of his family. *How can I know?* He seeks answers the Patriarch cannot give. It is obvious in his mind what he needs to do.

'Let's go, Mushtar,' he instructs his dog, turning back from the edge of the ridge.

They make their way down the slope and along a slender path forming a natural staircase down which he descends. Ahead of him there is a tunnel. A howling gust of wind rushes through it. He notices a figure coming in his direction. The person is backlit by cressets hanging inside the tunnel. As the man draws close Kaivan recognises Vard.

Dressed all in black, the snarly-faced assassin offers him one of his sardonic smiles.

'It is not too late, Kaivan. Embrace the will of the Patriarch,' he says.

Kaivan regards the assassin with a measured gaze. 'And when did I not?'

'Ah, you are far too readable. The look on your face when the Patriarch distributed the list of names! I embraced my list. You however appeared uncertain, regretful. This is not the way of an assassin, to show feelings towards prey.'

He and Vard are the same age, but Kaivan has never liked him. Vard has an air of superiority over the others on the mountain. Vard likes to rile up other assassins by spreading lies and rumours. The Patriarch permits it, even encourages this type of behaviour: rivalry amongst assassins keeps everyone on their toes. It also maintains the old man's position at the top of the hierarchy. Kaivan learned very early that you never know when there might be a dagger in the night. It's why he sleeps with his knives and Mushtar curled next to him. The dog has often alerted him to danger with a growl.

Mushtar growls now. The dog detests Vard. Most people do, but Vard pays no heed.

Kaivan has no desire to speak with Vard and brushes past the troublesome assassin, who catches him by the arm, stops him in his stride.

'The Patriarch is getting old, Kaivan,' Vard whispers. 'He does not have the energy to go up and down the mountain every day. We have few assignments these days. Until the Teuton arrived yesterday all we were doing for weeks was practise with one another. The others are restless. They want a change of direction. The arrival of the Teutons is an opportunity we should seize. Ally with them, and we will have plenty of work to keep us occupied.' Vard pauses. Looks around. 'Only,' he says. 'I'm not sure the Patriarch has it in him to seize this opportunity.'

Kaivan narrows his gaze. 'What are you suggesting, Vard?'

'I think you know,' Vard replies.

Kaivan shakes off Vard's grip and takes off down the tunnel, not looking back. But he can imagine Vard standing in the same place with that insufferable smirk plastered across his face.

Kaivan descends the mountain, emerging at the level where the assassins train. It's a large open area, sheltered by high mountain walls. Seating is chiselled from the rock so observers can watch training. The ring is full of young assassins, mostly around his age, some much younger. The Patriarch likes to purge his older assassins when they get beyond thirty. This is well known. He says that after thirty, assassins have too many opinions about how to run things. He gives them two options. Leave Arön or try their luck in a knife fight with the Patriarch. Half of them choose the latter but few last longer than a few minutes with the old man, before he sends them plummeting from the stone bridge into the ravine where their bodies remain, plucked by vultures and food for the worms. Kaivan still has ten years before he hits thirty, but he hopes to have left long before then.

Mushtar looks up at him and he tickles the dog's ear. The enormous mastiff has been with him since he was a puppy. He found the dog down on the lower slopes, abandoned. The Patriarch let him keep the dog, though he does not permit other animals on site. Kaivan still does not know why an exception was made for him.

'Kaivan,' a voice calls out.

He turns, notices a small group of assassins together. Juud, Ayu and several others. Juud beckons him over. She keeps her hair in a neat braid.

He leaps down from a boulder to join them.

'Kaivan,' Juud says. 'Show the others the defence to attack move.'

He smiles. He's been working on a new fighting technique, based on manuals from cultures in Cin. It is minimalist and practical in form. No flowery movements, but direct and functional.

'All right,' Kaivan says. He looks around. Turns to Ayu. 'Attack me with your sword.'

Ayu, a tall broad lad with a tree trunk neck, shares a perplexed look with Juud.

'Just do it,' Juud sniggers. 'See what happens.'

Ayu raises his practice wooden blade into a guard position. The others take a step back. Kaivan bounces on his toes, his left leg placed before his right, both knees bent. His palms straight. Pointing slightly upwards.

Ayu lunges, aiming the blow at Kaivan's chest. In a deft show of speed, Kaivan dodges the strike, wraps his right arm around Ayu's leading arm, neutralising it, then strikes with his fist at Ayu's cheek. He stops, an inch from Ayu's face.

'Woah!' Ayu says. 'What was that?'

'In one move you turn defence into attack,' Kaivan says.

'I told you,' Juud says. 'Your speed, Kaivan, is remarkable. You seem to be getting faster every year.'

'Show me that again,' Ayu says.

They go through the same movements, yielding the same results. Kaivan then shows them at a slower speed, how he anticipates Ayu's movement by watching his feet. How he swings his body away from the strike, then grabs Ayu's arm to lock it, whilst at the same time striking a deadly blow at Ayu's cheek with his left arm.

Pleased with the display, the young assassins practise what has been demonstrated and Kaivan continues further into the mountain complex, ordering Mushtar to remain outside.

The Patriarch is lodged deep within a cave system, a set of tunnels leading to a location where he dwells in the daytime. It's minimally furnished – a rug, table and chair. Kaivan finds the Patriarch sitting cross-legged, his back against a set of cushions, eyes closed, practising breathing.

'Kaivan,' the Patriarch says, as he approaches. The old man's eyes remain shut but he can recognise his disciples from their footsteps.

Kaivan sits on the carpet opposite the Patriarch, his knees tucked back, hands on his lap.

The Patriarch opens his eyes, looks at him. 'You have questions.'

I give away too much from my facial expressions, he thinks. *I must learn to hide my thoughts.*

Kaivan takes out the list the Patriarch gave him.

'Ah, the list,' the Patriarch says.

'I …' Kaivan starts.

'You are uncomfortable with the names, the religious scholars,' the Patriarch says.

He nods.

'You have a compassionate heart. No matter what I put you through, however hard I try to bend you to become pitiless and callous, your kindness shines through. It's your weakness; it will be the death of you one day.'

'So you tell me,' Kaivan says.

'Now, take Vard,' the Patriarch says.

Kaivan freezes. The Patriarch could not have overheard the conversation he just had with Vard, could he?

'Vard is selfish, an unpleasant, brutal and malicious thug. He enjoys inflicting pain on others. He is also competitive and deadly. A perfect assassin. I have no doubt he has already started plotting how he will one day depose me, throw me off the stone bridge between the two mountains and take my position as Patriarch.'

The old man studies Kaivan's face. Kaivan tries to hide his surprise, but the Patriarch is canny and shrewd.

'Once more your face gives you away. Vard will end up like other pretenders. Throat cut, bleeding to death, before I roll him off the stone bridge.'

'But these names, they are good men. They bring people together, give charity, are generous. It would be—'

'It would be right to kill them now,' the Patriarch interjects.

'Why?' Kaivan asks.

'Because of what's coming.'

'Which is?'

'Anarchy, confusion and chaos. The Teutons and their Syndicate are a force of disorder and upheaval. They will strip Arön of all good – its people, its resources, its ideas. They will turn each race and tribe against one another.'

'But …' Kavan says.

'Is it not better for the honourable and forthright to depart this world now and not witness the breakdown of society, suffer the cruel indignities of rupture, see the common man, woman and child suffer under a tyrannical foreign overlord?'

'The Teutons will bring such devastation?' Kaivan asks.

'Yes,' the Patriarch rasps. 'But there is, I fear, more to them than just the Syndicate. The one who came yesterday …'

'Yes,' Kaivan asks.

'He was …' The old man trails off into silence.

Kaivan studies the Patriarch's face. He has shut his eyes, leant back against the cushion and resumed his breathing exercises.

He waits, but the Patriarch does not say anything else. *What was he about to tell me?* he wonders.

Kaivan looks down at the names on the list, then back at the Patriarch. He will get nothing else from the old man on the subject. As he leaves, he puts the list back in his tunic pocket.

-19-
TRADE DEALS

An ego in a mind of little intelligence is liable to create trouble.

A FOOL'S PARADISE

'WHAT IS HE DOING HERE?' grumbles General Ramin.

The sight of Zorar has annoyed the General as Zorar enters the circular meeting room at the eastern end of the palace and comes to stand beside Negin. Its vast glass windows overlook the magnificent city of Urua below. The room is elaborately adorned with *cuerda seca* tilework depicting the trees and fauna of Arön.

'You know the answer,' Negin replies. 'Especially after the recent theft at the palace and the inability of your soldiers to prevent it. If it wasn't for that young girl ... what's her name?'

'Alifa,' Zorar says quietly. *Who was incarcerated in a metal underground prison. Are you aware there are other Conduits there, Negin?*

'Yes, Alifa, poor child. She not only prevented further theft but also saved the lives of two soldiers, Ramin.'

The General nods in acknowledgement.

'And what did we do? We imprisoned the poor child for a week,' Negin says, more to herself.

Zorar exchanges looks with Ramin.

'General, we should talk about the prison you have there,' Zorar says.

'What is there to talk about? It's for the monarchy's protection,' Ramin replies.

197

'Yes, but ...' Zorar starts, when the Sultana's attention is drawn to a group entering the room.

The bankers, led by Almas, approach.

'Your Majesty,' Almas says, bowing. The others follow suit. The middle-aged head banker has a healthy pound of flesh on him, though he could not be called fat, just well-fed. His face shines and his slick black hair is combed into a quiff. His pinstriped dark blue *sherwani* coat is understated, as is the rest of his attire. Expensive, but not flashy.

He is probably as wealthy as the Sultana, if not more so, Zorar thinks.

Almas is known to have several lucrative contracts in Cin and elsewhere. Rumour has it that he is planning to open a trade finance operation in Teuton.

'Almas, I am so pleased you could make it,' Negin says.

'I'm travelling tomorrow, as the Emperor wants to see me, so the timing is perfect,' Almas replies.

'Do give my cousin Behrooz my best regards. Tell him I often think about him and only want the best for him,' Negin says. 'Will you do that?'

'Of course. For us here in the south you are our Sultana and anything that serves your interest, serves our interest,' Almas says.

The bankers are ushered to a set of chairs, in front of which there is a round table for their beverages. They engage in dialogue with some of Negin's ministers.

'Sycophant!' whispers Negin.

Zorar leans close to Ramin and whispers so that only the General can hear. 'Be wary of Paxon's deputy; his name is Brant.'

'Why?' Ramin asks.

'He is a Grand Conduit.'

The General stares at him, as though he's announced the return of a dead ancestor.

'Apparently so,' Negin seethes. 'Paxon must know.'

'He must,' Zorar says. 'Brant is their most lethal weapon. But he also plays another game, which I'm sure Paxon is not aware of.'

'He's the one you fought at the docks?' Ramin asks.

Zorar nods. Word has got around, then, about his fight with another Grand Conduit.

Ramin is about to ask something when the Teutons arrive, Paxon and Brant at the front, their entourage behind. There is also a tall, angular man, wearing robes of silk, and a straight topee embroidered in gold.

'The Emperor's vizier,' Ramin declares. 'What is Kansabar doing with the Teutons?'

The sight of the vizier catches Negin off guard and Zorar notes her annoyance before she regains her composure. Zorar thinks, *Is it a coincidence they arrived at the same time, or has Kansabar been meeting with the Teutons, scheming with them and wants it to be known?*

Paxon wears a satisfied grin, as he approaches the Sultana. 'Your Majesty,' he murmurs. 'We are honoured to see you again.'

Negin nods, remains silent, observes the Emperor's vizier, who has taken to hovering some feet away from the Teutons, as though assessing which side to sit with.

'You know my deputy, Brant,' Paxon says, motioning for Brant to approach.

'An honour, Your Majesty,' Brant says, bowing. As he raises his head he shoots a glance at Zorar, smiles a cold sickly grin.

Beside Zorar, General Ramin grows tense, his hand resting on the pommel of his sword. Zorar knows it would do little good against an opponent as powerful as Brant.

Ushers approach, direct the Teutons towards their seats, offer drinks and snacks, then depart.

'Vizier Kansabar,' Negin says, as the vizier approaches.

'Your Majesty,' Kansabar replies. His face is implacable, devoid of emotion, until he exchanges looks with Zorar and he scowls. If there is one thing the vizier hates more than anything else, it is Conduits with their *Kha* abilities.

'How is my cousin Behrooz?' Negin enquires.

'The Emperor is well, but troubled by your slow acceptance of the Syndicate. He cannot see why it takes you so long to seize this opportunity to work with the Teutons.'

Kansabar shoots a glance of hatred at Zorar once more.

'My cousin should not fret for us in the south: we are used to going at our own pace. We might be slow, but we stay the course,' Negin says.

'The Emperor wants you to move faster, open economic ties with the Teutons, give them better access to your ports and ministries. There is much to gain by allying with these northerners,' Kansabar says.

So far, Zorar has only seen an influx of Opius. The Emperor is being led a merry dance by the Teutons and fails to see it, or he sees it but is apathetic about doing anything about it.

'Shall we sit, discuss it with the larger group?' Negin offers.

Kansabar nods and takes a seat between the bankers and the Teutons. Almas grins familiarly when Kansabar approaches. Zorar knows the Emperor is deeply indebted to the bankers and without them, the imperial treasury would be short of its annual budget. Fortunately, Negin has run a prudent ship in the south. She provides tax income to the Emperor, whilst maintaining livelihoods for her people and continuing to invest in her cities.

The Teutons wait long enough to be polite, but not a moment longer.

'Your Majesty,' Paxon declares, leaning on the lacquered walnut table. 'We must be allocated more capacity at the ports, at Onogur and Shabaran. Just last week three of our vessels were turned away and ended up having to sail to the imperial port of Hatra. In other cases, our vessels have remained at sea for weeks, unable to dock. As for the perishable items on board, well, they perish! We cannot continue like this.'

The forthright way in which the ambassador addresses the monarch surprises Zorar, but Paxon is an experienced career diplomat, and this is not the first empire he has broken..

'And you have taken this matter up with the Commerce Ministry?' Negin asks, knowing full well they have, but that under her instructions the ministry drags its feet.

'We have been caught in red tape for weeks, Your Majesty. I would not bring this matter to you. But it is impacting the hitherto cordial relationship we have had between Teuton and Arön. We would not want to jeopardise the hard work so many have put in to get us to this stage.' Paxon glances at Kansabar, but the imperial vizier is gazing into empty space.

He cannot be seen to be too close with the Teutons, Zorar thinks. *But he was probably the one who put them up to this, knowing Negin will need to comply with the Emperor's wishes.*

The Sultana nods at her finance minister, shifts her gaze back to Paxon and says, 'We will increase capacity, but in stages. We cannot flood the local market, as we have our own merchants and traders to protect, and many livelihoods depend on the goods they sell. If you dump cheap items into our markets this will cause civil unrest. Slowly, we will give you greater access, but be warned, our own local traders and craftspeople will always be my priority.'

'As Her Majesty wishes,' Paxon says.

Zorar observes the subtle signal from Negin to her General.

General Ramin clears his throat. 'The Sultana has been magnanimous in granting you greater capacity,' Ramin declares, 'but will this increase the volume of Opius flooding our market?'

The room goes quiet.

'What do you mean?' Paxon asks.

'With the arrival of the Syndicate we have seen a staggering increase in Opius addiction in our cities,' Ramin says. 'Yes, the drug existed before the Teutons arrived, but it was used recreationally by a minority of affluent pleasure seekers.'

The statement catches the attention of Kansabar who scoffs. Zorar thinks *The Emperor is a known Opius addict – perhaps Kansabar is also.*

The General continues, 'Now entire communities suffer from the addiction, even the lower-income ones, and I hear entire villages have also fallen under its spell. Our intelligence says Opius is being smuggled in via Teuton-owned vessels. Does the Syndicate have anything to say about this?'

This time it is Brant who speaks. He is calm, confident in his delivery. 'Opius is a tragic blight on any society. Our people suffered its misery for decades. The drug originates in the Northern Wastes, to the east of Teuton. It is grown in high-altitude areas of the Waste and harvested by the northern tribes, the Zandal, who occupy the land. They have used it for thousands of years and have developed a sort of immunity. A micro dose for them would knock anyone else out. Recently it has come to our attention that Cin criminal gangs are working closely with the Zandal, importing vast quantities into the Cin empire. The very same groups now turn their attention to Arön.'

'That is a fine history lesson, Deputy Ambassador, but what role does the Syndicate play in all this?' Ramin presses.

'We create affluence, wealth and livelihoods where we trade. When people have greater disposable income, then drug cartels, such as the Zandal and Cin gangs move in. We cannot be held accountable for trying to raise people up,' Brant says.

'And when your ships come into port, will you declare all of your manifests to our authorities?' Ramin asks.

'Of course,' Brant says, smiling. 'All of our inventory is currently audited by imperial inspectors, is it not, Vizier Kansabar.'

All heads turn to the vizier. He looks to Brant then across to the General. 'I will assign a team of imperial inspectors to your ports in the south – Onogur and Shabaran,' he says. 'They will check all of the Syndicate's manifests and cargo.'

Brant smiles, as does Paxon.

Was that planned? Zorar thinks. *The imperial inspectors will not serve the interests of the south, but of the Emperor and most likely the Syndicate.*

Negin's face is a mask of displeasure, but she keeps her temper. Almas the head banker has a coy smile on his face. Zorar imagines shipments of Opius will only increase. He decides to ask an unsanctioned question.

'Ambassador Paxon,' he starts, but Kansabar cuts in.

'What is *his* capacity here today, Sultana?' the vizier asks.

'Zorar is my advisor,' Negin replies, her lips pursed in politeness.

'Advisor regarding what?' the vizier pushes back.

Negin puts her finger to her chin, smiles. 'Subjects with which the vizier is unfamiliar. But after this meeting I can always sit with the vizier and enlighten him.'

The Sultana has used the third person to address Kansabar. The vizier grinds his teeth but remains silent.

Zorar acknowledges the intervention, turns back to Paxon. 'Ambassador, what need has the Syndicate of our seed? Farmers and villages have been coming in with reports that officials from the Syndicate are collecting native Arön seed. Why would the Syndicate require this?'

'Oh, it is merely archival evidence,' Paxon says. 'You see, in Teuton we have built large museums dedicated to documenting the world's different regions. We want to show the native seed of Arön, so that it can be displayed for our public, for visitors and schoolchildren to learn more about your culture and its agriculture. That is all.'

Zorar knows Paxon is lying and a quick glance at Brant tells him he knows it too. He is tempted to using his Calming on Paxon to loosen his tongue but cannot. Negin would not forgive him and how would Brant react? He persists with more conventional methods.

'I see,' Zorar says. 'What proposals does the Syndicate offer regarding agriculture?'

'We have,' Paxon says, 'been commissioned by Vizier Kansabar to undertake a full review of the agricultural methods deployed in Arön, with a view to modernising them. Your yields are very low for such fertile soil. We have some ideas and will be sharing them with the Imperial Agricultural Ministry in due course.'

Paxon looks towards Almas, as though he is ready to move on. 'Now,' Paxon declares, 'as part of that overall modernisation of Urua and Arön, I believe our friend Almas has an announcement to make.'

All heads turn to the head banker.

Almas' associates look nervous. He himself exudes calm. He clears his throat and declares: 'As you well know, your Majesty, the Sethee is a private bank, the largest of its kind on our continent, one of the largest in the world. Every year we issue an annual bond for regional governments in the south and the north, and of course an imperial bond. We will continue to issue these – they provide a reasonable return for investors and are seen as safe instruments to invest in. But this year, we are pleased to announce we will be issuing a bond on behalf of the Syndicate. It is a riskier investment vehicle, one for the sophisticated high net-worth investor, but it offers very attractive returns.'

The banker surveys the stunned looks on the faces of those who did not expect this news.

'Now, I would like to affirm, the bond we issue for her Majesty will continue to be attractive. It will be a mechanism for the royal treasury to raise capital for its infrastructure works. That will not change. However, the Syndicate with its global scale of operations presents for our high net-worth investors a very attractive return. *Very.* I expect the offering to be heavily oversubscribed.'

The room is silent. *They all knew,* thinks Zorar. *This is a dangerous road the bankers take. Less capital flowing into the royal treasury will impact investments Negin can make to support her subjects.*

'When?' Negin asks.

'It is ready. Investors have already been warmed up, so we will announce it later this week,' Almas says, glancing over at Paxon.

Negin controls her fury, but Zorar can see it rising. One does not have to be a Conduit to recognise she is angry. She closes and opens her fists. Zorar knows the Syndicate will not invest in Urua or Arön. They will extract their profits and they will not circulate them back into the local economy.

'There is one more thing I should mention,' Almas adds.

Negin's cold gaze could kill, but Almas retains his cheerful manner. *Why not?* Zorar thinks. *He is one of the richest men in the world.*

'Unlike conventional bonds, the bond issued by the Syndicate will be held offshore.'

'What do you mean?' Negin asks.

Paxon now comes in. 'The Syndicate has found a more tax-efficient method of issuing bonds through some of the offshore islands we control, such as the Warbler Islands which are partway between Teuton and Arön. This jurisdiction, as it is offshore, means investors in the bond will not be taxed by any onshore treasury, such as yours in the south or any across Arön. I am sure you can appreciate this tax-efficient structure makes it more attractive for high net-worth investors.'

'The investors will not pay any tax to the royal treasury on their investments?' Ramin asks.

'No,' Almas smiles. 'Ingenious, really. I wish I had thought of such an idea. I must hand it to the Teutons for coming up with such creative financial structuring.'

Negin clasps her fingers on the table. She presses them together then releases them. Her thumbs play rings around one another.

The meeting continues with no other shocks, but Negin has had enough and leaves. The others continue with minor procedural matters until the meeting ends.

Zorar steps out onto the balcony adjacent to the meeting room. The air is clean, the city of Urua stretched out below him. It's beautiful, an architectural and cultural marvel, underwritten by the royal treasury and private endowments from the wealthy held in trust funds. *Is this all about to change?* he asks himself. *The financial engineering of the Teutons is going to upset the commerce of the kingdom. What will be the effect on ordinary people? Not good.*

He hears footsteps, turns to see Brant idling his way across, hands clasped behind him. The Teuton smiles, leans on the banister, peers out across the city.

'Didn't get too wet, did you?' Brant asks.

'I needed a swim,' Zorar retorts.

'Well, you saved those dock workers. So reliable,' Brant says. 'So predictable.'

'What games are your people playing, Brant?'

'We are all wretched and in need of civilising by a firm hand. This is what modernisation looks like. You change the levers of power, slowly but surely. Governance, finance, food, healthcare, technology, information — standardising them as you go along. And when they are all in your hands, you squeeze and keep on squeezing, till you draw the last drop. Only then, do you let go and rebuild anew, somewhere else. This is the way of the new world. Why does this surprise you?'

'Your version of modernisation seeks unity through uniformity. This grounds the individual to a pulp. We allow differences but seek unity through the hearts,' Zorar says.

'The words of a man who sees the world changing and doesn't like what he sees.'

'No, I don't like it and does Paxon know what you are *really* doing?'

'Paxon,' Brant glances behind him, looking through the glass into the conference room, 'is merely a pawn on the board. Mörtan will use him how he sees fit. It is Mörtan we truly serve, not the Syndicate nor the Teuton federation. And you should know this too.' He faces Zorar. 'Look,' he says. 'I'll be honest with you, Zorar. I like you. You have a good way with yourself. You're an exceptional Grand Conduit, your powers unmatched by most, not all. So, I make the same offer I made to you when we were dancing on the crane over the docks. Will you come and work for me?'

Zorar shifts his gaze away from Brant. Examines the city, its people, its culture, the very things he loves, he holds dear. The memories of his wife; he remembers walking through the Blue Souk with her, in happy times, long ago. *Will I ever see such again?*

He turns back to Brant. 'Since you understand me so well Brant, you'll know my answer remains the same.'

'It is a shame. Life can be simple for you, why make it complicated?' Brant muses.

'Maybe it is and maybe it could,' Zorar says.

'But ... to be a slave of another slave is not to be a slave at all,' Brant says.

Zorar arches his eyebrow. 'What is it, then?'

Brant smiles. 'In the new world slavery will be called freedom.'

'Freedom? From what?'

'Anything you want to be free of,' Brant retorts. 'Yet all will be slaves of Mörtan, only they will not recognise their state. That is true slavery: to be a slave and not even know it.'

Zorar turns to leave.

'One more thing,' Brant says.

'What?'

'We already have more Conduits in Urua than you. And the ones you have, you've sent on a life-threatening mission into the Isthmus.'

'What do you mean?' Zorar asks.

'Your precious Azadeh, the agronomist and Nimar, the trader. Did you not think we would notice their absence, notice how they ventured to the fourth level of the Isthmus to check on the Seals? Well, I can tell you this, Zorar, the Seals have broken. Mörtan is emerging from his prison, and as for your friends, the Djüne are expecting them.'

-20-
THE RUINED DRESS

Be a servant not one who wants to be served.

THE BOOK OF HERALDS

THE DINNER INVITATION from Hale arrived via the dispatch system to Alifa's scroll-light when she was in prison. When he did not hear from her, he sent a reminder two days later. A third reminder arrived the morning she returned to the safety of the Lodge.

Zorar initially refused to send her into the Teuton embassy alone. When Alifa explained the host was an amiable young man called Hale who was throwing a dinner party for his new friends in Urua his attitude changed. When she explained that Hale's Uncle Paxon, Aunt Orinda, and most of the senior embassy delegation were away for a few days, Zorar relented and agreed. Within two days Jamshi arranged for Alifa to be measured and fitted for a special dress by a famed local seamstress.

The shimmering dress, all in black, is delivered the morning of the event. Alifa has never worn such a fine piece of stitching. It is long-sleeved, high necked, embossed with patterns running down the front which is studded with faux pearls.

Shame I'm going to ruin it this evening, she thinks, as she watches the streets pass from inside the vehicle. Alifa sits with her back to the oncoming traffic. Durayd is opposite. In the front cabin, shut off from the passenger section, a driver sits at the wheel.

'Durayd,' Alifa says. 'The spare dress.'

'Yes, what about it?'

'Did they pack matching shoes?'

The Calmer looks over his shoulder into the back of the transport where luggage and items are stored, as it chugs along on chunky tractor wheels down one of the main roads of the capital.

'Ah, I forgot, despite Zorar's reminder.' Durayd smacks his lips. 'But it shouldn't be too much of a problem, should it?'

'Shoes are important for a girl's outfit,' Alifa says, hardly believing she's having a conversation with him about fashion, having spent the last week in prison. 'I suppose it will have to do.'

Durayd shrugs.

'Where is Zorar this evening?' Alifa asks.

'He said he had a dental appointment, some pain in his tooth or something,' Durayd says.

'Dentist? It must have really been hurting,' Alifa says.

She adjusts her headscarf to how she likes it, with some of her hair showing at the front, the rest of it hidden under the fabric. She glances in the mirror, checks her face, eyes, lips. When she turns back, Durayd is grinning.

'What?' she asks.

'Alifa, you look delightful,' Durayd beams. 'If my wife and I had children, and we had a daughter, I would want her to be just like you.'

Father. Daughter. Relationships Alifa has never thought of, as she had never known her parents. The sudden possibility of having a father, albeit a surrogate one, triggers dormant emotions. Alifa's eyes well up.

'Oh,' Durayd says, leaning forward. 'Did I ...'

'No,' she snivels.

Durayd passes her a handkerchief. She accepts it.

'I ...' Aifa says, her voice settling, 'have no memory of my parents. I would love to be someone's daughter.' Her voice cracks as she utters the last word.

Durayd leans forward, takes her hand in his. 'I know I can never be your father. But in his absence, maybe I can play a fatherly role. From now on, if you wish it, I will regard you, Alifa, as I would my own daughter.'

She grips his hand.

'I wish it very much,' Alifa says, tears flowing down her cheeks.

They hold each other's hands, and she thinks Durayd is calming her, for she feels his subtle touch on her emotions. She lets him, and soon Alifa smiles. Durayd leans back, as does she.

'Now, all that expensive mascara, eye shadow, foundation, whatever concoctions ladies apply to their faces, is going to be ruined,' Durayd says.

She glances at the mirror, dabs away the wet spots on her face. It takes a few minutes to regain her composure. The damage done to her foundation is tolerable. She takes a deep breath. Looking at Durayd, she feels a genuine sense of love and affection for him. Then she thinks: *Is he still calming me?*

'Zorar wanted to be here this evening. He's very nervous about sending you to the embassy. Anyhow, after his dental appointment he's visiting Azadeh and Nimar. They're not in a good state after returning from the Isthmus. The Djüne were expecting them, but they made it out alive. Apothecary Belal is giving them his full attention. It will take time, but if the Creator wills it, they will recover.'

'How bad are they?' Alifa asks.

'For another time. Now, focus on your task. You have the embassy map memorised?' Durayd asks.

'Yes: get to Paxon's office, second floor, on the western side of the building,' Alifa says.

'Good,' Durayd says. 'My sources in the catering company tell me the dinner will be in the grounds, in the enormous glass conservatory the Teutons have built. There are no *facilities* there. When you ...' he pauses, looks at her dress, grimaces, 'need a new dress, you will have an excuse to enter the main building. Make sure they take you to the ladies' facilities in the eastern wing of the ground floor. There is a frosted window set high on the wall of this facility facing the garden, just large enough for you to squeeze through. The other facilities have smaller windows, so you need to get to this specific one, otherwise the plan falls apart. A member of staff will most likely escort you. That will be your chance.'

'I understand,' she says. Alifa reaches for her *tasbeah*, loosens a bead, watches it empty, a glow form, then she reaches for it with her heart. She connects with the Source.

The vehicle draws to a halt outside the Teuton embassy.

'All right,' Durayd says. 'If you sense any danger, or encounter any difficulty, I want you out of there immediately. Leap over the wall if you must. I don't care if anyone sees you. Just get out. We'll be parked on the western side of the embassy wall. When you need the second dress, send one of the embassy staff to look for us.'

'I understand,' Alifa says again, reaching for the door handle.

'And Alifa,' Durayd adds with a smile, 'enjoy the evening.'

She nods.

Durayd pats her on the shoulder as she exits, and she squeezes his hand. She likes Durayd. Likes him very much.

At the gates, the security guard checks her name against the guest list, then ushers her past the embassy, through the grounds. The gardens are manicured, all straight edges and squares, unlike gardens in Urua whose designs are full of waves, spirals, swirls and curves. How strange, she thinks, that the Teutons design their gardens like you would a highway.

Ahead of her is the glass conservatory. It is an impressive sight, all aglow with lights and at least fifty yards across. She notices several guests entering through a secure door, which she thinks is meant to keep the building free from insects. About twenty people are already inside. *Hale has been busy socialising*, she thinks. She checks the position of her scarf and heads for the entrance.

Warm air radiates around the glasshouse, and all heads turn as she enters. She notices the looks of admiration from most, envy from some, before Hale bounds in her direction.

'Alifa!' he cries ecstatically. 'I was so worried when I hadn't heard back from you. I hope everything is okay?'

He reaches out to shake her hand.

'I'm sorry, Hale, I was out of town for a few days and forgot to take my scroll-light. It's still so new to me, I'm not used to carrying it around.'

'Of course,' he says. 'I'm so pleased you could make it.' He examines her, as though for the first time. 'That dress, Alifa – you look stunning!'

She blushes. He is very sweet and genuine but he is a Teuton after all.

'Thank you,' she replies. 'And you look quite dashing this evening.' *He does indeed*, she thinks to herself and feels a warm glow in her chest.

'Not at all, I just … anyway, let me introduce you to some of the others. Come.'

Hale escorts her towards a small group of people holding drinks, who are talking amongst themselves, but she knows they're waiting for Hale and her. A server approaches: she chooses water, unsure what's in the cocktail.

Turning to the five people standing together, Hale says. 'Friends, I'd like to introduce you to Alifa.' They smile. 'She is quite a delight, a local of Arön, a healer by profession,' he adds.

'Just learning,' she adds.

'Alifa, this is Lin, daughter of the Cin ambassador.' It is the first time she has met a Cin. The girl is tall, about the same height as her. She wears a red silk dress with sequins along the front. She offers a serene smile, not too friendly, but welcoming, nonetheless.

'And this is Ikal, the son of an Aztlan diplomat visiting Arön.'

Ikal immediately steps forward, takes her hand, bows, presses her hand to his lips and gently kisses it. 'I am at your service, Alifa,' he says in a deep husky voice.

Alifa reddens, feeling a bead of sweat form on her temple.

'Well yes,' Hale stumbles. 'Aztlanians are, ah, very forward I suppose, eh Ikal?'

The Aztlanian beams, tries to catch Alifa's attention, but Hale is introducing her to several of his Teuton friends: Cooper, Kelver and Amber, children of other diplomats who work at the embassy in some capacity.

Finally Hale approaches a robed figure, whose hood masks much of the person's face.

Clearing his throat, he makes the introduction. 'This is Dassin, from Koemox.'

The girl under the hood wears heavy mascara and her lips are dark red. She barely acknowledges Alifa. 'Nice to meet you, Dassin,' Alifa says.

'She's quite intense,' Hale whispers in Alifa's ear, as they withdraw.

Looking up, Hale notices new guests arrive. 'Excuse me, Alifa,' he says before making his way over to them.

Alifa turns to Lin, trying to avoid the gaze of Ikal, who strikes up a conversation with the Teutons.

'How long have you been in Urua?' Alifa asks the Cin girl.

'Less than a year. And you, are you local?' Lin asks.

'I'm from the north of Arön. I'm new to Urua,' Alifa says, sipping her water.

The Cin girl turns her body away from the nearby Teutons, speaks more quietly to Alifa. 'Hale really likes you. All he's talked about since I came is his quest to find red algae and when his friend from Arön would arrive. He has a crush on you.' Lin winks.

By the Creator!

Alifa takes a gulp of water.

'Look, Hale, he's a lovely young man,' Lin says. 'If he weren't a Teuton, I'd say give him a chance, but I'm from Cin, so trust me, we know what these Teutons are capable of. The Syndicate has wrapped its tentacles around the Cin empire and like a bloodsucking leech, it's draining us dry. He may be a dashing adorable bachelor, but he is a Teuton. He will remain with his kind.'

'Well, I hadn't even thought about ... I mean, but yes, I'll keep my distance,' Alifa says, taking another swig of water.

Lin arches an eyebrow. 'Hale described you as the most beautiful woman he had seen since arriving in Urua.'

'He said that!' she gulps more water, realises the glass is empty and motions to a waiter for a top up. *How many other women has he been looking at?* she thinks.

'You do look quite stunning in that dress,' Lin adds. 'I can see why Ikal is desperately trying to get your attention.'

'Is he?' Alifa says, turning away from Ikal without appearing rude.

Feelings long suppressed pop up. Her brain is foggy and her

heart races. *I'm a Calmer,* she reminds herself. *Why don't I calm my-self?* She reaches for the Source, calms her nerves, slows her breath-ing.

As she does, the Koemox girl, Dassin, looks up. Dassin's pene-trating stare bores through Alifa.

Hale returns. 'Alifa,' he says. 'Sorry about that – I just wanted to pair up the newbies with some of my buddies. That way I can spend the whole evening with you.'

'Oh,' she says. *Am I really the most beautiful woman he has seen in Urua?* Staring into his eyes now, she knows he thinks it, though she knows that it is far from the truth. *I was in prison last week. If he but knew, he'd have me escorted from the premises.*

She calms herself. She needs her wits about her, if Hale is going to be so close and Ikal so overbearing.

A waiter taps Hale on the shoulder. He nods.

'Wonderful,' Hale enthuses. 'Everyone, can I get everyone's at-tention?'

The guests in the glass conservatory look to their host.

Hale raises his voice. 'Thank you, old friends, and new. I'm so pleased you could come this evening. While my uncle and aunt are away on business, what else can a young man do but invite his friends over?' He glances at Alifa. 'Please make your way to the tables on the other side of this building. Dinner will be served shortly.'

With that, the guests head in the direction he has indicated.

'Alifa, stay with me,' he says. 'I'm so looking forward to your company this evening. I want to hear what you've been up to since we last met and want to share my latest research into red algae.'

What have I got myself into? thinks Alifa, as she accompanies the young man towards the dinner tables, laden with plates, silverware and glasses.

Hale helps Alifa to a seat, stands beside her, watches his other guests take their places. Ten guests sit either side of the table. There are servers waiting at both ends. Hale sits in the middle, Alifa is to his left. The space to the left of Alifa is vacant, till Ikal sneaks in and grabs the seat.

'We meet again,' he says, then looks her up and down with an appraising eye.

Noticing Ikal sit next to Alifa, Hale momentarily scowls, but he composes himself. Across from Alifa on the other side of the table sits Lin, and next to her is Dassin, whose cloak and hood still lend her an air of mystery. Alifa has never seen a Koemox; perhaps they all dress like that.

Starters are served, the conversation switches between Hale and Lin and her, with Ikal trying to break in and start a solo conversation with Alifa. Dassin says nothing, but Alifa feels the Koemox's inquisitorial eye on her, as though studying her in some way. Alifa is sure she has barely seen Dassin move, but her starters are finished. *My concentration is not what it should be this evening*, she tells herself.

When the main course arrives, she seizes her opportunity.

The beef dish is served with a sauce and vegetables. Hale tells them it is a famous and popular dish in Teuton. Alifa keeps a close eye on Ikal beside her, who is in animated hand-waving conversation with a Teuton girl to his left. Alifa draws on corallite and threads a weave behind Ikal's chair. Then she yanks it and almost simultaneously yanks his gravy-filled plate towards her. Ikal falls forward, arms flapping, and his movement implies that to stop himself hitting his head on the table, he has thrown his arms out and inadvertently sent the entire plate of beef and gravy over Alifa's lap.

'Oh!' she cries, as she takes the full brunt of the spillage.

'By the Creator!' someone exclaims.

The front of Alifa's sparkling dress is soaked in gravy, and chunks of beef are lying on her lap.

'Ikal!' Hale shouts.

'Huh?' The Aztlanian looks up to see what a mess he has made of her dress.

Waiters rush towards her, with cloths and plates to catch the dripping meat, but that won't be enough, she's made sure of it.

'Alifa, I am so sorry!' Hale says.

Ikal is dumbstruck. 'I ...' he cringes, standing up. 'I apologise profusely.' He bows, reaches to help wipe the gravy off her dress.

'Hands off,' Hale interjects.

'I think I need to go to the ladies,' Alifa whimpers.

'Of course, yes, please,' Hale looks around, catches sight of one of the female waiters. 'Over here.'

The woman approaches. Hale instructs her. 'Take Alifa, to ...' He pauses. The embassy is shut, as Alifa knows. 'Better take her to the staff facilities in the eastern wing.'

The woman nods.

'Let Alifa clean herself up,' Hale says. 'Stay with her. Offer whatever assistance you can.'

'Yes sir,' the woman says.

As Alifa rises from her chair, gravy dripping onto cloths the waiters have placed around her, she notices Dassin smiling. It's faint, but it's a smile, nonetheless. *Who is that girl?*

'I'm so sorry,' Hale says as she leaves.

'It's okay,' she says tearfully.

Behind her there is a flurry of activity as waiters clean the area. She almost feels sorry for Ikal, but he had it coming. Walking as briskly as possible, Alifa follows the woman into the eastern wing. Alifa is directed towards the ladies' facilities on the ground floor.

'Through that door – you can have a proper clean-up in there. There's also a bath, plus a shower if you need it,' the woman tells her, grimacing at the sight of her dress. 'Not sure what you're going to do about your dress.'

Alifa, now more composed, says. 'Actually, I had two dresses made. They were both so good, I couldn't decide which one to wear when I picked them up from the dressmaker before coming here. The other dress is still at the dressmaker who is not too far away. My driver is outside, parked on the western side. His name is Dur: the dressmaker is his sister. If you ask him to fetch it, I'm sure he will be able to drive down there and collect it. He could be there and back in thirty minutes. That will give me enough time to clean up. Can you do that?'

'Yes, of course,' the woman says.

The bathroom is large. She locks the door, then strips off her dress, to reveal another layer of clothing, all black and grey, fitted for combat. She removes her headscarf and pulls the hood of the tunic up, so that it covers her head. It has a sewn-in mask, which now covers her eyes, apart from two slits so she can see.

She tosses her dress into a corner, strides past the shower cubicle. The frosted window is where Durayd said it would be. It does look tight, just wide enough to wriggle through. She threads herself up, opens the window and is soon outside. Behind her a line of birch trees blocks the view into the garden. With the trees camouflaging her, she threads herself onto the balcony of the second floor. Crouching low, she approaches a door. Removes a picklock, then taps into her Revealer abilities. Threads of near invisible lines appear, revealing the shape of the lock. She manipulates her tools to synchronise with the locking mechanism. The door lock clicks, she opens and enters. Alifa finds herself in a living room, with easy chairs, several sets of low tables, and a bookcase running along one wall. Exiting the room out into the hall, Alifa is making her way to Paxon's office, when she hears heavy footsteps coming up the stairs.

Alifa ducks into an alcove. It's dark. The footsteps approach and she can see the huge form of a Hefter striding past. Probably one of the ones I fought, she thinks to herself. The man remains oblivious to her presence and is soon out of sight. She peels away and shimmies towards her destination. Paxon's office is locked and once again she needs to pick the lock, which takes a little longer this time. Once inside, she silently shuts the door.

It is a large office, with a mahogany desk and chair close to the window, along with a set of chairs around a meeting table. The walls are decorated with several paintings and large maps. One is of Arön, the other of Cin. Little pins are stuck into several locations on each map. Examining the map she can see most of the markers are beside ports, major roadways, and in the capital. There is very little marked in Urua, or anywhere else in the south.

There will be a safe, Zorar told her. Tapping into volcanic ash she amplifies her Revealer abilities and near invisible lines criss-cross before her, revealing the make-up of the items around her. The wall opposite the desk is the one with the built-in safe. It's behind a painting which depicts a beach scene, with several people pointing at a magnificent ship. She approaches the painting, lifts it away from the wall, gently places it on the ground. It's heavier than she expected.

She hears a sound from the corridor, tilts her head to listen. No, it's quiet. It's a combination safe and she uses the knowledge she has gleaned from her sessions with Cinan to unlock it. Using the white lines to guide her, she turns the lock in one direction, stops, hears it click, moves it in another direction, hears it click. She repeats this several times till finally the door releases. Inside the safe Alifa finds documents and dockets, all with the seal of the Syndicate. She removes a wedge of the papers and places them on Paxon's desk, without disturbing any other items on it.

The first manifest is a ledger of commercial transactions between the Syndicate and various individuals, who are not named, but there is a cipher. There are pages and pages of payments to people or entities. She draws on obsidian and taps into her Imbuer skills and begins to memorise them. It's a hard skill and she has practised extensively with Kaşifa , but still feels she's barely scratched the surface of what is possible as an Imbuer.

The second manifest is a set of contracts, which shows agreements between the Syndicate and the Sethee Bank concerning a Bond. She does not know what this is but memorises the details. It might be helpful to those who know what a Bond is. Other agreements are in place with several imperial bodies and she tries to commit as many as she can to memory – she only has thirty minutes before she needs to be back at the ladies' facilities.

Turning back to the safe, she removes several scrolls placed against one side. The first two refer to a land registry transaction the Syndicate has made with the Ministry of Agriculture. The Syndicate has purchased farmland in the south of Urua: this is a very fertile location, everyone knows this. Much of the food for Urua comes from the south. *Did the farmers sell their plots to the Syndicate*, she wonders. She unfolds the third scroll. It has a hand-drawn image on it, in the form of an organisational diagram. At the top, written inside a box, it says 'The Syndicate'. Below this are four other boxes, at the same level, which are connected back by a series of lines to the Syndicate.

The first box has a title at the top – it says 'Agrilleon' and in brackets beside it someone has written 'food'. The next box says 'Epsilon' and in brackets 'comms'. The third 'Morgrock' and in brackets 'health'. The final box is 'Sonark' and in brackets 'war'.

Alifa studies the diagram again. She is aware of the Syndicate, but these other names are unknown to her. She thinks Zorar or Durayd may know, so she commits it all to memory. She is about to reach for another set of documents, when she hears voices coming down the corridor.

Someone says, 'Sure, I heard something.'

Hurriedly, she replaces the items in the safe. She clicks it shut and puts the painting back in front of it, just as the knob on the door of Paxon's office starts to turn.

She realises she didn't lock it!

'Door's open – he never leaves it open,' the voice says.

'Careful,' the other voice adds.

Alifa grabs a gold-coloured letter-opener and slips under the desk. She watches two enormous Hefters enter. She taps into ochre, feels the energy flow to her muscles. The two brutes leave the door open as they enter, glance about. One stands close to the door, whilst the other approaches.

'See anything?' the Hefter by the door asks.

'Turn the lights on. It's too dark,' the other one says.

A switch is flicked and the algae-powered bulb flickers, then radiates a glow around the room. Alifa does not move. With the lights on there will be no way to get out of the room unnoticed.

The Hefter draws near. If she moves, his friend by the door will see her. If she remains, he will see her. She throws the letter-opener into the air, threading it for the light. The glass breaks. The room plunges into darkness. Alifa rolls from under the desk, comes right up under the Hefter, who stands more than a head taller than her.

With all her strength she cracks him under his chin. The huge man lifts off the ground, seems to hang momentarily in the air then crashes onto his back. Alifa has already moved, threading the letter-opener back at the Hefter beside the door. It plunges into his stomach. He doubles over. Alifa is beside him, clubbing him on the back of the head. He falls flat on his face.

She slips out of the door, relocks it. Threads herself at speed down the corridor, through the room she entered, onto the balcony and then over it and back to the ladies' bathroom. She crawls in through the window. She removes her face mask, tucks her hood back into a roll under her suit. She turns on a tap, takes a towel, wets it, before replacing it on the rail. She makes her way to the door, calls out.

'Hello?' she says.

'I'm here, Madam,' the attendant replies.

'Did you find Dur?'

'Yes, he managed to get the dress from his sister, I have your dress here with me.'

Alifa rolls up the sleeve on her suit, runs over to the tap, wets her forearm, returns to the door, sticks her arm out to take the dress.

'Thank you,' she says, taking it from the woman and locking the door once more.

Alifa lets out a deep breath, walks over to the sink, washes her face, then begins the task of dressing, adding her new purple dress over the combat suit. She takes her scarf, puts it back on her head, adjusting it once more. Finally, she wipes her face clear of water, straightens her dress, removes the slender phial of perfume she had left in a secret pocket within its folds, applies it to her wrists and neck.

On opening the door, she finds the woman waiting for her.

Alifa smiles. 'Thank you for bringing me my dress. My other dress is over there – could you put it in a bag and I can take it with me on the way out?'

'Of course, Madam, but I think Master Hale will insist on it being cleaned and returned to you in the best of condition.'

She nods. 'I can find my own way back to the party,' Alifa says, as she retraces her steps out of the embassy. She can hear some shouting from the floor above and she quickens her pace, threading herself down the corridor. Soon she is back at the conservatory, where she makes a dazzling entrance in a purple dress this time.

Her fellow guests have just finished their desserts.

'Alifa,' Hale is immediately on his feet. 'You managed to change?'

'My driver was able to get the second dress I had made from the dressmaker, who is his sister. She is not too far away.'

'Well,' he looks her up and down. 'This one is even more fetching on you.'

He guides her back to the table, this time seating her on his other side, so that she is next to Lin.

Ikal avoids looking at her. She's grateful for that.

Her main course is presented.

As she picks up her utensils to eat in the customary way of the Teutons, she catches Dassin smiling at her.

The girl simply says. 'Did you find what you came for?'

PIERCING
A HEART

*When it is dark all around you,
even a glimmer of light is noticeable.*

THE WISDOM OF THE WAY

WALKING THROUGH URUA reminds him why he detests cities. Crowds. People jostling in markets, all crammed in confined spaces. Unfamiliar sounds and noises, strange smells and vapours. For a mountain boy, Urua is troubling. Yet work brings him here this evening. Kaivan scans the streets – an assassin is always suspicious – an occupational necessity, so the Patriarch tells him.

He pulls his cloak tight around him, hood up, face down. Leather gloves keep his fingers warm. An assortment of knives adorns his belt, hidden from the casual observer.

Kaivan had never seen a Teuton before the two men came up the mountain. He's curious about them, these men from the north. His curiosity and some locals direct him to the district housing the new Teuton embassy. He's not sure what he is going to find, but he wants to know a little more about his benefactor. After all, in his line of work, today's benefactor might become tomorrow's target. *There is no loyalty, expect no loyalty,* the Patriarch is prone to saying.

Kaivan turns a corner. Across the street is the embassy. A flag flutters over it – a black eagle with its wings spread out against a white backdrop. Algae-powered lights emit a greenish glow down the street. Several vehicles with rollerblade tyres are lined up on the side roads. A stone and metal boundary wall runs around the embassy, on the other side of which are several tall birch trees. Kaivan stops under a streetlight, observes the embassy. There's movement on the upper levels, where he can see shadows against a lit backdrop. But it's the two figures walking slowly towards the entrance who catch his attention. There is a tall young man, a Teuton. He is fawning over the girl beside him – and what a girl! She's wearing a shimmering purple dress and just her walk beguiles Kaivan. Her scarf hides most of her hair, but some of it shows at the front.

His mouth goes dry. Kaivan knows he should move, get out of the light, but he remains. At the exit, the Teuton awkwardly says goodbye to her, leaning forward then shifting backwards. She re-mains regal, sure in her posture. In his opinion, her feelings are not the same as the man's, but then what does he know about love? The girl places a hand on her heart and says goodbye. It's a ceremonial parting, not a lover's one.

The fumbling Teuton mimics the salute, clearly unsure of what he is doing. As the girl comes out onto the street, she looks up, she sees him. Those eyes, deep, like pools of ink. Kaivan gulps. He should be gone, but he cannot move.

The girl stops in her tracks, her eyes narrow, fists clench.

'Alifa,' the Teuton calls out to her from the gate, drawing her at-tention.

Kaivan moves back into the shadows.

By the time she looks again, Kaivan is gone. She hesitates, star-ing at the spot he was standing in, then turns to look at the Teuton.

'I did enjoy this evening very much,' the Teuton says. 'I hope we can do this again.'

'As do I, Hale, thank you,' the girl says, waving to him then glanc-ing one more time at the spot where Kaivan had been. She shakes

her head, then continues walking. Silently Kavian moves to follow her movement. There is a waiting vehicle around a corner. A plump fellow gets out to greet her and she gets into the vehicle with him.

'By the Creator!' he whispers.

Kaivan wipes his brow. He feels hot and bothered on a cold evening. 'Alifa! Is that her name? What just happened there?' He shakes his head. 'Cities,' he scolds himself. 'It's why I hate them.'

Composing himself, he marches down several streets to refocus his mind before he turns towards the home of his victim. The name of the target is General Ramin, some high-ranking officer who reports to the Sultana herself.

Walking for a further half-hour brings him to the location. Conveniently the Patriarch has been sent a map of the interior of the house and Kaivan has been informed that the soldiers who normally patrol the rear wall will be absent this evening. *Someone close to Ramin wants him dead. Either a family member, such as a disgruntled wife, or jealous son, or a rival in the military. But it's always someone on the inside.* Work would be so much harder if assassins didn't have someone on the inside.

He easily scales the outer stone wall and drops down into the grounds. He looks left and right. No patrols. He crouches low, remains hidden, moves in silence towards the house. It's a two-storey home. Ramin, he was told, is a man of routine, so at this time he will have retired to the library in the western part of the house. Kaivan checks the route, stays on the grass, away from the pebbled path that might give him away. He spots a ledge halfway between the ground and first floor. He accelerates, leaps, lands on the ledge, then propels himself upwards, gripping the edge of the balcony on the first floor. Slowly he pulls himself up, balances on the edge of the balcony, then clears it, landing safely on the other side.

He's always had an instinctive ability to leap, spot footholds, then launch himself. The Patriarch says it is a unique skill he possesses. Sometimes it works better than other times, but he doesn't know why. Today it's done the job for him. He approaches the balcony door, removes his pick and works the lock, finding success after several minutes of trying. Inside, he enters through an empty bedroom. Soon he is in the corridor, moving towards the study. The lack of a patrol around the house is another sign that someone on the inside wants the General dead.

At the door to the study, he leans in, listening intently. It's quiet. With a deft hand, he turns the handle, opens the door, slips in. Ramin is in a leathered upholstered chair facing the window, a book in his hand. He has not seen Kaivan. Mahogany and oak shelves fill two walls, furnished with an impressive collection of books that would sit well in the home of a scholar. The sight makes Kaivan pause. To know his library is to know his mind. He prefers to see Ramin as a military officer: it makes it easier on his conscience to kill him.

Kaivan approaches the General, readies himself.

Ramin's chair swivels. Kaivan spots the sonic revolver in his hand. As Ramin goes to fire, Kaivan moves. The General rises, fires again as Kaivan leaps onto one of the bookshelves, launches himself into the air, twisting over and around Ramin. He lands behind the General, who swivels to confront him, but it's already too late.

The poison-tipped needle, his preferred means of assassination, has already penetrated Ramin's neck. Kaivan withdraws the needle, then replaces it in a pouch attached to his waist belt. The poison needle is less mess and for the victim, it's far less gruesome than having your throat cut.

Ramin's mouth is open in shock. Another harmless shot is fired, before the weapon slips from his hand. Kaivan catches the falling General behind the neck, lowers him into his chair.

The fast-spreading poison has paralysed Ramin's limbs. The General tries to raise his right hand.

'Don't fight it, it's more painful,' Kaivan says softly. 'Just surrender to it.'

'Why,' Ramin croaks. 'Zorar, why?'

Zorar does not sound like the name of the Teuton: the General must have the client mixed up with someone else. *Let the real mastermind's identity remain a secret, it's better for the client*, thinks Kaivan.

'Father,' an approaching child's voice says.

Kaivan sees fear in Ramin's eyes. 'Don't worry, General, I'm not here to kill your family, only you.'

Kaivan pads away, opens the window, slips onto the ledge, waits out of sight of whoever enters.

'Father!' a young boy shouts.

Kaivan winces. He'd have preferred not to have known the General had children, but what else did he expect?

Ramin splutters. He is trying to say something to the boy.

'Who did this, Father?' the boy cries.

'Conduits...' Ramin gasps, before silence seizes him forever.

'No!' the child screams, as Kaivan hears other steps approaching.

He leaps from the window, somersaulting down to land on the lawn. He sprints across the grass, leaps over the wall and continues running till he is clear of the scene.

As he begins to tuck his robes about him, catch his breath once more, he remembers the girl he saw earlier. *Alifa. Who is she?*

-22-

CALLED TO ACCOUNT

*Busy yourself with worldly matters and death will take
you before you have time to reflect on its coming.*

A FOOL'S PARADISE

ORNING BRINGS LIGHT RAIN and a mist. Zorar
arrives early at the Lodge; he did not sleep much. His
mind is weighed down by thoughts of Azadeh's and
Nimar's injuries. Belal has worked tirelessly, but both Conduits
have a long arduous convalescence ahead of them and neither can
currently access the Source. Belal says they should recover but it
will take time. Something Zorar does not have.

Problems pile up.

In the inner courtyard he sips his *kahwa*, watching water circulate in the fountain. The raindrops do not bother him: he will go
inside soon enough. He rubs his jaw; the recent dental surgery was
more painful than he'd expected. He has been drawing on limestone for healing, but still feels the scar tissue and has occasional
blasts of pain in his teeth.

A game is afoot and he does not know the rules. Larger players
are on the board and he, Zorar, is merely a minor piece, preparing
for an assault and weary of being sacrificed. He recalls his morning
litany, running through it seven times.

The others start to arrive, so he gets up and heads for the *majlis*. Alifa, Durayd, Jamshi, Kaşifa and Cinan are present. The mood
is sombre: everyone knows the damage done to Azadeh and Nimar
who are recovering deep in the forest south of the city. Zorar looks

at Belal for a further update.

'It will be a while,' Belal declares. 'I cannot say how long, but expect several weeks of inactivity, before they, the Creator willing, can once more access the Source. Let us be hopeful. Hope is also an aid in the recovery process.'

Zorar nods.

'Do we know what they encountered?' Jamshi asks.

Zorar looks at the troubadour, shakes his head. 'They haven't been able to speak about what they faced.'

Silence.

He never thought the run-up to the Final Standing would begin in his lifetime. This was something for history books, chroniclers, legends and eschatological treatises. Something for theoretical study, not a practical matter to deal with.

'Oh well,' Durayd says. 'I suppose sales of *kahwa* will be up, with everyone drowning their sorrows about impending doom.' He chuckles, trying to bring some humour to the gathering.

Zorar feels Durayd's deft touch on his emotions, calming, reassuring him. He lets the Calmer do his work.

'And there will be lyrical lamentations, melancholy music for lovers whose future bliss has been taken from them,' Jamshi adds.

Zorar smiles. 'And you, Cinan? Anything you will miss?'

The architect leans back in his chair, cups his chin. 'I was rather looking forward to going on that speaking tour of Teuton.'

'Tah!' Durayd says. 'Is that it? Always work.'

Cinan shrugs his shoulders.

'So, you should,' Zorar replies.

'I should?' Cinan asks.

'This news changes nothing and it changes everything,' Zorar says.

They direct questioning looks at him.

'We cannot sit around and let things happen to us. We must act to shape what is within our ability to shape. If going to Teuton for several weeks will help defeat the Syndicate by your learning more about their ways, then go. At the same time the breaking of the Seals changes everything – the clock ticks very loudly now.'

Cinan nods thoughtfully. 'I will make final arrangements for my trip, then.'

Zorar turns to Kaşifa. 'How long do we have till the Final Standing?'

The chief librarian usually barely smiles and this is not the time to change the habit. Solemnly she puffs out her cheeks. 'The archival records say that after the breaking of the Seals, events happen quickly, like grains of sand falling from one's hand. One after another. We should expect to see tumultuous change. It really is like a countdown timer. Are we talking years? Maybe. Are we talking decades? Probably.' She throws up her hands, expressing her lack of knowledge.

'All right,' Zorar looks at each one of them, reserving his warmest smile for Alifa. He wonders what she must be thinking. To discover that you are a powerful Grand Conduit and then to find out the world is ending unless you do something about it – that is quite a challenge. *She probably wishes we never found her,* he thinks. 'We need to plan. How do we respond to the threat of the Syndicate, the Teutons in general, and now Mörtan?'

'It's a pretty big ask,' Durayd says, sipping his *kahwa.*

'Decades go by when nothing happens. Then days go by when decades happen,' Cinan drolly adds.

'I suppose,' Durayd says.

'All right, let's break it down, then decide who takes what,'

Zorar says. He rises, goes to the chalkboard and begins to write. He makes three columns, drawing a straight line of partition between each one. In the first column he writes 'Syndicate and Teutons', in the second column 'Arön', and in the third 'M', which he explains stands for 'Mörtan.'

'Let's detail the issues,' Zorar says. 'First the Syndicate. The problems it presents.'

'Opius,' says Belal. Zorar writes it down.

'Exploitative trade deals. Emperor's support. Banker's bond. There's three,' Durayd says.

'This seed business,' Cinan chimes in.

'And tea,' Alifa says.

Durayd smiles. 'Yes, let's not forget this ghastly tea they want to bring in to replace our beloved *kahwa*.'

Zorar has written these down. 'Any more?' he asks.

'Zorar,' Alifa says. 'I haven't had a chance to tell anyone but Durayd. Last night at the embassy I came across several contracts and ledgers, which I will share with Kaşifa. But there is one piece of information which needs airing now.'

'Go on,' Zorar says.

'In Paxon's office, in the safe, there was a document, on which was drawn a box with the name of the Syndicate at the top, and under it were four other boxes, with the names "Agrillion", "Epsilon", "Morgrock", "Sonark" on them. The first said "food", the second "comms", the third "health" and the final one "war".'

Cinan leans forward, having drawn the diagram on a piece of paper. He shows it to the others. 'It's like an organisation structure,' the architect says. 'With the Syndicate at the top and these other entities sitting below it. I, for one, have not heard of any of them.'

The others shake their heads. Zorar adds the Syndicate

organisation to his list. 'Anything else?'

Taking their silence as confirmation, he turns to the second column headed 'Arön'. 'All right, what are the problems we're facing at the moment in the empire?'

'Division and enmity which the Syndicate is exploiting,' Kaşifa says.

'At court,' Jamshi says, 'there are many stories that the Zandal from the Northern Waste are sailing down to the north of Arön and raiding and pillaging Artay's kingdom. They carry off his wealth as well as his people. Some say they take slaves to serve in the production of Opius.'

This is news to Zorar as it is to the others. He adds 'Zandal' to the suggestion already made by Kaşifa .

'I'm afraid to say it, Zorar,' Durayd declares. 'But the Emperor is a problem. His neglect of his empire, his hedonistic lifestyle. He is dependent on the Syndicate for his Opius supplies. How else can I put it – but the Emperor needs to change his ways, or he needs … to go.'

There are nods from the others around the table.

Zorar moves his chalk hand across to the third column headed 'M.'

'He's coming,' Durayd says nonchalantly.

'Yes, it is rather inevitable,' Cinan adds.

'The Sultana should know,' Jamshi says. 'We owe it to her – she has, apart from allowing Alifa to be locked up for a week – been good to us. You should tell her, Zorar.'

He agrees. 'I'll take care of it,' he says.

'The hooded figure in the Isthmus you and Nimar fought. I think I know who he might be, now that we know the Seals have broken,' Kaşifa says.

'I was hoping he was a travelling tea salesman,' Durayd says. 'But by the look on your face, apparently not.'

Kaşifa purses her lips. 'At the time of the Heralds in the second epoch, there were four powerful Harbingers, whose abilities were almost equal to those of the Heralds. Each Harbinger is a Grand Conduit, a very formidable one. Aside from the Heralds themselves they might be the strongest Grand Conduits ever. They sided with Mörtan, who promised them immortality and an abundance of power from *Dhulmi Kha*. They swore allegiance to him but were also taken down into the lowest levels of the Isthmus with their master. I think the one you fought was Darrick, harbinger of war and pestilence.'

'Darrick,' Zorar says, turning the name around in his mouth. 'Together, Nimar and I had not even a tenth of his strength. He brushed us off like flies. If he is one of four ...' Zorar trails off into silence.

'The others are first, Rasa: she is known to be persuasive and ruthless. Then there is Limòs, a harbinger of famine and finally Dìyù, a harbinger of death. Together these four, if they were to escape from the Isthmus ... well, I'll leave it to your imagination.' She lowers her head, staring back at her books.

The room is quiet.

'Well, that cheers me up no end,' Durayd says. 'We might as well all get intoxicated on Opius if things are that bad. I might even try some myself!'

Alifa gives Durayd a firm stare as a daughter would her father when his jokes are no longer funny. *Something parental and wholesome is happening between those two*, Zorar thinks. *Long may it continue, but how long have we got?*

Zorar writes 'Harbingers' on the chalkboard, then steps back to look at the list of problems. He shakes his head and is about to say something, when there is a knock at the door. It is the watchman of the lodge.

'Master Zorar,' the watchman says.

'What is it?' Zorar asks, thinking, *the watchman has never interrupted a meeting before.*

'You had better look outside. The army is here.'

'The army?' Zorar says, exchanging a glance with Durayd.

They make their way towards the main entrance of the building, where there are glass windows. He can see soldiers outside, hundreds of them. Armed, sonic rifles aimed at the Lodge.

'What in the name ...' Cinan says.

'Zorar!' a loudspeaker voice says. 'Come out immediately.'

Zorar removes a bead from his *tasbeah*, draws on the Source. He turns to the others.

'This doesn't look good. Let me go outside, find out what they want. In the meantime, Cinan, conceal the entrance to the basement. We don't want the army finding it. Durayd, take everyone out via the emergency tunnel. Whatever you need from the lodge, take it in the next two minutes, then leave.'

'I can stay,' Alifa says. 'Help you.'

He smiles. 'I don't intend to fight the soldiers, nor do I intend to give myself up. You go with the others. We will rendezvous at Belal's surgery in the forest.'

'Come, Alifa,' Durayd says.

Reluctantly the girl leaves. Durayd looks back at him. 'Don't do anything reckless, eh!'

'It's not how long we live but how we live,' Zorar says.

Durayd is about to respond, but then waves his hand in dismay and follows the others.

Zorar smiles, draws on the elements, pulls his robes about him and steps out of the front door, just as the loudspeaker voice is shouting his name once again.

The courtyard housing the lodge and its neighbouring buildings is circular, and every position is taken up by soldiers with sonic weapons. There are several snipers on rooftops, with their rifles aimed at him. *This will be interesting*, he muses.

He recognises Brigadier Bousan, a short portly figure, second in command of the Sultana's army after Ramin. Bousan is a man with a nasty reputation, nasty indeed.

Zorar takes a few steps towards them, stops. 'How can I help you this morning, Brigadier?'

'General Ramin was assassinated last night,' Bousan says. 'You are wanted for his murder.'

'Murder!'

'Come with us, or we'll open fire,' Bousan declares.

'You have the wrong man, Brigadier,' Zorar protests.

'Conduits have been implicated, Ramin's dying words incriminated the Conduits and since you are their leader, you are wanted for his murder,' Bousan declares triumphantly, jabbing a finger in his direction.

Zorar does not know why Ramin in his dying words would accuse him, but Bousan is not in a mood to negotiate.

Zorar looks around the circle with the buildings around it. Maybe two hundred soldiers including the ones on the roof. All armed with sonic weapons. The Lodge is a beautiful building and it has served the Order for decades, but nothing lasts for ever.

'I – ' Bousan is saying.

Zorar yanks the panes of glass from their window frames, propelling thousands of shards at the soldiers standing before him, whilst at the same time threading himself up into the air, avoiding the spray of glass, momentarily landing on the top of a streetlamp. The sound of a hundred sonic rifles is deafening. Zorar disintegrates the glass shards before they wound any soldiers, then launches himself onto a nearby rooftop. The snipers on the roof take aim, but he anticipates their shots, yanks their rifles from their hands, and flings them towards the crowd of soldiers below.

Zorar lands on the rooftop where two snipers, now minus their weapons, stare at him. One draws a revolver. Zorar effortlessly threads the weapon into his own hand, then throws it over his back. Other snipers nearby turn their weapons towards him, but he does not give them time to aim. He has already leapt to the next rooftop, then the next and is fast disappearing from range and view.

-23-
SHOW OF
STRENGTH

The heart is sick when it is driven by want.

THE WISDOM OF THE WAY

THE SMUGGLERS' BAY is east of the capital on the coast, but north of the royal port of Onogur. On its edge is a nondescript village inhabited by forgotten people. Mostly old, a few young, no families. A place that will likely die out within a generation.

Brant has accompanied Paxon on visits outside the capital in the past week and this is his last stop before they head back to Urua. Travelling with them is a small unit of fifty soldiers from the newly formed Syndicate militia. These trained soldiers come from Teuton, with some locals amongst them. Hanging around the fringes of the militia are some of Brant's Conduits: two Threaders and one Hefter. He also has a Revealer who has been helping him locate Gateways from Arön into the Isthmus. Paxon is aware of these extra bodies, knows who they are, and regards them as specialised resources.

That is all he needs to know, thinks Brant.

They walk downhill along a pebbled path towards what constitutes a village inn. Cressets and the glow of a few algae streetlights provide faint illumination.

Paxon addresses him. 'Your field agents did an outstanding job securing the seed from the local farmers.'

'Indeed,' Brant says.

'The seed will be shipped back to laboratories in Teuton later this week,' Paxon informs him.

'How long before we receive the modified shipment?' he asks.

'Scientists can replicate the seeds within two harvests, after which they molecularly alter it. I've been told that within two, maybe three years we should have the new eradicator seeds back in the soil of Urua. With the Syndicate being the only source of seed provision, along with the chemically produced fertilisers the farmers will need, we'll be able to control the kingdom's food chain. We'll charge what we want and increase supply and demand as we please.'

'Most satisfactory,' Brant grins.

'What it also does, Brant, is give us a timeframe. In a few years this empire will be in ruins. With the populace desperate the Syndicate will be regarded as saviours. They will adopt our ways, our beliefs, our education. Once we have their minds, we will capture their hearts.'

Brant nods and thinks: *And when the Syndicate has established control of Arön and the other kingdoms of Ikleel, built the infrastructure, the technology, the economic systems, the governance, then my true Lord, Mörtan, will take it from the Syndicate. Without even knowing what they are doing, they will be laying the groundwork for Mörtan.* He smiles.

'Good job.' Paxon pats him on the back, as they walk towards the village.

They enter a crumbling inn. Their soldiers arrived early, tidied the place up a little, paid the innkeeper to make sure the venue was empty. Some drinks and food are laid out on a table in the middle of a large hall. Other tables and chairs are pushed back against the walls. From the inn's high roof, a decaying iron and wood chandelier hangs.

Konrad clears out the other soldiers. Brant and Paxon sit down on the rickety wooden chairs, sip the ale. It's awful. He's got too used to higher quality spirits. *It doesn't hurt to be reminded how the less well-off live*, he thinks.

There is a commotion in the doorway, as two militiamen are thrown into the room. A giant Zandal, possibly seven foot tall, with an enormous mane of black hair, a thick beard and a muscled torso packed into metal body armour, strides in. A long double-handed axe is strapped to his back. He surveys the room, spots Paxon and Brant in their fine attire sipping cheap ale in the centre.

'Humph,' the brute says.

The Zandal steps aside. Behind him enters a man of medium height and build, intelligent eyes, a straight nose and long chin. He has a golden-brown beard. This man wears a sword belt and his breastplate bears the symbol of a wolf's head. When he spots the two men, he smiles.

'Gentlemen,' the newcomer says.

'Chief Kerbasy?' Paxon asks.

Kerbasy approaches, shakes hands with Paxon, followed by Brant. The chief takes a seat and Paxon offers him ale, which he accepts. The giant Zandal stands guard a few steps away.

'Bah!' Kerbasy spits the ale out. 'What is this?'

'Best the house has, I'm afraid,' Paxon says.

Kerbasy pulls out a small canteen from within the folds of his robes, takes a swig from it, rinses his mouth, then swallows. 'Much better,' he says. 'Next time, Paxon, pick another place to meet. I hear Urua has some nice venues.'

Paxon smiles. 'All in good time, Kerbasy.'

'All this sneaking around, sailing up and down the coast at night-time, it's cowardly,' Kerbasy says.

'It's part of the plan. Be patient,' Paxon says.

'You're not paying us enough to be patient. We've spent a month

of nights raiding the Arön coast. Night work costs more,' Kerbasy slaps his palms against the tabletop.

'We're putting pieces in place, with the government, the bankers and other levers of power. It takes time to topple an empire – to do it well, that is. You can always raid and leave things in a mess as the Zandal are prone to do, but to do it well, to make it permanent, to ensure the enemies never get up off their knees again, requires subtlety and guile.'

'Yah!' Kerbasy waves a hand around. 'Teutons, you're all words, finances, and ideas. It's strength and power that get results.' He pounds a fist on the table.

'Last time I looked, it's the Teutons who employ the Zandal, not the other way around,' Paxon says.

Pointing a finger at Paxon, Kerbasy says, 'Only because we don't have the stomach to live in a world gone soft, unlike you.'

'I can assure you …' Paxon begins.

There is a whoosh of air: in one swift movement the giant Zandal has taken out his battleaxe and it's coming down at speed on Paxon.

Brant moves faster. He is up, as the brute swings the axe downwards; with his right hand, Brant catches the handle.

'Hah!' Kerbasy exclaims.

The giant Zandal's eyes go wide in wonder. He pushes with more weight. Brant holds firm. He starts to push the Zandal back; the giant digs his heels into the floorboards but is not able to withstand the pressure. Slowly the Zandal is nudged back, his boots sliding on the wooden floor. Brant stops. He fixes the giant with a stare. The Zandal is pushing with all his strength, not understanding how a man of Brant's physique can withstand his strength. Uncertainty leads to fear.

In one swift movement, Brant releases the handle. As the giant tumbles forward, Brant pushes the handle of the axe up, so it spins out of the giant's grip. He grabs the handle, then swings it at the falling giant, who lands on his knees, sweating. As the man crashes to his knees, the speeding axe-blade halts an inch from his neck.

'I'm the dog that eats the other dogs,' Brant says. 'On your feet.'

The giant looks over to his chief, who nods vigorously. As he rises, Brant flips the axe around in his hand, so that he catches it by the blade and presents the handle back to him. The Zandal hesitantly reaches out and grasps his weapon. When it is firmly in his grip, in the blink of an eye, Brant fires a roundhouse kick straight into the giant's stomach. It lifts the brute off his feet, and he is sent crashing into a cupboard full of stained crockery.

The room goes silent. The giant groans, holding his stomach. He winces as he begins to stand again.

'So, you remember it,' Brant says, calmly returning to his seat beside Paxon. He turns to Chief Kerbasy. 'Not all Teutons have gone soft.'

'Hah!' Kerbasy tries to laugh off the situation. 'Hilderbrandt was just aiming his axe at the table. Didn't mean no harm.'

Paxon leans forward, takes the jug of local ale and fills the chief's cup once more, placing the cup before him. He puts his fingertips together. 'Shall we get down to business then, Kerbasy?'

Kerbasy takes a swig of the ale, grimaces, but this time does not complain. He nods.

'We need to double the production of Opius for the Arön market,' Paxon says.

'We've already doubled it for exports to Cin,' Kerbasy says. 'We don't have enough able-bodied Zandals to farm the plant. None of the chiefs do.'

'Use the children,' Brant suggests.

Kerbasy glances at Hilderbrandt, who stands slightly bent in one corner. He grimaces. 'No, it would not be honourable to use our children. The young are taught how to survive in the Northern Wastes, how to hunt, to fight. You need those survival skills. We will not make our children farmers, or else they won't be any good for hunting and defending the Waste.'

Brant is about to say something, when Paxon waves him down.

'I understand, Kerbasy. Though I have no children of my own, I do have a young nephew who lives with us, and the attachment of blood is strong. What else can we do to double production?'

'Give me workers,' Kerbasy says.

Paxon mulls over the point, interlocks his fingers before him.

'I will give you slaves,' Paxon says.

Kerbasy raises an eyebrow.

'Brant,' Paxon turns to him. 'I think it's about time we lend a hand to Kerbasy and the other chiefs. We will establish holding centres, mini-fortresses in remote coastal towns of Arön and I will tell the Governor General Amery to do the same in Cin. These holding centres will be for captured slaves: men, women and, if required, children. We will trap them like animals, take them in chains to these holding centres. When there are enough of them, you, Kerbasy, will send ships to pick them up and take them to the Northern Wastes to farm the Opius fields.'

The chief nods his head. 'You Teutons are industrious and by the Creator I swear I would rather be your friend than your enemy, for Mörtan's demons have spawned your kind.'

Brant smiles. *My Lord will be most happy with such a compliment.*

'As for Urua, we will need you soon. I will only be able to give you short notice, so start to bring your fighters ashore. There is a place not too far from here, remote. Brant will show your man

Hilderbrandt. We will provide your army with food and board whilst they wait. When I send one of my men to you, you will immediately mobilise.'

-24-
SULTANA
OF HEARTS

*Happiness can be found in pursuing
the happiness of others.*
THE BOOK OF HERALDS

THE FRAGRANCE OF JASMINE blows in the still night air. Dew settles on the lawns of the winter palace on the outskirts of Urua, within striking distance of the mountains. The peaks loom large in the background.

It's a trap.

The words echo in Alifa's mind. *How can it not be? Yet Zorar can't see it, or he doesn't want to see it. Why?*

She perches on the edge of a cliff, long having got over any fear of heights now that her mastery of threading has matured. To her left, Zorar waits, watches the distant walls of the winter palace, the wind catching his robes.

Zorar has received a private dispatch from Sultana Negin, on a secure channel that only he and she use. She has asked him to meet her at the winter palace this evening. It's far enough away from the city to avoid suspicion. It's also a perfect place to capture a Conduit with minimal damage. *Why can't Zorar see this?*

'It is time, Alifa,' Zorar says, wrapping his robes around him.

'Are you ...' she says.

'Sure? About this reckless move, walking into the winter palace, a citadel which can hide an army, which can be configured to trap a Conduit? No, I'm not sure, but yes, I am sure that Negin ...'
He pauses.

Then it hits her. *They love one another!*

She scolds herself for not noticing earlier, but then she has never seen the two of them together, other than briefly at the Teuton embassy. Now that she thinks about it, she recognises the way their eyes met, the understanding of lovers.

'You care for each other, don't you?' Alifa asks.

He whirls round, but his gaze is soft. He lets out a deep breath.

Alifa thinks about Hale, an amenable young man, who is falling over himself trying to please her. She doesn't feel the same about him. *Should I?* Then she remembers the young man she saw under the streetlamp outside the Teuton embassy. *I felt a powerful pulse from him. Was he a Grand Conduit? I should tell Zorar, but how can I be sure? Zorar already has too much going on.*

'We ...' he begins. 'After the same sort of tragedy befell each of us, we found comfort in each other – in a shared conversation. That is all. It was not possible then and it is not possible now, for there to be anything else.'

'What happened?'

'She lost her husband and son.'

'And you?' Alifa asks.

Zorar takes a deep breath. 'My wife and daughter ...' his voice cracks, 'were taken by raiding Vanimals. I searched for them; for years I looked everywhere, without giving up hope. I still have hope. They might be alive.'

'Oh! I didn't know. I'm so sorry.'

'Do not fret, child. It was destined. All we can do is show poise and grace when faced with adversity. Everything is in the hands of the Creator and He gives and He takes. He knows what is best for us, we do not.'

'It must be difficult, to lose ones you have loved.'

Zorar studies her, places a hand on her shoulder.

'I love Negin, but I love my wife. She was like the sun, all warmth and splendour. Even though I cannot see her, I see her in the cosmos of my eye. Until I know what has truly happened to her, I cannot ...'

'I understand,' Alifa says. She places her hand on his arm.

He smiles.

'Your daughter, how old would she be?'

'About your age, I'd say,' Zorar replies.

'Then, if I may be so bold, like a daughter, I ask you not to go to the winter palace this evening. You know it is a trap.'

'Alifa,' he takes her hands in his. 'You have come a long way these past months. I am so proud of you. All of us are. The entire crew loves you.'

He glances at the winter palace, then continues. 'If anything should happen to me tonight–'

'Don't–' she starts.

'Let me finish,' he says softly. 'You will be the only Grand Conduit of the *Nurani* Order in the whole of the south. I have high hopes for you, but you are young and inexperienced. You have much to learn from those who have travelled this path before you. If anything happens to me tonight, then you must seek out Master Quezai in the Qwaqeetul province of Koemox. He will be able to pick up where I left off. Unfortunately, where I go tonight, you cannot follow. We cannot risk both of us getting captured.'

'Nothing is going to happen to you, because you aren't going into the palace, are you,' she urges, desperation now in her voice.

'As you say, love blinds us,' he says, letting go of her hands.

'Zorar, please.'

'When we transcend this world, we wake up, and everything that came to pass, will feel like a dream,' Zorar says before stepping

off the cliff edge and threading himself away over fields of golden chrysanthemum. She watches him leap away, heading towards the walls of the palace.

'Don't follow me? Right!' She clenches her fists, then leaps off the edge.

Threading herself over the golden flowers below, she follows Zorar for several minutes, before he approaches a river and leaps it in a single bound, continuing at pace towards the outer defensive walls of the palace. Alifa keeps up. She is unsure whether he guesses she is following him, but she doesn't care. Having been found by him, she is not about to let him slip out of her life. At the white stone walls, Zorar threads up to a portcullis before leaping for the top of the wall. The lack of patrols on the roof is suspicious enough. Any palace is guarded by a night watch, with sentries covering all entry points. The winter palace has no guards in sight.

It's a trap.

Following the trajectory of his leaps, Alifa lands upon the battlements of the upper defensive walls and drops into a low crouch. Her black scarf is tucked back within her riding robes. Tonight, she is a dark wraith, hidden in shadow. She intends to keep it that way. She scans the empty ground ahead of her, where a courtyard leads to a lower inner wall. Zorar has just gone over it. She is about to leap from the outer defensive battlements to follow him, when she sees an entire legion of soldiers emerge from various points within the palace grounds. They push sonic cannons and the soldiers carry sonic rifles. Her heart sinks when she sees a reinforced metal box being taken on a cart towards the inner courtyard. Other soldiers carry nets, with wire and razors. She counts at least two hundred soldiers, possibly more, coming from other parts of the palace.

This is the mother of all traps. *Love is blind!*

She punches her fist into the palm of her hand, grinds her teeth in frustration. *What can I do? What should I do? We need Zorar.*

The soldiers march into the inner courtyard. She follows. Threading off the battlements she lands softly in the grass courtyard, then threads herself into a leap of fifty yards, quickly crossing it. Ensuring no one is behind her, she launches herself up onto the inner walls, crouches as low as she can, concealed in shadow.

Peering around a minaret, she notices soldiers assembled below. They have come through the gatehouse and are holding their position in the entryway to the inner courtyard. They are hidden from Zorar. In the centre of the inner courtyard, there is a garden. In the midst of some acacia trees, she observes Zorar. He stands ten yards from a finely dressed woman, whose back is to him. The Sultana?

It is then Alifa notices three other gatehouses with entry ways into the inner courtyard. *Are they also filled with soldiers?* She breaks into a cold sweat.

Zorar takes several steps towards the woman, who turns and pulls out a sonic weapon which she fires into his chest. Zorar takes the full blast and is thrown back but manages to roll and leap back onto his feet. Suddenly soldiers who have been hiding in gatehouses, under barrels, even in trees, open fire at him. He dodges, threads himself left and right, but there are too many snipers. Several shots catch him. Horrified, Alifa watches as he is thrown back, tumbles, rises, falls, skids across the ground.

Near-invisible threads fly from his hand. She can see them. Soldiers are yanked from trees. More and more soldiers pour in through the four gatehouses; the courtyard is full of sonic firepower, with hundreds of rifles all trained at Zorar. The sonic cannons are rolled in.

No!

Zorar is cocooned in sonic blasts. Popping sounds puncture the air. He tries to thread himself up, but shots catch him, throw him ten feet into the air. Then the cannons go off. Tree trunks split, branches shatter. The entire garden is being pulverised, shredded by the army in its pursuit of one man. The imposter pretending to be the Sultana has left. Alifa spots her running behind the soldiers for safety, before she picks up a sonic rifle and fires it at Zorar.

Alifa's mentor is flung about like a ball, as wave after wave of sonic discharges catch him, coming from every direction. Alifa clenches, unclenches her fists.

Enough!

Alifa launches herself off the roof. She lands beside one of the sonic cannons. Startled soldiers turn, raise their weapons. Drawing on ochre, she slams into the side of the cannon, toppling it, before she spins and threads multiple invisible lines around her, drawing soldiers and yanking them to where she stands, seconds before she leaps into the air. The soldiers' bodies collide, as she lands back amongst them. Her fists and feet do the talking. Soldiers are thrown in every direction. She floors an entire regiment, before a group of soldiers line up and fire their rifles at her. Threading herself back, she somersaults and lands on the other side of the cannon. Then she leaps away, as rifle fire is aimed at her.

How much more can he take? Alifa tries to reach him. He looks up, their eyes meet. She freezes. He shakes his head, urging her to go back. *Why?* Her mind yells. *Why?*

The metal box is behind Zorar. He does not heft it away. *Is he so beaten?* The sound of booted feet surrounds her. Sonic rifles pop. Sound waves hit her in the side. She does not care, launching herself away from the soldiers targeting her. She lands on a turret, then leaps higher onto the inner perimeter wall. Sonic blasts continue to pulverise the masonry around her.

When she next turns to look for Zorar, he is gone. The iron box is shut. He is inside it.

'No!' Alifa screams.

Sonic fire comes at her from below.

With glassy eyes she glances at the iron prison, then threads herself into a series of long leaps, heading back towards the outer defensive walls of the winter palace. Around her cannons sound, but she is out of range, journeying back to the city, her heart heavy and her cheeks wet.

-25-

RASA

'It can be rather discomforting when you realise others consider you a clown.
A FOOL'S PARADISE

IN THE LATE AFTERNOON, Brant and Konrad thread over the rooftops of Urua. They land on the ridge of the abandoned lodge of the *Nurani* Order before dropping down into it. The guards outside notice nothing.

Brant feels the rhythmic throb of a Gateway into the Isthmus. A gift from a Grand Conduit, he muses. He leads Konrad into the basement. A skilled Revealer has hidden the entrance, but it does not take him long to see through the deception and they find themselves exiting out into a corridor within the basement. Konrad, beside him, smiles.

The winding tunnel slopes downwards. They follow it and emerge into a chamber which houses the gateway.

'Oh, look at this, Konrad,' Brant crows with satisfaction.

He saunters across to the training circle, tapping cylinders brimming with elements. 'Supplies. Enough for years and years,' he says.

'Relics as well,' Konrad says, gesturing towards a glass trophy cabinet. Konrad walks over to it, finds a small notebook in one corner. 'Properties of each of the relics on display; some are written in a sort of cypher, most likely the powerful ones, but we can crack it with the Revealer on the team.'

'Good, see what else we can harvest,' Brant takes a deep breath, stares across at the Gateway. 'I'm going to explore a little.'

Konrad grins, gets to work.

Brant stands before the Gateway. *This is one. Where are the others in Arön?* It's like every Gateway he's encountered, with a floral border running round the door. *Why do they do that?* With a confident stride, he enters.

Immediately a cold chill envelops him. He knows he is in *Dhulm*. *I should have brought a warmer coat*, he thinks. He draws on ochre for strength.

As the mist fades, he realises he is in a cold, bleak room, where shabby furniture is layered with dust. White walls surround him and the wooden floor is worn. There are no windows in this room. When he leaves it, he finds he is in an opulent house, with a black and grey-patterned marble floor in the central hall. A golden door, which has long lost its lustre, indicates the exit.

He listens attentively. Nothing but the rustling of the wind against the windowpanes.

After taking a tour of the lower level and finding nothing of consequence he ventures outside. He is met by a bleak garden, all patchy grass, broken fences, trees devoid of greenery. In fact, everything has an element of grey. A blast of wintry air rattles down the street, and he pulls his raincoat tight. He thinks he hears the sound of bats flying overhead, but when he looks up, he merely notices a shadow passing.

'What a miserable place!' he says.

Outside on the street he discovers the other houses look the same as the one he's just left. His Revealer ability orientates him north and he heads that way. Overhead, clouds hang low, and the air is heavy. A light drizzle falls, just enough to place a sheen of wetness on his raincoat. On the horizon a shard of light breaks through the clouds – the way to the *Nurani* portion of the Isthmus. It's always there, but he knows he will never take that path.

He threads himself to the end of the road. Soon, he has left this street and similar streets behind and is heading towards the centre of this city. He knows he needs to find a way to get to level two of the Isthmus. *Much more interesting down there*, he thinks.

The pulsing throb coming from the Gateway to the second level of the Isthmus emanates from a structure which to his eye looks like an abandoned library. It is in the centre of a set of similarly designed buildings – museums, galleries, and such. The library is five storeys high, with a large dome at the top of it.

What is this place? A real image from the past or a glimpse of the future? Where is it? Who designed it? Why did he emerge here and not somewhere else?

Too many questions and too few answers. He waits for the coming of Mörtan, when all will be revealed.

He enters the library's cavernous entry hall: above Brant is a dust-covered dome. Several doors lead to halls on either side. Tens of thousands of books, maybe hundreds of thousands of books, maybe even millions, fill the shelves. A part of him wants to browse the collection, but he is drawn by the throb of the Gateway. It is in the basement. He takes the stairs downwards and emerges into an assembly hall, which he guesses is directly below the entry hall. It is of a similar size, and in the centre of it, he sees what he is looking for.

It's a circular iron-bound gateway, built into a wall, twenty feet high, which appears completely out of place in the centre of the room. He walks across to it. Nervous energy fills him. He draws on sand, calms himself. Opening the door, he peers through it. A blast of icy wind causes him to shudder. Steeling himself, he draws on ochre and enters. The passageway is opaque: a sheet of ice envelops the circular tunnel as it slants downwards. Streaks of light pass him, mere flashes, like lightning on a distant horizon. High-pitched screams emanate from around the passageway, in this place between two places. It takes considerable presence of mind and bodily strength to pass through a gateway to a lower level. He clenches his fists, grinds his teeth against the cold air.

As Brant exits the passage between the two levels, he shakes his head, a momentary sense of disorientation having gripped him. He stares about him. He is inside what appears to be a huntsman's cabin. Spears and maces line one wall, nets and chains lie in one corner. The enormous head of a deer is displayed over the doorway, and bear-paws line the mantlepiece. A large double-handed axe and shield hang beside a second door, which he assumes leads to a bedroom. A massive overcoat is draped on a peg in the wall. Twice his size at least. He tries to smile but the cold keeps his lips pressed together. Leaving the lodge, he finds he is in the lower grounds of a colossal palace of pearly white spires.

Brant marches for the palace; the gradient is steeper than it looks. Dressed as he is, the cold is almost unbearable. Ten-foot-high statues of people, none of whom he recognises, stare at him as he passes through the grounds. *Legends from a bygone age or heroes to come*, he wonders. A strong gust of air catches him from behind and when he turns he realises that behind the huntsman's lodge is an ocean, so wide and vast that it seems to meld into the grey sky. Icebergs float off the coast as the tide is jostled by a stiff deafening breeze blasting across the water.

He directs his attention back to the palace. The chill is too much, so he decides to run. He needs to warm up, otherwise he will freeze to death. Momentarily he considers the folly of having entered the second level of the Isthmus without the proper preparation. *What was I thinking? I wasn't!* He speeds up. A blast of cold air hits him in the back and he thinks he hears giant chains being dragged along the ground. He dares not turn around, for it feels to him the ocean will reach out and pluck him into its embrace. It's a stupid notion, he knows, but there is something terrible, so malevolent that exists close by that he grows more anxious by the moment. He reminds himself he is a Grand Conduit, but this has little effect on his dread. He runs faster.

He skids to a halt as he enters the palace. Brant looks behind him, towards the ocean. It swells and for a moment he cannot see the icebergs. A boom sounds like thunderous waves crashing against a shore. What manner of place is this?

Brant!

He turns: someone called his name. A woman's voice, commanding yet beguiling in its tone. *Who?* It rings again through the high-ceilinged halls of the palace. He begins to walk in its direction. Around him platinum engravings and rings of iron adorn colossal marble pillars. He is pulled by the enchanting call of his name.

Brant!

More forceful, yet attractive in its allure. He is tugged like a puppet, further into the palace. He takes to running once more. Deeper and deeper, through more halls and courtyards, through intricate chambers bedecked with jewels and engraved with mythical pictures of heroes in battle. He wants to stop, but the magical sound of his name propels him onwards. He threads himself. Everything is a blur as he moves quicker. A terrible force draws him nearer like a firefly to a flame.

Then Brant sees her.

Fifty yards away is the most beautiful woman he has ever laid eyes on. She wears a shimmering white gown and her locks of brunette hair cascade like a waterfall down her shoulders. Her light olive skin is a stark contrast to the whiteness of the palace. She slowly raises her arm, a single finger beckoning him. He threads himself into a huge leap, lands before her.

Brant, without realising it, kneels before her. He enthusiastically turns his gaze upwards, looks into her face. It is so stunning, he is lost for words. A shiver runs down his spine, his heart races and he longs to be with this woman, to please her in any way she demands. To upset her would be a travesty, he thinks.

Seductively, she arches an eyebrow, and his legs turn to jelly. He places a hand on the cold marble floor to steady himself.

He will do anything for her. The woman leans forward, as a master would over a pet. She strokes his slick hair with her soft caressing hand.

'Brant,' she whispers into his ear.

His heart races. He nods like a well-trained dog.

'You ...' she eyes him up and down, her eyes tempting him with every look, 'are a Grand Conduit!'

He nods vigorously. Brant wants to please her.

Her finger strokes his left cheek. Her touch sends a cold shiver down his back, whilst his heart burns with emotion. 'You are a pretty boy aren't you, Brant. I like handsome men. They keep me warm at night. Would you like to stay with me this evening?'

Like a foolish puppy he nods again.

There is a fiendish growl – he is not sure what it is, but it sounds terrifying, emanating from far down the corridor. The woman shrugs. 'Maybe on another occasion. I had forgotten I already have another waiting for me tonight.'

Her finger moves slowly from his cheek, to his chin, then softly down his neck. He wants nothing in the world more than to be with her. Her finger stops, gently moves back to his chin.

Then with the flick of her index finger, she strikes Brant square on the chin. He is propelled ten feet, landing heavily on his back, before skidding across the ground and hitting his head against a pillar. For a moment he blacks out and when his eyes open, the woman is standing over him, her heel on his chest, pressing him to the floor.

Brant is no longer under her spell for she is no longer agitating him, manipulating his emotions, arousing his desire.

Embarrassment overpowers him. No matter how beautiful this woman is, she has been toying with him. He begins to regain control and anger rises. He tries to get up, but with little apparent effort she keeps him pinned to the ground. He draws on all his ochre, to propel him with strength enough to overcome several Grand Conduits. Nothing. She is not even fazed, whilst he sweats. He can feel his bones straining under her heel.

'Don't bother,' the woman purrs. 'Or else I'll just enchant you again. Besides, I'd rather you hate me for what I am, than love me for what I'm not.'

Immediately Brant relaxes, lies back. He does not want to be made a fool of again.

'Who are you?' he says through clenched teeth.

She takes a step back; her heels click on the marble floor. Her dress swishes around her legs as she strolls away, then stops. She turns her head, those gorgeous locks of brunette hair cascading over her perfect shoulders.

'Be sure Epsilon is ready. Be sure of it, Brant, and I may keep you by my side. You are a pretty boy. I think I have use for you.'

She saunters away. But now, her every step sends a chill through his veins.

'Rasa.' Her name escapes his lips, before he shuts his mouth in fear. *One of the four Harbingers!*

-26-
THREADS
OF HOPE

You are a blueprint of the cosmos,
and the cosmos is a blueprint of you.
THE BOOK OF HERALDS

THE COTTAGE IS A SIMPLE ONE, with a single living
room, kitchen and study on the ground floor. It is furnished
in soft auburn and forest green, with an assortment of herbs
and plants in spaces between chairs and tables. A thick rug with a
design depicting the forest floor in autumn is in the centre of the
living room, where Alifa sits, head in hands.

It was a trap. He knew it, so why did he fall for it? The question has
troubled her for days. It does not make sense. Zorar knew the message to be false, he knew the woman he was meeting was an imposter, he even knew the winter palace was an ideal location for hiding a
mini-army. *So why did he go ahead!*

Her head throbs. It has done so since Zorar was captured. She
leans back, adjusts her loosely-tied headscarf. Crossing her legs, she
sits back on the sofa, picks up a velvet cushion beside her and presses it against her chest.

'Why?' she whispers.

'Indeed,' the calming voice of Durayd says, as he approaches
with a cup of soothing *kahwa*. She gratefully accepts it, sips it. He
has added extra cardamon as well as an additional helping of fennel
seed. Both have cooling properties. She needs to calm down. Durayd
parks himself opposite her in a high-backed leather chair. Soon,
the owner of the cottage, Belal, joins them, then the immaculately

dressed and well-groomed Jamshi saunters in.

'It is truly perplexing that Zorar let himself be caught,' Durayd says.

'Did he have anything else with him?' Belal asks.

'Like a weapon?' Alifa queries.

'Yes, like a ... relic,' Belal says.

Once more she casts her mind back to the details of that fateful night. Journeying out to the winter palace, the patient waiting game, the entry, the battle, the parting and loss.

She shakes her head. 'I didn't see anything,' Alifa says. 'Besides, before they put you in prison, you have to ... umm ... remove your clothes, which they check. They take out anything they want and then give you back the garments.'

'Oh dear,' Durayd says. 'Alifa,' he clears his throat. 'They ... they didn't touch you or do anything else, did they?'

'No, thank the Creator. It was, as the female guard told me, just procedural, to ensure I was not carrying any weapons. I had my privacy, while they went through my clothes.'

'Thank the Creator,' Durayd says blowing out air from his cheeks. 'Decency at some level still prevails.'

'Where do you think they will take him?' Alifa asks.

'Most likely the same place they held you, unless they have other similar prisons, which I doubt as the running cost would be too high – security, housing, feeding, transporting, and above all keeping the location secret. No, I think there can only be one such prison in Urua.'

'I wish I was more helpful, but I can't remember where it was. There were mountains, a lake, a valley. And we were deep underground.' She rubs her forehead. 'I'm sorry.'

Durayd leans across, takes her hand. 'Do not fret, child.

Everything that happens is the Will of the Creator.'

'But if I ...' Alifa says.

'You did what you could. Life gets harder as you age but you be-come more durable,' Durayd interjects.

Jamshi picks up the *oud* guitar beside him, strums a melancholy chord, sings:

Even if you had this world. What would it be? Nothing.

Even if you had the palaces and the streams? Nothing.

Even if you had the forests and the seas? Nothing.

What if you had intimacy with the Beloved? Everything.

What if you had ascendency to Liyuün? Everything.

What if you had felicity with the unseen? Everything.

Jamshi looks at her and smiles. The others do as well.

When Durayd sees a smile return to her face he lets go of her hand and addresses the apothecary. 'How are your patients doing this morning?'

'They will join us soon,' Belal replies. 'They have started to make progress, but their recovery will take time.'

'They will get their Conduit abilities back, right?' Jamshi asks.

Belal nods slowly. 'If it is the Will of the Creator.'

Alifa cannot imagine living without her abilities. Not being able to thread herself over buildings, or use her strength to shift objects or people, or to calm another. *Yet I lived my whole life without them before. If I were to lose my abilities, could I return to the way I used to be?*

'Any word from Cinan?' Jamshi asks Durayd.

'He took the Teutons up on their offer. He has gone to their lands. I hope that by the time he returns, Zorar will also be back,' Durayd says.

'And Kaşifa?' Jamshi says.

'I received a dispatch from her. She is fine, but deep within the

imperial archives,' Durayd says. 'Slowly she is constructing a picture of what might befall everyone on Ikleel. She has been in communication with archivists in Cin and Aztlan but official dispatches through the Ministry of Information are operating at a snail's pace.'

'Why is that?' Jamshi asks.

'The Teutons have been given priority over cross-border communiques, equal only to that of the imperial court. There is only one official undersea cable system between Arön and Cin which runs along the eastern borders and one in the west which goes to Aztlan. Of course, there are some unofficial cabling systems for dispatches, and it might be that we need to resort to them at some point. But for now, we wait for the ministry to send our dispatches.'

'What do we do in the meantime?' Jamshi asks.

Zorar would know, she thinks. *He was the one with a plan, writing ideas up, setting things in motion, chalking timelines, and setting budgets.*

'What was the name of the Brigadier who came to arrest Zorar?' Alifa asks.

'Bouson,' Durayd replies.

'What say we pay Brigadier Bouson a visit during the night,' Alifa says, smiling.

'You mean kidnap him?' Belal asks.

'Only temporarily,' Alifa replies. 'He will know where Zorar is being kept.'

'And then?' Belal asks.

'We get Zorar out,' Alifa says triumphantly.

'Alifa,' Belal says quietly. 'I want Zorar back just as much as you do. But to go to an all-metal underground prison, heavily guarded by the military with sonic weaponry, where none of our powers work – how exactly do you think we are going to break him out?'

She opens her mouth to reply, then closes it.

'Belal is right. Zorar would not want us getting caught,' Durayd says.

'But we can't leave him there!' Alifa cries.

'No, we cannot,' Belal says. 'But he let them capture him. He has a plan. Zorar always has a plan. He never does anything on a whim. Let it play out.'

'What if he's dead?' Alifa whispers.

'We all have a certain amount of time. Then we go through a door, that is somewhere in the world. We do not know where, but there is a door destined only for you, and when you pass through it you go from the finite to the infinite world, so it's best to be always vigilant, to be at peace with yourself and the Creator, and to be content. I do not believe Zorar has gone through the door that waits for him,' Belal says.

'Then, what do we do?' Alifa asks.

'We have a lot to do,' Belal replies.

'Like?' Alifa asks quietly.

'Stop the Syndicate taking over Arön,' Belal says.

The room is silent.

Alifa's head pounds at the thought of the mounting problems: the Syndicate, *Dhulmi* Conduits, the loss of the lodge, Opius, seeds, bankers, Zandal raids, the Sultan of the north, not to mention the breaking of the seals and the impending emergence of Mörtan.

She shuts her eyes, recalling there are dispatches from Hale waiting her response. He must think her rude. Since the dinner she has not been in touch with him. *Maybe he thinks I'm angry at my dress being spoilt. No, I made it clear it was an accident, an accident I caused.* But Hale does not know this. He will never know. *I should send him a dispatch; he is very sweet after all.*

Alifa recalls the girl from Koemox, Dassin. She did not say much but seemed to guess at the reason for Alifa's prolonged disappearance at dinner.

'Durayd,' Alifa says. 'The Koemox, what kind of people are they?'

'Traditionally a nomadic people, always on the move with the changing of the seasons. They keep themselves to themselves. You never hear from them, nor do they want to hear from you. Their land is harsh, with impassable mountain passes to the north and south, and a series of giant ergs in the centre which are uncrossable on foot. And of course, they have the great rift, where the battle of the first epoch took place between Volgorok and the Heralds.'

'And they have sandstorms that can take the hide off cattle,' Jamshi adds.

Alifa looks startled, which is the response Jamshi expected, by the look of his face. 'Sandstorms can be so powerful?'

'When a sandstorm approaches, you run, you hide, you let it pass, or else they say there are whispers within it which take you, drag you into the desert, never to be seen again.'

Alifa gulps. 'I need to go to Koemox,' she says.

'What!' all three of the Conduits say simultaneously.

She takes a deep breath, looks at Durayd, then at the others. 'Before Zorar left, he told me that should anything happen to him, that I should seek out Master Quezai who will finish my training.'

'Quezai,' Durayd exclaims. 'Is he even alive?'

'I thought he was just a legend,' Jamshi adds.

'Oh no,' Belal interjects. 'Quezai is a true master. But to find him. Now, that is a task in and of itself.'

'What do you mean?' Alifa asks.

'No one has seen or heard from him in decades, besides you

cannot cross the desert without a guide,' Belal says.

'Zorar must have – why else would he have told me to seek him out?' Alifa says.

'She has a point,' Durayd adds.

Belal smacks his lips. 'Even if he was alive and you found him, convincing him to take you on as a student would be tricky.'

'Why?' Alifa asks.

'He only trains Koemox,' Belal replies.

Alifa is about to respond, when two weary figures appear in the doorway.

'Nimar, Azadeh!' Alifa leaps off the sofa, rushes over to embrace them both.

Durayd and Jamshi greet their old friends, assisting them to a set of high-backed chairs either side of the mantel. Belal hands his patients steaming cups of something that smells as awful as it looks. Nimar winces at the sight of his, then gulps it in one shot. Azadeh sips hers slowly, grimacing as she does so.

The others gently break the news of Zorar's capture . They need to know, thinks Alifa. After an initial slump, quiet determination settles on their faces. Nimar slowly clenches and unclenches his fists, testing his strength.

That's the spirit, thinks Alifa. *When you think you are getting better, you get better.* On several occasions she'd seen patients with a cheerful approach to life recover faster than those who wallowed in self-pity and misery.

Eventually the conversation turns to what the others want to know.

'What did you see?' Durayd asks.

Nimar and Azadeh exchange glances before Azadeh says, 'We entered the *Dhulmi* part of the Isthmus through the ground fog. It is a difficult journey. Even on level two, there is a change. It's not just the cold, or the grey and icy wintry winds. There is a foul stench in the air, a mist that clings to the body. Screams suddenly pierce the air, then die away as quickly as they came. You see ...' she pauses, looks carefully at Nimar. He nods.

She continues. 'You see Djüne shoot past on the horizon. Often so fast, like a blur, that you think you imagined it. Like a black spot that appears before your eyes, then it's gone. We were not sure at first, but as we went deeper to the third level, to the point where the Gateway opens to the fourth, we were left in no doubt. The Djüne of Mörtan are on the move.'

'Djüne!' whispers Alifa. 'Real demons?'

'I'm afraid so,' Nimar chimes in. 'Fiends, ghouls, devils of all kinds. If I had not seen it, I would not have believed it. The Isthmus has changed. There is an edge to it. A sense of imminent threat pervades every level. Entering the Isthmus will make you anxious.'

'But the Djüne and these fiends, can they leave the Isthmus?' Alifa asks.

The Conduits remain silent.

'Can they?' she probes.

'It will take time,' Belal says. 'But as the Seals have broken, eventually Mörtan will pass through the levels, emerging with his Djüne. In the Isthmus at the lower levels their bodies age very slowly, so they would not have aged very much. When he has massed his forces in the first level, all it will take is an invitation, an opening of a single Gateway somewhere in Ikleel, and that will be enough for them to pass through and enter our world.'

'And then?' Alifa asks, voice quivering.

The room is silent.

-27-
AN UNHOLY OFFER

The best sort of betrayal is when the betrayed is not even aware.

A FOOL'S PARADISE

THE THRUST IS CLEAN, a slim poison-tipped needle piercing the neck of the judge, before the heavyset man collapses. The public official is simply another name on Kaivan's list. He reminds himself: *it's the Teuton's list. Who is to say how virtuous or not these victims were.* Yet it still feels wrong.

Brisk steps remove him from the scene of the crime and soon his dog Mushtar pads along beside him, glancing up at his master as he tucks in close to him. He rubs the crown of Mushtar's head. The mastiff was a puppy when he found it, abandoned and lost in the mountains. He loves the dog. Loves it more than anyone else in the world. *Is that healthy* he wonders, *to love an animal more than any person? Probably not.*

The image of the girl, Alifa, outside the Teuton embassy, comes to mind once more. He has been thinking about her. He can't get her out of his head. That face, her manner. *Who is she,* he wonders for the umpteenth time. It's been weeks since their encounter; maybe she's not even in Urua anymore. He knows he should move on, forget her, but there is something she represents which he longs for – an alternative path in life. Another future which does not involve being an assassin. Companionship, friends, family, all the things he craves, but none of which he has tasted. He fears a future in which, like the Patriarch of the Peak, he ends up a miserable old man, alone and dispirited, surrounded by young assassins.

This Alifa is most likely a decent law-abiding daughter of a wealthy merchant. She probably comes from a good home, with nice parents, siblings who love her, a future – a promising one no doubt. What could he offer a girl like that? *My life is full of danger, uncertainty, risk at every corner, enemies at every turn. No, a decent girl like that, she's better off with the right sort of person. Certainly not that Teuton fellow turning to jelly as he escorted her out. Fool sap of a boy!*

He's left the affluent part of the city where the judge lived, and now heads south, out of Urua, towards a poorer neighbourhood, where he keeps off the crowded thoroughfare, taking the back streets between old tenements. The wind rushes down the alley he's on and he pulls his cloak tighter around him, fastens his hood around his head. Mushtar suddenly stops. Kaivan also halts.

'What is it?' Kaivan says, scanning the area around him. He has learned to trust the dog's sense of threat over the years: it's saved him many times.

The mastiff growls, its eyes fixed on the path ahead. Kaivan peers through the mist and as it clears, he notices a hooded figure, standing at the other end of the alley. It's a solitary man, no one beside him. Kaivan's fingers move to his daggers. Mushtar leaps, bounding for the stranger.

'No, wait!' Kaivan calls after his mastiff, but the dog has its blood up and does not heed him.

Kaivan grimaces, running after Mushtar. As the hound draws closer to the person, the hooded figure leaps away, onto a sidewall, then seems to run at an angle on the wall, his arms held out. Kaivan cannot see any ropes: it's as though the figure is threading himself through the air.

'What the ...' Kaivan says.

A thought crosses his mind. *An assassin has come for me!*

He skids to a halt, spins, runs in a different direction. Turns down a narrow alley, then right, left, right again. He hugs the edges of the walls, making sure he is silent, does not disturb anything or anyone in his path. He reminds himself he's a trained assassin, who moves like a shadow. He will soon shrug off the attentions of another killer, no matter how good they might be.

Slipping between buildings, Kaivan slows down, turns to look behind him. Nothing. Then he sets off again. Freezes. The hooded figure, a tall man by the looks of it, is perched on an algae-fuelled lamp post waiting for him.

'No way!' Kaivan says, turns, sprints, skids around several corners. He keeps going for many more minutes, even crossing into a different part of town, one with fewer houses and more apartments, higher buildings, easier to conceal himself in. He knows Mushtar will track him down: the dog always finds its master. For the first time in his life he feels hunted and he does not like it.

As he turns a corner, he sees the hooded figure ahead of him. There must be more than one. How can it be the same person? *Is he flying?* He runs, then stops, waits in an alcove. *I'm an assassin, this is what I do,* he reminds himself. He does not make a sound, but draws his daggers. Statue-like, he waits. *Let the hunter come,* he thinks.

Minutes pass. The wait is an anxious one. His palms sweat and he breathes slowly. The sound of a cape flapping gives away the approach of the stranger. He tightens the grip on his weapons. Waits. Ears tuned, he listens. Footsteps: he's locked on to them. He knows the man is only a few yards away from him. *Wait,* he tells himself. *Wait.*

Now.

Kaivan rolls, rises before the hooded man, plunges his daggers at him, but misses. The hooded figure moves faster, steps back, cape billows out, flaps in the wind.

Kaivan lunges, daggers flying right to left, then back again. He spins around, strikes high, then cuts low. Each time the hooded figure dances away with ease. *How can someone move so fast?* Kaivan tries a new tactic. He leaps into the air, throws his smallest dagger straight at the man's chest.

The stranger sticks out his palm. Takes the full brunt of the blade on his skin. The blade bounces off, falls to the ground. The man's white palm is held out flat: there isn't a single mark or cut on the skin.

Impossible.

'We could do this all night,' the man says, lowering his hand.

Kaivan throws another dagger. Aims it at the man's head, but the stranger swings his hand, as though swatting a fly. The dagger bounces harmlessly off a wall.

'Or we could talk,' the man says.

Kaivan clenches his fists. He has several more blades he could try, but at this distance it's not going to have any effect on this fellow. Kaivan needs to get close, really close, then stab this man through the heart.

The stranger lowers his hood.

'Huh!'

It's the Teuton. Kaivan recognises him from the time he came to meet the Patriarch.

'You're the employer – why are you trying to kill me?' Kaivan gasps.

The man calmly folds his arms behind his back. Casually, he walks to one side, then back to where he was.

'Who said I was trying to kill you?' the Teuton says.

Kaivan hears Mushtar bounding up the street.

'Here, Mushtar, heel,' Kaivan says, as the enormous mastiff comes to stop beside him. It still growls at the Teuton, but listens to Kaivan and does not move.

'Dogs are loyal. Had one myself when I was a boy. Died. It was tragic,' the Teuton says.

'What's your name, Teuton?'

The Teuton rubs his hands together before him, as though he were relishing what was about to follow.

'That's more like it. Let's get down to business. Brant is the name. And yes, I am your employer in the sense I paid the Patriarch to do some work for me.'

'And he gave the messy end of it to us,' Kaivan says.

'Someone's got to get their hands dirty, I suppose,' Brant says.

'You're a bag of tricks, running on walls, evading blows like you were floating, parrying a metal dagger with your palm! You don't need us; you could do it yourself.'

Brant grins. 'It's a fair point, but there are more important matters needing my attention.'

'Humph,' Kaivan grunts.

The man fixes him with an unpleasant smile. Next, Kaivan feels himself growing agitated, at the Teuton's face, that smirk. He wants to punch the man in the face. He clenches his fists, is about to take a step forward to do just that, when he feels another emotion wash over him, a calming, peaceful sense of serenity. The Teuton doesn't look so annoying anymore, not a threat or an irritation, just a man going about his daily business. In fact, Kaivan starts to think highly of the fellow. He's probably a decent family man, who helps others. Why, he's a role model for Kaivan.

'Wait a minute,' Kaivan growls. 'Stop whatever you're doing!' He steps towards the Teuton, reaching for another dagger on his belt.

The Teuton holds up his hands. 'What am I doing?' he says, innocently.

'Manipulating my emotions. Get out of my head.'

'Good,' Brant says. 'You spotted it quickly. Most people wouldn't know they were being manipulated at all. But I expect more of you. What's your name, assassin?'

'Why should I tell you?'

'I suppose it's a risky affair giving your name to someone in your line of work, but there is a reason I ask it. You and me, we're the same,' Brant says.

'What do you mean?' Kaivan asks.

Brant points back behind him. 'What you saw me doing earlier, running along that wall, stopping your blade with my hand, manipulating your emotions. You can do all these things, and much more, much, much more.'

'How do you know this?'

'You are,' Brant takes a step towards him and Kaivan grips the handle of the dagger, 'what is called a Grand Conduit of *Kha*.'

Kaivan waits for Brant to say something else. Evidentially this should mean something to him by the look on Brant's face. 'Never heard of such a thing.'

'I see,' Brant responds, rubs his chin with his fingers. 'Have you always lived with the Patriarch?'

'As long as I can remember.'

'And he never mentioned Conduits?'

Kaivan shakes his head.

'Then you have not lived,' Brant smiles. 'You are unique. We are all unique in our own ways. But you have capabilities which few possess.'

'How do you know this?'

'I am also a Grand Conduit of *Kha*.'

Kaivan cuts him off. 'What is this *Kha*?'

'All in good time,' Brant replies. 'And as a Grand Conduit, I can recognise another Grand Conduit, because we release a pulse – think of it like a murmur in your heart. It's very subtle and few can pick up on it, unless they're Grand Conduits too. But it is the signature that allows us to recognise each other.'

'You're saying I'm sending some signal, and you can detect it?'

Brant nods. 'It's how I recognised you when I met with the Patriarch on the stone crossing. Your *Kha* is strong.'

'It's how you found me, despite me running.'

Brant smiles.

'How do I hide it?' Kaivan asks.

'For that you need to tell me your name,' Brant probes.

'Kaivan,' he says.

Brant raises an eyebrow. 'Kaivan.'

'That's all you're going to get,' he replies.

'All right Kaivan,' Brant says. 'I will show you how to hide this pulse, but first I want you to know something. I have your best interests at heart. I feel we can work together and accomplish many things in Urua, in Arön and beyond. But there are others, other Grand Conduits who would regard you as competition. See you as a threat. You're lucky I found you. If one of them discovered you, you would be dead, Kaivan. They are merciless.'

Kaivan huffs. 'And you're not merciless?'

'When I need to be, I am, but what I'm offering is to help you learn your abilities. You can do a lot. More than you can imagine. Become whoever you want to be.'

'Maybe I'm happy being just myself,' he says, knowing it's a lie. He wants a way out and this Teuton has piqued his interest.

'Oh really, I think not. I saw you at that last kill, of the judge. The hesitation, the uncertainty. You question your actions, you question your purpose, you question your function as an assassin. I can train you to become something else.'

'What?' Kaivan asks.

Brant smiles. 'An icon, Kaivan. A symbol of hope in a world gone mad.'

Kaivan listens to the Teuton's words. He does not trust Brant. *The man is devious – he has to be if he came to the Patriarch. But then the Patriarch isn't the epitome of compassion and benevolence either.* If this Brant can train him to unleash his potential, then maybe this is the opportunity to forge a new path, do something different.

He thinks about the girl once more.

'What do you say?' Brant probes.

'You can train me in the things you spoke about?'

Brant nods.

'What do you want in return?' Kaivan asks.

'Your loyalty,' Brant says.

Damn, there's always a catch.

'I'll think about it,' Kaivan says.

'Don't think too long,' Brant says. 'Things are about to get messy in Urua, and this is only the beginning. You can either shape the world or be shaped by it.'

'How can I prevent another Grand Conduit tracking me?' Kaivan asks.

'Brant removes a ring from the folds of his coat. He shows the ring on his right index finger. They are a match. He throws the original ring to Kaivan, who catches it.

'When you wear this ring, you are invisible to another Grand Conduit. Like wearing a black cloak on a moonless night.'

Kaivan turns the ring in his hands. He looks back up at Brant.

'Maybe together, we can set the world on fire,' Brant says, bends his knees, throws his hands in an upwards direction, leaps. Kaivan's jaw drops as he watches Brant soar to the top of a four-storey building. Landing on its edge, his cape whips around him, before he disappears into the night.

Kaivan lets out a deep breath and crouches to rub Mushtar along his back.

'Why is it, Mushtar,' Kaivan says, 'that the ones who promise you the world are always the creepy types?'

-28-
FINDING THAT GIRL

Do not grow morose at losing some worldly matter.
Truly, the one who is lost is the one in whose heart
there is not the remembrance of the Creator.

THE WISDOM OF THE WAY

TRACKING DOWN ALIFA is harder than Hale anticipated. His dispatches are met with silence. Frustration at having lost contact has driven him to take matters into his own hands. People do not simply disappear off the face of the earth. Unless an awful event has happened. He would rather not think of such a thing. Hale knows little about Alifa, the girl he cannot get out of his head. He realises he is being foolish, but love does this to one's heart, he knows.

His enquiries lead him to the old quarters of Urua. He has a tip from someone who knows someone, who heard from another person, that they saw a girl fitting Alifa's description moving around with an eclectic group residing in a lodge of some distinction in a part of the city where many of the less well-known Guilds are based.

After going around in circles for half the morning, before some strangers take pity on him and direct Hale to the right place, he thinks he has arrived at Alifa's lodge. Only, when he sees it with his own eyes, his heart sinks. It's in utter ruin.

The entire front is cordoned off as though major building works are underway. Scaffolding has been erected against the exterior walls. He notices that what glass remains in the windows is shattered or cracked. Pockmarks pattern the wall, as though a series of sonic blasts were fired at the building. *Who would do such a thing? Maybe he is in the wrong place.*

I've come this far, might as well see what's behind all that hoarding, he thinks.

The midday winter sun peeks over several of the taller rooftops, casting an eerie light across the courtyard housing the lodge and two other buildings, which also appear empty. Outside the abandoned lodge there is a working fountain and the pebbled paths are in immaculate condition. Hale spots a soldier, loitering at one end of the building, almost hidden.

It's then that Hale notices another soldier at the other end. Both men are armed with sonic rifles. *What is going on? Since when do soldiers guard building sites?*

There is more to this than meets the eye. Uncertainty grips him. He shouldn't meddle, but he wants to find Alifa. If she did come and go from this dwelling regularly, maybe there is a trace of where she went.

Hale observes the soldiers for a while. They are not particularly alert. They like to chit-chat with passers-by. He can't blame them: standing around a building site is not the most engaging of occupations. Spotting his moment when both soldiers are preoccupied, he scoots across the courtyard, marching at pace. He approaches the scaffolding, and climbs up it, so that he is parallel with the hoarding.

He is about to leap down when he freezes. The ground is covered with thousands of shards of glass.

He hears movement to his right where one of the soldiers patrols. *Nothing for it now,* he tells himself, and leaps down, landing as softly as he can on splintered glass. With caution at the forefront of his mind he steps on the shattered surface. For what feels an eternity he tiptoes in his leather boots towards the interior. An enormous entrance door with intricate carvings is singed. He pushes it open and he enters an elaborate hall bedecked with fine mosaics. Feeble sunlight leaks in through a skylight, casting a sorrowful glow on the ruin of a once magnificent interior.

Several rooms lead off a central hall. There is also a staircase spiralling upwards. It's quiet. *Is this where you lived, Alifa? What happened?* His heart beats faster, as he realises the reason Alifa has not returned his dispatches is that she may be gone, even perished. He scolds himself for such foolish thoughts. No, he knows she is alive, she has to be.

As he makes his way toward one of the rooms on the right side of the building, he hears his name called.

'Hale.'

Heart nearly in his throat, he spins, then calms himself when he sees Brant and Konrad. *But what are they doing here?*

'Brant, good to see you,' Hale says, trying to disguise the nervous energy in his voice.

Brant has that know-it-all smile on his face, as though he is already five mental steps ahead of him. *He probably is,* thinks Hale. *I need to keep my wits about me.*

The two men saunter in his direction.

'What brings the nephew of the ambassador to this ruin?' Brant asks.

'I could ask the same thing, could I not, of the deputy ambassador,' Hale replies jokingly. *Brant is like a coiled cobra: he can strike at any moment. Of course,* Hale tells himself, *he would never do that – we are all Teutons, after all, and he works for my uncle. But every time I'm around him, there is a sense of imminent danger. Why?*

Brant turns to Konrad, who smiles. 'The lad has a point, does he not Konrad?'

'He does,' Konrad says.

Brant rubs his hands together, blowing into them. 'Well, Hale, we're following up inquiries. There was a criminal gang based in this building, a very dangerous one at that. They were known as the best burglars in Urua, organised, determined: high calibre light-fingered thieves. Also deadly, taking a life without a second thought when they needed to.'

'Criminal gang? Here?' Hale says, looking around at the fine trappings and exquisite architecture.

'Don't let the façade deceive you, Hale. Sometimes the people you trust the most are the ones who will bury a blade in your ribs and twist it.'

Hale flinches at the image of Alifa holding a knife close to him. She probably doesn't even know how to hold a weapon, he assures himself.

'Isn't that a matter for the local authorities? They have law enforcement in Urua. Why are you getting involved?' Hale asks.

'Good point,' Brant says, taking several steps closer to him. Konrad moves slightly away, as though taking up a position to one side, should Hale try and make a run for it. *Why would he do that?* Hale asks himself.

'We have reason to believe the criminals based here were the ones responsible for the theft at our embassy,' Brant says.

'Theft? What theft are you talking about?' Hale asks.

'We've kept it quiet for various reasons, but the night you threw a party for your friends, there was a break-in at the ambassador's private office. It was bravely thwarted by two of our men, who took a severe beating from the felons. Some items were taken, valuable in themselves, and some information may have been compromised –

trade secrets and confidential matters.'

'I didn't know,' Hale says, thinking back to that night.

'I've seen the guest list,' Brant continues. 'All young men and women like yourself, nothing suspicious about it.'

'No, it couldn't be one of my friends – they wouldn't!' Hale says.

'Sure?' Brant probes.

'Probably an opportunistic set of thieves who used the occasion to break in.'

Brant comes closer. Hale straightens his back, but there is an ominous presence to Brant, which makes the younger man want to cower. Hale feels uncertain and his heart grows agitated. He tries to think positive thoughts, but Brant's gaze is so overpowering. Hale glances at Konrad, who has a similar slick smile on his face as the deputy ambassador.

'Hale, did any of your friends leave the glasshouse for an extended period of time?' Brant asks.

'No,' he snaps.

Brant tilts his head to one side. 'Really?'

Hale swears to himself he will not give his friends away, but remembers clearly that Alifa was absent for an extended period. But then so was the Koemox girl, Dassin, who left to use the ladies shortly after Alifa and came back just before her. At the time he thought nothing of it, but now, with this new information presented to him, he questions her motivation. *Dassin is very secretive. Perhaps she's involved with this gang of criminals. Who else can it be? It's not Alifa – she is such a sweet innocent girl. It must be Dassin.*

'They remained in the glasshouse except for when they might have had to use the facilities,' Hale replies.

He will not give his friends up. In part he does not trust Brant and Konrad; they might take too heavy an approach in resolving this matter. He will track down Dassin as well as finding out where Alifa has gone.

'If you say so,' Brant says, suddenly turning away from him.

'Brant,' Hale asks. 'The people who were living here, where did they go?'

'Why would that be of interest to you?'

If he says he is looking for Alifa, Brant will know he met her at the embassy. He'd rather find Alifa himself than have Brant haul her in for questioning.

'Nothing, just wanted to know if they had been arrested so that the city is safer, or whether they are on the run, and I should take more precautions.'

Brant smacks his lips. 'They are on the run. If you come across any of them, make sure you tell either me or Konrad, before you tell anyone else. These are very dangerous people, lethal in fact, much more than you can ever imagine.'

'I will,' Hale says.

Brant turns to go, then addresses Hale once more. 'I'd suggest, Master Hale, that you sneak back out the way you came in, making sure the soldiers don't spot you. Your aunt will be telling you of plans to leave Urua later this week, for a short time. We have been invited by Almas, head of the bankers, to spend a few days at his winter retreat by the lake. It will be a pleasant few days out of the capital. Be sure to pack.'

Hale nods. He wants to find Alifa; he *needs* to find her before Brant does.

𝒦

-29-
TWO DOZEN

*A teacher is worthy of the title when they can
gain new insights from what they already knew.*

THE BOOK OF HERALDS

C HECKING HIS REPLACEMENT MOLAR TEETH is the
first thing Zorar does every morning in prison. The dental
appointment he attended on the night of Alifa's visit to the
Teuton embassy is his lifeline to escaping prison.

His interrogators are restrained, even cordial in their questioning. They treat him as a contemporary and equal, not a prisoner. It means the sunstone relic from the Isthmus taking the place of his old teeth are working. He has access to the full range of his Grand Conduit abilities. He regularly calms his interrogators, without them suspecting their emotions are being nudged.

The extra beauty of the sunstone relic is that they work through metal. Of course, there is a downside: they run out faster, as every relic does with use, but these more than others as they must connect to the Source through the metal barrier. He has been restrained in their use: calming his jailors, healing his lower back after the pounding he took from the sonic weapons which were set to wound, not kill, discovering his cell position within the prison complex by using his revealer abilities.

The latter has offered considerable insight. He is deep within a mountain complex of several floors. A long lift shaft ascends to the exit, alongside of which is a stair with hundreds of steps. Few guards occupy these lower levels, but at the exit there is a regiment of soldiers with sonic weaponry.

He wonders what Cinan would think of such a place. He would no doubt call it a monstrosity but might grudgingly acknowledge it as a feat of engineering. *Negin, do you know such a place exists? I cannot believe in my heart you do, or else you would have told me. Surely you would have told me.*

The door to his cell opens.

Zorar stands, straightens his clothes. Four guards, sonic rifles trained on him, enter the cell in pairs. Outside, he knows there are four more. He is ushered out, where two of the four men clamp handcuffs on him. A quick glance up tells him there is a precision-guided sonic cannon at one end of the corridor. If a prisoner were to get out, they would be pulverised. He will need to think about how he deals with that.

For now, he is cuffed and the eight guards, with their rifles pointed at him, slow march him to the end of the corridor, take a left down another passageway and continue for several minutes till they reach the familiar interrogation room. He is directed inside, then the guards all step back and the door is locked. In the centre of the room is a chair and table, which faces another chair and table set, but in between the two are sets of metal bars running from floor to ceiling. No elements but metal. Nothing a Conduit can use to harness the Source. The architects of this jail knew what they were doing.

His regular interviewers come in. He has been calming them this past week, and now he barely needs to touch their emotions, for them to become easy in their methods. He even knows how many children they have and has made suggestions about their education. The interrogators approach and are about to greet him when the door on their side reopens and Brigadier Bouson appears.

'I'll conduct the interview today,' he tells the two, who look disappointed at having to leave Zorar, who gives them a calming nudge as they exit.

Bouson marches across to the seat on the other side of the bars, waits for the door to close at his end, then turns to Zorar with an indignant grin.

'It seems, Zorar, that my jailors have been soft on you. I've read the transcript of their conversations with you. They are more interested in sharing their family problems than in finding out why you murdered General Ramin.'

'Ramin, despite our differences, was a good man,' Zorar says. 'I had nothing to do with his death.'

'Why then were his dying words to his son, "Conduits"!' Bouson snaps.

'I have been asking myself this question. Maybe it was a cry for help: "Call the Conduits!"'

'Rubbish. It was a cry of complicity.'

'What does the Sultana think?' He almost called her Negin.

'Her Majesty has given her full support to hunting down all Conduits. We have already shut your precious lodge, confiscated materials and driven away any who are loyal to your cause.'

Zorar decides to calm Bouson with a slight nudge. 'Have you caught any of the others?'

'No,' Bouson snaps, then shakes his head, surprised he would give away such information. 'But it will not be long, as we know where they are.'

Bouson is likely bluffing, yet if he has located Belal's community in the forest, then Zorar will need to break out soon.

Zorar gives him another gentle nudge. 'So, none of my friends are in this facility?'

'No!'

'Who is here?' Zorar asks.

'Conduits and Vanimals,' Bouson replies.

'Vanimals?' Zorar asks.

'Vicious beasts,' Bouson says. 'We keep them in the lower levels, under this section. You wouldn't want one in your cell with the door closed, would you now, Zorar?'

It would be a convenient way to arrange his death, mauled by a Vanimal. The incident could be blamed on a random prison fight between two convicts. These things happen when aggressive men are locked up in confined spaces. It would be a convenient way for Bouson to dispose of him. 'How many Conduits are here?'

'Two dozen,' Bouson replies.

'All on this level?'

Bouson nods, then shakes his head, suddenly questioning why he is giving Zorar all this information. Zorar draws a little more from the relic, adds a bit of Clarifying to the Calming. Tries to get Bouson to stay focussed.

'Yes, all along here,' Bouson says, waving his arms around to indicate where the cells are along the corridor.

'How many Vanimals?' Zorar asks.

'About the same.'

There is a knock on the door. Bouson turns to see the two interrogators there.

'Brigadier,' the shorter one says.

'Yes, what!' Bouson says.

'Sir, we have been listening to the conversation from the adjacent room, and we thought ...'

'What?' Bouson barks.

'Well, we were not sure whether it was really appropriate to be sharing the number of prisoners with the inmate.'

'Huh!' Bouson spins, his attention back on Zorar. He glares at him suspiciously. 'What did I tell you?'

Zorar shrugs his shoulders.

Bouson rises, backs away, keeping an eye on Zorar. As he exits, he tells the regular interviewers. 'Take him back to his cell. No more interrogations.'

The door shuts and soon the eight soldiers escort him back to his cell, as he ponders how he will know which of the Conduits is *Nurani* and which is *Dhulmi*. He won't. It also dawns on him if he is to create as much chaos and confusion as possible, he will also need to release the Vanimals. Containing them will keep the guards busy, allowing more Conduits to slip away.

He enters the cell, the door shuts. Zorar has a sliver of a smile on his lips.

-30-
MANY SCHEMES

*Everyone will have a day that reminds
them what a fool they have been.*

A FOOL'S PARADISE

THE SUN WILL SET SOON. A chill draught of air swirls around Urua, piercing streets, boulevards and souks with an icy touch. Threatening rain clouds gather and the mood is pregnant with anticipation. The assassins, including the Patriarch of the Peak, have assembled in a dilapidated warehouse in the south of the city. The Teutons want all the remaining assassinations to be carried out tonight.

Kaivan crouches besides Mushtar, rubbing the dog's head. Its tongue lolls, hangs limp, and its eyes look expectantly at its master. Footsteps approach; Kaivan hears a growl in Mushtar's throat.

A glance up tells him it is Vard. No other person repels Mushtar as much as this snarly-faced fellow.

'Easy, boy,' Kaivan says, as he rises.

Assassins are dotted about the warehouse, hidden within robes and hoods. Most like to prepare themselves in isolation. Not so Vard, who swaggers about and whose manner grows haughty. Kaivan knows Vard's showmanship is intended to remind others he is number one behind the Patriarch. Vard is highly skilled and adept; he moves faster than anyone apart from Kaivan himself. The Patriarch lets Vard get away with his bluster. Maybe, Kaivan thinks, Vard is equal to the old man. *Maybe he wants me to challenge Vard, so he won't need to.*

Vard stops a few yards from him, looks disdainfully down at Mushtar. 'That dog will give you away one of these days. It'll get you killed.'

'That dog,' Kaivan says, 'has saved my life on countless occasions.' He rubs Mushtar on the crown of his head.

'Humph,' Vard dismisses the comment. 'An assassin always works alone. You don't need support, unless, of course, you aren't up to the job in the first place.'

The comment draws the attention of some assassins nearby, who tilt their heads to catch the response. The animosity between Kaivan and Vard is well known. Unlike the other assassins, Kaivan does not bend to Vard's will. Most expect their enmity will come to a head at some point. *Maybe I can get clear of all this soon.* The picture of Brant running sideways along the wall appears in his mind. *He said I can do that. But there's a catch – there is always a catch when someone promises you power like that.*

'Maybe. Not everyone is a born killer,' he replies. He doesn't want an argument today. A feeling of nausea washes over him – the city is edgy, the army is away on a training drill, the assassins have convened, Brant can sense him when he is close unless he puts that ring on. He feels it in his inside coat pocket. *Not just yet, not just yet,* he counsels himself.

'Maybe,' Vard says with a flick of his fingers. 'It's good to know your place, Kaivan.'

The door at the far end of the warehouse opens. Several hooded assassins walk in, faces hidden, before the Patriarch appears, lowering his hood to reveal his distinctive white-grey beard and hair. He strides towards the group, taking centre stage in the middle of the warehouse.

'Draw closer,' the old man instructs.

His assassins approach, emerging from shadows and gullies. Kaivan exchanges a look with Juud and Ayu before they move towards the Patriarch. Vard stays beside him, whispers, 'And sometimes it's good to move your place.'

Kaivan glances at his fellow assassin. *Was that a comment directed at me, or about his plans to overthrow the Patriarch,* he wonders. The assassins under a man like Vard will become a brutal outfit. Then it will be time to move on, as far as he is concerned. Kaivan only remains out of loyalty to the Patriarch. The day the old man leaves him or dies, is the day Kaivan knows his time with the assassins will be over. The problem is that once an assassin, always an assassin. He knows he will need to leave Urua, or else they will track him down. He will then have two choices: return to the fold, or die.

Maybe I can find that girl and start a new life.

The Patriarch sweeps his gaze across those assembled, settles his stare on Kaivan. Notes Vard beside him.

'Our employer,' the Patriarch says, 'wants the remaining hits completed this evening. Each of you will be given a name, an address and a time. Complete the assignment, then return to the mountain. Do not linger in the city.'

'Why is that, Patriarch?' Vard asks.

The Patriarch's eyes narrow, observing Vard with suspicion, before momentarily resting on Kaivan.

'The Zandal are massing on the outskirts of the city. With the army away, our employer wants us to complete their work here. We will then be assigned a second imperial city.'

'A second,' Vard whispers beside him. 'What's the old man planning?'

Kaivan is silent. He senses disquiet. Sacking a city is different to killing one person. The effects of it are catastrophic to ordinary people, their families, their livelihoods. Cities rarely recover from such an event. This is what they will do tonight – assassinate Urua's prominent figures, leave the city leaderless, let the Zandal, notorious wild men of the Northern Waste, loot and pillage. *What will be left?*

'Now, collect your target names,' the Patriarch orders.

The assassins form a queue and approach the Patriarch one by one. Each takes the master's hand and kisses it before the Patriarch slips him a piece of paper. Kaivan decides this is the perfect time to put some distance between him and Vard, who eagerly makes his way to the front of the queue. Kaivan strolls across and brings up the rear, taking the last position in line.

When it comes to his turn, he takes the Patriarch's hand, kissing it, then takes the paper the old man has assigned to him.

Kaivan reads the name on the slip and his throat goes dry.

Sultana Negin.

Alifa hopes that this, her second visit to the palace, will be a more benign affair than her first, when she was arrested and imprisoned. Beside her, Jamshi is dressed in long blue and yellow robes, and a golden scarf sits elegantly around his neck. Alifa and three other vocalists are dressed in the same colours as Jamshi. She will need to sing tonight and clap. Jamshi has taken her through the routine, and she has a basic understanding of what to do. She has never sung before, but Jamshi says she has a pretty voice.

With Zorar's whereabouts unknown, she is the only Grand Conduit in the team and her unique skills are required to fathom where he might be. Durayd has advised her on the personalities at court who might know of Zorar's whereabouts. She will need to calm them to loosen their tongues.

Durayd is too well known a figure to accompany Jamshi as part of the singing troupe. She, on the other hand, is unknown to all but a few guards who saw her on the night the *Dhulmi* Conduits broke in.

Entering the palace, the troupe is directed towards the grand hall where the performance will take place. They wait in an antechamber, where they run through final preparations, tuning instruments, testing their voices. Alifa tests her vocal cords, but only when the others are doing it so that her voice is subsumed amongst the rest.

Jamshi speaks with the *oud* and *duff* players. There is a pleasant camaraderie amongst this group of trusted performers. *They train with instruments, I train with elements, but we all need to train to perform,* she thinks.

Nimar and Azadeh are close to the palace. Some of their abilities have returned. In their current situation, even a half-ready Conduit is better than none. But tonight, she reminds herself, will be a time of music, song and pleasant conversations. No one expects anything else. It will be nice to unwind for once.

Jamshi takes Alifa by the elbow and draws her to one side. 'Don't get too near to the Sultana. She's very intuitive, and remember she is … close to Zorar, so we don't want her suspecting who you might be,' Jamshi says.

'But she's a supporter, I mean …' she trails off.

Jamshi raises an eyebrow.

'With the state of the empire as it is, don't assume we have any friends. Focus on the lower-level officers, get them talking. Seeing such a beautiful young woman as yourself will, I'm sure, loosen their tongues. Your charm and a little bit of calming might be enough for you to discover where Zorar is being kept.'

'Loosen their tongues,' she smiles. 'I'll have them singing like nightingales by the time I'm finished with them.'

'Good girl. Keep it subtle, keep it simple, don't draw attention to yourself.'

Alifa nods. Jamshi goes over the song list with the other performers. They practise some lyrics, and Alifa tries her best to sing in tune. She has hardly practised her Clarifier ability, but knows that when she does, it will be a skill she can use.

A royal footman appears at the entrance. Waves them over. It's time.

The troupe enters the grand hall, to be directed to one end. A wide high-backed chair is set for Jamshi. A luxurious thick carpet laden with soft cushions is set for the other performers. The musicians sit on Jamshi's right and the vocalists on his left. In the hall, there are several rows of low-level cushioned seats, spread out on an enormous carpet patterned with the wildlife and fauna of Urua. Servers stand alert at the sides of the hall, waiting for guests to arrive. Overhead a chandelier with gold trimmings and sparkling crystal hangs from the centre of the domed roof. Several smaller versions are positioned in a circle around the central one.

From the far end of the hall there is a flurry of noise, as the Sultana is sighted. Alifa is once more impressed by how strikingly graceful the monarch is. Poised, regal, resplendent. She and Zorar would make a wonderful match. *Why did he let himself get captured?*

Directed by her footman, the Sultana sweeps into the hall. She is wearing a long velvet dress, all eyes on her. It dawns on Alifa – the people here adore Negin. The looks on their faces tell her. *May the Creator give her long life.* As the others in the entourage take their seats with Negin, the servers immediately mobilise, presenting them with sherbets.

The footman approaches Jamshi. 'You may begin,' he says to the troubadour.

Jamshi looks to each member of his troupe and offers them a nod of encouragement. He clears his throat, then gives the signal to the musicians. The *duff* player begins with soft beats against the stretched goatskin. A rhythm for the *oud* player to join, as he begins to strum his strings with nimble fingers. The *riq* and *zurna* musicians join in.

Jamshi begins the preamble to the song, with some *oh* and *ahh* vocal stretches, to the tune of the music. It prepares the audience for what is to follow.

Then Jamshi throws back his head and begins to sing:

Never will I forget that one starry night,
The night I witnessed a luminous light.

Alifa's jaw momentarily drops, before she steadies herself. She has never heard Jamshi perform with a real audience.

A radiance moved in the darkness around me,
Unveiling my heart for me to see.
For a moment I felt expansion and ease.

His voice touches her very soul, reminding it of the primordial promise, of the journey back to the Creator, of the return that awaits every person when they leave the boundaries of the physical world to transcend to the metaphysical. The audience is overwhelmed by a powerful burst of clarifying. It is as though his words are all that matter, his voice the only one in the room, his instructions the only ones to follow.

I must learn the skills of a Clarifier, Alifa thinks. *There is much good that can be done with the voice.*

With the other vocalists she joins the chorus:

Never will I forget it for the rest of my life.

Tears well in many people's eyes. Sultana Negin is one of them. Jamshi continues:

Brightness from a hidden realm burst through,
Filling horizons I never knew.
I had never experienced such a starry night before.
Never will I forget it for the rest of my life.

A carefree cheerful clarity took me,
Beams of brilliance pouring into me.
My heart's elation was not like anything I knew.
Never will I forget it for the rest of my life.

A night that kindled a flame.
It is the star on the horizon I see.
The day I remembered my destiny.
Never will I forget it for the rest of my life.

As the troubadour draws the first song to a close, Alifa realises that after Jamshi has clarified the audience members, there is very little calming she will need to use to loosen the tongues of those from whom she seeks information.

The singing is interrupted.

Cries echo from the far end of the grand hall through which guests entered. Soon a Captain in the Royal Guard approaches the Sultana. The hall is hushed. All eyes are on the soldier. The Sultana is up on her feet. She exchanges a look with Jamshi. Alifa knows that look: it's a plea for help. It's a cry for the Conduits. Negin whirls, then strides out of the grand hall.

Commotion follows.

'What's happening?' a voice cries.

The Captain of the Royal Guard raises his sword high in the air, silencing all those about him, then shouts: 'The city is under attack!'

Up on the rooftops of Urua, Brant perches on the edge of a four-storey building. His burgundy cloak flaps as gusts of wind streak through it. Beside him Konrad and the other Threaders wait.

Screams and shouts drift in from the east of Urua. It's where the Zandal attacked first. By this time the wild men of the Northern Wastes will be ripping their way towards the central square of the eastern district. He smiles.

Konrad says, 'Hefters are in position, outside the palace walls, waiting for our signal.'

Brant nods. In the confusion the Patriarch of the Peak will finish his work this evening before his assassins are moved to the second city as planned. By the morning Urua will be leaderless. It will be primed for the Syndicate to step in under an imperial decree, which has already been issued, stating that in the event of all recognised leaders in Urua becoming incapacitated, the Syndicate, on behalf of the Emperor, will temporarily restore order for the people, until the Emperor appoints a new ruler of the south. Thereafter the Syndicate will continue to serve under the new ruler.

Brant chuckles to himself – it helps that they have already chosen the new ruler, who is entirely loyal to the Syndicate. Bouson may be a buffoon, but he is remarkably loyal to the vision of the Syndicate. He did not even question the removal of the army from the capital this evening. He just did as he was ordered.

Oh, what decrees an emperor signs, when under the influence of Opius, muses Brant. It helps that the Syndicate has bought off the ministers around the Emperor and the bankers are finally on side.

'Get everyone ready,' Brant says.

Konrad addresses the other Conduits on the rooftop behind Brant.

Brant feels his chin: it still hurts from when Rasa the Harbinger flicked her finger at him. *How powerful must she be?* And what of the others, Darrick the Black Rider and Harbinger of Pestilence, Limòs the Harbinger of Famine, and Dìyù the Harbinger of Death? How can he stand against any of them? He cannot. But if Mörtan were to grant him *Dhulmi* power to equal that of the Harbingers then he would show Rasa how it feels to be humiliated. In fact, he will become the hands, ears and eyes of Mörtan. *Yet is such a thing even possible?* Not for the first time when he thinks about Mörtan a shiver runs down his back.

Konrad returns. 'We're ready.'

With a grin, Brant turns to address his Conduits.

'To the palace.'

Ҝ

-31-
ONLY
WAY OUT

The best moments in life are those that
remind you of your ultimate destination.

THE WISDOM OF THE WAY

DEEP WITHIN SOLID ROCK, inside a shell of metal, there is a prison. Zorar remains in it, meditating in his cell as he lies on a bedroll. His litany is interrupted by grunts in the corridor outside his cell.

Several booted feet congregate on the other side of his door. These are not the usual prison guards: there is a different tempo to the way they move.

Click.

His cell door is unlocked. Several deadbolts slide apart. Algae-fuelled light from the corridor casts a greenish hue into his cell. He remains motionless but is alert to danger. His eyes are trained on the open door.

Zorar smells them before he sees them. Vanimals. The bestial things lurk in the recesses of the corridor. Zorar remains motionless, his back against the wall.

A howl is followed by a huge bear-like Vanimal entering his cell. Behind him is one with wolfish properties. The larger one spots him, smiles, its teeth glimmering in the light. It strides in Zorar's direction.

Zorar rolls off the bedroll, threads himself against the wall, snaps back and with Hefter-flared strength, sends a bone-crunching punch into the jaw of the enormous Vanimal. With a crack, the giant hits the floor. Howling, the wolfish Vanimal leaps for him. Zorar swivels, kicks the Vanimal in the ribs, driving him into a wall. He crashes against it, bounces off it. Zorar follows up with a nose-breaking punch which floors the brute.

Two more Vanimals leap in. They are fast. One grabs his arm as the other approaches. Zorar leaps up, propels himself at the newcomer, dragging along with him the one who holds his arm, swings it into the door. He hits it flush in the forehead, drops it against the doorframe. The other Vanimal receives a flat kick in the chest and is sent backwards, tripping over the bear-like Vanimal. As it lands, so does Zorar, smashing the back of its head into the ground.

Click.

The doorway begins to shut. Zorar leaps through it. He kicks the Vanimal partly blocking the cell door into the wall, saving the creature from being crushed. Zorar spins, faces another Vanimal. Strong, face as hard as iron, with black curly hair and a thick beard, it stares down at him. There is no malicious intent in its eyes.

He notices behind the Vanimal are several prison guards, all knocked out. The Vanimal turns away and makes its way down the corridor towards the stairwell. He would like to follow, but he needs to get the others out. Behind Zorar, several cries go up. Guards charge in, ten of them, sonic rifles pointed at him.

'Fire!' the command is raised.

Zorar sprints at the guards, threads himself against the ceiling, then onto the right wall, back to the ground, up to the ceiling, onto the left wall. He moves faster than the guards' ability to aim. They shoot where he *was*, not where he *is*. All around him he hears the sonic *pop-pop-pop* going off, knowing that each of those shots would be like a painful punch to the gut. Even having the sunstone relic he is not immune from pain.

Whack! He lands beside the guard closest to him. snaps his rifle from his hand, kicks the man away, swings the butt of the rifle in several swift movements, knocking weapons from the hands of others, before he threads the lot of them behind him, sending them crashing down to the far end of the corridor. The corridor is awash with weapons.

'Stop him!' another shout goes up.

Zorar, leaps, threading himself to the end of the corridor. Inside a reinforced glass cubicle sits a prison guard. The man cowers when he sees Zorar.

'Open them,' Zorar says, motioning to the two dozen cells.

The prison guard shakes his head, terrified.

Zorar pulls back his fist, draws from ochre and hefts a punch at the toughened glass. It shatters, sending shards spraying in all directions. The guard screams. Tries to run. Zorar grabs the man by the collar. 'Now, open them all,' he says.

The prison guard hesitates.

'All?'

'Every single one,' Zorar seethes, teeth showing.

'Ah!' the guard screams, reaching out for a set of controls.

Zorar hears several clicks and deadbolts open along the length of the corridor. He throws the guard against the wall; the man collapses on the ground.

He turns to look back at the opening cell doors. Figures emerge into the corridor. Conduits, wielders of *Kha*, imprisoned in this dungeon.

He notes men and some women, some very tall and broad, others of medium stature, some waiflike. Using his ochre-fuelled strength he amplifies his voice.

'My name is Zorar. I am like you. If you want to live, I will show

you how to get out of this place.'

He steps back into the corridor, walks in their direction. He does not recognise a single face. Who are these people? Where were they taken from? When were they taken?

An enormous shaven-headed man, not more than twenty, steps forward.

'You will show us the way out?' he asks Zorar.

'I will,' Zorar replies. 'What's your name, lad?'

'Pedram.'

Zorar nods. 'Anyone else want to join Pedram and me on the surface, then come now.'

Then Zorar hears boots running round a corner close to the glass booth. More prison guards arrive, many more than before, this time wielding additional weaponry. Zorar leaps in the air, threads all the previously abandoned weapons around him, drawing up every sonic rifle, knife blade and baton and sends them like an oncoming tidal wave straight at the soldiers. One sonic handgun he threads back to himself and slots it into his pocket. There are screams as the prison guards are thrown back into the debris.

Zorar lands, skids, turns and runs back towards the other Conduits, noticing the shocked looks on their faces. *Good, they needed to see that, see what they are capable of,* he thinks. *Better move fast before they decide to use the sonic cannon.*

Sprinting through their ranks, he heads for the stairwell the Vanimal took. He knows they are an easy target ascending stairs when the other side has powerful sonic weapons. *Maybe the relic's power will last long enough to get us to the surface.*

Bursting onto the first flight, he turns back to the twenty Conduits following him. 'Can any of you thread?' Zorar asks.

One short skinny man steps forward. 'Not down here I can't,

but up there, oh yeah!' he says. His roguish smile displays his yellow teeth.

'Stay close, then. We will need you when we get to the surface.'

The Threader nods.

'Anyone else know about their *Kha* abilities?' Zorar asks.

Pedram says. 'Yeah, just give me some ochre,' he says, knocking his fists together.

'Good,' Zorar says. 'Get to the top as fast as you can,' he tells the group, then starts to sprint up the stairs. He dare not use the relic because he needs it to last till they get out. The stairwell is endless, lit by low banks of algae lighting. Flights of stairs are followed by flights of stairs, uniform in every respect. Every now and then he sees a number on the side of the wall, telling him how many floors they are from the exit. Still five to go.

The Conduits, despite their lengthy captivity, do a good job of keeping pace. The opportunity to escape spurs them into motion. At minus level three, Zorar draws to a halt. He can hear prison guards assemble a few floors up.

Behind him the Conduits stop, with heaving chests, tired faces, exhausted limbs. He addresses them in a low voice.

'There are guards stationed three floors up. Lots of them, with sonic weapons that will injure you, perhaps even kill you.' He studies their faces: there is determination there. *Maybe some will join me in the battle against Mörtan. After all, it's why I came here, to free these Conduits and bolster our numbers.*

'We're not afraid,' Pedram says, standing a little taller.

The skinny Threader makes his way to the front. 'Just get me out there, I'll show you what I can do.'

Zorar hesitates. This man is not to be trusted. Right now, he has no other choice. 'All right,' he looks at the group, then back at the stairs. 'I'm going to take out the lighting. It's going to be very dark but get to the top. Stay as close as you can, I'll need your help when we reach the surface.'

Zorar threads himself up the stairwell, drawing the sonic handgun and shooting out the lights as he goes. Ahead of him darkness descends, and he draws on his Revealer abilities to orientate himself.

'He's coming!' he hears a panicked soldier cry.

'Fire!' someone shouts.

In the pitch black the prison guards cannot see a single thing. He threads himself upwards at awkward angles they would not think to fire at. Sonic pops go off around him; he takes a few shots on the arm, draws on Hefter strength within the relic, heals any wounds he takes with limestone.

Zorar lands on a step beside the first soldiers, disarms them, throws several men back down the stairwell. Weapons scatter in all directions. A soldier gets lucky, fires at him point black. He ducks and rises to crack the man's jaw. The soldier flies back, crashing into several behind him. Zorar threads over the next group of soldiers, grabs a soldier by the arm, uses him as a battering ram, and takes out several other soldiers who are thrown down the stairwell. He ducks, leaps, fist-fights his way up. Soldiers back off.

'Retreat!' a command is given above him. 'Seal the door!'

He expected it. Zorar draws deeper on the fragments of sunstone relic which have taken the place of his molar teeth; he threads, hefts, reveals faster than he has done before. He is a blur of movement, ascending the stairs, heading for the summit, advancing to freedom. He sees a crack of light – lamplight streaking in from the open yard.

The guards abandon the fight, scramble towards the exit. As he leaps over them, one grabs his leg. He kicks the man with his other leg, sends him careening back into a mass of bodies.

He hears Pedram roar. The others are close. He backhands a guard, brushes another aside. He feels a rotten taste in his mouth. *The relic is leaking: it's getting to the end of its power. So, close, so close, come on, just a little more.*

The door slams shut; bolts fasten on the other side.

He reaches the doorway. Soldiers still left in the stairwell move away from him, backing off further down the stairs. Pedram and other Conduits bellow, turning the remaining soldiers into whimpering babies. They fall on their knees, surrendering themselves.

Zorar draws on all the remaining power of the relic. Every single last drop into his arms. He fuels them with as much hefting force as he is able to bear. He leaps, threads himself as fast as he can, draws hefting strength into his body, making it firm like iron, propels himself at the door, with as much force as he can muster.

Smash.

The reinforced door flies off its hinges. Zorar follows it, landing on the door. He looks up in the evening dusk, green algae-light permeating the scene before him. A hundred sonic rifles are trained on him, as well as two sonic cannons, on either side of the yard.

The power of the relic has gone. 'Light and Kha,' whispers Zorar.

'Whah!' A bestial scream sounds. Vanimals, led by the one he encountered earlier in the corridor, surge out of the stairwell, ahead of the Conduits. The guards turn their weapons at the new danger. Zorar rolls forward, jumps, grabs a firearm from the nearest soldier, fires the weapon into the soldier, throwing him back.

Pedram charges out, followed by the Conduits. Now the guards have fifty prisoners to deal with. Soldiers panic, firing shots in random directions. Discipline has disintegrated. Without access to his *tasbeah*, Zorar must fight his way out purely on his martial skill. He punches, pushes, kicks, rolls, leaps, twists, thumps, throws. Pedram is by his side. The big man's presence reassures him. They weigh into the guards. The Vanimals have collectively toppled over the two sonic cannons, which are now out of action.

The square yard has a tower, where he sees officers watching the unfolding fight below them. It's where they took his belongings when he was processed. His *tasbeah* and other items might still be there. He needs to check.

'Push the guards towards those reinforced gates,' he says to Pedram. 'I'm going for my elements.'

The big man nods and delivers a pulverising punch to the side of a guard's face: the man spins and drops. Sonic pops are exchanged behind him. Zorar sprints for the tower. At the door, a terrified guard raises his weapon. Zorar rolls, ducks under the man's attempt at a rifle swipe, then delivers a knockout blow to the side of his head. Zorar opens the door, goes inside. Two guards fire at him; he rolls away, taking cover behind a set of tables. He knows any direct hit, when he cannot draw on his Hefter and healing ability, may prove lethal.

'Where'd he go?' one soldier says.

Zorar crawls under the table and when he sees soldiers approach, grips both sides of the table from underneath. Raising it above his head, he hurls it at the men. He leaps at them, disarms them, then slams their heads together, knocking them out.

His personal belongings were taken in a room close by. He enters it and picks up a file which is attached to a chain on the wall. Scans the names on the roster. His name is there and beside it, the number of a locker. Twelve. He picks up a bunch of keys, finds one with '12' embossed on it. Goes to locker number twelve, unlocks it.

'Thank the Creator.' His items are inside.

He throws on his robe, checks the *tasbeah* is intact. Takes one bead, removes it from the collection, watches it empty. The fire-fly-like light glows for a moment, then draws from the Source. He is alive!

'Right,' Zorar says, smiling. 'Let's get that gate open.'

Outside the soldiers are pinned against the gate. They have drawn reinforcements around them. The yard is occupied by the Conduits and the Vanimals. *They are waiting for reinforcements to arrive. We need to end this now.*

'Threader,' Zorar calls out to the skinny man, threading him his *tasbeah* which he plucks from the air. Though the man, not being a Grand Conduit, will not be able to draw on any of the other elements but corallite, it will be enough.

'Pedram,' the wiry man calls out, threading the *tasbeah* to the big fellow.

Pedram rolls his neck. 'Oh yes,' he says, crunching his knuckles after drawing from the Source. Pedram charges guards cowering behind a reinforced barrier, knocks them aside. The Threader busies himself yanking, thrusting, sending prison guards in all directions like a demented puppet master.

Now for the gate.

'Pedram,' Zorar says. 'With me.'

He approaches Pedram who hands him back his *tasbeah*. Zorar bends his knees, then threads himself and Pedram up to the top of the prison wall. He perches on it momentarily; Pedram wobbles at that unfamiliar height. Zorar catches the shocked expressions of several newly-released Conduits, before he threads himself and Pedram down and out, landing on the other side of the reinforced gate.

'Together,' Zorar says.

He and Pedram sprint at the gate, throw their bodies at it. *Smash!* They've made it shudder, but the gate holds.

'Again,' Pedram says.

Together they attack it. This time, the iron gate loosens, before flying off its hinges and skidding across the open ground. They enter. Terrified prison guards drop their weapons, fall onto their knees, hands raised in the air.

'That's more like it,' Zorar says.

Soon, the yard is cleared, All the Conduits and Vanimals are out, jumping into vehicles parked in the yard. The group drives down the mountain, along the twisting road, till they come out at the fork with the forest to one side, and the highway to Urua the other way. The lake where Zorar collected Alifa lies to his left, and he thinks about his young apprentice.

The Vanimals are massed at the edge of the forest, as Zorar emerges from his vehicle. The one who aided him stands beside another.

Zorar goes over to him. 'I didn't get a chance to thank you.'

The Vanimal nods.

'I'm Zorar, what's your name?'

'Gurgen,' the Vanimal says. He has a deep resonant voice.

'Thank you,' Zorar reaches out with his hand. Gurgen shakes it.

'Thank you,' Gurgen replies.

'How so?'

'We were sent to kill you. If you hadn't disabled the others of my kind in your cell, I might not have had the courage to take out the guards. It is I who owe you, Zorar.'

Zorar studies the Vanimal. It is the first time he has spoken to rather than fought with one of their kind. *Maybe there is more to these beings than I thought.*

'I would like to ask you something, Gurgen.'

'Ask.'

'Some years ago, my wife and daughter were captured by Vanimals. I searched for years for them but could not find my family nor the Vanimals who took them. If you should hear anything ...'

'We do not take human women and children for our use. It is not our way. Are you sure they were taken by Vanimals?'

'There were several witnesses,' says Zorar.

Gurgen mulls over his words. 'Then it would be for a human overlord. A contract of a kind, in return for payment.'

'Contract? Who?' Zorar says.

'You have human enemies?' Gurgen asks.

Zorar nods.

'In the north of Arön?' Gurgen asks.

'Several.'

'Then it is there I would search for them,' Gurgen suggests. 'If I come across the wife of Zorar and the daughter of Zorar, I give you my word, I will send a messenger to you, or I will come myself, for this is a matter of one's family, of one's honour. It is not a light thing; it is a heavy burden to carry.'

In my ignorance I have considered these creatures incapable of intelligence and feeling. What folly.

'Thank you, my friend,' Zorar says. He reaches out his hand once more and Gurgen grips it. 'If there is anything I can do for you, Gurgen, simply ask.'

The Vanimal nods.

'Where will you go now?' Zorar asks.

Gurgen looks at the other Vanimals waiting behind him. 'We've had enough of human lands, we're headed home to Küor Araz, back to our kind.'

'May you have a safe journey.'

Gurgen smiles, revealing a set of perfectly sculpted wolfish teeth. He turns, walks back towards the other Vanimals, before they descend a hill into the forest.

'What now?' Pedram says, coming to stand beside him.

'Now,' Zorar says, placing a hand on Pedram's shoulder. 'We get ready for the Final Standing.'

'The final what?' Pedram asks.

Zorar smiles as they head back towards the other Conduits.

RECOVERING
A RELIC

Seek out the sages, for their virtuous conduct will inspire you.
Avoid the unworthy, but if you cannot, then reflect on yourself.

THE BOOK OF HERALDS

THE ZANDAL ONSLAUGHT on the central district leaves the reservists scattered. The full-time corps is out of town on a training exercise and the voluntary guard has little stomach for the fight or ability to hold off the brutal assault by the wild tribes of the Northern Waste. From what Kaivan can see, the reservists have abandoned their positions, taken off their uniforms and disappeared, blending into the civilian population.

He uses the pandemonium to slip through the streets. Swift progress takes him to the sparsely patrolled southern palace gates, where he catches the guards unawares, knocking several of them out. He refrains from killing any.

Once through the postern he enters the herb garden in the southern grounds. Crouching low, he angles towards the palace. Soldiers run past him but fail to notice his presence. To them he is merely a shadow within the darkness, where they dare not look. A sound catches his attention, the sound of fabric billowing in the wind. He glances up, notices several figures leaping impossible spans high over his head.

Then he remembers Brant. He did some impossible things, like running along a wall. *Maybe they are his people?*

He asks himself again: *Do I want to be the man who killed the Sultana?*

If he wants to quit this lifestyle, he is going about it the wrong way. After this job, his reputation will spread. Others who want monarchs and rulers assassinated will come knocking on the door of the Patriarch. This thought gives him pause, and he is nearly spotted by a soldier. Kaivan lies as low as he can, feeling the wet grass under his fingers, the smell of the soil. The soldier investigates, does not see him, moves on.

Hesitation will get you killed, he remembers was one of the Patriarch's sayings. *Don't think, do. Knowledge without action is useless.*

'Damn the old man,' Kaivan whispers to himself. He despises the Patriarch in so many ways yet loves him for teaching him the skills to survive in a brutal world, where people pay a premium for men like him.

What can Brant teach? he wonders. *I haven't even scratched the surface of what is possible. Maybe it's time to move on.*

To the rear of the southern palace, there is a window: in the chaos it has been left open. He makes his way toward it, stays low, back against the wall, surveying movement around him. When he senses it's clear, he rises, peers through the window to the room beyond, which is a store of some sort. He widens the opening and goes through it, into the palace.

The personal bodyguards of Sultana Negin have ushered the monarch away to a secure chamber within the inner palace. Jamshi, his troubadours and Alifa are left in the grand hall. Jamshi dismisses the others in his troupe, bidding them to go to their families, to stay inside, remain out of trouble. He turns to Alifa.

'We must defend the Sultana. Her guards will be no match for *Dhulmi* Conduits should they use this commotion to attack the palace,' he says.

'We could do with Nimar's and Azadeh's help.'

Jamshi nods. 'I will get them through the gate. Come.'

The troubadour leads her back towards the exit, where a thin line of soldiers stands guard. Their terrified faces search the streets ahead: the sound of the Zandals approaching has them rattled.

Jamshi says to the guards: 'Good evening. Allow my friends passage into the palace: they are here to help.'

His tone is melodious; with a soft vibratory quality in his voice that is not normally there. He is using his clarifying ability, Alifa realises.

'Yes, sir,' one of the guard responds enthusiastically. 'They are here to protect the Sultana.'

'That's right,' Jamshi's melodious voice says.

Alifa reminds herself she must develop a melodious voice like this; it is a skill she can use when the moment requires it.

Soon, the four of them are back inside, moving through the abandoned outer palace, heading for the inner quarter.

Removing the mediocre security around the primary entrance to the inner palace is easier than Brant anticipates. Brigadier Bouson assigned all experienced personnel to the training exercise, leaving the city with only fresh-faced reservists. Mighty handy as far as he is concerned. His Conduits make short work of the guards.

'This way,' Konrad instructs. The Threader is familiar with the palace layout from his previous visit when he left behind the relic for use on this very evening.

Brant follows Konrad through the palace. A couple of soldiers spot them, but by the time they raise their sonic rifles, they've been yanked from them. The men are quickly put to the sword.

Without breaking stride, Brant tucks in behind Konrad, as the Threader follows a series of corridors, taking them to a hall filled with glass cabinets. Dazzling jewels and treasures are on display.

Brant estimates there are hundreds of these cabinets. The loot from these will nicely embellish the treasury of the Syndicate for several years.

'My, Konrad,' Brant says. 'You did choose a rather fetching location to leave the relic.'

'Hidden in plain sight,' Konrad says, leading him to a cabinet, within which is a vase. Konrad picks the lock and lifts it out. He gently tips it over and an object the size of an apricot, sparkling like a ruby, tumbles into his hand. 'Here, you have it, the moonstone,' Konrad says, handing him the relic.

Brant slowly wraps his fingers around the moonstone, gripping it in his palm. He feels the pulsating power it emits, this object brought from the fifth level of the Isthmus. Several Conduits were sacrificed to get this relic to them. *Rather them than me.*

'Oh yes,' Brant whispers. 'The war hammer.'

Konrad removes a silver war hammer from his belt, hands it to Brant, who takes it and slots the moonstone expertly back into a groove in the iron head. It clicks. Brant smiles.

'Where next?' Konrad asks.

For a moment, Brant is lost in the spellbinding allure of the moonstone relic. *How much power does it give me? Enough to withstand the lure of Rasa, enough to overpower Darrick?*

'Sir,' Konrad says.

'Yes, of course, the reason we're here. The Vessels of Nur. Come, they are located within the lower levels.'

Brant leads them from the magnificent chamber, back into the corridor. Konrad is by his side, the six Threaders close behind, when he hears a voice.

'Stop!'

He turns slowly, then a smile forms on his face.

'Ah, Zorar's people,' Brant chuckles. *Only four, what a shame. Soon there will be none. Yet they do have a Grand Conduit with them, albeit an inexperienced girl.*

'What are Teutons doing in the palace,' the darkest amongst them says. By his build Brant assumes he is a Hefter. Though he seems to grimace at times in his movement. *Ah yes*, he remembers.

'You must be Nimar,' Brant says. 'Recovered yet from your meeting with the Djüne?'

'She's the Threader who went with him,' Konrad comments.

'I asked you a question,' the man repeats.

'We don't have time for these underlings,' Brant says, turning to his Conduits.

The Threaders around him leap forward, producing weapons from hidden places. Brant heads straight for the Hefter, but before he can reach him, the girl blocks his path.

'Oh, really, child,' Brant scoffs. With the relic in his hand, he could pulverise this waif, but the reserves of its power are required for another task, so he latches the war hammer to his belt. Meanwhile the Hefter and other Threader face his Threaders who zip around them like hornets. The other fellow appears to lack any physical skills and is doing his best to support the Threader by fighting with a sword. Pathetic.

The sound of fighting draws Kaivan's attention. He stops at the corridor, peers inside. He spots Brant. Facing him is a woman in an elegant outfit. Kaivan cannot see her face as her back is to him, but she moves with incredible grace. Around them swords, blades, shields, whirl at terrifying speeds. The combatants leap onto walls, then off them, as though invisible vines were placed there. There is also a large dark man: his muscles seem strong, but he looks tired. The men around him are wearing him down.

Kaivan reaches for the ring Brant gave him. Looks at it carefully, then back at Brant who is busy with the woman, before he slips the ring on. He would rather none of them notice him. Kaivan takes one last look; he still cannot see the face of the woman fighting Brant. He decides to leave, jogs down the corridor. To his surprise nobody follows him. *Maybe Brant was telling the truth: maybe this ring does camouflage me. Can I trust him?*

He ventures deeper into the palace. The Sultana will be under heavy guard. He knows where to find her; the instructions are clear about where she will retreat for safety. It's not far. He turns a corner, runs into a guard who raises his sonic weapon, but Kaivan rolls under him, chops the soldier on the back of the neck. Knocks him to the ground.

He collects the sonic rifle, reduces its blast level so that it will not kill anyone, aims it at the guard at the other end of the corridor. The man drops. Kaivan sprints forward as two more soldiers emerge. Kaivan fires the sonic weapon at the first, before dodging to one side as the soldier takes aim at him. He leaps into the air, throwing a dagger that strikes the soldier's thigh. Three more soldiers converge on him, and he drops the first with a kick to his knee, followed by a heavy blow to the head. The second and third fall to the sonic rifle blast. He turns around: seven soldiers lie motionless behind him.

He doesn't feel good.

These men have families, loved ones. *An assassin can't think like that*, he reminds himself. He sets about tying them up with cords he carries. He binds their wrists and feet and bundles them into a storeroom, shuts the door, and slides a broom handle through the latch on the door to secure it.

He is one chamber away from the Sultana, but his instructions were clear: *remain hidden till you hear the rumbling*. He has no idea

---

what it means, but it sounds like it could signify an earthquake.

Kaivan tucks his daggers away, withdraws into a dark alcove, crouches, waits.

-33-

VESSELS
OF NUR

True glory is in those things that do not vanish,
so do not seek glory in that which vanishes.

THE WISDOM OF THE WAY

THE GIRL IS SPRIGHTLIER than Brant expects. She has taken well to harnessing the skills of a Grand Conduit. He occupies her by pretending to be flustered by her textbook attacks. Eventually he grows tired of the charade. He reaches for the war hammer, and with but a fraction of the power of the moonstone relic, hits her with the blunt side of the war hammer full in the chest. She is thrust to the other side of the chamber, lands on her back and does not get up. *What a shame. With time I could have turned her to our path.* He takes one last look at the girl, then leaves Konrad and his Conduits to deal with Zorar's crew. More important matters need attending to.

Brant makes his way down an eastern corridor; which he knows has a flight of stairs at the far end. Reaching these, he takes them two at a time. The chamber he seeks was built first, then the palace was built around it, so it occupies the precise centre of the building. In fact, on the same vertical axis above the chamber is the Sultana, hiding one floor up. *She is about to get a nasty surprise*, he thinks.

Weaving through corridors, he arrives at the chamber, with its ornate door carvings. To everyone else in the palace, including the monarch, this is merely an old archive, where historical records and artifacts are kept. It is opened biannually with a ceremony performed by minor court officials, who do not know why they still undertake the ritual.

He knows.

Twice a year the room is cleaned and serviced, after which it is sealed once more. The door is heavily armoured and he does not have the key.

Brant removes the war hammer from his belt. Grips it in his left hand, drawing on some of its power, then charges at the entry. *Smash.* One of the doors comes off its hinges and hangs limply. The other remains in place. He slips through the gap.

Brant studies the war hammer. 'I hope this holds together.'

He advances into a circular chamber. Shelves containing archival records form a ring around the outer wall of the room. In the centre is a tiled area, set a yard below floor level. In the middle of the depression is a green marble pillar, rising to the ceiling above him. It is an odd design, a single column by itself. He looks to the roof.

'Negin, you won't be expecting this,' Brant says. 'No one will.'

He walks around the pillar, which if five people surrounded it and stretched their arms around it, would just about allow them to interlock their fingers. What he seeks is under it.

Brant removes his robe, grips the war hammer with the moonstone relic in his left hand. He knows he will be dangerously weakened by the effort, but is relying on Konrad and the other Threaders to arrive soon. He pulls back the war hammer then strikes the pillar with all his strength. It shudders and cracks start to appear. His hands feel raw, but not painful. Not yet. Merely numb. He hits the pillar with another hammer blow. This time, some of the marble splits from the main structure, crumbles to the ground. He pounds it, faster and faster, till cracks appear up and down it.

He continues to pound the pillar, till a part of it falls away entirely. Now he sees what he is looking for – an iron rod. He reaches out, grips it tightly, then leans back, yanking it with all his strength. It begins to shake, coming away from the foundations. Brant leans back further, hauling at it as hard as he can. It does not bow or snap, but merely leans to one side, loosens further from the base. Brant continues to pull on it, dislodging it further.

There is an almighty *snap* and the base of the iron cylinder ruptures from the structure of the pillar. The entire pillar, which is a central support column for the palace above, disintegrates with a shuddering boom. He immediately threads himself backwards from the crumbling structure.

'They would have heard that everywhere in the palace,' Brant says, wiping the sweat from his forehead.

Above him the ceiling splits. Fissures and cracks form. He lets the debris and dust settle before venturing forward. At the base of the pillar, there is a brass box, covered in dust. He goes over and lifts it.

He carries it to a marble table by the entrance. He wipes away the dust from its surface. Dizziness grips him. His strength fades and he must use all his willpower to remain conscious. He leans against the table for support.

'Damn it, stay awake,' he orders himself.

The relic is drained and Brant with it. His arm gives way, he falls.

'Sir,' Konrad appears by his side, catches him. Steadies Brant. The dizzy spell passes. Brant takes a deep breath, calms his nerves.

'We have it, Konrad,' he says, supporting himself against the brass box. He sways once more but does not pass out.

'Sir?' Konrad studies him.

'Give me a moment,' Brant says. He knows he cannot draw any more from the Source at this time. He is too weak to do that. He just needs time to recover. 'Open it,' he instructs Konrad.

Konrad sets to work. There is no lock and the Threader slowly, with delicate fingers, prises open the box.

'The Vessels of Nur ...' Brant says.

'Huh?' Konrad says, looking inside.

'What?' Brant stares at the box.

Konrad removes an envelope, lying on top of a padded velvet cushion, where there is a round indent, which once held one of the seven Vessels of Nur.

The box is empty. Except for an embossed envelope. Konrad slices it open and hands him the slip of paper. He unfolds it.

A mere six words are written there.

In the custody of the Custodians.

'Custodians!' Brant snaps. 'Who in Volgorok's name are they?'

Alifa wakes to find herself alone. Her chest aches, as does her head. As she tentatively rises onto her elbows, she feels pain in her back and neck, as well as her legs. *What did he hit me with?* she wonders. *A relic?* With a tremendous effort, for the pain is almost unbearable, she rises, wincing as she studies her surroundings. A terrible rumble and shaking throws her back on the ground. It passes and she rises again.

He could have killed me. Why didn't he?

Her chest aches and she grimaces when she moves her left arm. Taking a deep breath, she collects the folds of her dress around her, and leaves the chamber. She tries to run, but each step is like someone hitting her back with an iron rod. She slows to a skip. The Sultana is in danger. For Zorar's sake – for everyone's sake – she must try.

Several corridors and chambers take her to the heart of the palace where the Sultana is lodged. As she draws closer, the absence of soldiers concerns her. This should be the most heavily-guarded part of the palace.

She arrives at the secure room, only to find the door wide open and unguarded. Inside she sees the Sultana, standing on a slightly raised podium. She is staring defiantly at an approaching figure. A man, who has a knife in his hand.

He is going to kill Negin!

Alifa threads herself into a leap, then in mid-air doubles over as it feels like a giant hand has squeezed her ribcage. She lands, skids, collapses beside the assassin. Through tear-filled eyes, she stares up at this man.

It is a handsome face. Not what she would consider the face of a killer. A thoughtful, regretful face.

She has seen him before.

'You!' the man says. He freezes, mouth open.

Then it hits her. Outside the Teuton embassy. Their eyes locked, then he was gone.

The assassin gulps.

'I ...' he hesitates.

He turns to look at the Sultana.

'No,' he shouts, hand rising.

Alifa turns to see an old man, too old for her to think him a danger, move at a speed belying his years. He plunges a slender sword into the Sultana's back. The point emerges from her chest.

The blade is yanked out. The Sultana falls.

The old man stares indignantly at the man with the knife, then at Alifa, his ancient eyes burning with hatred. She tries to summon the energy to reach for the Source but the pain stops her.

Addressing the young man beside her, he says, 'Our work is done. We leave.'

The old man strides away.

The young one turns to her. His face is filled with remorse. She stares back at him. As he holds out his hand to help her, someone slams into Alifa's side and she is sent sprawling across the marble floor. She tries to rise but a Teuton Threader is on top of her. His knee presses into her chest and he takes out a knife. Raises it above his head.

A blade plunges into the side of the Threader's neck. The young man shoves the Threader off her. Crouches beside her, takes her hand in his.

'Who are you?' he asks.

Her heart beats faster than she can imagine. A surge of emotion overwhelms her.

'Alifa,' she whispers.

'Kaivan,' he says.

He glances towards where the old man exited. 'We will meet again. Alifa,' he says, then with one last smile, he turns and runs.

Alifa watches him go, wondering what just happened.

Then she remembers.

'The Sultana!' Alifa exclaims, scrambling to her feet to rush across to the fallen monarch and crouch over her. Negin is barely alive, but when Alifa grips her hand, she holds it tightly. The Sultana's eyes open. They are tear-filled, agonised and grief-stricken.

'You are Alifa,' she says.

'Hush,' Alifa says. She tries to summon her healing, but the pain is too much and she almost blacks out from the effort.

'Zorar spoke of you, like a daughter.'

Tears streak down Alifa's face. *A daughter.*

'Tell him,' Negin says, her voice laced with loss. 'Tell Zorar, I would have said yes, if he had asked.'

Alifa gasps as the Sultana's eyes close and her hand goes limp.

'Sultana Negin,' Alifa whispers, as her tears fall. She has witnessed death many times, held the hands of dying soldiers as they took their last breaths, but she has never felt like this before.

With all my abilities, there is nothing I can do!

Silence cocoons her. She sits motionless beside the dead ruler.

The sound of boots draws her attention. She looks up to see a group of soldiers rush into the room. They take in the scene.

One of them shouts, 'She killed the Sultana!'

'Murderer!' another shouts. 'Arrest her!'

Alifa looks back at Negin's body, then tries to stand, but the strength in her legs is gone. She collapses. The soldiers approach. She remembers the metal prison.

The soldiers draw nearer. She still cannot run.

Then the soldiers are thrown to one side. Azadeh threads herself into the hall. Nimar rams his body into another group of guards, sending them sprawling. Meanwhile Jamshi picks her up in his arms and shouts behind him to Azadeh and Nimar.

'Follow me!'

As she catches one last glimpse of the slain monarch, tears blind her. *Oh Zorar, I'm so sorry I couldn't save her.*

Kaivan's heart beats in an unfamiliar rhythm. It's love, he knows it. He catches up with the Patriarch of the Peak outside the palace. Around them soldiers pass in confused bands. Zandals run amok on streets close to the palace. The city of Urua burns this night; screams emanate from every corner. The smell of smoke wafts through the air. *What have we done?*

When he draws close, Kaivan grabs the old man by the elbow.

'You disappoint me, Kaivan. That girl bewitched you, made you weak,' the Patriarch says.

'She made me think,' he replies.

'Think! You're an assassin for hire. You don't think about the rights and wrongs of a target, you execute. Tonight, you failed.'

The Patriarch shrugs him off, walks away.

Kaivan does not follow. Stands hands on his hips. Calls after the old man. 'You knew.'

The Patriarch freezes. Turns his head to one side.

'About Conduits,' Kaivan says.

The Patriarch remains silent.

'And you knew, I was … one of them.'

The old man does not reply.

'Answer me!' Kaivan implores.

Still facing away from him the Patriarch says, 'It's what made you the best assassin I ever trained.'

Kaivan lets out a breath. He remembers the times he could do things others merely dreamt of: how he could move faster, balance on heights, leap higher, even recover faster from injuries. He feels a sense of relief wash over him.

'You will be hard to replace,' the Patriarch says, before walking away towards the burning city streets. Kaivan watches his form disappearing into the night, till he is only a shadow against a burning flame.

Motionless, he stares at the mayhem. Screams of anguish and despair come from every direction. Lecherous mobs of Zandals are pillaging the beautiful city of Urua, destroying its cultured homes, gardens, artifacts. He feels the ring on his finger. He looks at it.

To his left several men emerge from the eastern end of the palace, making their way towards the now unguarded perimeter. He recognises Brant, plus the other man who came with him to the mountain. *If I am a Conduit, if I have these powers, I need someone to train me. Who? This man Brant? But I don't trust him. Who else is there?*

Reluctantly, he makes his way towards Brant, who he notices is walking with some difficulty. The group comes to a stop when they see him approach.

'It's okay, let him pass,' Brant says. The Teuton stands straight, pain etched on his forehead.

'Hard day at work?' Kaivan asks.

'You could say that,' Brant says in a smooth laconic tone.

Kaivan spins the ring around his finger, says. 'This Conduit business.'

'Yes,' Brant says.

'Can you teach me some of it?'

Brant's lips curl into a smile and Kaivan thinks *I hope I don't live to regret this.*

END OF BOOK 1

APPENDIX A:
A TUTORIAL

I N T H E L O D G E, at the start of Alifa's training, Zorar conducts a tutorial with Alifa, in which he explains the history of Ikleel. He begins in the following manner:

'Our divine history informs us that in the first epoch, there was a great rivalry between the Djüne, who are like fiery demons and Vanimals, who are humanlike in form but have animalistic natures and properties. Both the Djüne and Vanimals live very long lives.'

'How long ago was that first epoch?' Alifa asks.

'We cannot be sure, but it may have been a hundred thousand years ago or perhaps even several hundred thousand years ago when the descent took place, that is, when humans, Djünes and Vanimals descended to Ikleel. Possibly even longer than that. We really don't know.'

'Descended?'

'We believe it was from a divine abode.'

'Where?'

'We do not know, nor is it important to know where it was. When we leave this realm upon our deaths and return to the Creator it will be revealed to us.'

'The first epoch was such a long time.'

'For humans, but not for the Djüne and the Vanimals.'

Zorar continues. 'The Djüne occupied the land of Nar-as-Samum, which would be to the extreme west of us, and Vanimals made Küor Araz, a territory north of Nar-as-Samum, their habitation. For thousands of years, they fought across their borders. Till one day, humans appeared in their territory. At first, they ignored such

weak beings, but slowly humans spread into their lands, set up trad-
ing posts, and began to set down roots. We do not know precisely
what happened, but the arrival of the humans caused the Djüne and
the Vanimals to set aside their rivalry and unite to repel humans
spreading in Ikleel.'

'There was a war between humans and the Djüne and Vanimals?'

'Like no other,' Zorar says. 'Under the leadership of Volgorok,
ruler of the Djüne, the Djüne and Vanimals engaged humanity at
the Battle of Rift on the western shores of Koemox. The humans
rallied around the Heralds. Yet even before the battle they knew
they were outnumbered and did not possess the physical prowess
of the Djüne and Vanimals, so a great quest was undertaken to recover the seven Vessels of Nur which also came down at the time
of the descent. Many Heralds and other great heroes were lost in
the quest for the Vessels. Yet find them they did and with the light
of the Vessels the armies of the Heralds overcame Volgorok, who
was driven back to the shadowlands of Nar-as-Samum. As for the
Vanimals they retreated to Küor Araz, vowing to never engage with
either Djüne or humans again.'

'But this Volgorok, I'm guessing he came back?' Alifa asks.

'He did,' Zorar says. 'Historians label the period after the Battle
of the Rift, the second epoch – the golden age of humanity, where
under the guidance of the Heralds, humans spread to all corners
of Ikleel. Trade routes were established, centres of education and
learning built. Some of the greatest Heralds of the time came together to construct the Isthmus, a parallel realm to the physical
world, to remind humans of our eventual return to the Gardens of
Liyuün.'

Alifa has heard of Liyuün, but in tall tales of valour and heroism.

She wishes she'd paid more attention.

'Yet deep in the shadowlands of Nar-as-Samum, Volgorok and his deputy Mörtan plotted and schemed. Their envy of humans knew no bounds,' Zorar says. 'Having learned from their mistakes, Volgorok and Mörtan recruited men and women to their cause, through the promise of *Dhulmi* powers. Over the centuries their acolytes secretly rose to prominent positions and matters came to a head when their human helpers took control of several major cities, thereupon declaring fealty to Volgorok.'

'What happened?' Alifa says.

'The humans rallied behind the Heralds. Volgorok was slain. Mörtan and the remaining Djüne escaped into the Isthmus.'

'The Isthmus, this parallel realm?' Alifa asks.

'Yes, unbeknown to the Heralds, Mörtan the Conjurer had created a *Dhulmi* part, and corrupted the remainder of the Isthmus as he descended deep into *Dhulm*. Mörtan has also made other changes which you will learn about when you enter the Isthmus.'

'I can go into this Isthmus?' Alifa asks.

'Of course: you are a Conduit.'

'Are there still any Heralds?' Alifa asks.

'No,' Zorar says. 'The last Herald died several thousand years ago. In this, what is known as the third epoch, we have only ourselves, should ... Mörtan and the Djüne return.'

'They can come back?' Alifa asks.

Zorar grimaces. 'We can cover this topic another time.'

Alifa studies Zorar. *He does not want to tell me. Not yet.*

APPENDIX B:
THE CONDUITS

THE CONDUITS BELIEVE the Source emanates from the Divine realm. The primary *Kha* Conduits are:

NURANI KHA	DHULMI KHA
Calmers Settle people down, soothing their anxieties and worries, making them reflective and thoughtful.	Agitators Incite people to become aggressive and impulsive, rousing a sense of narcissism within them.
Clarifiers Remind people who they are and what is their purpose – souls on a journey back to the Creator.	Distractors Confuse and befuddle people so that they lose their focus and purpose and are stirred by the frivolous.
Nourishers Regenerate living matter. Helpful in recovery from illnesses and wounds.	Decayers Degenerate living matter that already has some decay within it. Where an illness or wound is detected they can cause this to worsen.

Threaders
Use *Kha* to propel themselves or objects across short and longer distances. Near invisible white lines emanate from their fingertips which only Conduits can see, so enabling them to tug or thrust.

Hefters
Tap into *Kha* to lift and shift heavy weights, taking on the work of several people. Helpful in a fight when outnumbered.

Imbuers
Infuse an inanimate object with memories, so when another Imbuer touches it, they can access the memory of what was left. Helpful for sending messages across time.

Revealers
Have the ability to perceive matters that are hidden. This may be as simple as a blueprint, traps, locks. More importantly to spot patterns which appear obscure.

Conduits can access one of the *Kha* abilities. A Grand Conduit is one who can access and use all of the *Kha* abilities.

Conduits cannot access the Source directly but must harness it through an element. Conduits access their *Kha* abilities through:

ELEMENT	KHA ABILITY
Sand	Calmer/Agitator
Silica	Clarifier/Distractor
Corallite	Threader
Ochre	Hefter
Obsidian	Imbuer
Limestone	Nourisher/Decayer
Volcanic ash	Revealer

The elements are stored in either the beads of a *tasbeah* made from ironwood or cartridges made from ironwood.

𝒦

APPENDIX C:
THE ISTHMUS

THE ISTHMUS IS ENTERED through physical Gateways which are scattered across Ikleel. Their locations remain a secret carefully guarded by Conduits. It was originally constructed to allow every person, the opportunity to spend forty days and nights reflecting on their journey back to the Creator. After the corruption sown by Mörtan, the Heralds warned that only Conduits should enter it.

The Isthmus itself is a point between two realms, the physical and what lies beyond – the metaphysical.

In the *Nurani* part Conduits ascend through the levels. In the *Dhulmi* part Conduits descend through the levels. The state of the Conduit's heart determines what he or she experiences when entering the Isthmus. However, those who have sworn to take the path of *Nur* will always enter the *Nurani* and those of *Dhulm* will always enter the *Dhulmi*.

Within the *Nurani* part of the Isthmus a Conduit can enter *Dhulm* by willingly submitting to the ground fog at any level. In the *Dhulmi* part a Conduit can enter *Nur* by stepping into the shard of light that is always breaking through the clouds. However, their 'letting go' of *Dhulm* must be genuine, or else they will be obliterated by the light.

Each Mökam (station/level) of the Isthmus holds different relics, which often take the form of jewels, or old artifacts which may even look like junk to the casual observer. Relics can amplify the powers of a Conduit in the physical world. A relic obtained from a higher/lower Mökam of the Isthmus will be more potent than others. An Imbuer is key to understanding the potential of a relic.

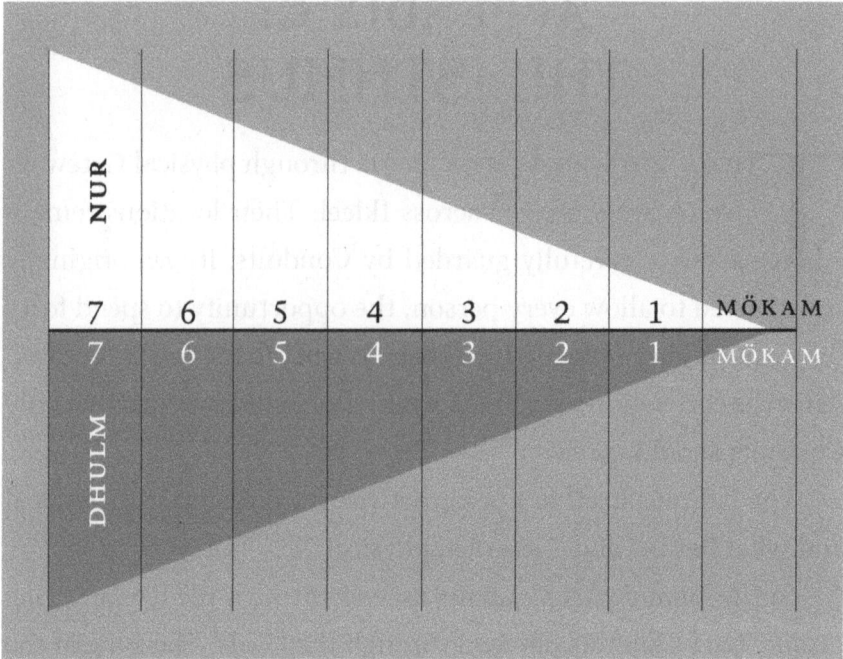

LEVEL	DESCRIPTION
1	Similar to the physical world, but powers are amplified.
2	Firmer connection to the Source, greater *Kha* abilities.
3	Stronger connection to the Source. Lifespan starts to lengthen. The relics associated with this level are thumb rings and signet rings.
4	Deeper connection to the Source. The relics associated with this level are anklets, armlets and bracelets.
5	Still deeper connection to the Source. The relics associated with this level are artifacts such as pendants, celestial orbs, astrolabes, moonstones and sunstones.
6	Isthmus contains relics from the first epoch. The divine primordial script becomes apparent in the architecture of the Isthmus. The relics associated with this level are sky discs.
7	The uttermost horizon of physical possibilities. Any further progress results in annihilation via *Nur* or *Dhulm*. The relics associated with this level are tablets inscribed with the primordial language of all beings.

Each Mökam, whether it is on the *Nurani* or *Dhulmi* side has a unique resonance to it. The sound heard aligns with the position of the Mökam, as well as the relics that can be found there. Every Mökam of ascension in *Nur* will cause the sound to become further harmonised with the divine realm, which resides across the celestial sea. The converse is true of the sounds of descension in *Dhulm*, which constrict the heart and thoughts.

At each level there are also relics which contain unique sounds that can be used by Conduits in the outside world. Nurani and Dhulmi sounds have been imbued into certain relics and can be harnessed in the world outside the Isthmus. In a similar manner a relic with a sound from the Isthmus can be a shield against a sonic weapon, as it muffles the vibratory impact.

Each Mökam has a particular attribute – in the first waystation of *Nur* it is resolution, whereas in *Dhulm* it is indecision.

APPENDIX D:
CAST OF CHARACTERS

The primary cast of characters within Book One are:

Alifa	Grand Conduit, Nurani Order, apprentice to Zorar.
Almas	Head of the Sethee Bank.
Artay	Sultan of the north of Arön, leader of the notorious Black Axe army division.
Ayu	Assassin in the service of the Patriarch of the Peak.
Azadeh	Threader (Conduit), Nurani Order, serves under Zorar. Agronomist.
Behrooz	Emperor of Arön.
Belal	Healer (Conduit), Nurani Order, serves under Zorar. Apothecary, acupuncturist.
Bouson	Brigadier in the armies of the south of Arön, serving under Ramin.
Brant	Grand Conduit, Dhulmi Order, Teuton deputy ambassador to Arön.
Cinan	Revealer (Conduit), Nurani Order, serves under Zorar. Imperial architect of Arön.
Dassin	Traveller from Koemox.
Daria	Scroll-Master in Urua.
Darrick	One of four Harbingers who serve Mörtan.
Durayd	Calmer (Conduit), Nurani Order, serves under Zorar, owner of Dallah Wala.
Gurgen	One of the Vanimals.
Hale	Young geologist and phycology enthusiast, nephew of Orinda.
Hildebrandt	Bodyguard to Chief Kerbasy.
Jamshi	Clarifier (Conduit), Nurani Order, serves under Zorar. Troubadour to the royal court in the south of Arön.
Juud	Assassin in the service of the Patriarch of the Peak.

Kaivan	*Assassin in the service of the Patriarch of the Peak.*
Kansabar	*Imperial Vizier to Emperor Behrooz.*
Kaşifa	*Imbuer (Conduit), Nurani Order, serves under Zorar. Chief Librarian of the royal archives in the south of Arön.*
Kerbasy	*Chief of the Zandal, wild tribes of the Northern Wastes.*
Konrad	*Threader (Conduit), Dhulmi Order, serves under Brant.*
Lin	*Daughter of the Cin ambassador to Arön.*
Mörtan	*The Corroder, disciple of Volgorok.*
Negin	*Sultana of the south of Arön, ruler of Urua and patron of the arts and sciences.*
Nimar	*Hefter (Conduit), Nurani Order, serves under Zorar. Merchant and trader.*
Orinda	*Teuton noblewoman, wife of Paxon.*
Patriarch	*Patriarch of the Peak, head of the order of assassins, located outside Urua.*
Paxon	*Teuton ambassador to Arön, husband of Orinda.*
Pedram	*Hefter (Conduit).*
Ramin	*General of the armies of Negin.*
Rasa	*One of four Harbingers who serve Mörtan.*
Vard	*Assassin in the service of the Patriarch of the Peak.*
Vartez	*Member of the Black Axe army division.*
Zorar	*Grand Conduit, Nurani Order, serves Negin.*

APPENDIX E:
GLOSSARY

Dhulm	Darkness, a veil cast over, an absence of light.
Duff	Drum, musical instrument.
Himma	Resolve
Ilkidee	Ancient language of the first epoch.
Isthmus	A place between the physical and the metaphysical realms.
Kamish	Writing instrument, used with a scroll-light.
Kha	Originating from the Source, a divine energy, conducted by conduits.
Khidmat-gars	A place of refuge for the destitute.
Liyuün	Heavenly abode, highest paradise.
Majlis	Assembly hall for hosting guests.
Nur	Light, illumination.
Opius	Narcotic with highly addictive properties.
Oud	Fragrant scent from a wood origin
Oud guitar	Fretless guitar
Scroll-light	Rollable screen with an algae liquid display, used to send and receive data.
Sherwani	Long form of jacket or coat.
Souk	Marketplace for trade.
Tasbeah	Beads upon which a litany is performed.
Vizier	First minister to the ruler.

ACKNOWLEDGEMENTS

THE CREATIVE DEVELOPMENT PROCESS of bringing *Tales of Khayaal* to life has involved contributions from a gifted global team of inspiring artists, creatives and designers, supported by Gould Studio and a community of like-hearted friends and fans. Specific mention should be made to the following individuals.

Our dear friend Neil King for connecting the two of us together. Our publishers Sadia Anwar and Mehnaz Anshah have been tremendous advocates for the series. Special thanks go to the delightful editing skills of Lorna Fergusson, who Rehan has had the pleasure of working with for more than a decade. Thanks also to our diligent proof-reader Samira Issa.

Special credit and gratitude go to Mukhtar Sanders of Inspiral Design, who designed and typeset the entire book—bringing cohesion, elegance and clarity to the project from first page to last. For the mesmerising *Tales of Khayaal* logo and book cover, we must thank the calligraphic prowess of Salwa Faour as well as valuable input from Ruh Al-Alam, Kais Al Kaissi, Hira Ali and Nada Maktari. The map was crafted by the deft hand of Asya Leztizia, and the industrious illustrator Emil Salim took on the challenge of working with us for thirty-three key moment visuals.

Finally, we would both like to thank our families for their ongoing support and commitment to ensuring we have a stable base from which to allow our creative work to develop.

All Praise is to God. With peace and blessings.

—REHAN AND PETER,
SEPTEMBER 2025

www.talesofkhayaal.com

BY THE SAME AUTHOR

KHAYAAL

"The capacity of the heart to give forms to spiritual realities that don't have any form, and to spiritualise material realities that do have form."

DR SAMIR MAHMOUD

www.talesofkhayaal.com

9 789948 684732